Print VERSION ONLY

Original Ebook/Print Cover: Carol Marques Design
Alternative Cover: Sandra Maldo Designs
Map: Honeyy.Fae
Editing, Proofing, backgrounds, & Formatting: Dirty Sexy Words/ Storm shield
Editing/Little Tailfeather Publishing
Cassandra's logos: Pretty in Ink Creations/Artlogo
Goosebusters Alpha team: Kat Silver, Becky Ross, Erica Taryn
Duckhunters Proofing: Jackie H, Jaemi Serrano
Sensitivity Readers: Brit Mason, Gail Jericho
Translation Consultant: Mo Jacobs
Legal Services: Joshua Farley, esq.
Images/Fonts: Depositphotos, Shutterstock, Canva, & Photoshop

No GenAI was used within this book. All errors and greatness are by an ADHD muppet.

Little Tailfeather Publishing

DISCORDIA UNIVERSITY

COGERE EVOLUTIONE PER MUTATIONUM

DISCORDIA
UNIVERSITY

Quiet BURN

INTERNATIONAL BESTSELLING AUTHOR
CASSANDRA FEATHERSTONE

Content Information

This is a *paranormal whychoose romance with poly elements*—our FMC, Kat, will not have to choose between love interests.

I *purposefully* include **all** pertinent information in this section from tropes to triggers to included content to silly things. It's an attempt to cover my bases which is probably futile since some will be upset with *and* without it.

However, it's my book, and I'll do what I want, so here we go.

There are many situations included that are intended for <u>mature audiences (18+).</u>

In this book/series, there may be instances/references (be they small or lengthy) that could trigger some individuals such as:

- a *lot* of discussion of mental illness
- demons
- attacks on the FMC (physical)
- discussion about past non-consensual sexual event in FMC's past (description not on page, not MMC)
- sexy shifting
- within series: MM, MF, MMMMMMFM, and more
- bullying (light from MMC)
- foster kid
- consistent discussions of consent
- non-binary MC

- alphahole/possessive MCs
- cinnamon roll MC
- girl disguised as a boy
- slightly unhinged chaotic MC
- big tough guy MC
- unhealthy coping mechanisms
- spoiled, rich MCs
- extremely aggressive boundaries
- age gap (unknown)
- cute familiar
- pre-existing pairings
- BDSM discussed (D/s relationship)
- horns, tails, and forked tongues
- traumatic childhood
- alcohol use and abuse
- threats of bodily harm
- death
- body modifications
- physical assault by non-MCs
- treacherous authority figures
- bullying (in person)
- PTSD
- blood
- emotional abuse
- body dysmorphia
- adult language
- pop culture references
- literary references
- emotional manipulation
- power play
- adorable nicknames
- physical intimidation
- emotionally abusive/manipulative parents (MCs)
- markings/tattoos
- Easter egg character cameos from other series in the universe
- family dysfunction
- absolute disrespect for shitty parents
- brief mentions of non-body positive dieting culture
- very liberal re-imagining of history
- ancient secret society who only cares about bigger picture
- official corruption
- discussion of arranged marriages

- rituals
- inappropriate professors
- name calling
- occasional misogyny
- shitty mothers and fathers
- discussion of parental physical abuse
- elitism
- bribery
- corpses
- drama
- physical threats to FMC and others
- species-ism

No practices in this book should be taken as safe or appropriate for real life application.

Content information is important to me and I do my best to include things people might enjoy and not enjoy.

READER'S NOTE
A FEW THINGS YOU SHOULD KNOW...

Quiet Burn is book **two** of the *Discordia University* series. There are five books planned and they will start on Ream, then come to print/KU after they are re-edited and formatted. The books don't *change* from one medium to the other so much as get refined, etc.

Note: This book is an **exception** to that general rule in that several chapters in the middle were previously in the *All Hallows Eve* anthology and not published serially. They are included in *Quiet Burn* as they belong within the story.

This is a multi-book series, so *everything will not be revealed at once.* Some plot lines will continue through series in a larger arc and not get resolved in the first or even the third book.

I write lengthy books with intricate world building, strong character development, and *lots* of tiny threads that stretch throughout a series that may not always seem important at first glance. However, I promise nothing I put to paper and leave in the book is unimportant; it may simply become *more* important later on. There is no 'throwaway' detail in my worlds, so every scene will mean something eventually.

For information on the larger universe reading order, go to https://cassandrafeatherstone.com/pages/legends-of-the-ouroboros

I promise it will all get tied up and have a HEA; don't worry!

Quiet Burn is a why choose/poly romance, which means our FMC will not have to choose.

I would consider it a **SLOW** burn—the slowest I've ever written. It will get spicier—slowly—in the following books as Kat's situation changes. If you're looking for porn with little to no plot, no judgment, but this isn't the series for you. It won't be closed door or FTB, so I believe the spice will be worth the wait. I realize spice scales are subjective and everyone has different opinions on it, so forgive me if mine and yours aren't totally aligned.

Note: In the South (where I'm from), it is fairly common to call people by their full names when you're being condescending to dressing someone down. It's not just family, and if they don't know your middle name, sometimes they even make one up! It's an authority flex to do so. This happens in my books a lot—even if they are not set in the South—so I'm just giving you a heads up that it's stylistic and purposeful.

There are some characters and creatures that speak in other languages. I made the *translations clickable end of chapter notes* to help.

There are some words that are slang, jargon, or foreign that may seem to be spelled wrong—*please email the author or find her on social media rather than report to Amazon* if you find a typo. This has been proofed and edited *several* times, so the error could be a stylistic or dialect choice. Every effort is made to find these pre-publication and since the publishing industry standard is below two percent of word count (and my books are almost always over 100K), I promise what you find is not out of the accepted range for the editors and teams who have reviewed it.

Please do not email critical feedback that is not a simple typo or formatting issue—this book is written and released. It will not be changed after publication to suit personal requests.

If you see this book *anywhere besides Kindle Unlimited in ebook format,* please reach out to me via social media or email. Pirating kills my ability to write full time and I am so grateful for your help.

Contact my team for typos or to report piracy: teamcassandrafeatherstone@cassandrafeatherstone.com

Author Ramblings

Readers, your fierce love for Kat and her demons makes my feet kick in glee.

You accepted her broken pieces and came along for the ride as we watch her —and maybe the guys—heal from a tragic past. She's doing the work, but as you know, it's a slow process when you're crawling out of the pits. Kat is doing it the right way, but doesn't have much support—then her world turns upside down.

If you have issues with discussion of consent, her mental health, and the way that shapes her entire world, this may not be the series for you. I'm absolutely not willing to cheapen Kat's tale for anyone, especially when it comes to the way she behaves as a result of her trauma.

#sorrynotsorry if that feels boring or overdone—it's **real** *and I know that from* **experience.**

There are Easter eggs for those of you who are inclined to read the faster burn series *Faetal Attraction* and some for *Secrets of State U,* but if you don't, those references won't leave you behind the curve. You might even catch some more coming up; keep your eyes peeled.

As usual, I've done a lot of research and added quite bit of mythology, depth, and information to my rich world. But if I get something wrong, know I did the best I could to make certain I had the right information.

*Plus, you know… magic. Magic explains everything. *wink**

While I definitely cannot ever make every reader happy—and that's *okay*—I'm so grateful for all of the people who enjoy my books in my group, REAM, and other venues. You guys are the sunshine in my day when I happen upon less than kind opinions on the internet by mistake.

For that, I can never repay you.

However, I never give up, so I'm going to be here with silly puns and smart FMCs who aren't afraid to show how big their hearts, libidos, *and* brains are.

Enjoy the next installment in this series in the *Legends of the Ouroboros* universe, and fall for the bad boy demons one by one.

Blood and guts,

Cassandra Featherstone

A Note To My Loving Family Members and Their Friends...

THANK YOU FOR SUPPORTING ME BY BUYING THIS BOOK!

WE'RE IN A SLOW BURN SITCH STILL, SO THIS ONE MIGHT BE OKAY TO READ.

HOWEVER... I'D HATE TO EXPLAIN THINGS LATER ON SOOOO... MAYBE JUST DON'T?

I MEAN, XERXES ALONE IS GOING TO RAISE TOO MANY QUESTIONS IN THIS ONE.

CAVEAT: IF YOU CHOOSE TO KEEP READING, KNOW THAT AT NO TIME WILL I EXPLAIN TERMS, POSITIONS, THEMES, TROPES, OR ANY OTHER PART OF THIS NOVEL AT FAMILY EVENTS, IN GROUP CHATS, OR ON SOCIAL MEDIA.

DON'T ASK.

Quiet Burn Playlist

CHAPTER TITLE SONGS

Quiet Burn Chapter Playlist

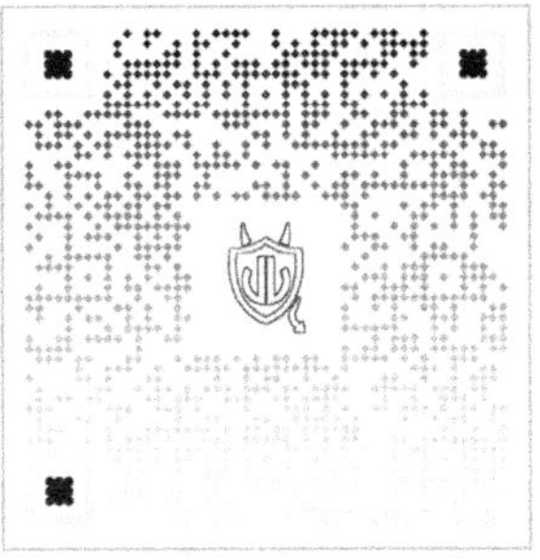

BONUS PLAYLIST

The Demon Boys Mix Playlist

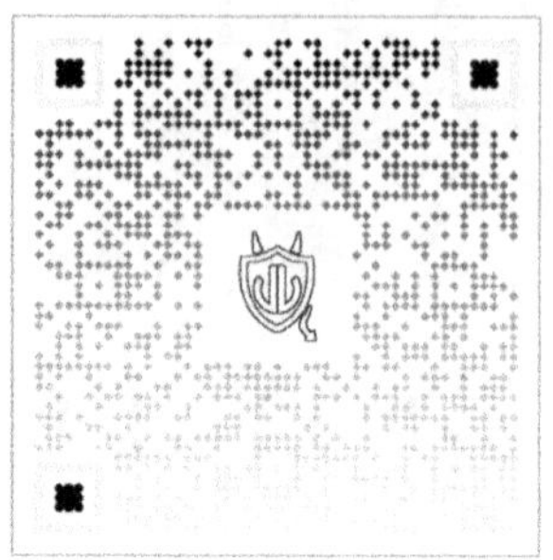

IT'S NOT WHETHER YOU GET KNOCKED DOWN;
IT'S WHETHER YOU GET UP.

~VINCE LOMBARDI

Discordia University
Student Dormitories
Library
of the
Ancients
The
The Wastelands
Staff Housing

Canto V
Region: Hell
Arena of Lost Souls
gic Enclave
Knowledge Enclave
Administration
& Health Annex

CLASS SCHEDULE

All class schedules subject to administrative and professorial approval.

time	monday	tuesday	wednesday	thursday	friday
8:00 AM	Intro to Demons & Supes	Curses & Hexes 101	Intro to Demons & Supes	Curses & Hexes 101	Arms & Battle 101
9:00 AM	Lillibet	Wormwood	Lillibet	Wormwood	Eversore
10:00 AM	Deconstructing Human History	Mythology 101	Deconstructing Human History	Mythology 101	Free Period
11:00 AM	Alabaster		Alabaster		
12:00 PM	Free Period	Lunch	Free Period	Lunch	Dueling
1:00 PM	Lunch		Lunch		Lunch
2:00 PM	Ancient Demon Lineage	Free Period	Ancient Demon Lineage	Free Period	Dark Magic
3:00 PM	Kindervelt		Kindervelt		Salazar
4:00 PM	Literature of Dark Ages	Weapons & Tactics	Literature of Dark Ages	Weapons & Tactics	Intro to Fae
5:00 PM	Romero	Eversore	Romero	Eversore	Cedar
6:00 PM	Drama	Supe Law	Drama	Supe Law	Hackers Guild
7:00 PM	Dinner	Dinner	Dinner	Dinner	
8:00 PM	Thieves' Guild	Caliphate Mtg	Government	Caliphate Mtg	Dinner

COGERE EVOLUTIONE
PER MUTATIONEM

WAIT!

A FINAL REMINDER BEFORE YOU READ…

My series typically have prequels, gap novellas/novels, and bonus material that are integral to your having a satisfying reading experience.

If you have not read the other pieces in this series, you may feel as though you have missed critical details, developments, plot points, and other information. This will cause the book to appear to have continuity gaps that it does not have.

If you have not read the bonus material for this series, it is available online here, in audio versions (if applicable), and in print special editions (if applicable).

I highly recommend consulting the bonus page prior to reading this new title so you're up to speed on all the things going on in this world.

Happy reading!

Previously On Veiled Flame

Katarina Camponella, or Kat, to those who aren't trying to sound like a Victorian governess, has spent most of her life being unwanted.

Shuffled from foster home to foster home, she learned early on that people don't keep her around for long. No one ever told her why. She wasn't a troublemaker, didn't flunk out of school, and never stirred up drama. She did everything right. It didn't matter. Every year, she was sent back, traded in like an outgrown pair of shoes.

Now, stuck in a dull suburban town with foster parents who care more about their star-athlete sons, Bryce and Blake, than the quiet, nerdy girl they took in, Kat is ready for her escape. College is supposed to be her way out. She has the grades. She's done the work. But when the acceptance letters start rolling in for everyone else, she opens her application system to find—nothing. No rejections, no offers, not even a simple acknowledgment that she exists.

Then, out of nowhere, a mysterious letter appears on her doorstep, offering her a full-ride scholarship to a place called Discordia University. The name alone is suspicious, but what's even stranger is the fact that Kat never applied. Even worse, the letter isn't addressed to her. It's for "Mssr. Kit Camponella." Whoever Kit is, it isn't her, but the offer is too good to ignore. They promise tuition, housing, meals, even spending money—all things she desperately needs. The only catch? No one has ever heard of Discordia

University. It's not in any college database. Google doesn't recognize it. Her high school's guidance counselor insists it doesn't exist.

That should be a red flag. A big, flashing, neon-colored red flag.

But when the alternative is staying in this dead-end town with people who don't care whether she's there or not, Kat takes the risk. She signs the letter and waits to see what happens next.

She doesn't have to wait long.

Discordia University isn't just some ultra-exclusive school hidden from the public eye. It's a demon academy in another realm, a place where power is everything, students are more predator than person, and survival is far from guaranteed. Kat, who has spent most of her life fading into the background, suddenly finds herself surrounded by creatures who could rip her to shreds if they ever suspected what she really was—a girl.

Because girls don't belong at Discordia—it's all boys school.

Now going by Kit, because apparently that's what the school thinks her name is, she scrambles to figure out how she got accepted, who signed her up for this, and—most importantly—how the hell she's supposed to stay alive. Blending in is her only option, but that becomes increasingly difficult when she catches the attention of Jasper Eversore, a demon prince with entirely too much arrogance, entirely too much suspicion, and entirely too much interest in her presence at Discordia.

Jasper is ruthless, powerful, and used to being the smartest person in any room. He knows something about Kit isn't right, and rather than letting it go like a normal, decent person would, he pokes at her secrets until they bleed.

Unfortunately, he isn't the only one monitoring her. His caliphate, an elite group of demon hybrids, has also noticed that Kit isn't exactly fitting into the mold. Salem, the quiet protector who seems far too kind for a place like Discordia, watches her with concern. Oriel, the sharp-eyed thief, has a knowing look that makes her want to check whether she still has all her belongings. Slash, the deadly and predatory shark shifter, sizes her up like he's waiting for her to make a wrong move. Zavida, the nervous but perceptive kitsune, seems to puzzle her out, while Anton, the silent and enigmatic observer, says nothing but sees everything. And Xerxes, the eagle-eyed cobra shifter who seems like the most affable of all.

None of them should care about her. None of them should be interested in her existence at all.

But they are, and that's dangerous.

As if being under their constant scrutiny wasn't bad enough, Kit soon learns that Discordia University has reinstated the Caliphate Games, a brutal, cutthroat competition that hasn't been held in years. No one knows exactly what the Games will entail, but everyone understands one thing: they will be deadly. Jasper's caliphate is preparing, whether they want to or not, and by some unfortunate twist of fate, Kit is now tangled up in their chaos.

The more time she spends at Discordia, the worse things get. Someone in the administration knows exactly what she is, and that makes her a target. A mysterious figure from her past seems to have orchestrated her arrival, but she has no idea why. The worst part, though, is what's happening inside her own body. She's changing. Something is waking up in her, something she can't explain, and that she might not be as human as she's always believed terrifies her.

With the Caliphate Games approaching, the school growing more dangerous by the day, and Jasper and his crew closing in on her secrets, Kit has to decide who she really is, what she's willing to fight for, and whether she can survive long enough to uncover the truth.

But Discordia University isn't a place where people walk away unscathed.

It's the kind of place where secrets kill, and Kit has too many of them.

If she isn't careful, she won't just lose the game.

She'll lose everything.

Splish Splash

Beep. Beep. Beep. Beep.

I groan when the alarm goes off, my entire body aching as I shift slightly. The painkillers Dank gave me wore off while I was sleeping and they make me too loopy to take them during the daytime. Any other time, I would consider emailing someone to take the day off, but after the announcement yesterday…

Nope, I can't be seen as weak.

Sighing, I look up at the ceiling, smiling when Dottie scurries up and peers down at me happily. "Hey girl…"

The kinkajou chitters softly, dancing a little on her hind legs. I don't know why she's so excited, but maybe she's trying to help me stay positive. I pet her gently a few times, wincing at the pull on my healing scrapes, bruises, and injuries. It's a miracle I wasn't burned, so I guess I should be thanking someone—demon, deity, whatever—for that.

"Rise and shine, Kit Kat!" I blink as the oddly cheery voice of my room-mate echoes in the dorm as he bustles in. He walks over to my closet, yanking a uniform set out and places it on the bed nearby. Salem also grabs my shower basket, making my chest fill with alarm until he sets it down next to my clothes. "You have thirty minutes to get decent for our big *Triclinium* appearance. I won't repeat Jasper's words, but you'll want to look sharp."

Is he fucking kidding me? I look like shit microwaved.

A groan slips from my lips as I slowly push to a sitting position, hoping the world doesn't start spinning. When it doesn't, I let out a long breath of relief. I'll be able to stay upright in my damn classes without someone supporting me. That's a fucking miracle, and I'll take it. "Salem, you are *way* too chipper for this time of day."

"You just need some caffeine, Kit Kat. Now hustle up so I can help you to the showers. I've got breakfast and snacks all packed up for you and Dottie."

I frown at him, confused by his sunshiny 'mama bear' routine. "You made things for us to take so I don't have to eat that food? Why?"

"Because you're hurt, dude, and no one should have to survive that shit on empty while nursing wounds. Don't be dense." He ruffles his bed head messy black and white hair, making it look ridiculously hot—and I didn't think that was possible. "Come on. I'm sure the others will crash our gates if I don't get you in there soon."

Son of an ale-swilling goat-man.

Swinging my legs over the side of the bed, I grunt but wave my hand when Salem gets closer. "No, no. I have to do some shit myself. I don't like feel-ing… dependent… on people."

His eyes widen and he looks sad for a moment. "You really had a number done on you, man."

"Lucky me," I mutter as I prepare myself for the pain, then I slowly lift up until I'm on my feet. The ache intensifies and I have to plant myself in place firmly to make certain I don't sway. "The Universe just *loves* giving me chal-lenges to rise above."

Dottie chitters again, scampering on the floor as she waits for me to move. I realize I'm not quite steady enough to do so on my own and the panda demon gives me a crooked smile. He holds his arm out for the kinkajou, who climbs him like a tree and positions herself on his shoulder.

I might be jealous of my companion animal; how weird is that?

When I don't move, Salem pads over to me, giving me the other arm to hold onto. "You'll have to grab your stuff, Kit Kat. I'm more concerned about making sure *you* get to the bathroom. Everything else is icing, you know?"

Nodding, I swallow my discomfort as I scoop up the clothes and basket. It's light enough that I manage okay, so I look up at him. "Okay. I think I've got it."

Together, we shuffle towards the door, exiting my room and making our way across the living area at snail speed. I hope I get less stiff as the day goes on or I'm going to have *a lot* of trouble in the hallways and from professors. Since Jasper fucking obliterated the assholes in the study room and we've not heard a single word about them, we can't mention my attack to the administration or anyone else.

"Did Jasper say if he'd found anything out about the…" I drop my voice even though we're on our own floor. "…bodies?"

Salem grins at me as we walk towards the bathroom. "That's a good question, Kit Kat. You're a lot more cognizant than last night. Although, off-his-tits Kit is pretty awesome, too."

Oh, no. What did I say? Or do? Fuck.

The demon seems to sense my fear and he laughs softly. "Don't worry. No one saw you do anything stupid and O made sure you went straight to bed. You're safe."

"Thank fuck for small favors," I grumble. "I've never been high in my life and I have zero clue what crazy things I'd do or say. I don't… remember… a lot from the hospital in the past, so I don't have a frame of reference."

A shadow flickers over his face and I carefully squeeze the bicep I'm holding onto. Salem rumbles next to me, and I get the feeling he's going to press for more information about my attack at some point. "Well, the birdie and I escorted you to your room then tucked you in. It wasn't hard to imagine you wouldn't want anyone interrogating you in that state."

Now I definitely owe them some sort of reward; Jasper could have asked me anything.

"That must have made him really pissy. You guys did me a huge solid," I say softly.

He winks at me playfully, then stops to pull open the bathroom door. "I'll take a K. I. O.U for it."

Damn these guys for being interminably hot, *and* stupidly clever. I suck in a deep breath as the voices echoing from inside the bathroom carry. "I guess it's time to see how well I do standing on my own."

"But I can—"

Uh… fuck no, you can't. I'll die on the spot.

"ARE YOU OKAY IN THERE, LITTLE DEMON?"

Slash's question makes me freeze up and I hold my breath so I can hear whether or not anyone is coming close to my stall. When I confirm that they're all still doing their own thing, I go back to scrubbing my skin hard. I feel like there's a layer of filth I can't access with the loofah and spicy soap, but I know that's not true. It's the same feeling I had after the incident and no matter how hot the water, or how strong the scent of the body wash, I didn't feel clean for months.

My shrink damn near locked me up when I burned myself with bleach wipes trying to get him off.

Suffice it to say, I know *why* I'm acting like this. but engaging my logical brain when my anxiety and PTSD are flaring is really difficult. If I'm doing okay, I can think like this and try to talk my lizard brain off the ledge. It's when I lose control of the animalistic part and go feral that I need to be watched. I should probably talk to Oriel and Salem about how to tell I'm headed in that direction *before* I wig out.

"I'm okay, big guy. Thanks for asking."

A huff bounces off the walls, and Oriel's low tones get closer to my door. "I wanted to give you space, so I'm not *bothering* you, Kit Kat."

"Same," X and Anton chorus in unison and I blink.

What the hell is with all of them this morning? This isn't the Sound of Music.

Shaking my head, I go back to scrubbing until my skin is pink and angry, then I finally give in. I close my eyes, sinking into my mind to push the fear and fury from the attack into a closet until I'm alone. I can't allow anyone to know how affected I am, even the guys, because we don't have the luxury of time. The announcement this weekend opened up a whole different can of worms that we'll have to face, plus this harebrained scheme makes my ass twitch.

How am I supposed to pretend I'm a guy dating these guys? I don't even know how to be a girl dating them.

I let that question roll around in my mind while I finish washing my hair with cold water. The icy blast helps neutralize my stinging skin as I think about how I'm going to play this shit. If I wasn't even a tiny bit attracted to them or pretending to be a boy, this wouldn't be a big deal. But alas, that's *not* my situation so I can't let this playacting get too realistic. After all, even if some of them did find me appealing, I'm *not* a guy. They'll be furious when they find out my secret.

"Okay, Kit, you just need to be careful and cautious. Don't let them get to you," I whisper to myself as I grab the towel to dry off.

"What was that?"

The growl makes my eyes widen and I wrap the luxe bath sheet around me tightly as I tiptoe over to peek through the crack in the stall. I was right —that was His Royal Pain-in-my-Assness, Jasper. My breath hitches as he passes by only clad in a small towel barely clinging to his hips. His tatts and scales are on display with water trickling down his huge, muscled back.

I'm gonna pass out, no lie.

When no one notices my peeping, I cut my gaze from the huge, impressive dragon bully to the others. X's lithe form is willowy with compact, cut muscles on pale skin like that vampire on Buffy. They're hot in a way the others couldn't dream of, while Salem and Slash are beefy and stacked. Wiping my mouth just in case, I scan for Anton, noting he has an oddly athletic form—like a swimmer, and Zav is smaller, but definitely built for speed and stealth.

Oriel's swirls of tattoos are even more gorgeous than Jasper's and every inch of him is covered in art that would make a tattooist on Earth weep. He looks like an avenging angel of darkness now, so I can't imagine what he looks like half-shifted.

I am so fucking screwed.

A thought occurs to me and I back away from the crack, dropping my towel to look at myself with a frown. I'm okay, I suppose. My boobs are decent when unbound, but I'm not a model, and I have a lot of scars. They're from a lot of different things, including the *incident,* but I know this look isn't conventionally attractive. I won't get any open-mouthed gapes from guys, regardless of whether they're demons or humans.

But that's not why I'm here, nor is it why we're doing this stupid game of pretend. I just need to survive, not hook a sex partner. It doesn't matter that I'm damaged goods because they can't see through my damn clothes anyway.

"Fuck, Kit," I grumble as I pull on my boxer briefs then wriggle myself into my binder. "You're losing your focus."

The sound of a palm slapping against my door makes me jump and without thinking, I slam my palm back on my side angrily. The intake of breath from the demon outside my stall is quick, but then comes out in irritation. "What are you in there talking to yourself about? Why does it take you so damn long? Do I need to send Oriel in to help?"

"*No!*" I shout quickly then realize how insane it was. "I mean, I'm fine. Go away, Jasper. I can talk to myself if I want. It guarantees I hear less bullshit, anyway."

There. That should teach him.

The huff of indignation makes me grin, but his feet on the floor give away his path. "Fine. But you have *five more minutes* before I send someone in after you. Pray that it's not me."

"Fuck off."

My retort is full of resolve, but his words make me move quickly despite the aches it causes. I *cannot* have some well-intentioned demon come bursting into my stall to find my boobs hanging out. Yanking my clothes on, I get everything back in my basket and open the door, slowly moving toward the sink like a little old man. Salem blinks, rushing over to help me despite my batting him away.

One peek of that barely clad set of guys is enough and now I have to look them all in the eyes—fuck my life.

Lean On Me

sälem

"Kit Kat, take it easy. Dr. D said you can't over-do it for a couple of days, dude." He gives me a sulky look that I have a stupidly hard time not reacting to as I guide him to the counter. "It's not a sign of weakness to need help when you're injured. Is this a human thing?"

My gaze cuts to the rest of our caliphate and they shrug, obviously not sure, either. Oriel tilts his head, watching Kit pull items out of his basket carefully. Once he's got what he needs, the crow shifter frowns a little. I want to ask him what the hell his problem is, but the expression on his face tells me to keep my big yap shut. I guess he doesn't want Prince Prickface to hear his question, and I don't blame him.

Jasper's behaving for the moment, but most of us don't trust that to last as the day goes on. His churlishness is too ingrained as a defensive mechanism.

"Why is everyone staring at me? That's going to draw attention, you know," the smaller human grumbles as he preps his toothbrush. "You can't study me like I'm a damn bug under a lamp all day."

The Prince snorts, walking to his private station to apply aftershave. "It's hard not to. You're moving like an invalid and you snarl anytime someone touches you. I don't know *how* we're supposed to maintain this facade."

"Behave." Slash's single word makes all of my dorm mates straighten, even the grumpy royal. "They will believe what we tell them to."

That's easy to say when you're sporting a fin and razor teeth all day.

"Slash, you have the ability to silence a room with a look. Not all of us are so formidable," Zavida says as he ruffles his rusty hair.

"Let's map the flow for today, then," X says as they roll their stockings up their legs. "They said the classes will flip to prep for these stupid games, but not change. It's Monday, so who's where?"

Kit pauses his brushing, his eyes wide as he looks at us in the mirror. Spitting quickly, he rinses his mouth before replying. "I have Intro to Supes and Deconstructing History *alone* on Monday and Wednesday."

His admission gets a chorus of groans or growls depending on the demon, and the tension in the room ratchets up. Oriel lifts his hand, clearing his throat, "Let's not forget I found him being cornered by Lilibet in there last week."

"Fuck," Anton mutters. "We haven't had time to deal with that mess yet."

"I have a free period during the first slot," Slash says with a toothy grin. "I can deal with the Cubi. She'll back off once I'm there or I'll make her suffer."

Jasper rolls his eyes, sighing as he pulls his uniform on, adjusting it for his preferred shift. "Fine. What about the second class?"

"Guys, I don't really need…"

"We all have class." Zav looks up from his phone, his eyes dark as he fixes his tie. He's always the first one dressed, but Kit has him beat by a landslide. "That's an issue, but I don't believe we can solve it this semester without a great deal of administrative power."

X wrinkles their nose as they lace their knee-high boots. "We will *never* get Darkstar to sign off on that. He's definitely up to something and if he hates Kit and us, he'll never approve the moves needed to make it work."

"*Hello!*" We all spin to see the guy in question glaring at us in annoyance. He's clenching his fists at his sides and there's frustration rolling off him in waves. "Just because you have a plan that I agreed to does *not* mean you get to dictate my entire life. I will be okay in one class alone, especially since it's not Lilibet. If I'm *not*, I'll tell you. How about that, douchebags?"

I blink, a slow smile creeping over my face as I yank my shirt over my head then move closer. "Okay, Kit Kat. You're right. You agreed to do this shit because you're not an idiot, but treating you like fine china is off the plate."

"That's not what we—"

Oriel shakes his head at Anton. "It's not what we meant, but it's how he felt. I get it. But Kit, you gotta know we're worried about someone hurting you again. Until your shit emerges, you're a lot more breakable than the rest of us."

Our leader grunts as he finishes up his routine, and I take that as agreement until he says otherwise. Slash nods, then the rest of my brothers fall in line with our thief's assessment. Kit sighs, gathering his things with his shoulders slumped. I frown, not liking the loss of his spitfire, so I take them from him gently.

"Let's drop these off and grab the rest of your stuff, dude. The rest of these dicks can argue about whatever they want until we meet at the elevator."

My answer is a tiny grin, and when I whistle, the kinkajou comes running out of a pile of towels where she was curled up. Her big eyes blink as she stares at the group, then she chitters loudly and shakes her paw again. I really think that's her method of telling us all to get fucked, and Kit chuckles before holding his arm out.

"Alright, Salem. We'll take Dottie and get supplies. Clearing all this testosterone out of my lungs is probably a good thing."

Before anyone can shoot back, I lead him away from the sink, looking over my shoulder at the caliphate with narrowed eyes. They need to give the poor kid some fucking space or we're all going to go down in flames. Our discussion about the shared interest in Kit was a good first step, but we can't let our instinct to protect him alienate us.

As we walk back to the dorm, I look down at our new obsession. He's moving better, but he's definitely not going to classes without an escort. Jasper wouldn't tell any of us how the fuck Kit avoided getting roasted, but I'm glad he's not lying in the infirmary with burns while Dr. D hovers over him.

"You know, if you need to talk about what happened... before Jasper showed... all you need to do is tell me," I say softly. "We don't have therapists here and shit, so..."

His crooked smile makes my chest tighten in that odd way, but he shakes his head. "Not yet. I'm still... processing it all, especially Jasper's help. It's hard to explain, but I'm not completely sure which details are real and which ones I maybe... imagined?"

"Fair enough, little dude. But I'm here if you need one ear who'll shut up to listen."

Strangely enough, I mean that—even the part about doing it without everyone else around.

A knock at our door tells me it's time to head for the elevator, and I close up the container of fruit Kit and I were tossing to Dottie. "Time to face the music, girl. Your master and I have to put on a show for the crowd, so you gotta behave."

My roommate snorts and shakes his head. "Dottie will do what she wants, no matter what. I trust her judgement by now."

"Oh, that's going to go over so well," I mutter. Looking at the kinkajou, I shake a finger playfully. "You have to let people touch him, young lady. It might not be comfortable for him at first, but that's the only way we can sell this shit."

Kit gives me an amused look. "You're talking to her like I do. I can't really decide if she understands everything or not."

"Either way, I hope I got the message across." Rising to my feet, I wait for him to hook his bag over his neck and hold my arm out for the rodent. "Let's get this show on the road, folks."

"Okay," Kit sighs as he grabs my bicep. I tuck it close to my side, smiling when he doesn't shrink away. "Time to face the executioners."

Guiding him out the door, I grin. "I like music as a metaphor better, Kit Kat. None of us want to kill you, you know."

"Speak for yourself, panda," Jasper grumbles. "I'll definitely want to murder him if this shit goes sideways."

"Shut up, Prince."

Kit snickers at Slash's irritated grunt as we all fill the elevator. The big guy is showing up for him in the best way possible since the incident, so I'm inclined to let him into the inner circle with X and Oriel. Everyone else is close to joining, except the grouchy dragon who simply refuses to admit to himself what we all know.

Well, everyone but Kit, but that's no surprise.

"So tell me what I should expect this time." We all look down at Kit—except Zav—as he demands our attention. "If I can prepare, I'll handle it better."

"We're going to sell the idea that you're dating us, one by one. It won't all be at breakfast, but it's a good place to start," Oriel says softly. "Salem is already close, so if he behaves like he is now but amps it up a bit, it will get tongues wagging."

Zavida pushes his glasses up, flushing a bit. "Then Slash can take him to the first class and it will reinforce it, right?"

"Yes."

Grinning a little, Kit looks over at the shark shifter. "You're not going to force feed me, right, big guy? I promise Salem sent me food I'll eat at the table."

Jasper arches a brow at his second, who pointedly ignores him for our charge. The shark rumbles a bit, studying him for a second. "I'll get fresh coffee, then."

"Lillith's dirty thongs," Jasper mutters as he stares at the ceiling. "This is going to be interminable."

His grunt tells me someone socked him in the side or gut, and I'm strangely pleased with that. "That works, Slash. We'll start with those two hints, then Kit Kat goes to History on his own. Who's got him after that?"

"I'm *not* a football you can pass around the field."

"Nope, but you are someone we want to ensure stays in one piece," Zavida says shyly. "So Oriel should join you and you can head to the *Triclinium* for lunch, right? You'll meet Jasper and me there, but by the end, Anton should be there, too."

Anton nods, watching Kit digest the information carefully. "Correct. I can drop him at Lineage afterward."

Fuck. That's another class he's got on his own.

"O and I have Lit after that, so we'll get him then," I muse. "I wonder what these assholes are going to do since they're canceling all the damn extracurriculars? Think they'll tell us in class or…?"

"No. I think they'll tell us in the *Triclinium*," Jasper says as the doors pop open. "Hurry up so we don't miss anything. I don't like how quiet it's been since the announcement."

That's our leader—missing the forest for the fucking trees. He's so intent on *not* letting anyone know how worried he is about Kit after the attack that he's gone full scale laser focus on the games. His ability to narrow the field is great when it's helping develop strategy, but it's shit when it makes people feel like they don't matter.

I look down at Kit, hoping the dragon hasn't upset him again. Luckily, he's too busy chewing his lip and mouthing something to himself as he holds onto my arm. He doesn't seem to be going into one of his episodes, so I don't interfere.

Maybe he just needs to get in the right mindset.

After all, this is going to put an even bigger target on his back, but it's the only plan we've got. Nothing else will keep all the lower level idiots off his case. And Satan forbid, when the admin figures out which damn demons are missing from their crispy end this weekend, it will keep eyes from turning to the new kid—hopefully.

We march up to the double doors of the cafeteria and Jasper looks at the entire caliphate seriously. "This is it, gentleman. The curtain is going up, and we have to make sure everyone believes the show. There's no room for error, or the newbie could get killed."

"Thanks for the inspiring speech," Kit grumbles. "Can we go in and get caffeine now? I can't take anymore of your bullshit without an injection into my veins."

Damn, he's fun; I'm going to enjoy this.

Somebody's Watching Me

kät/kit

J asper throws the doors open, striding inside as if he owns the place—which he kind of does, I guess. His head is held high, chin tilted arrogantly, and his posture reeks of entitlement. It's no different than normal, but I know this day is definitely yet another that's going to change my entire fucking life.

I hate having men be responsible for my world tipping over, by the way.

The low roar of demons chattering dampens a bit as he crosses the floor with Slash and Zav at his side, followed by Anton and X, then Salem and I, and Oriel at the rear. It's almost a military formation, so I assume the shark is the creator of this plan. He seems to take presentation seriously when people perceive the caliphate's power, and Jasper made it clear he listens to his friend when it comes to that shit.

"Everyone is staring," I mutter out of the side of my mouth to my partner.

He chuckles softly, barely jerking his head in a nod. "They didn't gawp this much last week."

"Last week, the school hadn't announced a millennia-old tradition returning to a population largely unprepared for that kind of brutality—except for the children and relatives of royals. They've come to the realization that caliphates such as ours are primed to survive, while many of them will not."

Oriel snorts. "Not to mention no one is used to you having someone clutching your arm so confidently."

Great. That means Jasper and the others were right about how quickly this shit will spread.

I suck in a slow, calming breath. Rumor mills were vicious after my attack, and I was bitter about the fosters sending me back like a poorly cooked steak, but I wasn't sad about leaving that school. Humans are pack animals, no matter what anyone says, and their innate desire to belong leads them to be absolutely dog shit when it comes to compassion. It's especially rough in preteen and teen years—not that being a fucking sociopath is ever okay—so the girls tore my reputation to pieces defending that piece of shit.

Their instant acceptance of a false narrative about me without a whiff of proof destroyed what little self-esteem I had left after the incident. My abuser got off scot-free, making sad faces like a wounded dove while I was castigated by his minions every day. Their betrayal wasn't personal, my therapist told me, but it felt like it was. These chicks saw me all the time, minding my own business and not being troublesome, but they bought into a shiny cover story from someone they thought had more social sway. It took a long time to accept that it was more about their own fragile psyches than mine and I needed to let go of my anger towards the flying monkeys to focus it on the instigator—the true abuser.

"Kit?"

I blink, coming out of my trance to look at Salem as he holds a chair out for me. Shaking my head slightly, I lower myself onto it carefully and force a smile up at him as he scoots me in. Dottie jumps from his shoulder to the table, standing in front of me chittering softly. She knew I was having a moment, I think, so I reach out to let her grasp my finger. The touch is soothing and after a second, I'm able to clear my throat and murmur, "Thanks."

The panda squints at me briefly, but nods and smiles so the people around us don't see any strain. "Anytime, Kit Kat."

Now that I'm seated, Jasper takes his chair at the head with a huff of impatience, then Slash and Zav flank him. Oriel sits on my other side, so X drops down across from me with Anton between him and Slash. They all look at me expectantly and I frown. "What?"

"Tell the big guy to grab your coffees, KK," X says with a wink. Their flashy blazer has sequins that wink in the bright lights, and I have the strongest urge to ask them to fix my frumpy shit for me.

I can't, obviously, or my stupid secret will be out, but damn, their shit is hot.

"Sorry," I mumble. "I didn't know I needed to… lead this?"

Anton shakes his head. "Not lead, per se. But… guide. You *have* seen people dating before, right?"

The groan I want to release is full of irritation. Apparently, these assholes don't have a damn clue how to 'date' someone and are using outdated bullshit from… TV shows or something as reference. They want me to act like a stereotypical girlfriend, sending them to fetch things and shit. This is going to be a pain in my ass; I'm pretending to be a dude, and I'm just not that kind of chick. No shade to women with those expectations; Kat Camponella is simply not high maintenance but for my stupid issues.

"Um…" I lick my lips, looking to the end of the table with what I hope is a pleasant smile. "Slash, can you get us some coffee? Salem packed my breakfast, but I'm dying for some caffeine."

Oh, how stupid I feel right now. Shoot me… just shoot me in the face, please.

The big guy grins toothily, rumbling with what actually seems like pleasure. "I would be honored, little demon."

My jaw drops as he stands, posture puffed up and proud like I handed him a medal. "What the hell?"

Salem snickers as he helps me get my delicious smelling food out of the 'to go' bag. "You're about to find out some *really* interesting shit about demon hybrids, Kit Kat."

Burying my face in my hands, I groan as I rub my palms down my cheeks. "I am *so* not ready for this crap. It's too early and I hurt way too much to try to figure that statement out."

"Relax," Oriel says as his hand drops to squeeze my knee. "We'll help you navigate it. You're doing well so far. Everyone is whispering, and that's what we wanted—them to watch this, not question why you look beat to hell."

Perfect. That's just what I was hoping for—not.

I'M SPARKLING FROM HEAD-TO-TOE WITH ANXIETY BY THE TIME WE FINISH eating. There were more eyes on me for that half-hour than I've had on me in a *long* time. It was creepy as fuck, but I have to give Salem and Oriel credit for helping me stay anchored. Between them and Dottie, I was able to eat so Slash didn't snarl at me, parry verbally with Jasper, and not toss my cookies all over the table.

It's a Christmas miracle, Charlie Brown.

As we head for the doors of the *Triclinium,* I feel my chest get tighter. The bulk of the group have to head to their own classes, and I'll have to endure this bullshit on my own. Dottie's clinging to my neck, making soft sounds near my ear. I know she's working to keep me level, and I appreciate it, but this charade and my aching body are making it tough.

"Okay, Kit Kat. This is where we all split except for the trash compactor," X says with a smirk.

"Niiice *Jaws* reference," I mutter with a small grin. "Good distraction."

"I try," they say, preening playfully and even Slash grins a little. "But seriously, you have the chat. If you're in trouble, what do you say?"

My eyes flutter shut and I growl softly, "I'm going to kill you for this, but 'cherry pie' is the code word."

The dragon laughs darkly, just as he has every single time I've had to repeat that since yesterday. "Perfect, pleb."

"Stop calling me that," I grit out as I turn to Slash. "Can we get the fuck out of here before I blow this by slugging him in his extremely punchable fucking nose?"

All I get is a nod and the tiniest glint of mischief in his dark eyes, so I let go of Salem's arm to take the shark's. I hate that I need the help, but honestly, I'd be moving like a senior citizen if I didn't hold onto someone and push the pain of moving normally into my feet.

They all wave, heading in various directions as Slash leads me away from the cafeteria and towards the academic building. The distance has never seemed this daunting before, but I also haven't had to do this when someone healed my bones the day before. The crowds milling about are much more subdued than they were last week; there's no one jacking around, shooting magic at one another or hanging out on the Gothic architecture of the buildings.

The campus atmosphere is like a damn funeral home now.

"It's weird, right?" I ask the shark hybrid as we walk toward the building where my class is. "This quiet?"

"Very." He pauses at the base of the steps in front of our destination when we reach it, studying me. "This will be okay?"

"Dude, you gotta use more syllables," I grumble. "I know you only say shit when it matters, but that doesn't mean you have to be damn near mute."

His smile is bigger this time, and his huge hand lands on top of mine on his bicep. "I find people listen harder when you talk less. They assume what you say is important."

I frown, tilting my head as I look at him. "X talks all the time and people listen."

Jerking his head to the steps, he guides me up the first one as he replies, "X is sparkly. Everyone enjoys shiny things."

The snort that escapes my lips is followed by a giggle, and I slap my free hand over my mouth. *Fuck, fuck, fuck.* That was incredibly stupid, and it might have blown my cover. When Slash doesn't comment, I force out a fake cough. "Well, that's definitely true. But Jasper never shuts the fuck up, either."

He huffs and I know this time, *he's* trying to cover a laugh. "Jasper is the Prince."

"Oh, I know. He makes sure *everyone* knows," I shoot back grumpily. "I meant that despite the stupid shit he spews, people don't take him less seriously because he talks a lot. Salem and O are similar, but they're not assholes like the prince."

Slash stops in the middle of the steps, turning to look down at me seriously. "You are mistaken."

"About what?" This seems like something I should listen to regardless of how much he does or doesn't babble—his expression is very firm.

"Those two were very quiet, though not as much as me, prior to your arrival."

My mouth drops open and I blink for a second. "Really?"

"Indeed. Oriel in particular often stayed quiet for days unless he was filling Jasper in on assignments. Their behavior is surprising to all of us." A gentle tug on my arm gets me moving again and as we ascend, he continues, "X and Anton flittered off to their own world a lot. It is very different now, and I believe that is what scares my old friend so much."

Well, shit. I told him to talk more and I'll be damned if he didn't listen.

Licking my lips nervously, I realize that while we've been talking, I completely ignored all the whispers and eyes on us. We're standing at the doors to the academic building, ready to walk in, and I stopped thinking about how much I hurt and who was watching me. I simply felt safe while he was by my side. That hits me like a smelly trout to the face, and I draw in a shuddering breath.

"What's wrong, little demon?" Slash asks as he pulls the huge door open.

"I… It's nothing." I shake my head, barely able to comprehend the situation, much less explain it to anyone. "We should get in there before Lilibet goes bonkers. I think she's going to be pissed about you hanging around as it is."

"No, she won't."

I frown, giving him a doubtful expression. "How do you know that?"

"Because if she gives you trouble again… I'll eat her."

The worst part is, I believe him without a doubt.

DANGER ZONE

oriel

Sitting through my first two classes was a pain in the ass. Slash isn't known for being verbose, so we didn't get updates during his turn at being bodyguard in the separate chat we started. I know it grated on everyone, but not a single complaint filtered through, even from the Pissy Prince.

Slash keeping our new inductee safe was a foregone conclusion, anyway.

Once he had to drop Kit at his Human History class, all bets were off. We all poked our heads out to check on him, which went unanswered because the guy is nothing if not stubborn about his education. The rest of us are much more *laissez-faire*, but I suppose it's because much like knowing Slash would keep him safe, we all know we'll be leaders whether we flunk classes at Discordia or not.

Not that anyone would dare fail us, of course.

I cut out of the spy craft lab early to lurk outside his classroom so the ache in my gut would shut the hell up. As the minutes tick by, I fiddle with the ring on my thumb, spinning to quell the anxiety building inside of me. When he comes out of Kindervelt's class looking relatively unbothered, I sigh in relief.

"Heya, Kit Kat. Time for the big table again." He wrinkles his nose and I shrug. "We would be almost done with the show for the semester after a week, but the Games changed everything. It's especially important with your attack."

Brushing his longer hair out of his eyes, Kit sighs heavily. "I know, O. The stares are beneficial this time, but it's hard to… keep my brain on that wavelength. You know?"

"Yep." I hold out my arm, grinning a bit as Dottie chirps a 'hello' to me when her human takes it. "We'll survive it, though. I think after another week, our claim on you will be cemented enough to forgo the *Triclinium* for Salem's cooking instead."

His squeeze on my arm makes my smile wider. "Thank fuck for that. I sort of learned not to be a big eater early on, but with Slash growling at me every time he thinks I look hungry and this injury sucking my energy, I guess I need food more. Luckily, Panda-man never lets me leave without provisions."

I chuckle, shaking my head. "It's easy for us to forget how much he does for the group because he used to be asleep like eighty percent of the time. He's awake more in the past week than I've seen since we were kids. You're too amusing to nod off."

"I'm more fascinating than snoozing—what a review," Kit snarks, his eyes dancing with mirth. "You really know how to compliment a dude, man."

Was that a bad thing to say? Fuck if I know; this isn't my forte.

"You know what I mean," I mutter as we leave the academic building to head across the campus to the *Triclinium*. "Salem and Slash hovering over you that way is both interesting *and* complimentary, I think."

"Really?"

"Absolutely. It's not like the big guys fawn over every person in our path, you know."

Kit hums under his breath, not answering as we cross the middle of the quad area. He's right—the amount of eyes I feel on me has multiplied by a large factor. His grip on my arm is likely part of it, but since I cling to the shadows more often than not, my being in the open is drawing curiosity as well. But the sensation of being watched instead of being the watcher is pretty annoying and now I get why he's so ruffled by it.

It makes you feel vulnerable.

"Someone said you barely spoke before last week. Are you secretly a hermit, Oriel?"

"Not remotely secretly, Kit Kat. I've never been shy about preferring solitude and staying out of the limelight. It helps with my function in the group, obviously, and I can gratify my own needs better there as well."

"Gratify…?" he chokes out.

I almost bark an amused laugh before I realize he might think I'm poking fun at him. It takes me a second to get myself under control before I reply, "The crow part, man. I like to hoard things, and I love to steal them. Anything not needed for the caliphate is fair game for my collection of shiny shit that makes the bird happy."

Damn, I never tell people that. What the hell?

"Oh… oh. Got it. Sorry," he says. His face is flushed bright red and it literally delights me when he ducks his head. "Yeah, that makes sense. The shifter sides of you guys are really fucking cool to learn about."

"Huh. I guess I'm so used to all this…" I gesture at the landscape of Discordia and Hell in general. "…that I've never given thought to how cool it must seem to someone who didn't know it existed."

Kit snorts, rolling his eyes at me as we get to the steps of the cafeteria. "Oriel, two weeks ago, I thought my future included either an Ivy League school and a bunch of rich dicks with double popped collars or being stuck in my small town working in a diner until I could find enough money to get out. Demons, shifters, and magic would have been cool to anyone, but to me, it's a goddamn miracle."

Leaning in, I tap my finger on his nose with a pleased smile. "Then regardless of the sucky ass circumstances that lead you here or the ones we face now, I'm stoked as fuck to be part of that so-called miracle."

The color rises in his face again, making my chest tighten, and he's about to respond when a voice calls out in front of us.

"Hey, guys! Do you not check your phones? Sheesh."

I blink as I pull back, looking at the twitchy kitsune as he comes down the stairs in a huff. "What's the problem, Zav?"

"Jasper says they're going to start talking games during the lunch periods. Get in here—*now*."

Once again, the Prince of Pain manages to ruin a moment—it's like he has a sixth sense for this shit.

BY THE TIME KIT AND I REACH THE BIG TABLE, I CAN TELL JASPER'S stressed as fuck. He's clenching his hands on his silverware as if he's going to stab the next person that aggravates him. Not a good sign, in my opinion, but lately, the prince is impossible to catch in a decent mood. His eyes narrow as I get Kit settled, then flick to the crowds.

He's checking to see if they're noting that this time, I'm the one helping our newest member.

"Oriel, leave the runt here while you fetch the food."

I roll my eyes, giving Zav a *look*, but the kitsune shrugs. Maybe Jasper's worried about appearances *and* the trials. He certainly seems more tense than he was after he formulated the plans for this week. "Got it, boss," I say drily.

"Don't be a pain in the ass," he mutters as I turn to leave. "Remember what we discussed."

As if I could forget that ridiculous meeting by the next afternoon.

I shake my head ruefully wishing I had more than the wishy-washy gamer to support me. Zav is definitely sorry and I think he's going to make up for his dumbassery, but standing up to Jasper will take time. It's a lot easier to get him to back off when there's a full caliphate present. Sighing to myself, I trudge over to the food service area and scan what's on the menu. None of it is as appealing as what our personal chef would make, but I see a few things that will do.

Filling two plates with meats and savory vegetables, I pause as I hit the dessert area. I have no idea if Kit has allergies to anything, especially since Hell has its own flora and fauna, but I know Salem said he loved crunkleberries. I grab a huge piece of crunkleberry cobbler topped with loads of black

Underworld cow whipped cream and sparkling dark Fae dust. It looks girly as shit, but it's delicious, so I think he'll like it. I swipe two pieces of pitch black chocolate silence cake for myself, then move to the drink station.

My hackles raise as I catch the whispers floating through the air. Lower demons are wondering which of us Kit is fucking, while the mid-levels are more interested in what the deal with the Games is. I whip up a couple of iced mochas and two glasses of water, listening for the upper tier rumor mill carefully.

They're the ones who are the most dangerous if they don't buy our story.

"I heard he's working his way to the top the hard way—if you get my drift."

Covering a snort, I duck my head as I continue eavesdropping on one of the court tables. They're all so criminally easy to manipulate because they're so desperate to be part of the in-crowd. It would shock every damn one of them that Kit could a give a fuck less about Jasper, and actively *tries* to avoid the prince at all costs. He's certainly not being friendly with the rest of us to get Jasper's approval.

"Morons," I mutter to myself as I turn and head back towards our table. It won't be too long until Anton joins us, so I hope whatever bullshit the admin is going to trot out doesn't happen until he's here.

When I get to our spot, I put the tray in front of me, off-loading Kit's half before I even touch mine. Demons can be quite old fashioned about courtship and all seven of us were raised with the appropriate behavior drilled into our skulls by our families' tutors. He looks at me curiously, then at his plate.

"Does this dessert thing have the mouth-party berries in it?" His eyes widen as a broad grin takes over his face. "I've been *dying* for more of those!"

Score one for the crow—it helps to notice shit from the shadows.

"Crunkleberries? Yes. The cream is a delicacy, too, and very rich. Maybe be—"

Before I can warn him, he digs into the sweet treat, ignoring the rest of the tray as he groans softly. A flare of energy sweeps over our table and my eyes jerk to Zav and Jasper. They're watching Kit as intently as I am, and I decide my earlier statement isn't true. Perhaps they *are* as interested as everyone else, but they're too fucking stunted to figure out what to do about it.

The chitter of the kinkajou brings me out of my reverie and I look at the creature giving me an awfully skeptical expression for an animal. That damn thing is *definitely* magical, but I haven't quite worked out how yet. My knowledge of familiars is limited because they're rare, but one of the Fae casters at home has a bloodbird familiar. I need to send her an email to ask a few questions about their origins and what types of hybrids and supes attract them.

"Oriel? Are you with us?" Zavida says, his voice edged with strain.

Damn. I spaced again. This being social shit is harder than I imagined.

"Yes, yes." I wave my hands as I put my focus on the prince and the kitsune. "I'm here; I was just… noodling a few things. There's a lot going on and even more we don't know. Thinking about shit is how we find inconsistencies we might be able to use to our advantage."

"This isn't finding a flaw in a security system, O," Jasper says with a frown. "I know thinking is the 'go-to' for you and Zav, but…"

Kit clears his throat, looking up with a face full of berries, cream, sparkling dust, and zero self-awareness. "I dunno, Prince Asshole. Thinking is something you guys don't do often enough."

No one says a word as we all stare, and after a minute, I grab my napkin. Kit looks surprised when I turn his head, but he lets me clean the mess off of him before it short-circuits every brain cell at the table. The sight is both adorable and hot at the same time; I know those two have no idea what the actual fuck to do with the image.

"There. Now we can take you seriously." I grin and let go, allowing him to pull back with a cough. "Go on, Kit. Tell us what you really think."

That's probably a dumb suggestion, but I enjoy chaos and my dick's hard…. sue me.

Nerd Rage

Kat/Kit

Everyone acted really fucking *weird* at lunch after I devoured my dessert, so I backed off my blunt assessment of their critical thinking skills. Dottie kept sniffing around and giving me looks I couldn't interpret; I have no idea what got into her. The entire thing was so damn bizarre, and it didn't get any better after Anton arrived. He looked at everyone, then at me, and dropped his tray with a clatter that even made O jump a little.

Satan help me with a pack full of fucking dudes, man.

I blink when I realize they've got me switching my colloquialisms already. If only the snot-ball people at my old school—including the stinky twins—could see me now… No one would believe it; Kat Camponella being social, eating, and not slinking around trying to be invisible would be too far-fetched. Still, I don't feel like anything is changing for the worse, so it's okay. Everyone has to grow up at some point, and this is my new era.

"Keep telling yourself that, Kit," I mumble to myself as Zavida walks beside me. The kitsune was assigned to walk me to Ancient Demon Lineage—another class I have on my own—and he's been quiet as a mouse.

"What did you say?"

My head turns and I feel heat crawling up my neck when he catches me talking to myself. "Nothing. Don't worry about it."

He frowns, scratching his chin. "You can talk to me, you know. I know I have shit to make up for, and I will, but I'm not going to do anything bad."

Oh, we're going there, huh?

"Zavida, I appreciate that sentiment, but trust has to be earned. You're in the negative in that column because of your dumb shit, so it's going to take time." I see him wince and sigh, feeling a pang of pity for the guy. "That doesn't mean you won't get there. Just… start thinking for yourself and stop letting that fuckwad lead you around by the dick."

This time *he* turns red and my eyes widen when I realize I've probably hit on something very private. He coughs, then finally nods. "I know what you meant. It's not an excuse, more of a reason, but Jasper has been a big support system. He's rough in public, but he's… not the same when we're alone. That makes it hard to separate, but I'm determined to do it."

We come to the doors for the academic building and I grab one before he can get to it. He frowns, trying to communicate something to me with his eyebrows that I don't get. I roll my eyes at him and point to the open space. "Dude, just go in. I got it."

The huff he lets out is puzzling, and I follow him to the elevator with a puzzled expression. Sometimes, I think males of *every* species are so damn odd that no one should be expected to figure what the hell is up their ass. They're so fucking sensitive about the weirdest shit that it's impossible to know what the right move is. He fidgets as we wait for the car, then we pile in with a group of other students. The bulk of them get off on the second floor, so we're alone after they exit.

That's when the small fox shifter pushes the button, jerking the elevator to a stop abruptly.

What the fuck?

"I'm going to be late," I grit out. "The professors are not exactly forgiving with me like they might be with you dipshits."

Zavida walks closer to me, looking at me seriously. "You have to let me do things."

"Huh?"

He rakes his hand through his rusty locks, looking frustrated. "I know you don't know how all of this works, so I'm trying to be patient. But… people already see me as weak."

I frown, making a confused face at him. "So? Who the fuck cares? Random people's opinions don't mean shit. The only people you should worry about are your family and friends, Zav."

My words seem to agitate him more, and he throws his hands up in the air. "That's not how this world works, Kit. Appearances, reactions, and emotions are how you're measured, especially now that the Games are in play. Notice how Lucian was supposed to make some big announcement and then *didn't?*"

Damn, he's right. The guys were being so strange that I forgot about it.

"He did that to get everyone's attention. Failing to follow through means it could come at *any time*, which will put him and his power on every demon in Discordia's mind all day. He's toying with our perceptions and emotions, especially the fear some of the lower level guys are feeling."

"Ohhhhh…" I say as it hits me. "Fuck, that asshole is smarter than I gave him credit for."

"Pit demons *always* are, Kit. They were created to torture and extract things from demons for the King. Lucian is ancient as hell and he knows how to do his job extremely well. This won't be the last time he manipulates the entire student body for his own entertainment or gain."

I scratch my forehead, muddling through his words carefully. "I badly need to catch up on demon types. Like, I have to learn their powers, their strengths, their weaknesses…. everything. I'll be a hindrance if I don't know how to think around these idiots."

Zavida smiles and I see the hint of color surrounding him perk up. "I could help with that. Studying is one of my less unsavory skills. Maybe I could make some flashcards?"

The excitement on his face is kind of cute, so I lick my lips, considering his offer. After a moment, I nod slowly. "Okay. You make some stuff up and maybe some of you can quiz me? I think Salem and Oriel would help if you make them a set."

He stabs the elevator button, starting its progress upward again with a bright grin. "I'll make enough for everyone. Colorful, laminated, maybe with pictures… Yes, this will definitely work! We're going to get you up to speed so fast."

I love the enthusiasm, but the guy is delusional if he thinks their pissy prince is going to do a damn thing.

Kindervelt is a pompous asshole, but at least he treats everyone the same. His demigod half is probably from a Roman or Greek, I've decided, but he refuses to tell anyone. The weird ethereal glow I'm seeing around him is why I landed on the Mediterranean pantheons—he seems to glow slightly gold around the spotted skin of his shifter side. I guess a giraffe shifter isn't any weirder than a panda, but damn, looking up at the guy makes my neck hurt.

"How was class?"

I blink at Oriel as he materializes out of nowhere. "Shit, man. You're going to give me a heart attack." His slow smirk makes my body tighten and I have to take a second before I answer. "Fine. Kindervelt's an ass, but he doesn't single me out."

Before I know it, he's draped an arm over my shoulders and is guiding me to the elevators. "I guess you can't ask for more than that at a demon school. We're not exactly known for being soft."

I'm too busy waiting for my typical reaction to being this close to a guy to kick in to refute his statement. It doesn't happen, just like with Salem, and we walk into the car together. People crowd in around us and I take a deep breath, causing my escort to tighten his hold by pulling me to his side. Again, it doesn't trip my wires and I internally high-five myself. My brain might still be locked in danger mode, but my attack didn't set me back to the beginning of therapy.

Fuck, yeah.

"Are you okay, Kit Kat?" Oriel whispers in a ridiculously low tone.

Dottie moves around in my bag, making soft sounds as she finds a spot where she can press against me through the material. My lips curve up and I look at my feet so he can't see my goofy smile. "Yeah. All good. Thanks."

A cough echoes in the quiet elevator—one combined with a word that isn't any nicer in the demon world than it is in the human one. Oriel tenses next to me, and I feel a zap of dark energy fill the air. The demons around us shift uncomfortably, some of them pulling at the collars of their shirts and others digging into their book bags like they're looking for something. The fidgeting increases as we continue to the ground floor, and I frown as the crow shifter moves me until I'm standing in front of him out of their reach.

"Shhhh…" he says with a wink.

Once I'm settled, he puts his chin on my head, and I watch the boys continue to search for things, their movements getting more frantic until the bell dings and the door opens. They spill out into the lobby, looking around the room briefly before lunging at one another.

"You stole it!"

"No, you did!"

"I'm going to kill you. Give it back!"

The shouts echo off the marble and within seconds, the entire group from our ride starts pounding one another in a pile of limbs and snarls.

"There's a lesson here," Oriel says as he leads me around the mass of dudes beating each other with wild abandon.

I snort. "Don't piss Oriel off?"

"Well, yes… but a deeper one." He grins darkly as the shitty demons keep wailing on each other even though staff members are arriving. "Greed isn't just about physical items. Sometimes, it's about status or power. Those who try to take others down to elevate themselves are open to more manipulation than they think."

Ducking my head as we head out the doors to the steps, I mutter, "I didn't care about the slur, man. Guys are idiots, especially spoiled rich ones, and calling me gay isn't the insult that douche thought it was."

"It's not, but that doesn't mean he gets away with using sexuality that way. For fuck's sake, Kit Kat, it's 2024. Humans might be that far behind the times, but demons aren't." He arches a brow as we walk towards the library building for Lit class. "He only said that shit because everyone still thinks *you* are human. And that's un-fucking-acceptable on another level entirely."

"O, I'm not worth—"

"Stop that sentence. You're part of our caliphate, which means, you *are* special and they *should* fear you. Magic or no, we don't allow disrespect like that to stand."

I have to swallow hard again, trying to distance myself from emotions I haven't had in a very long time. Actually, I can't even remember how long it's been since I felt like someone cared enough to do that, so it's messing with my head.

Gotta back away, Kit.

"Thanks. I'll… try to remember that. It won't be easy, though. Be patient with me."

That said, I turn my gaze on the path to the library. I don't think I can look at him right now. My heart is doing weird flip-flops and my gut is churning with anxiety. Dottie pokes her head out of the bag, waving a paw at me as she scrambles out to sit on my shoulder. The little rodent is so attuned with my emotions that I'm not even surprised anymore.

"Ooh, there's the pretty girl…" Oriel coos and my head whips around. "What? She is. Dottie's a pretty girl, isn't she?"

Motherfucker, that was scary as hell—what am I going to do about this shit?

"Salem's meeting us inside, right?" I ask, hoping to cover up my new mini panic attack.

Oriel stops making silly faces at my animal and grins. "Hopefully. But you know how he is… he could have fallen asleep and lost them for all we know. We may have to fight off more of your admirers to claim them."

Admirers… right.

"Ha, ha. You're so funny, Oriel. A real laugh riot," I grumble as we reach the huge doors. "You should do stand-up on Netflix or something."

He snorts and shakes his head. "Oh, no. There's a crossroads demon with a really ugly deal in place regarding those, and I can promise you, not being funny but still making money isn't a coincidence."

Huh. I guess that confirms everyone's suspicions—selling their souls is the only way those idiots can make a buck.

Puttin' On The Ritz

Xerxes

This day has been a major buzzkill: no classes with Kit, edging Headmaster keeping info from us, and the OG caliphate chat going bonkers with Jasper fretting about us 'keeping up appearances'. I'm still pissed that Darkstar canceled all the extracurriculars for this nonsense, as Drama Club is one of my main outlets for my creativity that isn't tied to a grade.

Hopefully, Kit survived Dark Age Lit with Salem and Oriel. I know Romero is a fun professor—surprising given her status as a Fallen—but dealing with those alone in the afternoon can't be easy. By the end of the day, Oriel is usually fidgeting, aching to find things to steal, and the bear falls asleep. It has to be like baby-sitting more than getting educated.

Perhaps I'll steal him away for a tour of the costume lab? I bet he'd like—

The squeal of magic precedes a loud boom intended to get our attention and the campus-wide announcement system stops everyone in the quad in their tracks. I roll my eyes, hating the insane dramatics of the fucker who runs this place; this could definitely have been a mass email or text.

"Attention, loyal demons of Hell and Discordia students! There will be a caliphates-only meeting in the Triclinium in five minutes. If you are in a caliphate, your class, studio, or lab is now canceled for the evening so you may attend. Make your way to the Triclinium in an orderly fashion, but do not be late."

"Fuck," I mutter as I reverse the direction I'm headed to go straight to the cafeteria without freshening up first. "I *hate* being grubby around food."

Stomping across the last half of the quad, I climb the stairs, noting Kit making his way up with Oriel and Salem. Anton and Zav will have to finish whatever they're doing in their labs, so they'll be cutting it close. A quick glance behind me to the open area I came from lets me find Jasper and Slash tromping over with veritable lines of steam coming from their heads. This last minute bullshit is pissing everyone off, and if Lucian doesn't show again, they're going to have a riot on their hands.

Not the smartest move when gathering the strongest demons on campus in one place.

By the time I get to the door, Kit and his bodyguards are even with me, and we form a group as we march into the big room. I hold up my hand, pausing for effect so the demons in the room before us note our presence. Oriel snorts, and Kit arches a brow, but once I'm satisfied, I move again. We have to make an entrance, even if these two think it's stupid, and I know the Prince would agree. The other groups *need* to fear us and what we might do if they disrespect anyone in our caliphate.

"X, I know we're supposed to—"

"Shh, KK. Let me work this. Tell one of them what you want from the line before we get to the table. Make it look good."

He makes a face, but turns to Salem, laying his hand on the big bear's arm. "You know what I like, so you also know what else I haven't tried that might work. Just… grab me whatever you think is good."

I roll my eyes. Not quite the display I'd hoped for, but good enough when Salem beams and peels off to head for the food and drink lines. It's easy to forget Kit doesn't know everything about our history or food or whatever because outside of pissing Jasper off, he's slipped into our lives without a hitch. It's like he's a perfect fit, and the thought makes me a little giddy.

Fuck only knows why it tickles me so much, but I don't question my instincts.

We ascend to the high table slowly, and Oriel shakes off his derision to pull chairs out for both Kit and me. I give him a dazzling grin, pleased with his compliance, and sit in the seat to the left of our newest member. He left space on my other side for Anton, though it means he'll be next to the Prince. Salem is going to pout for sure—the crow shifter is sitting on Kit's other side with a grin of satisfaction.

"You know, I'm starting to think this entire thing is a big mind fuck," Kit says as he lifts Dottie out of his bag to let her perch on the table. "That dude is going to take away shit everyone likes, yank our chains frequently, then come up with some lame excuse for not having the Games that's our fault."

I grin at him. "*Now* you're thinking like a demon, dude."

He snorts, pulling a baggie of some Salem-created mix to start feeding the kinkajou. "Nope. Feels like something authority figures would do in my world, too. Humans are definitely as devious and manipulative as demons, just in different ways. I don't know if that's a chicken or egg thing, but it's true."

"It's not like *any* supes—even deities or primordials—are any less inclined. We all came from somewhere, man. Down here, we're grouped into lineages that reveal what our darkest desires and greatest weaknesses are, which levels the playing field somewhat." Oriel shrugs and pushes his dark hair out of his eyes. "Humans aren't, which makes them much more dangerous than they look."

Kit scoffs as he tosses a dried berry to the small animal. "Duh. You don't have to remind me of that, O. If I met a goddamn lion shifter, in theory, I'd know what to watch out for. With people, you have no idea what lurks behind smiles and pretty faces. Being able to tell how shitty people are is a blessing."

Salem walks up, frowning at the seating as he sits across from Kit. He slides the plate of roasted black cow, veggies, demonic gravy, and grains over, but doesn't release the delicious looking desserts. "Now, Kit Kat, I promised Slash I'd make sure you bulked up with protein and nutrients before the sweet stuff. He was very specific when he texted me."

Kit's eyes narrow as he swivels his head to glare at the approaching Prince and his shark companion.

This is going over like a lead brick; I can feel it.

"Who gave you jurisdiction over my food?" he asks, fuming as they take their normal seats at the head of the table.

Slash arches a brow and shrugs. "You don't manage it on your own."

The new guy looks around with a pissy expression, but none of us can argue Slash's logic. Kit doesn't know how to manage intake for a human, much less an emerging demon or hybrid. He's spent too long living under the thumbs of shitty fosters in that world. I sigh, deciding to take one for the team before he jumps over the table to smack the shark.

"KK, he's right about your diet, though maybe… not how he chose to handle it?" I cut my eyes to Slash, who doesn't look sorry in the slightest. "It *is* important to keep your calorie and nutrient intake up. We've talked about that before and I know Salem sends stuff with you for during the day."

He throws his hands up in the air, growling softly. "I eat them. I'm following the plan."

"You need more after the weekend." Slash sniffs, then rises to his feet. "I will fetch our dinner, Prince."

Kit gives him another dirty look, but digs into the food Oriel brought him regardless. Both Salem and the crow look pleased, so the tension in the air fades. When I realize that, I turn to look at the astonishingly quiet Prince at the head of our table. He hasn't once taken a swipe at Kit, nor did he give Slash shit about monitoring the kid's diet.

Something is off with him.

"Jas, you're uncharacteristically quiet," I say as my eyes roam over him. I'm looking for evidence of magic, though I'm not nearly as good at it as Annie. "What's going on?"

The dragon huffs, blowing a smoke ring from his humanoid nostrils and I know he's upset. "I don't like the idea of Darkstar gathering all the most powerful Discordians in one place. I highly doubt *this* meeting is a feint, but if this becomes a common occurrence for this Games, it will be more dangerous each time."

"Shit." We all look at Kit as he drops his fork with a clatter. "You think they're laying the groundwork for some kind of secret attack later on. Normalize things that aren't normal, then use that predictability to create a vulnerability."

Slash gives him a toothy grin as he drops trays in his place and in front of the Prince. "Good, little demon. Excellent strategy."

The dude flushes and mutters something about listening to books as he's falling asleep to catch up. I had no idea he was working quite this hard even when he's not around any of us, but I think we need to find something fun to do this weekend if all Hell doesn't break loose—literally.

"You know, it occurs to me that we should do something fun this weekend." They look at me as if I'm crazy, but Annie and Zav finally arrive as I'm speaking. They both concur as they drop their bags, and I go on. "Even if we don't leave campus this time, we should do something that isn't training, studying, or prepping for these stupid Games. I think we *all* need a break, even for a couple of hours."

Jasper tilts his head back, thinking for a moment, and nods slowly. "You're probably right, X. Whatever Lucian is about to announce will bring shit to our doorstep, and the accompanying danger will only add to the stress."

"We can plan it," Anton says and I grin at him happily. "Xerxes loves this shit and I'm willing to put up with the nonsense involved if it gets everyone to stop being so fucking intense for a bit."

Kit pokes at his roast, slathering it in the gravy. "I'm down for that. What are you gonna do?"

"No idea," I reply as the doors to the *Triclinium* open. "But I'll think of something."

Lucian Darkstar strides up the center row of the cafeteria in the exact same way Jasper insists we do, his cape flutters behind him as his contingent of lackeys and lickspittles strain to catch up. His eyes rake over our table, but he makes a sharp right to ascend the tall podium against the front wall. Other than our sheer power and Jasper's hatred of him, I have no idea why he'd single us out. We're not the only people looking at him like we want him to disappear, especially since the revival of the Games.

He's not exactly popular and never has been—that's not Jasper's doing, either.

"Finally," the Prince snarls. "This asshole said no one could be late then showed up twenty minutes later than he said he'd start. Fucking bullshit power moves."

"Not surprising," Salem says with a sigh. "This is going to take forever if that asshole has his way."

Zavida frowns. "We all need to eat and study. None of the professors seem to give a shit about this yet. They're proceeding as normal with the workload."

"Word," Kit said as he nods at Zavida. "And I have like a thousand other things to catch up on while I'm keeping up with it. I want out of here."

"Keep calm, and don't let him see that it is bothering you, Kit Kat," Oriel says softly. "You know he feeds on the bad mojo now."

He grins at the panda, waving his beet root at him. "I'm always anxious; it's my reverse Hulk power. The person you need to warn is Prince Prickface. He's going to launch into outer space if the dumbass doesn't start talking soon."

We all look down to see Jasper's smoke rings gathering in formation in front of him—a telltale sign that the new kid is absolutely right. When Jasper gets angry *and* compulsive, he's almost past reason. Annie pushes to his feet, abandoning the seat next to me and gestures for Zav to switch with him. The kitsune hurries over and I sigh as my love ends up on the other side of the wood.

"That's not fair, you know. He's plenty old enough to mind his own temper."

Kit snorts and his kinkajou prances in front of him happily. I smile as it *seems* like the animal is working to keep him calm just like Zav is by cuddling up to the Prince. Annie catches my eye and winks, making me take a deep, calming breath.

I guess we're all a bunch of neurotic nits when it comes to our family being in danger.

kät/kit

Aloud *crack* echoes through the room and it startles everyone into silence—even Jasper. He doesn't flinch, of course, but his scowl deepens as our Headmaster cuts his icy gaze around the room. Dottie scrambles close to me and I cuddle her while we all wait for the pompous dickbag to speak.

"Good evening elite students of Discordia," Lucian begins. His voice booms without a microphone and I arch a brow at Oriel, who grins and mimics waving a wand. "Tonight you will receive materials outlining the changes we will implement throughout the week to support your caliphates in their quest to conquer the upcoming challenges. It is your responsibility, caliphate leaders, to ensure your team members review this thoroughly and prepare themselves."

I frown when I realize that he's called a gathering of maybe a hundred or so people who are already the richest, most powerful demons in school to give them a cheat sheet. "What a fucking douche canoe," I mutter under my breath.

X snickers next to me, then slips their hand over to squeeze mine. "Nice."

Keeping my eyes on the psycho at the podium, I wink. Jasper gives both of us a reproachful look, then aims his displeasure at Salem. I forgot to pay attention when the dramatic villain entrance happened and the panda dozed off within the short span of time. I elbow him in the ribs, waiting until his eyes open. "Stay awake, man. Between the pouty prince and this prima donna, you'll get your ass beat somehow if you're caught."

He gives me a sleepy grin as he shrugs. "Arrogance bores the hell out of me and it *is* my low energy time. Not my fault, Kit Kat."

"I know, but I don't want you to end up scrubbing toilets or stuck in some weird prison." I tilt my head, realizing I have no idea what kind of punishment Lucian would hand out. "There aren't torture rooms here, right?"

"Later," Oriel hisses. "You're going to get us all bitched at guys." The crow shifter glares and I make a motion like I'm zipping my lips, tuning back into the long-winded speech about the long tradition of the Caliphate Games.

Leaning down, I grab my tablet out of my bag and pull out the stylus so I can take notes. The thoughts racing around my head are hard to pin down, and I know I'll want to come back to this. Zav grins at me slightly as I start scribbling my random questions and concerns on the app. His shy efforts are slowly chipping away at the ice wall I built up when he was so cowardly. I'm surprised to find I want to repair that bridge and find the funny gamer I saw on the first day.

The speech drones on and I realize Headmaster Darkstar is extremely full of himself. Some people just like to hear themselves talk, but there's something more sinister in this speech. He's mentioned the 'glorious outcome' twice now, and I know the guys told me the current royals of Hell waged war after they won. It's not a big leap to think he has plans for the end of the Games, but who the fuck is he going to use to accomplish them?

If he'd shut up, I could try to figure out who his pawns are.

I blink when Lucian stops speaking suddenly. The room seems to freeze in place around me and panic rises in my throat. I don't know what the hell is happening, but when I look at the guys, they're also stuck. Sucking in a deep breath, I let it out slowly as I try to get my heart rate under control. Obviously, I can move, but everyone else, including Dottie, is as still as a gorgon gallery. A soft chuckle escapes me when I realize I wouldn't have used that simile a week ago, so I'm definitely assimilating to this damn school.

"Okay, Kit," I whisper. "You have no idea why the fucking shit everything is paused, but you wanted time and you've got it. The only way to keep from having a full blown panic episode is to distract yourself. So who is Darkstar looking at? What teams are in his pocket?"

Pushing to my feet, I cradle Dottie in my arms while I run my gaze over the pre-formed caliphates. If I'm correct in my assumptions, there are about forty or so, ranging from four to six team members. No one is sitting in a group as big as ours, and I wonder if the only reason we're getting away with it is because of who Jasper is. That would paint the target on the Prince bigger since he has more back-up. But then, when the guys formed their boy band as kids, no one expected these games to ever happen again—at least, that's what I assume.

Will they let the smaller teams pull in more members?

I put that on my list of questions to talk to the guys about later. Zav needs to add the entire process behind forming caliphates and the history of these damn challenges to those cards. I can't be an effective team member if I'm both a knowledge and a behavior liability. Not having magic is bad enough; adding ignorance and lack of control to it means I'll be their weak spot. I don't like that idea one bit.

Shaking my head to clear those intrusive thoughts, I go back to studying the people in the *Triclinium* before whatever magic bullshit this is wears off. There's a group in the back that has my new nemesis, Roquefort, in it, and I'd bet my favorite fidget ring he's one of Lucian's lackeys. That might be wishful thinking because it would make me feel better about the guys raining fire on him now that I'm 'theirs', even if it's pretend.

A weird vibe makes me shiver and I turn, looking at the table behind me near the left wall. The demons sitting there seem intense as fuck, and their expressions are determined. I'm not good at identifying demon types by sight or scent yet, so I don't know what they are. What I do know is they're not all the same, and they exude a vibe that makes my skin crawl.

Whoever they are, they're going on my suspect list.

I pin-point a few more options, then drop back to my seat to make a brief sketch of the room with all my question marks notated. My pulse slows as I look at it, feeling a lot better about who the competition is and how we're going to identify Lucian's puppets. That was all I needed; a little time to gather my thoughts so I can move forward.

Just like that, the room unfreezes like nothing happened and my jaw drops.

Did I do that?

"DID YOU GUYS NOTICE ANYTHING WEIRD ABOUT THAT SPEECH?"

My eyes widen as I turn to look at X. They pluck a bit of their salad off their plate, holding it up for me to try, and I lean in, taking the bite automatically. I was hoping they'd expound so I'm not worried I dreamt the whole 'time skip'. The dressing they put on this is delightful—light, tangy, and sweet—so I raise my hand to give them a thumbs up while I chew.

"Good on you, Kit Kat. The nightshade greens are death for humans, but for us demons, they're magical enhancers. You should definitely eat more of them," Salem says as he watches me with a proud smile. "I can't believe you're so willing to just try shit without knowing what it is."

I shrug. "What else am I going to do…. starve? I think not."

Jasper snorts, looking up from his now clean plate of unidentifiable Hell fare. "To answer your question, X, I agree. It was weird as fuck and there's… something… about it bothering me. I feel like I missed something."

Like a ten minute span of time where I played detective?

"Yes. It is puzzling." Slash looks at the prince, his brow furrowing for a moment, then he turns back to the rest of us. "Salem is right. Nightshade intake should increase."

Sighing, I squint over at the big guy. "You're not my trainer, and I can hear just fine."

"That's an idea," the prince says as he snaps his fingers. "A good one, in fact. Slash, you will help us train the pleb. You're already doing some of the work, and this is one of your most useful skills."

I can't help the look of horror on my face as the shark shifter gives me a smug, tooth-filled grin from his seat. My palm slaps the table and I hiss, "You don't get to assign people to harass me, Eversore. That's not what I agreed to."

He shakes his head, looking amused as he sips his coffee. "I believe you'll find that you agreed to a *very* open-ended bargain in reference to the dating situation. Your caliphate oath placed you under our protection and training you for this life-threatening event *is* within our purview. As the leader of the caliphate, I'm giving that task to the person most capable."

God fucking damn him, he's right. I want to punch him in the nuts so hard he pukes.

"Ugh," I growl as I throw my hands up. "Fine. Slash can *confer* with Salem then because he's the one who does the most with food. But the first person who keeps me from eating dessert is getting their balls turned into an earbuds case. Got it?"

I want to look threatening, so I point my fork at the Prince, stabbing the air a couple times. He merely smirks, and Oriel chuckles behind his hand. Looking at the rest of the guys, I notice their sheepish expressions, and I know Jasper has won this round. That demon just sicced his fucking mother hen general on me and I don't have a leg to stand on if I complain.

"As for the rest of your training, I believe Zavida will be the best one to—"

"Ha!" I stab the air again, my expression triumphant. "Zav and I already planned to study together. You're too late, asshat. Suck on that."

X chokes, picking up their napkin and wiping their mouth. "Damn it, Kit Kat. You can't say that shit when I'm drinking."

Shrugging, I give the Prince a smug smile and bat my lashes. He frowns, tilting his head and panic races through me. *Shit, too girly… fuck, fuck.* Clearing my throat, I paste a scowl on my face as I glare back. "Stop staring at me, dickface. It's not my fault you're too slow."

Please let that distract him.

"That's the kind of initiative you should be taking," Jasper says in a non-committal voice. "I wouldn't have to take charge if you'd focus, Kit."

Anton snorts this time, giving his leader a wry look. "Dude, you always take charge, even when we have shit handled. But I think Zav, Slash, and Salem are good picks. What I don't like is the shared odd sensation we had during that meeting, and our theories about why Darkstar held it. He's definitely up to something."

"Yes, he is." Jasper scratches his jaw, his handsome face marred by the warring emotions on it. "I don't know if he intended to size up the teams, scare people, or simply soak up glory like the self-centered prick he is. But putting all the powerful caliphates in this room has a purpose beyond giving us early insight into the Games structure."

"What the fuck is with that, by the way?" I ask as I spear a tomato-like thing on my plate. "I get that it's Hell, and that all the fuckers in here are probably rich, but what's the point of having a competition if you're stacking the deck? Won't it be boring?"

Oriel finally gives up the dessert he'd been withholding when my tray looks pretty empty and I squeal happily, only to turn bright red when they all stare at me. "Uh, you really like this shit, huh?"

Why am I so stupid tonight? I'm going to fuck everything up and I have no idea how to stop it.

Ducking my head as I get myself under control, I rake my hand over my short locks then look up at them. "Dessert wasn't a foregone conclusion at most of my homes. I like having sweet things whenever I want versus an occasional special treat when I'm lucky."

"Damn it," Salem mutters as he bumps my shoulder with his. "Now I'm going to make as much sweet shit as I can and no one can stop me—not even you, Scrum."

Slash eyes me as I dig into the treat, his eyes glittering as he nods. "Agreed, chef. Provide things to make him happy and we will work around that."

That's not what I expected him to say at all—who would have known?

TROUBLE

slash

Something was off about the little demon after the meeting last night. He tried to play it off as being tired—which is believable given what Jasper told us about the fire in that study room. Kit's powers are emerging very slowly and until they're fully settled, he needs a *lot* of rest and fuel. That's part of why I'm so focused on making sure he doesn't burn himself out with poor self-care. A demon that is coming of age is like an energy vampire—every bit they use has to be replaced with twice as much to balance out the exchange.

I have this niggling feeling in the back of my mind that it wasn't simple exhaustion, though.

Glancing over at him, I tune out Professor Wormwood's lecture on the basics of magical spells and how they resemble math equations or cooking recipes. I've been constructing spells, hexes, and curses since I was a kid playing in the pee-wee version of magical battles. The mage-dhampir hybrid is well versed, but this lesson is way beneath my capabilities. Lucky for me, that means I can watch our newest caliphate member closely.

"What's going on with you?" Anton murmurs from his place on my other side. "I know you're above this level of discussion, but I *feel* the tension in you, man."

I grimace, looking at my sensitive friend with a shrug. "Intuition. Something's off."

Kit stops taking notes and elbows me in the side. "What's off? Is someone going to cause trouble?"

Definitely not the result I was looking for.

Patting his hand lightly, I shake my head. "No, Kit. No one is targeting us at the moment. You can focus on the lesson without worrying."

Anton grins as the tension even I could feel amping up in the air fades, and once Kit is distracted again, he whispers, "You can tell me later. But I'm not going to let it go now that I have the scent of a secret."

"Mr. Stryker!"

The sharp reprisal comes out of nowhere and I have to stifle a groan when Kit turns red and gives Salem a mean-looking pinch. It's only nine a.m. and somehow, the panda shifter is asleep at the wheel. You'd think the professors here would make accommodations for the biological natures of hybrids, but Hell doesn't have an ADA law. My need to move—sharks don't stay still— and Salem's sleepiness are just some of the problems they pretend are misbehavior instead of instinctual traits.

"Shit," Salem says with a yawn as he stretches. "You fell down on the job, Kit Kat."

A bolt of magic sizzles past our friend's ear, and we all turn back to Wormwood. "I'll thank you to *not* use my lecture as nap time from now on or you'll get dungeon detention for a month."

"He didn't do it on purpose!"

Damn it, Kit. That fucking humanity is going to get us all detention.

"Mr. Camponella, no one asked for your ill-informed opinion. Now if we can all—"

The kid stands and glares at the mage, crossing his arms over his chest. "I'm not 'ill-informed'. Anyone with an internet connection can research pandas and his snoozy issues are common even in non-demon hybrids. It doesn't deserve an admonishment or a punishment. Obviously, you could have used magic to get him up without even telling the rest of class."

Wormwood's teeth lengthen and his scent changes as he heads for the stairs to come up to the seats where we're camped out. "Since you're so well versed, Mr. Camponella, perhaps *you* should serve as the proxy for his punishment. You clearly feel powerful enough to intervene."

"That seems rather unfair," Anton says as he shifts in his seat. A fluffy feather floats past my face and I groan inwardly.

His peacock doesn't like the character of people he's fond of being challenged—Wormwood just insulted two in one go.

"Jasper's going to fucking murder me," I grumble to my companions. "But fuck it."

I rise to my feet, my bulk shielding Annie from people's view. His bird is too much of a draw not to cause a damn crowd, and I need to shut this shit down before it gets worse. My eyes cut to Salem, who's trying to get his sleep-addled brain back to non-hibernation mode so he's useless. Putting a hand on Kit's shoulder, I wait for the professor to get closer. If I need to block something, I will, but I'm not going to attack unless I have to.

"Mr. Scrum, are you vying for dungeon duty as well?"

Giving him a half-shifted, shark toothed grin, I stay quiet until he's within range. "I think this has escalated far enough. We should move on."

"As long as Salem isn't getting in trouble, I'm fine with that," Kit mutters as he leans into me slightly. "But once I figure out what the fuck I'm doing, I'm hexing this fucker's dick twelve ways from Tuesday. What a douche."

"What did you say, Mr. Camponella?" The dhampir's fury is increasing, and his speed is an issue if he uses that rather than magic. "Would you like to repeat it for the entire room?"

Kit snorts and shakes his head. "I highly doubt you want me to do that."

None of us do because it will get us sent to Darkstar's office for certain.

"Texting this mess to the group," Anton whispers from behind me.

That's helpful. It means if Wormwood decides to fuck with us via administrative complaints, Jasper will have it handled before we're out of our second class. "Again, we should move on."

"The time for moving on has passed, Scrum. Your puny recruit is now the proud recipient of my first month of dungeon detention." He turns to Kit, his fangs protruding creepily as he eyes the small guy. "Make sure you're wearing clothes you don't mind throwing away. I have very special tasks in mind for you."

A shiver runs through him, and my eyes widen as Kit grabs my hand to squeeze it. "I can take anything you throw at me, asshole. You're nothing more than a bully using your position to treat demons who are better than you like shit. Bring it on."

Is this kid trying to give me a fucking heart attack?

By the time Wormwood settles down and class continues, the word has a spread.

> Prince: What the hell is going on? There are three of you who are supposed to be watching him.

> Enforcer: Calm down.

> Chef: I fell asleep. Something threw my internal time clock off yesterday. Wormwood was being a dick.

> Designer: In other news, Kit Kat is happy to stick it to professors as viciously as he does with you, Jas.

> KitKat: ...

> Prince: Who changed his name?

> KitKat: I'm not stupid, Jasper. I know how tech works.

> Thief: Good on you, Kit. Don't let these idiots grind you down.

> Hacker: Can we get back to what happened in class?

> Prince: You'll see him in a few minutes in Mythology. He needs to tell me.

> KitKat: He's right here, assholes. Look, the fucker was being mean to Salem and you said we stick up for the people in the caliphate, right?

Everything goes quiet, and I chuckle to myself. The kid has a way of knocking the knees out from under my best friend, and I enjoy it more than I can let on. I look up from my phone, checking to make sure that the irksome mage isn't monitoring us anymore. Jasper will *have* to fix Kit's detention now that he's pointed out it was in defense of our brothers.

> Prince: Who the fuck knew you were listening, shrimp?
>
> Chef: The point is, he stood up and gave Wormwood hell for being a dick to me, then Slash joined him, and in the end, he muttered something creepy as fuck about his punishment.
>
> Sparkle Skirt: What? No way.
>
> Thief: Now we know how Kit Kat changed his name. X has been playing with the chat.
>
> SparkleSkirt: Whatever, O. Tell us about the creepy punishment.
>
> KitKat: Look, I'll take my licks; I earned them.
>
> Enforcer: Something about dungeon detention and needing clothes he doesn't mind throwing away. I am not comfortable with this situation.
>
> Prince: Fuck.
>
> Enforcer: Yes.
>
> KitKat: Is every teacher here a goddamn predator?
>
> Thief: Probably.
>
> Designer: Definitely.
>
> Hacker: Depends on what kind of predator.
>
> Sparkle Skirt: Unfortunately.
>
> Enforcer: We're not leaving him to that shit, J.
>
> Prince: Fine. Get to your next class. I'll handle this.

"I don't want him doing me any favors," Kit grumbles. "I meant it when I said I can handle myself."

Anton snorts and shakes his head. "No one in this group or the chat is going to allow that shit, Kit Kat. You're one of us, and an idiot like Wormwood isn't going to traumatize you. When you can defend yourself, then we'll talk."

That makes him hunker into his seating, cursing under his breath as he pretends to pay attention to the end of class. I'm not concerned about that as much as making certain Jasper keeps his word. Something about the way Wormwood went from zero to a thousand on the creep scale bothers me. It's like there's some sort of… compulsion for bad people to come after him when he stands up to them. I know that's far too complex to be an effective hex or spell, but there's something drawing the evil out of people when he's about.

I need to discuss this with X and Oriel; they're very good at hidden shit like this.

"Little demon, you need to let the Prince help as Salem allowed you to help. It is what we do."

He sighs heavily, his lip curling as his rodent comes out of the bag so he can put his books into it. "Fine. But you need to quit logic-ing me out of funks, big guy. People will think I'm soft on you."

Salem snorts. "People are *supposed* to think you're soft on *all* of us, man."

My eyes light up and I wait for him to get his stuff, then grab his small hand again. "It is my turn, then, it seems."

Anton gives me a wry look. "If you say so, big guy. I think it's mine, and we have class together next. X and Zav will be waiting."

Blast, the bird is correct, and Weapons is too far from where Mythology is held to detour.

"Don't worry, " Kit says as he squints up at me with a smile. "You can get us lunch again if it makes you happy."

"It *very much* does, little demon." I turn to Annie and nod, letting go of his hand. "Anton can escort you to Mythology. You must not irritate Darkstar before the Prince has a chance to speak to him about the detention."

Salem gives me a wry expression. "I'll be surprised if Annie and Zav can keep him calm, but maybe we should be prepared, just in case."

I nod, considering his suggestion. "Agreed. Hopefully, the Headmaster will get a TA to cover the class since he is busy with the Games now. That would be the best outcome."

"Holy shit, that would be fucking amazing," Kit mutters as he takes Anton's arm. "It would be the best news I've heard all week."

It's too bad the annoyance is Lucian; I'd happily make the thorn disappear to get him to look this excited again.

"Okay, we're heading for Mythology now. Everyone say 'good-bye' to Kit so we won't be late for Professor Dickbag," Anton says.

Leaning in, I pat the small animal on his shoulder, then Kit's head as well. "Please do not get yourself in trouble in the next two hours. Running in armor will be difficult."

"Aw, you do like me!"

I roll my eyes as the others laugh, turning on my heel to leave. They're still snickering as I walk towards the Arena, leaving Kit to Anton, and my brothers to head for their own classes. I've never worried about them quite as much as I do our newest addition, but he's also much more breakable. Even Zav has the power to zip in and out of places as a kitsune, so I've never thought he was too exposed when he's off in his geek classes.

Kit being alone, however, bothers the fuck out of me and I don't quite know what to do about it. Obviously, I need more time to strategize so he's never in danger—the more I plan, the more likely I will be to succeed. This is what I've been taught since Jasper and I were small demons. My role in the new court will be to ensure everyone in the kingdom and my Prince are safe. I can keep one unemerged demon hybrid safe, right?

It's in my blood to protect those I care about, after all.

Flowers

Kat/Kit

Anton is quiet as we head to Mythology. I assume he's figuring out what he'll do if I go completely off-script with Headmaster Dark-star. The jerk will probably do something to piss me off, so it's not a bad plan, but I hate that I'm such a wildcard. Before coming here, I was always worried about my issues causing a scene that I'd have to live down. Now I have to worry about those plus dragging the guys into my bullshit. It's enough to make me spill the damn lunch Slash insisted I eat, so I twist the spinning ring on my finger anxiously as we approach the door to our lecture.

"It'll be okay," Anton says with a crooked smile. It's not his usual suave-guy expression, and I find myself staring at his handsome features wordlessly.

I swear, Hell has turned me into a hungry bitch and it's not just for the delicious grub.

Pulling my lower lip through my teeth, I try to re-focus my brain on his words before I answer. "Will it? Coming here and finding out about this world was *a lot*, especially for someone with my problems. Somehow, I've kept my shit together about that, but now there's... so much more. Bullies, Prince Asshat, Headmaster Cockrocket, assaults, death games, evil professors...*fake dating!*"

The gentle grin stretches and his gaze softens as he chucks my chin lightly. "*That* is your biggest hang-up out of the entire list? Very interesting."

I stomp my foot and roll my eyes to the ceiling in supplication. Given that we're in Hell, I'm not sure *who* I'm asking for help with this dude, but someone has to be spying on us, right? "Anton, there's a long list of traumas and shit I've experienced in my comparably short lifetime, but I only dated one time." My voice drops at the same time as my gaze and I murmur, "You've all figured out how that worked out for me. I don't have a fucking *clue* what I'm supposed to be doing here—as a demon, as a dude, or even as a boyfriend."

Suddenly, I realize what I just said and the panic rushes through me like lava spurting from a volcano.

But whatever deity or demon who was listening took pity on me because Anton doesn't even flinch. Instead, he chuckles, bopping me on the nose. "Kit Kat, do you think those of us without their heads squarely up their asses haven't figured that out?"

Annnnd we're back to panic at the doorway... What am I going to do?!

Swallowing hard, I sneak my hand into the bag and stroke Dottie's head. "Um, what... what do you mean by that?"

"I don't know about Slash for certain, granted, and we know Zavida and Jasper are clueless as hell. But X, Oriel, Salem, and I definitely realize you have no positive experience with dating. Your symptoms and issues make it clear that your incident made you shy away from trying to find another guy." He winks and pulls the door open, holding it for me. "Not to mention, demon courting is a bit different, and that's something you're learning as well. We'll help you."

My heart stops hammering in my chest, and the hand petting Dottie stops trembling at his words. Damn, I thought I was screwed for sure. That was a close one. I need to be much more cautious about what I say when I'm already worked up. "Oh. Well... that's really nice of you. People don't usually try to accommodate my annoying quirks like that. I'm not used to it."

He waits until I walk into the classroom, then leads me over to where Zav and X are seated. "Then those people are fools, and even if it takes some of us a bit to get there, we shall endeavor to be better. Not that it's *hard* for demons to be better than humans…"

X gives me a bright grin as they make room for us to get settled into the seats they saved for us. "He's right. Demons and supes are much higher on the evolutionary scale, so whatever Annie thinks we'll do better—we will."

I laugh softly, enjoying his cheery disposition after the heavy atmosphere of lunch. "I'm sure you will. He can tell you all about it later. We have to be *very* careful what we say and how we act here today."

"I've got notes today," Zavida says as he gives me a shy smile. "That way, the two of you can focus on helping Kit stay calm. Does that work?"

Well, look who wants to go to the head of the class?

Anton nods. "That's a good plan, Zav. Darkstar is likely to be an ass—as usual—and Kit's natural inclinations will make this our most difficult class to manage all semester."

"Harder than Prince Prickface's Arms sections? I highly doubt that," I mutter as Dottie climbs out of my bag and sits on my shoulder. "I don't care what promises he's making—being in charge brings out the douchebag in him."

X snorts, covering their mouth with their hand. "He's not wrong."

"But… he's a professor…"

All gazes cut to the kitsune and he flushes. "Sorry. Force of habit. But… It is true that he's judged on how well he can teach and control the classroom. That doesn't excuse his behavior last time, though."

Baby steps, ginger fox, but you're coming along.

"That's definitely not wrong, either," Anton agrees. "Jasper needs to balance how he's been raised with what he knows is right. Honestly, no one's forced him to do that in such a bold manner before. Though, I suspect he enjoys the battle as much as the control."

Zav's blush gets deeper and he shakes his head. "I wouldn't know about that."

"Of course you wouldn't, Sammy Subby," X crows gleefully. "No shade, but your relationship with old Scaly Balls is less Spike and more Drusilla. But you'll get there, man."

I frown, considering that reference for a moment. "You have to mean in later sea—"

"Good morning, students. Please turn your texts to page one hundred fifty-seven. We will be discussing the mythology of the Greeks today."

Wincing as I flick the screen of my tablet to the right page, I look down at Lucian as he points to the big screen behind him. Pictured on it is a collage of mythicals beasts and he has a dark smirk on face as he looks at our group.

That isn't good.

"As you can see, many of the creatures we've discussed today are depicted in various cultures with different names and abilities. Hybrid demons can be created from any number of supernaturals, including the creatures non-humans have classified as 'mythical.' Can one of you who paid attention list the most *common* mythicals seen in our current age?"

Lucian behaved most of the class, surprisingly, but the information provided today has damn near blown my mind. Knowing that dragons, gorgons, unicorns, krakens, gargoyles and a host of things deemed 'made-up' in my previous world is hitting me especially hard at the moment. I know Zavida is Kitsune and Jasper's a dragon, but the rest of them are pretty normal animals, so their shifter thing isn't quite as awe-inspiring. This stuff is making me reel with questions and I can't ask a single one because it would draw attention to myself.

Fucking asshole is shock-blocking me and I want to punch him.

"Are you okay, dude?"

Turning my head slowly to look at X, I shrug. "This is a bit… difficult. So many things we're taught are myths—from the creatures to the stories of deities—are real. Maybe exaggerated for effect, but… imagining a unicorn striding into the room or Hades showing up for tea is mind blowing."

Zavida grins as he pushes his 'note taking' glasses up. "Pay no attention to the man behind the curtain isn't just a phrase, huh?"

I nod, running my fingers over Dottie's head gently. "Exactly. It makes me wonder how much 'fixing' goes on to keep them unaware of things."

Anton leans in, his eyes dancing. "That's handled by all the agents. Demons could give a fuck less if they find out about us. The others care a ton because they live among the meat bags *or* they'll be made to do shit when they pray. The jokers who work for the Society have all these rules and enforcers and cleaners to deal with it."

That's when my brain starts to melt a little.

"I think... maybe I need to leave that topic for much, much later."

"Gentleman! Since you're so loquacious today, perhaps one of you can list the five most common mythical creatures found on Earth right now?"

We all freeze as Lucian booms at us and I turn to look at the angry Headmaster with a blank expression. I've done so well at avoiding his ire, and now we're fucked. That's what I get for letting the woo-woo crap of Discordia distract me. None of us answer, and he glowers so darkly I can almost feel it.

"If you won't volunteer, I'll select which one of you owes me a response." His dark eyes glitter and he pretends to think about it, but I know what he's going to say. "Mr. Camponella, show me you've learned more than how to make a spectacle of yourself in the week you've graced our presence in Hell."

Son of a bitch rat-fucking cocksucker.

I take a deep breath, squaring my shoulder as I look down at the demonic despot. "Dragons and wyverns, gargoyles, hellhounds, sirens and mer-folk, and centaurs."

The shock on his face makes me smirk and I feel X's hand on my shoulder. Dottie chitters happily and even Zavida looks proud as I continue to return his nasty stare. Finally, the dramatic asshole nods and clicks the screen behind him to advance the presentation. "Correct. It seems with the right teacher, even the challenged individuals at our school can be taught. That said, read the sections on Romans by class Thursday. You are all dismissed."

Letting out a slow breath of relief, I grin at the guys. "I made it. I knew I could do it."

Anton winks at me, reaching over to grab my hand and squeeze it. "I did, too. I'm going to leave you with X until Oriel arrives to pick you up. I need to run to Alabaster's class and I won't make it if I dawdle."

"We have him, babe," X says before they exchange a brief kiss. "Skedaddle off to talk about humans while Kit Kat and I have things to do. Zavida, we'll see you in Weapons later."

The kitsune nods, gathering his things before he gives me a hopeful look. "Class was okay?"

I pretend to think about it for a moment, then nod. "Not too bad. Slow and steady wins the race, foxy friend."

His face lights up and he scurries off with his head down, making me laugh. The dude is *so* fucking submissive it's almost comical, but it seems to be masking an innate sweetness. Letting him figure out how to shine without Jasper being pissed is definitely the best solution, but I hate to think he's feeling cowed by my demands.

People are fucking hard and now I get why everyone is always so frustrated on TV.

"You're being pretty chill with him."

Picking up my bag, I stuff my things into it and let Dottie scamper up my shoulder. "I think his heart is in the right place, but his *cojones* haven't dropped."

X blinks then bursts out laughing as they lead me to the door. "Damn, you're savage sometimes, man. Not off-base, but savage as fuck."

"Sarcasm has always been my closest friend. It helps distance you from some of the bad shit, right?" The look we exchange is fraught with shared knowledge as we walk to the stairs. I like that X is willing to use them instead of trapping me in that shitty metal box. "Well, that, and books."

They bob their brows as we descend. "Which explains why I knew we'd be spending our free period there. I told Oriel to meet us in the stacks where we were before once he's free."

Picking favorites probably isn't a good idea if I'm supposed to be dating all of them, right?

9 TO 5

Looking at the row of seats I saved, I fidget a little. This thing with Kit is making my anxiety higher, especially because I know what I need to do to fix it. I could have followed my instincts from the day he walked into our lives, but instead, I let Jasper's unfounded hatred of the kid lead me. It's a failing, but I haven't had to control it before. Usually, the guys let it go and give me shit later on. This time, they're serious as hell.

That's without Kit serving me up a steaming hot truth sandwich that made my tails wilt.

"Backbone, Z. You have to show you have backbone and can be trusted," I mutter to myself as I set up my notes system.

Organizing my desktop with everything I need to feel like I'll be able to focus on the class helps a lot. I don't always use every single bit of it—in fact, I often use very little—but the routine of putting each thing out in its place and making my space comfortable helps me immensely. I suppose the humans would say I've got ADHD and perhaps, based on their diagnostic criteria, I do. I looked it up once to satisfy my curiosity and it's definitely very familiar. But after years of managing my tics and quirks, I've got it down to science much like Kit seems to with his issues.

Not that any of my other brothers have theirs on lock down because demons don't believe in labeling that shit.

Speaking of barely contained quirks, Salem lumbers up first, yawning as he takes the seat next to me. The bear has been struggling since morning, so I'll have to make sure the person to his right is on the ball with keeping him awake or Jasper will murder him. Today is lecture day in Arms & Weaponry, something that happens every other week, to familiarize us with the history and creation of the things we'll use for the classes afterward. The Prince will lose his shit if our brother is nodding off while he talks about whatever he's discussing today.

"Man, I don't know what the fuck is with me today. I'm having a bitch of a time with the narco, man."

"I regret teaching you guys the words for all your problems so much," I mumble. "Whenever you have problems, you end up sounding like internet psychologists."

He grins broadly, his eyes sleepy but amused. "I like having a better name for it than 'Salem's Sleepytime,' man. And like I said earlier, my internal clock is all kinds of fucked up today for no apparent reason. I even had trouble in my damn cooking classes—you know that never happens."

"You're right, man. That's super weird."

I look up as Anton takes the aisle seat, leaving space for Oriel, X, and Kit when they arrive. "How's your trauma doing today, then? My anxiety is off-the-charts."

The peacock shifter makes a face as he dusts himself off, adjusting his uniform fussily. I have to cover my grin as he does so because that *is* his issue, and he's definitely *not* in control at the moment. "I'm fine, but I'm sending a complaint to the laundry about the quality of care our uniforms are getting. It's abysmal."

A snort echoes in the mostly empty room as Kit approaches with X and Oriel in tow. "You could always press your *own* damn uniform. Then it would meet your exacting standards."

Annie looks puzzled, tilting his head in that avian way. "Press my own uniform? I wouldn't have the slightest clue how to do that. It would be a nightmare."

"For the love of crispy croissants, give me strength," Kit mutters as he scoots into the row and sits down next to the panda. "I don't even know where to start with *that* horseshit."

Salem sits up, turning to look at the new guy curiously. "Do you know how? 'Cause I forget to send shit down all the time, even in lower schools, and I'd love to avoid being bitched out all semester."

Kit puts his hands on his temples, dropping his head as he rubs them, and I chuckle. Oriel grabs the seat to his right and X plops down between the crow and the bird in the spotlight. Once everyone is settled, I lick my lips and venture the question on all our minds carefully. "Is that a weird question or something?"

"If I survive this goddamn school and these death games, I'm going to die of suppressed fury over you rich morons and your spoiled bullshit," he mutters grumpily. "*Yes*, most people know how to use a fucking iron where I'm from. It's not rocket science, for fuck's sake!"

X leans forward, batting their lashes. "That sounds like it would have been super helpful for Drama if they hadn't taken it away. Are you going to teach us?"

Oh, X. Now you've done it.

"It is not my responsibility to teach you fools to be self-sufficient beings." Kit whips his head around, looking at them, then turning to glare at us on his left. "And the first person who offers to *pay* me is going to have missing teeth."

Oriel shrinks back in his chair and I cover my mouth again. He almost fucked up but good. I wait for a moment, letting our new inductee seethe off the irritation before I ask, "Perhaps if we asked nicely you might be willing to trade? I'm doing the cards because I enjoy it and helping you, but someone else might have a skill they could barter."

"Oh." We all wait for him to ponder that, staying quiet lest we set him off again. "Well, I suppose I could do that. We'd need an iron and board and shit… but I don't know what the hell I'd trade it for. I don't know what any of you can do or what I don't know I need to know."

We can fix that—that is, if Jasper doesn't ruin this when he finally arrives.

A rush of students all flood the hall at the same time, and I watch who sits where. I have a feeling that the Games will change behavior everywhere we go. I need to help identify the patterns so we know which demons Jasper will want dossiers on before he asks. Slash sent me a text to remind me this morning and I started a database as soon as I got to a computer. Being prepared is the best way to help Kit get through this—not to mention us—so I want to ensure we have everything we need.

Jasper finally stalks in after the last wave of demons take their seats with a sour expression on his face. He didn't look this pissed this morning and he hasn't said anything about it before now. Something must have held him up and that's why he's late. "Since I'm three minutes late, every one of you had better be ready to learn by the time I get to the front."

Ouch. He's definitely right on the edge.

"What the fuck happened to him?" Salem whispers as he leans into me. "He's even more grumpy than normal."

I shrug, fiddling with my supplies nervously. "I don't know. He didn't say anything to me privately."

Salem arches a brow as he watches me arrange and re-arrange my desk. "Dude, you gotta breathe. It'll be okay. If he tries to make you choose something, I'll try to help. Got it?"

My face turns red, nodding because my weakness makes me embarrassed. The panda chuckles and squeezes my shoulder then turns to Kit. "You're gonna have to keep me awake *and* watch your temper. This room has a shit ton of the caliphates from that meeting; we can't let them see division."

"*You* remember that? Really?" Oriel says in surprise. "Damn, Salem, you are paying attention in between naps, man. Good job."

Before Salem can reach over to smack the crow, Kit intervenes with a stern look. "What did he just say? No division. If I can't give Prince Cockwaffle a hard time, you have to behave as well. I mean, didn't he say you guys are supposed to *help* me stay calm?"

"Very smart, KitKat. Use the Prince's order against them even though you'd rather swallow acid than follow them," Anton snickers as he holds his fist out for a bump. "You're picking up on demonic behavior quite nicely, I think."

"*Excuse me!*"

Our heads whip around to see the demon in question practically vibrating with rage at the front of the room and my tails pop free before I can stop it. Ducking behind them, I breathe slowly. I'm not afraid of Jasper; I *hate* disappointing people. My parents weren't great with that situation and it sends me into a spiral when I know I've done something wrong that upsets people I care about. Salem's big hand lands on my arm as I grip the chair and it's more soothing than I expected.

"Are you six *quite* finished with your off-sides conversation? I'd like to begin discussing the evolution of projectile weaponry throughout Hell's ages." Jasper blows four fat smoke rings in our directions and his eyes turn to slits. "But I could certainly demonstrate instead if you're inclined to continue interrupting my class."

Fuck. He's so goddamn pissed.

"Mr. Draven, would you like to start us off?"

My eyes widen as Jasper calls my *full name* and asks me to guess what the hell he might be starting this lecture with. I have no idea and I was already fighting my kitsune as it is. Damn him; he's taking whatever happened before class out on me. "Uh..."

"If it's like where I come from, I'd guess rocks were the first projectiles. He's not dumb," Kit says in a sarcastic tone. "Humans aren't as old as you guys, but I can't imagine Hell has a shortage of them."

"Oh, shit," Oriel breathes. "Now you've done it."

The Prince's eyes flash with his dragon and I tug my tails tighter. Kit just threw himself in front of the bullet for me without a second thought. Now I feel even worse about being a coward for the past week. Damn the guy is better than all of us—maybe even the best person we've ever met—and Jasper is going to raze him to the ground.

"Why are we discussing projectiles in lecture, anyway? It's different from last week."

Xerxes has entered the game... that's unexpected.

Our brother is fuming at the front of the room, but even he realizes that X doesn't often shout things out in class. A sarcastic aside or comment, maybe, but not something as outwardly aggressive as this. He lets out a long breath, obviously calming himself before he responds. "That may be correct, Xerxes, but the Headmaster has given every professor new lesson plans to discuss as we begin the ramp up to the Games. Despite not owing anyone an explanation of my curriculum, perhaps that will end this ridiculous conversation?"

"Sure as fuck will," Kit mutters in a barely audible tone. "No wonder the stick up his ass has shifted so high."

Every one of my caliphate tenses in place as we fight the urge to burst out laughing, even me. Kit is afraid of so much and nothing at all simultaneously. It's fascinating—he's perfectly willing to risk his ass to tell people off when they deserve it yet is so haunted by ghosts of his past. I guess none of us should be surprised he turned our entire group upside down. He's as broken as we are but totally unconcerned about tearing through life with little abandon.

Are humans right about that therapy shit? Now I'm curious as fuck.

"Yeah, that helps, Professor," Anton says loudly. He's still futzing with his jacket, but his tone is steady and confident like normal. I'm always impressed by his ability to don a mask so effortlessly, and hopefully, it backs Jas off until after class.

"Fabulous," Jasper says drily. "Now if everyone will shut the fuck up and pay attention to the screen, I won't have to send you on laps of the Wastelands as punishment."

A chorus of grumbles rises from the entire class, and Kit coughs over another barb.

It's like he really can't stop himself, and I'm kind of here for it—who knew?

Talk to Me

kät/kit

The rest of the class passes by like a turtle plodding along in a race with a rabbit. I do my best to keep my shit together and Jasper does his worst, occasionally mitigated by one of the guys preventing us from locking horns too badly. I got the insinuation that Lucian made him change his lesson plan from his careful retort, but that doesn't excuse his shitty attitude. That dude needs to quit taking his frustrations out on the most convenient target. He's a fucking adult, for Satan's sake.

Slash meets us at the arena, studying the group for a moment before jerking his head to indicate I should follow him to Supernatural Law. It's a short class—probably because it's so dreadfully boring that Professor Holmes would struggle to keep us interested for longer than an hour. The man redefines the term 'beige' and it doesn't help that his hybrid shifter species is a sloth.

I know this shit is important for someone like me, but man, I've almost pulled a 'Salem' twice now.

I follow the shark demon into the room, letting him pick our spot, and then settle in for whatever nonsense the professor has been redirected to teach. The Games is changing everything little by little, and even though I'd only been here a week before they were announced, it's fucking with my Feng Shui.

If I can make it through this class without snoozing, it'll be a miracle.

"WAKE UP, LITTLE DEMON."

My eyes pop open at a rumble and I take in my surroundings in a mild panic. We're in the Law classroom and if my fuzzy brain is correct, Holmes is winding up his lecture on—something I definitely slept through entirely. Lifting my head up, I turn bright red when I figure out I've been snoozing on Slash's big shoulder.

Oh, shit, am I drooling?!

A quick swipe of my mouth relieves me when I find no strings of embarrassing moisture there. I blow out a quick sigh, then squint up at the big guy. "Why did you let me sleep like that? Didn't he notice?"

"Psssh," Slash scoffs as he shrugs. "Holmes is so blind; he wouldn't notice if you walked up to him and bopped him on the nose, much less that you were sleeping in the back of the room. Didn't you see how thick his glasses are?"

My lips curve a bit when the typically monosyllabic shifter blabs an entire string of words at me. I kinda like that he's less reserved when it's just us. "Okay, but why didn't you wake me?"

"You wouldn't fall asleep at six p.m. if you weren't exhausted. The time change from up there to Hell can be rough for the new demons. Plus, you were injured two days ago."

I especially enjoy it because when Slash does talk, it's pretty on the ball.

"Ugh, fine. Did you at least take notes?" I look over his huge arm to see lines of chicken scratch that makes my brain fritz for a moment. "And if those are the notes, do you have a translator in our group?"

He grins toothily, nodding. "Zavida is able to take my scrawl and make it legible for everyone else, don't worry."

"That's in the demon language, isn't it?"

Nodding, he closes the notebook and gestures for me to pack up. "It is, and you will pick it up gradually. At least, I think that is how it works."

Dottie crawls up my leg from where I think she might have been napping in my bag, and I grin as she grabs my finger to hug it. "It looks like some weird mix of runes, hieroglyphics, and Latin, maybe? Did you guys make a pidgin language to keep everyone from being able to read your shit?"

"Around the Salem Trials, there was a movement in Hell to safeguard our works by making them impossible for those without demon blood to read." Slash frowns, pausing to think as I stand up. "You'd have to ask Jas or Zavida for more information, but I believe it was to keep those of our kind living on the other side from being burnt to a crisp by panicked humans."

"We're pretty stupid as a species," I agree as we head out of the classroom. "I'm not afraid to admit my people are the fucking worst."

"No." I look at him and he shrugs. "Storybooks and deities are the worst—trust me. Humans come a close third, but they do not hold the crown."

Gee, glad I sort of asked… more shit to assimilate.

"I should probably leave asking questions about them until I'm fully grasping the demon part. Just thinking about adding on more unbelievable shit to my plate is making my stomach turn."

The big guy laughs as he holds the door for me and we amble down the hall to take the stairs to the bottom floor. By the time we get down, we've moved away from supernaturals that make me want to hurl to discuss the laws I missed during class. The professor went over the official rules of the Games —not that anyone expects them to be followed, especially with all the loopholes purposefully left in the wording.

"Did he send us a copy digitally? I really want to read every damn word of this fucking nonsense."

"You, Zav, and Oriel will likely be the only ones to do so, but yes." Slash tilts his head, arching a brow at me. "You have an affinity for fairness, it seems."

I snort. "Mostly because nothing in my entire life has *ever* been fair. It's like an addiction to an unattainable object, my shrink said."

"I'm not a fan of doctors that dig in your brains," the shark says, his expression disapproving. "I think they mix up shit until a slight problem becomes much larger and less manageable. That gets them more appointments and more money. It's a self-fulfilling prophecy."

You know, I've never thought of it that way, but it is a bit like a pyramid scheme. Now I'm never going to see therapy the same way again—awesome job, big guy.

I'm surprised when our path doesn't take us to the *Triclinium* for dinner—no, we head straight for the dorms when we get in the middle of campus. We've been walking quietly for the past bit, and it was more comfortable than I would have imagined. I didn't spend a lot of time above jabbering because I had no friends, so finding out that Slash is a good person to be silent with is yet another positive tick in his column. But I figured Prince Dickhead would insist on being 'observed' again, and it appears that's not the case.

"What's with diverting from the norm?" I ask him as we approach the front of the dorm. "I thought we had to make a unified appearance or whatever."

He grins at me. "It is a caliphate meeting night, so Salem is preparing dinner in your room. Once Anton and Xerxes are out of class, we will combine the meal and our meeting."

That's not a terrible plan. Jasper's a bit less shitty when he's being fed—not by much, but it will help.

"That's actually cool with me. I like cooking with Salem; we have fun and it's very educational."

Slash snorts. "Educational? How is that possible?"

We walk inside, and he follows me to the elevator, snarling at an unfortunate freshman who tries to join us until the kid backs off. I give him a frustrated look and the shark ignores me. "Slash, how am I going to get people to quit hating me if you all growl at them? And to answer your question, Salem is teaching me about the various plants and meats and fruits and shit."

He looks surprised for a moment, then nods. "Okay, that makes sense, little demon. You are learning our food while you cook. That is actually very helpful given you are likely a magic user. Herbs and plants will be important to you."

Don't think I missed that he ignored my complaint about the alpha posturing.

"How in the… here… do you know I'm a magic user? I haven't shown an affinity for anything yet as far as I know."

His laugh is dark as he bumps my shoulder with his. "Because you are too small to be a shifter… even the less predatory animal hybrids grow larger as their animals develop. You're obviously not one of the Cubi or vampiric because you would have started to change your eating and sleeping habits. Thus, we are left with magic users, including demis and Fae."

"Have you… does everyone assume that and no one told me?" I scowl as I cross my arms over my chest, not liking that idea in the slightest. I *hate* being talked around rather than to. I'm going to punch every single one of them if it's true.

"No. They are all far too emotional about it, and I prefer to allow you the space to change without the pressure a guessing game would engender."

Shit. This dude is racking up points like a fucking Hall of Famer.

"Thanks, big guy. That's actually really nice." I bump him back, but I bounce off his big ass arm and he bursts out laughing. My eyes widen, as I've seen him chuckle a bit, but this is real laughter—it's kind of glorious to watch.

When he notices I'm grinning like a fool, his brows furrow. "Why are you staring at me?"

"You don't usually let loose like that. It's cool." Ducking my chin, I tear my gaze away because I can feel the heat rising up my chest to my neck and I don't want him to notice it. "I enjoyed seeing it; that's all."

"Kit, you don't have to hide every time you say something real. We won't make fun of you."

I wrinkle my nose as I look up at him, but his expression is serious. "Old habits, I suppose. The idiot boys I lived with in the last home were… not exactly touchy-feely, and it was probably the best one I ever stayed at. I didn't have any friends because of moving around a lot. I'm mostly an awkward penguin."

His lips curve up. "Sharks eat penguins, little demon."

Annnnnnnnd there goes the stupid color in my face again…

I press my hands to my flaming cheeks, looking anywhere but the big shifter shaking with humor. "Don't make it weird, man."

"We *are* supposed to be dating you. I assume we will have to get comfortable with innuendo and such eventually."

He has a point and I refuse to acknowledge it. "There's no one around but us!"

"Better for practicing, yes?"

The elevator dings right as he shoots back at me and I groan. The Universe definitely gets its jollies by tormenting me and this is a prime example. "I suppose so, but maybe warn me first so I don't…"

"Don't what, Kit Kat?" Salem is standing in front of the elevator, clearly waiting for me to arrive to help him in the kitchen. "Is Slash making you uncomfortable? 'Cause I'll—"

"You'll do *nothing*, slumber bear." The shark gives me a nudge and I trudge out of the car with a sigh of irritation. "I don't owe you an explanation, but I was practicing our banter as Oriel suggested."

Excuse me, what?!

"What the hell does that mean?" I growl as I whirl around and stalk up to the large demon, pushing up on my toes to try to look him directly in the eyes. It doesn't work, of course, but I feel a lot more threatening.

"Oriel said it would be easier for you to accept certain aspects of the dating gambit if we practiced them when others were not around," Slash explains. "It seemed logical."

I poke him in the chest, giving him a dirty look. "He might be right, but you dipshits need to quit talking about me behind my back. Talk to me instead of about me, or I'm going lose my temper. Got it?"

He looks confused, but he nods. "I do not wish to upset you, little demon. I believe Oriel was trying to ease the transition for you as well."

"I *know* your intent was good, which is why no one is getting a nut punch. But it makes me feel like a bug under a microscope, not a person. Does that make sense?"

"Yes, actually." Slash looks chagrined for a moment and when I turn to look at Salem, he's making the same sheepish face. "As the royal caliphate, we are often watched like humans do their reality shows. I find it uncomfortable, whereas many of the others do not. I will try not to make you feel that way."

"Thanks," I say with a small grin. I lower myself to the ground again and move out of aggressive range. "I appreciate it."

Salem smirks as he watches us, his head tilted. "You know, somehow you're getting him to say more words in this hallway than I've heard him say in *months*. You must share your secret, Kit Kat."

"Don't ask me, Salem. I just live here."

As if I'm going to spill the big guy's secrets—yeah, right.

Come Together

Jasper

The shrimp is in their room, cooking with Salem for tonight's meeting. He did his best to aggravate the fuck out of me during class; it didn't take a fool to see he might be testing my words from his hospital room, so I stayed just inside the lines. It irked the fuck out of my dragon and went against everything I've been raised to do—but he doesn't need to know that. All he needed to see was that I was serious about my declaration so I can figure out how to keep the annoying little shit alive.

I still haven't worked out why the hell I care, but who has the time for examining their navel? Not me.

"Zavvie, how did the rest of the day go?"

My kitsune looks up from where he's collating data for the meeting, his eyes bright under his glasses. I have to suppress a smile when his tails swish happily in response. "Mythology could have been better, but it wasn't too bad. You know how Weapons went, and because you asked me to skip to do this, I'm not sure how Law went."

I sigh, pondering whether I want to call my second in to ask before we all convene. "That's better than yesterday, I suppose. Were you able to make inroads with our newest member?"

He ducks his head, looking away as he shuffles some more papers. I arch a brow, knowing what *that* reaction means. Zavida likes the shrimp and whatever progress he made today pleases him. "Okay, I guess. I think he's waiting for me to prove I'm not going to…"

"Zav, if you stopped talking because you were going to say 'sell him out for me', or some version of it—I'm not stupid." I run my hand through my hair, pacing back and forth in front of my couch. "Perhaps I was pushing you too hard before."

Before I can say another word, he's rushed forward to wrap his arms around me and bury his face against my chest. I blink, surprised as fuck to find him hugging me like this. "What… what the hell?"

His voice is muffled in my shirt, but I make it out. "You *never* admit you're wrong, Jas. Sometimes, you reassess, but this is the closest I've ever heard you come."

Mother of ghouls, have I really been that much like dear old Dad? Fuck.

Resting my hand on his head lightly, I clear my throat as emotions zing through me. I can't parse them all and it makes my dragon angry, so I huff a few smoke rings to calm myself. This fucking kid is making the entire world topsy-turvy, even my meek lover, and he obviously doesn't have the slightest clue what he's doing. I chew on my lip ring for a moment, my brain warring between fury and confusion as I decide what to say.

"Don't get used to it," I say gruffly. "I'm very rarely wrong, you know."

Zavida chuckles and lifts his head, his lips curved up as he eyes me. "Obviously, my Prince. But I'm still glad you're reversing your opinion on Kit— even if it's slow. I think he's good for the caliphate."

That's questionable, but I'm not going to burst his bubble.

Letting go of him, I jerk my chin to his doom piles. "What have you put together in the past couple hours, then?"

The kitsune frowns, walking over to grab his research. "I shifted from Kit because you said I could. Instead, I dug into the lore around the Games prior to our parents' participation. Everyone knows it's the first time any team bargained with others to secure a victory. I wanted to see how they ran before that so we know what *could* be coming if Darkstar and his supporters are planning to use them for a coup."

"That's the worst case scenario," I mutter as I head for the bar to pour myself a drink. "We'd better hope he's not planning an actual onslaught during the Games; it will lead to a full-on war. We can kiss keeping ourselves out of the royal shit good-bye forever if that happens."

His tails flick nervously as he nods. "Agreed. But I don't know if he's really had time to prepare that kind of thing. I'm leaning towards using them to cull the strong loyalists and royals *before* he makes a move."

It's a smart play, so someone other than Lucian came up with it. But who?

"He has to have been working on this for a long time. You know the King banned the damn competition after he and the rest of your folks ascended to the thrones." Scratching my chin, I frown, my brain whirling as I spin the chessboard to figure out what vantage point I'm missing.

"Oh, definitely," Zavvie says as he pulls a bunch of print outs from the stack and hands it to me. "See here? This is the decree that outlawed them and the laws binding it. Someone had to comb this shit for a loophole to even bring it before the courts."

"So he has a legally savvy demon of high repute on his side—probably a crossroads demon because they're naturally good with contracts." The names of every high ranking bargain maker fly through my mind and I growl in frustration.

Too many options and not enough time.

"Maybe a full or hybrid Fae, too," my lover says. "I know he despises hybrids, but he could be convinced to use one for their talents, and dispose of them afterward with little effort. He sees other supes and mixed breeds like us as tools to be used and thrown away."

Snarling, I give him a sharp look. "That's a disgusting opinion and it should have blacklisted him from the position of Headmaster. There are more hybrids than pure lines in Hell now. He's a sad relic and my father should have sent him to the pits."

Which makes me wonder what the fuck Lucian Darkstar has on the King—he wouldn't allow him to be here, otherwise.

"Obviously, I agree, but you know I'm correct in my assumptions. Unless he has continuous use for the being who assisted him in this interpretation, he likely terminated their association permanently to prevent leaks. It's boiler-plate megalomaniac behavior."

Zav's right, unfortunately. My father definitely eliminates any possible squealers in his nefarious deeds as soon as they've outlived their usefulness. You don't wrest control of Hell and stay in that position for millennia without getting your hands dirty—though his are soaked in blood in ways that even I admit outweigh practicality.

"So he's got alliances built over… centuries… amongst various factions in Hell and maybe in other supe species as well," I murmur as I stroke my chin. "Again, not unexpected, but maybe more vast than I anticipated at this juncture. The question is… why now? What makes *this* the prime time for his moves versus any other time in the past or future?"

He shrugs, wrinkling his nose. "I don't know. Maybe it's because we're all coming of age? But I doubt even Lucian believes our parents will cede control when we graduate, so that might be incidental."

Frowning, I consider the board again, spinning it in my mind for a moment. "Maybe he's gotten a whiff of our plans?"

"No way, Jas. None of us would dare to leave even a minute trail to our work on that project." Zavida shakes his head, his expression serious. "You know we're all in and we'll be killed if anyone even suspects."

My gaze hardens as I consider what's changed. "Then I was *right* about this new—"

"Stop it." His tone brooks no argument and I can't hide the shock on my features as my submissive kitsune stands his ground. "You know Kit is not a fucking spy. The kid knows dick about our world and it's painfully obvious he barely interacted with his *own* world. Don't be an idiot, Jasper Eversore."

Wow. Full name—he's serious as fuck.

Licking my lips, I gather myself, pushing the angry dragon down. He doesn't like the disrespect that showed, but that's only because of the way I was raised as he emerged. Between animal instinct and the asshole who raised me, my animal is more reactive to that than I'd like. Zavida is loyal to a fault—hence his situation with the shrimp—and I don't need to smite him for speaking his mind.

"You're probably right, Zavvie." I hang my head, my frustration at peak levels. "But I'm also correct to assume Lucian has a specific reason or direc-tive to do this at this moment in time. It seems out of the blue, but there must be other factors besides the appearance of this kid."

"Good job, Sir," he whispers as he looks at me shyly, as his bluster from before is gone.

I stalk over, grabbing him and spinning toward the wall to back him into it with a hungry smirk. "You know, you've never defied me quite so bravely before, boy. I hated it, but it was hot just the same. I might enjoy the spark this clueless fool is bringing out in you. It will make punishment much sweeter."

He shivers against me, and I feel his cock twitch as he looks up at me through his lashes. "I'm not a brat, Sir. You know that."

Laughing, I shake my head in amusement. "No, and I wouldn't accept that for a second. Too much work to spank the annoying out of someone who's asking for it."

My hand creeps up to his neck, holding him in place as our bodies meld together. I see his tails flicking in excitement and his scent changes… cinnamon, red pepper and saffron. That's the smell of his arousal, and it makes my dragon snarl inside.

"Jas… Sir. Please."

Oh, fuck. How in the hell am I supposed to ignore pleading when I'm this close to the edge of fury?

"Eris, time!" I bark.

The Hell-based virtual assistant appears in a hazy hologram that looks like a small imp I customized to look like a sniveling version of my father that always makes me grin. *"Good evening, Prince. The time in Canto IV is seven thirty eastern underworld time. How else may I serve you today?"*

"Go away," I mutter as I look back at my lover. "We have enough time for you to please me, but only if you're quick."

The second the imp disappears, I let go of his neck and Zav drops to his knees like he's going to worship at my altar.

I suppose he is, technically.

The fiery haired kitsune gives me a sly grin, and I groan as his eyes fix on the bulge in my pants. His gaze gets hungrier as he pulls my dick out, licking his lips as the light glints off my Jacob's ladder and magic cross piercings. He loves the feel of them inside him, and I love when he plays with them as he sucks me off, so it was worth the effort. I reach out, grabbing the tail that twitches beside me, betraying his excitement. Zavvie gets immense pleasure from pleasing me and getting praised, plus he gives head like jizz is going to save his life.

"Now, Sir?" Zavida purrs, his voice dripping with lust and anticipation.

I grunt my approval, eyes blazing with my dragon as my other hand buries in his hair. Zavida leans in, pressing a reverent kiss to the tip of my cock, his tongue flicking out to taste my pre-cum. A low warning growl rumbles from my chest—he knows it means stop fucking around. Encouraged, my kitsune continues to lick and tease his way down my shaft, his tongue swirling around each piercing and eliciting shivers as blood pumps directly south without passing 'go.'

The little tease is enjoying this and I'm going to splatter his face if he doesn't get moving.

As he reaches the base, he does that weird fox-like scream that his kind do when they're fucking and I grin. Zavvie can't help doing it when he's aroused, and it's why I made sure my room was sound-proofed. No one else needs to hear that unless I permit it. I suck in a deep breath when he wraps his lips around the tip only to take as much of my girth as he can until I hit the back of his throat. I love that he doesn't have a gag reflex, as the bumpy ridges and vibration of my dragon would be a task for someone as small as him otherwise.

I wonder if... no.

Cursing my errant brain, I force myself to focus on the scent of my boy as he sucks me. His dick has to be pulsing with need because his scent is practically filling my room now. He bobs his head up and down, applying suction or teeth where I like and my head falls back on my shoulders. Struggling to maintain control as his efforts intensify, I wing a thanks into the void for figuring out that I was into him when we were in middle school. It's not acceptable at home, but this is the very best way I defy my father's wishes, and I'll be damned if I ever give him up. This man is mine, and I'll destroy anyone who tries to force me to give him up.

Possessive thoughts always make my dragon push at the reins, and I tug on Zav's hair, muttering dirty things to him as he works me over. His tongue and teeth are sharp and wicked, pushing me toward climax quickly. I'd be self-conscious about it if my boy wasn't the best cocksucker in the ten realms of Hell, but he's that fucking skilled. With a roar, I come, shooting hot seed down his throat in powerful spurts. White-hot pleasure courses through me as he eagerly swallows every drop, still making that screeching sound around me.

Fuck. Yes.

As my orgasm subsides, my grip on his head loosens and I pant heavily. Zavvie continues to lick and clean every last drop of cum from my softening cock, determined not to leave a single trace behind. His eagerness to drink me in is always a turn-on and I have to look away or I'll get hard again. we simply don't have time for the thorough fucking I want to give him, so I pull back a bit.

He looks up at me with a satisfied expression and a coy twirl of his thick tail. "Sir, did that... please you?" he asks with an adorable expression.

My eyes sparkle with humor as I look down at the kitsune. "Only you would ask that after blowing my brains out, Zavvie. Yes, you were a good boy."

Rising to his feet, he doesn't even ask to deal with what has to be a raging hard-on in his pants. He knows we'll work on that later, and my wicked grin confirms that thought. "Then it's time to see if Salem is done with the meal."

Imagine that. He's still hungry. I'm a lucky fucking Prince, indeed.

The Room Where It Happens

Salem is humming under his breath as we put the final touches on the dinner. I've been watching him while I carefully follow his instructions on each task I'm given, and it's adorable. He's got more energy than I would have expected for this time of night, but he did snack while he worked, so that might have helped. I grab the dish full of veggies I just finished and climb down from the stool he made appear in our kitchen earlier in the week. Walking over slowly so I don't drop my cargo, I step into his field of vision so I don't startle him.

The panda shifter gives me a big grin, pausing his rendition of 'Shake It Off' to take the platter. "You're a natural in the kitchen, Kit Kat. I swear, every single one of these is the same fucking size. I don't know how you do it."

My face heats and I shrug when the praise makes my body tingle with happiness. "Hell if I know. I've always had pretty good spatial awareness. It helps you figure out where to hide and how to squeeze your shit into small areas."

"Fuck, man," he says as he dumps the plate into the boiling pot then turns to face me fully. "It *kills* me when you say stuff like that. I want to… smash shit, and that's Slash and Jasper's departments."

What do I say to that?

"Um, I'll try not to—"

His hand waves at me and he shakes his head quickly. "No, no. I don't want you to *stop* sharing with me, man. I just hate that you've had to make yourself so small for this long. It makes my bear pissy and he's normally a pretty *laissez-faire* dude. I don't know how to handle it."

Flexing my hands at my sides, I feel my anxiety surge as I try to figure out what to do so I'm not upsetting him. My gut is clenching as he runs his hand through his hair in frustration and all I want at this moment is to make him feel better. "What can I do?"

"Aw, Kit Kat. You don't have to do anything; I promise."

Sure, he says that now, but I've heard things like that before.

I chew my lower lip for a second, then back up, deciding a little distance might calm my frayed nerves. "I'm… I'm going to change out of my uniform so I'm comfortable for the meeting. Are we good here?"

Salem looks at the counters and the place settings, then nods. "It's good to go. Thanks for helping me get everything done. I never get this much done so fast, especially at night. You're good company."

Now I'm pinging between happy flutters and guilt, so I give him a weak smile before I head to my room. The sound of tiny paws on the floor tells me Dottie is following along, so I wait for her to scramble inside before I shut the door. Once I'm in, I lean back against the wood and close my eyes. Calm doesn't rush through me like I expect it to, and I frown.

Why am I not calming down now that I'm alone?

It might be anticipation of the meeting we've been preparing for; that's definitely been on my mind the entire time we cooked. Jasper's mood is never predictable, and I have no idea what he'll do. The rest of the guys have been fairly supportive since my attack, so I'm not worried about them. I assume he's going to fill us in on whatever the staff has been told that students aren't privy to. That, I want to hear because the low hum of fear thrumming through me every time the Games are mentioned is driving me up the wall.

"They were supposed to be telling us what's expected of us, but all I've had so far are normal lectures and shit. It's ridiculous," I grumble as I push off the door and head over to my dresser. Opening it, I pull out a set of the sweats I was given and walk over to the bed. "I get that they're demons, but this feels evil even for them."

Dottie climbs up the bedpost, sitting next to me and looking up at me sympathetically. She makes soft sounds that I think are meant to be soothing and I smile as I run my fingers over her head. For a little rodent, she's surprisingly supportive of my condition.

"Yeah, I know, girl. This entire place is a death trap and I'm surrounded by beings I shouldn't trust as far as you could throw them."

Sighing, I tug off my clothes, tossing them into the hamper before I reach for deodorant and body spray. I need a refresher after the day and you can bet Prince Assface would be the first person to tell me I stink if I don't make sure I'm good. I pull on the sweats and rise to my feet, putting my laundry in the small hamper. I'll need to find the damn facilities for that this weekend without a doubt.

Fuck knows the spoiled brats coming to our room won't have a clue where it is, so I'm on my own with that.

I take my tablet out of the bag, my compulsive nature demanding I have the ability to take notes for later. Walking over to the mirror on the wall, I use one of my towels to wipe off the eyeliner, then brush my short hair so I don't look like a frumpy mess. My eyes focus on my reflection, so different from a couple weeks ago when I didn't know any of this even existed.

"You can do this, Kat," I whisper. "You are a survivor in every sense of the word, and these rich kids aren't going to take away this opportunity. Everything you've done so far proves that determination and stubbornness trump everything else in the end."

I just have to keep telling myself that until I believe it—fake it 'till you make it, Kat Camponella.

WHEN I GATHERED MYSELF ENOUGH TO LEAVE MY ROOM, I DISCOVERED everyone but Anton and Slash lounging on our couches. Jasper is sitting in the big armchair I like and every time I look at him, my lip curls into a sneer of annoyance. Of course he'd choose the place I want to sink into to feel safe and surrounded without the slightest compunction. I'd be mad at Salem for letting him, but he doesn't seem surprised by the choice. That might mean I've been sitting in Prince Twatwaffle's seat when he's not here, but I seriously don't give a fuck about that.

This is my room, too, and I'll sit wherever the hell I want.

Oriel tilts his head, studying me for a moment. "You okay, Kit Kat? Your aura is… wavy."

The crow shifter doesn't see auras, so whatever vibes I'm putting out that alerted him to my discontent aren't that. "Super awesome, thanks for asking."

A loud snort from the kitchen gets everyone's attention and when we look at the panda demon, he shrugs. "I'm not stupid. That sarcasm practically dripped on our pristine floor."

The Prince fixes his gaze on me, his eyes flashing with the dragon. "What are you irrationally angry about now, shrimp?"

What the hell? Irrationally angry? That motherfucker… he promised!

"I am not irrational. Every complaint I've lodged so far has been in direct response to *someone* treating me like shit and not respecting my boundaries. I've been exceedingly willing to compromise despite repeated dickish behavior, if you ask me."

Zavida looks up from his spot on the floor next to Jasper, pushing his glasses up as his fingers cease flying over the keys of his laptop. "I think that's true."

"Oh, for fuck's sake…" Jasper grumbles as he shifts in the chair with an eye roll and a dissatisfied expression. "He knows you're sorry, Zav. Don't kiss his ass just because you want him to forgive you."

I blink. He thinks *that* was kissing my ass? "Jasper, someone admitting you're wrong is not sucking up to the other person. It's just agreeing with the facts."

X winks at me from their perch on one of the barstools. "To the crown prince of Hell, that's *exactly* what kissing ass is."

"Can we move this along?" Oriel says as Salem brings a tray of drinks over. "I'm hungry as hell and the second the big man gets here, he's going to have a tantrum when he finds out Kit Kat hasn't eaten."

Now it's my turn to roll my eyes and look sullen. Jasper isn't alone.

"You're right," my roommate says as he hands me a glass of oddly sparkly liquid. "But this should help."

"Huh?" They all laugh as I look at the rocks glass, studying the contents. "How does it do that?"

Oriel scratches his chin, looking thoughtful before he speaks. "It's hard to explain what Sparkling Styx Tonic does because it affects us all differently. It's definitely good for our health in small doses like this, but when mixed with various demon alcohol it's euphoric."

"So it's both a medicine *and* a party juice?" I arch a brow as I look at each of them carefully, searching for signs of deceit. I'm not drinking anything they can quantify if I'm not certain their motives are pure.

Zav smiles shyly, then takes a sip of his to encourage me. "It is, Kit. I'm surprised Dr. D didn't give you some after he treated you."

"He didn't, but it seems like Salem has some on-hand so I should be okay." I watch them all drink theirs before I put my glass to my lips. It tastes *amazing* though I couldn't describe what the flavor is like if someone asked. All I know is that it feels like my entire body is humming with energy and light in a really good way.

Damn. If this affects humans the same way, someone could be making a fortune putting Big Pharma out of business.

"Better now?" X tilts their head and I nod. "Fabulous. Jasper, get it rolling. I have stitches to do."

The dragon waits until we're all looking at him and clears his throat. "The staff wasn't fully briefed earlier, except for the changes to our curricula. I don't know if that's because I was present—though I wouldn't discount that possibility—or if they're determined to hide as much as possible until the moment we need to know."

"That means nothing has changed," I say with a frown. "Which, in turn, means we can eat and get to our damn homework."

"Hold your horses, Kit Kat. There has to be more," Oriel murmurs. "He's being a dramatic asshole."

Zavida snorts, then looks up from his screen to address the group. "I'm scanning a fuck ton of history to find Games lore and info. Once I have it all together, I'll email each of you a section to scour through and report back on."

"More homework? I'm going to die," I groan. "I'll never catch up at this rate."

"Now who's being dramatic?" Prince Asshat smirks and I have to resist the urge to fling my glass of happy juice at him in retaliation.

The door opens and Slash stomps in with Anton in tow. The shark shifter gives the smug royal a dirty look, then ignores the group to head for the kitchen. Anton drops his bag and makes a beeline for X, curling up with them as usual before he smiles at me. Together, their gaze on me is intense and I almost miss the big hand shoving a small plate of the cubed cheese and meat from the appetizer tray under my nose.

"Eat." I make a face at him, but I pick up a piece of cheese to nibble on and he grins toothily.

"You owe me fifty bucks," Oriel says to X. "I *knew* he'd do it, just like I knew Kit Kat would give in. Pay up, sucker."

"Get fucked," I mutter at them before chewing on one of the pieces of meat. "If I say I'm going to do something, I do it."

"Oh, good. That promise makes this part *much* easier," Jasper says with a pleased expression.

I take a sip of my drink, not wanting him to see how that ominous declaration affects me. "And what the hell is that supposed to mean?"

"Lucian has scheduled a Samhain ball to celebrate our most revered night of the year and the return of the greatest competition in Hell. It's in two weeks, and attendance is mandatory."

Salem groans. "That means he'll invite *all* the universities. I *hate* when they mix us up."

"Other universities?"

X and Anton whisper for a moment, then Xerxes looks at me sympathetically. "All of them. Brimstone included."

I wait for them to explain, but no one says a word and it finally becomes clear: Brimstone must be where the rich *female* demons go to college.

Oh, shit.

For What It's Worth

Danton

It's been two days since our meeting, and despite the odd determination of our professors to piss off Kit, it's been pretty quiet. I guess Lucian isn't announcing the damn Devil's Night affair to the masses yet, but since staff gossip as much as students, the whispers are running rampant. Jasper sent word for the royal tailors to visit this weekend, and X has been giddy with glee ever since. My effusive love is planning to make their own outfit, as well as our new member's, but the rest of us are stuck with using our families' employees. It would be an insult of epic proportions to not allow them to design our bespoke attire, and even though we'd all prefer *not* to get visits from what will definitely be spies… it's unavoidable.

Especially with the damned event so soon—a purposeful choice on Darkstar's part, I'd bet.

"Today we're going to spar with magic and weapons," Jasper says as he strides into the room brusquely.

My eyebrows shoot up and my panicked look at Zavida and Xerxes doesn't go unnoticed. Kit doesn't have magic to use and that will make him a *big* target. I'm fairly sure Jasper isn't doing this to punish him, but it's risky nonetheless. "Professor…"

Jasper's gaze slices to me, and all I feel from him is helplessness. He didn't make this decision on his own and he doesn't have a choice. When his eyes slide to the rest of the class, I groan internally. That might mean he's been warned about grouping his own caliphate together in his classes. This is going to be extremely bad if we're not careful.

"Not now, Anton." He gestures at the rack of dulled blades and lighter staffs on the wall. "Pick your poison, gentlemen, then we will divide into pairs to practice."

X sidles over, whispering, "At least he won't be with Bastian. Q is pretty far from C in terms of alphabet."

"We don't know that he'll use the alphabet," Zav says as he grabs a staff. "Kit, what weapon are you using?"

Our newest member looks at him blankly, and I curse under my breath. "X, help snap him out of it. He has to be focused."

Xerxes walks over to the wall, plucking two swords from it. "Kit Kat, you're good with the blade, so I got yours, too. Now take this pig poker and show your partner what you're made of."

Kit doesn't move to grab it and I realize he's probably rocketing into space with anxiety over the 'magic' thing. I step up in front of him, looking into his eyes as I put my hands on his face. "Dude, you *have* to get ready. I think Prince Asshat is being ordered to run this exercise in a specific way."

When he doesn't respond again, I look at the floor, asking every high demon deity in Hell to help me figure out what I need to do. I know he can't help it, but we have to help him get past this kind of incident so it doesn't happen *during* the Games and get him killed. Zav and X shrug, looking as helpless as I feel. Oriel would know what to—so would Salem, and maybe even Slash. Damn, we're so far behind in this situation.

Maybe…

I look directly at the freaked out guy and make an apologetic face before I dart forward to plant a kiss on his lips. Within seconds of our mouths touching, his eyes pop open, looking shocked and suddenly aware at the same time. I try not to notice how soft his lips are or the fact that just the barest brush of our tongues happened before he blipped back in as I pull back. His face turns bright red as people other than my caliphate start hooting and hollering, making this a much bigger scene than I intended.

"Don't forget we want them to think you're dating us," X says under their breath. They give me a smug grin as I recover from my likely ill-advised decision and I glare at my lover. Xerxes is not upset in the slightest, but they are *very* smug and that's going to last all day for certain.

"I... I..." Kit whips around, looking at each of us as he tries to find his bearings. "Um... I..."

Zavida takes pity on him. "It's fine, Kit. Take your blade from X and let's move on. I'm sure Jasper is going to intervene in about—"

"Mr. Camponella and Mr. Aldaric. Are you quite through?"

We all turn to look at the Prince, his dragon half-shifted as he grits his jaw and gives us looks like he's going to murder us all on the spot. His fists are clenched, his eyes are full of his beast, and he appears truly infuriated. I frown, unsure why the hell he'd be mad that we were getting Kit to focus *and* following the 'dating' plan in public. It seems like a win-win for all of us.

"Oh, boy," Zav says as he moves over to stand in line where the groups are normally assigned in Arms class. "This isn't good."

X joins him, and I follow, leaving a space for Kit to stand next to me. "What's up his ass, now, Z? He's impossible to predict lately and I can't see why he'd be pissy that we're doing what we agreed to."

The kitsune shakes his head, giving us a rueful smile. "I don't know, and if I did, I couldn't tell you this kind of thing."

Kit finally walks over, the sword clutched in his hand as he keeps his eyes on the ground. "Um, thanks. Sorry I... did my thing and you had to... do that."

I blink. He's sorry? I was worried I'd trigger some bad thing from his past, but it was the first thing I could think of that wasn't somewhat violent. "KK, it's cool, man. I didn't want to shake or smack you because it might make you spiral, but... this concerned me, too, even if it conforms with our plan."

His eyes finally move from the floor to mine and his cheeks go a pretty pink as he mumbles, "It was okay. I didn't... you know. You didn't make me freak. Obviously. It was... a good plan."

It might have been, but the way he's acting, I'm not so sure.

THE REST OF THE CLASS IS NERVE-WRACKING EVEN FOR ME. KEEPING AN EYE on my own partner, plus Kit, is hard as hell. I know the others are watching him, too, but something in my gut has attached his safety to my bird's deepest value—pride—and I can't allow anything untoward to occur on my watch. I'm normally not this edgy, except with X, but here we are.

My plan was a cock-up, after all.

"Annie, why are you scowling so much?" X asks as they dance around their opponent nearby. Luckily for us, Jasper put that fucker Ivan with demons other than the ones in our caliphate, so the distraction of keeping an eye on Kit didn't lead to disaster.

I dodge a perfectly aimed strike from Magnus Chilton, a drude from Zav's family line. He's not as obnoxious as many of the others in the room, so I don't bother with smack talk. X is using short daggers against his opponent, Kristian Hoebert. The incubi is from his own house, so it's not likely he's in any danger. Plus, despite the snarky bullshit Hoebert is spewing, Xerxes is owning his ass. He had to learn that shit early to defend himself from the less evolved demons in his family's court.

"You know why, X," I mutter as I duck a side blow from Chilton. "This irritates the bird."

Their eyes follow mine before we look away, and a bright smile appears on his face. "Ooooh. Now *that* is *much* more interesting than kicking Hoebert's ass."

"Get fucked, frilly ass," Kristian mutters as he continues to unsuccessfully defend his position. "I'm being careful because of who you are."

Snorting at his bullshit, I dart forward, knocking my partner's weapon loose. "Concede, Magnus. We're done."

The drude rolls his eyes, picking up his sword before he stomps away. His magic requires me to be unconscious, so he didn't have a fucking chance to do anything. X finally gets the best of his partner, too, and we both head over to put away our practice weapons. As we head for the other side of the field, Zav is struggling with the much larger brute he's fighting, but his kitsune speed and portal ability are helping. They have short bos, which I know Zavida is skilled with, so he should be able to avoid any real injury.

"Let's watch him. It's okay to be concerned, Annie," X says as they grab my hand. "I think he's doing pretty well considering Jasper put him with Aesyllian Furon."

My jaw tightens and I nod, the desire to be closer greater than my usual reluctance to share my emotions with anyone in public. "He was captain of the fencing team in secondary school. I don't know what the hell Jasper was thinking when he assigned that."

"Concede!"

The sound of Zavida finally getting control of his bout makes me sigh in relief as X and I stop in front of our dueling friend. Kit is holding his own, surprisingly, but he's getting slower. Unfortunately for him, the Fae demon is zinging magic *everywhere*, forcing him to have to dance around as he works in his shots. Not having magic is actively hurting his chances and if I were to bet on the purpose of this forced exercise, it would be to showcase how vulnerable Kit is. The rumors will get around before we even make it to lunch.

That's a damn good way to encourage attacks outside of the official Games to remove his piece from the board.

"Where the fuck is Jasper, anyway?" I ask Zav when he finally joins us. He's dripping with sweat and rubbing a towel over his fiery hair, a telltale sign that his fight took a shit ton of his energy.

"No idea. I noticed he disappeared after the assignments, but I was too focused on keeping myself from getting conked to see where he got off to."

I frown, noting that X and I were both likewise consumed by our opponents and watching out for Kit. "I think these pairings were given to him on purpose. I can't see him pairing me with someone who can barely use magic on this plane and Kit with a Hellympian, you know?"

"No shit," Zavida says as he finally puts his glasses on. "I'm fast as fuck, so I would have been a bigger challenge for Furon than Kit. This is definitely not a coincidence, nor is his disappearance. We should—"

A loud clang, then muttered curses force my brothers and me to pay attention to the battle again. When we do, Kit is standing there with his sword up, looking like he might keel over. Furon is on the ground under his foot and he's grinning broadly.

How the fuck did that happen?

"He cheated!" Aesyllian fumes from the ground. "I want the Professor to mark it. Where is Eversore, anyway?"

Xerxes walks over, giving the hybrid a small kick in the ribs as they lean down with a smirk. "No idea, Furon, but I definitely have to snap this for socials. Anyone ever tell you that you're an insufferable tool?"

"Shut up, you weirdo. I'm reporting this nonsense." Aesyllian pushes Kit's foot off of him after X's phone flashes, then rolls to his feet. "And that had better not end up online or you'll be hearing from our lawyers."

Ignoring his bluster, I walk over to Kit, my eyes scanning him carefully. He's going to have a few bruises, there are some magical burns on his arms, and that might be the start of a shiner, but otherwise, he looks okay. "Kit Kat, how are you doing? Do we need Dr. D?"

He shakes his head, pushing wet hairs off his forehead as he trudges up to our group. "No. I don't want to go running to the doctor every time some dick gets a few licks in. It just makes me look weaker. I have to suffer through this—at least in public."

A brilliant idea hits me and I snap my fingers. "You might have to in public, but you don't have to all day."

"Huh?"

"Slash has a free period with you next. He'll be here soon and he can follow you to your room. I'll handle the rest—trust me."

Hopefully, I can find Jasper quickly enough to make this happen.

Witch Doctor

Slash has been quiet since he arrived to pick me up, and while that's not unusual, I get the feeling it's not because he has nothing to say. He grunted at my condition, giving the guys who were in my class dirty looks as he asked the same question we all had: where the fuck is Jasper?

No one had an answer, even Zav, but when the big shark shifter jerked his head to say it was time to go, I waved and followed. I didn't see a reason to argue, especially since I'm a bit more wiped than I let on. The fight was extremely physical and while I'm not *out of shape*, per se, I'm definitely not ready to be sparring some athletic-ass automaton who came for me like I'd offended his ancestors. I'm still unsure how I won—it was like the fight was going on and suddenly, things turned despite my waning stamina.

It's fucking strange and I'm afraid to mention it lest we end up on another episode of 'what is Kit, really?'.

"Don't pay them any attention, little demon."

I blink, coming back to reality in time to wonder what the fuck Slash is talking about. It only takes a moment or two to figure it out, though. Demons are staring at me like I'm Amelia goddamn Earhart as we stride across campus. While being a famous missing person would be cool as hell, I know that's not the case. My injuries can't be the problem; people get hurt in classes all the time, according to the caliphate.

Bucking up my courage, I look up at the huge shifter with an annoyed scowl. "Why the fuck are they staring? I swear, I'm going to figure out how to buy a costume or some shit to get around if this doesn't stop. Every day, more people start—"

"Anton kissed you in class. It has spread already."

My frown deepens and I bark, "What the hell? Is it homophobia? You guys said demons don't give a shit. If you lied, I'm going to skin someone while they scream because I don't put up with that shit. Being shitty to someone because of who they are or love is absolute trash and—"

"Stop." That one word cuts off my flow, and I wait for him to elaborate. "That is not why, though even demons have… their own extremists to deal with."

I wait for him to open the door, used to his insistence that he has to make sure the damn lobby is safe before I go in. Fighting him on that quirk seems useless and for some reason, I don't want to quibble about things that may actually be in my best interest right now. What I really want is to get to the room I share with Salem and sink into the fucking comfiest couch ever and let my sore body have a moment to rest.

But I can't leave his statement alone, so I wait until we get to the elevator to ask, "Why is that a big deal?"

The big guy looks surprised for a second, then shrugs. "He has been with Xerxes since they were young. They did not… explore other options until now. That makes it very hot gossip."

That son of a bitch! How did he not realize his method of getting me to snap out of it was going to be the new headline?

Growling softly, I kick the wall of the elevator, then groan as the pain rockets up my leg. "Damnit. It's bad enough they think I don't belong because I'm human. Now I'm in your boy band *and* the dating thing is confirmed, so I'm not going to be able to go anywhere without an audience."

"Perhaps that is a good thing after this weekend."

I snort. "Exactly how is it good, Slash?"

He looks thoughtful, then says, "There are many who would like to be in our good graces. Helping to keep you safe by reporting things to our spy would be a good in-road for weaker demons."

The door dings and we walk into the hallway, my face shocked as I follow him. "Demons will watch me and report to Oriel if I'm in trouble? Really?"

His big hand waves in front of the sensor and our room opens. Once I'm inside, he closes the door behind us, facing me with a smirk. "Oh, not only to keep you out of trouble, little demon. They will also whisper to cause fractures in our group, but they can't do one without the other. Since they do not know what we have agreed to and what we have not, everything will get reported."

"Oh." I place my bag on the counter so Dottie can escape, then kick off my shoes. I have four hours to rest and eat before I have to meet Salem and Zavida at Dark Lit, so I'm going to take full advantage of that big ass break. Dottie wriggles out, scrambling across the island to the mini-feeder Salem set up for her. "I guess that makes sense. It's going to make me want to stab myself in the eye, but I suppose it could be helpful."

Slash laughs as he walks over to the refrigerator. "Indeed. However, you need to go rest on the couch as the others suggested. The doctor will arrive soon and I am sure you'd prefer to be ready."

My eyes widen as I look at him. "I said I wasn't going to the doctor. They'll think I'm even weaker, Slash."

He ignores me, pulling out a few labeled containers and setting them on the counters. The humming sound surprises me, but this guy seems to be full of those. Once he has everything out, he studies the instructions taped to the lids before he starts opening them. "Go rest. Anton spoke to Jasper, and they contacted Dr. D privately. He will come here via internal portaling to conceal his visit. Now, shoo, or I will be forced to carry you."

Um, no, I don't want that.

"I will punch you if you try," I promise as I scoop Dottie up and hobble to the couch. "And I don't care how much bigger you are—it will hurt."

"Sure it will." He sounds even more amused as I lower myself to the cushions with a whimper of pain and put my feet up on the big ottoman.

"Thank fuck Salem is so compulsive about his kitchen. I'm not a cook, but I can read."

I don't answer him; it's his own fault for being an ass about me punching him. If he needs to figure shit out in there, he'll have to do it on his own. It's petulant, but I'm not feeling very generous at the moment. I should have been able to celebrate my victory, but instead, I'm stuck waiting for Dank while Slash snarks at me. His bullshit isn't nearly as sharp as Prince Prick-face, but I'm not going to ask him to back off and let me calm down.

Fuck that noise; I'm no swooning damsel.

"You realize that I am not babying you for a reason, yes?"

"Are you a fucking mind reader?" I stroke my fingers over Dottie's head, pouting at my pet. "I didn't even say that out loud."

He snorts, shaking his head as he puts dishes in the microwave. "No, little demon. I am not a mind reader, but you are not disguising your emotions well right now. Your face is an open book."

Dammit.

"I'm usually very good at that," I grumble as I close my eyes. "But it's harder here, and somehow harder with you dipshits in general. Is that a thing?"

"Caliphate-wise?" I hear the fridge open again and glasses clink, then steps approaching. When I pry my lids open again, the shark shifter is standing in front of me with a tray that has a glass of fruity smelling liquid and two small pills on it. "Somewhat, I believe. It's been a long time since I was inducted, so my memory of the first few months where effects might be multiplied is vague. Take your medicine; I saw the reminder you left yourself."

My eyes narrow, but I take the pills and what I think is juice from him. "I don't need you to wait on me hand and foot. I'm fully capable of doing things for myself."

The knock at the door keeps him from replying, but I can tell by the look on the big guy's face that it wasn't going to make me happy. He sets the tray on a table, then stomps over to the entry to my room, pressing his face against it to see who is there. Once he's satisfied, Slash pushes the button on the panel, and Dank floats in, plague mask and all.

"Master Kit," he says as he moves across the room to get to me. "I am displeased to hear you have been injured again so soon after your last visit."

Dottie chitters at the weird demon, dancing a bit on my lap, and I give him a helpless shrug. "Arms class got a bit out of hand. It wasn't anyone's fault, but the members of my caliphate insisted that I be seen—despite my protests."

The demon pulls his mask off, setting it on the table before he joins me on the couch. "They are right to ensure your health, Master Kit. After your attack, and knowing your physiology is quite fragile in this stage… you could do more harm than you think by ignoring minor injuries."

"Fragile physiology? What the hell does that mean?" I ask as he prods my bruises, making me wince.

Slash comes back to the sitting area with the tray of food he heated up, placing it aside while the doctor examines me. "He means that your demon side—and whatever else you may possess, if anything—is in transition. It is why Discordia's seers could sense you in order to send the invitation. During this time, things are in flux, I believe."

Nodding as he continues looking over my limbs, Dank hisses a soft sound. "Yes. It is certain Master Kit's transition began very slowly and that called to those with the sight. However, I cannot say how long it will take to fully emerge and power to manifest. I also cannot say *what* will manifest since your young computer whiz has been unable to trace him."

I frown, looking between them with an exasperated expression. "That's why Zav was prying into me? To find out what I'd become?"

"That and because Jasper's a paranoid asshole," the shark says with a grin. "But yes, he was hoping to figure out who, where, and how you were left to fend for yourself for so many years above. It's uncommon for demons, unlike supes."

"That motherfucker *knows* I'm not human, but he's been torturing me about it?!"

The doctor taps my arm gently, pulling my gaze back to him. "The Prince may be protecting you without disclosing it, Master Kit. There are many demons with mind gifts in the staff and student body. The less you know that could engender fear or jealousy, the more likely you will make it through your transition period without being targeted."

Fuming, I cross my arms over my chest. "I'm not stupid. I *can* be trusted with shit. I mean, I've handled the whole 'you live in Hell now' thing pretty well, considering."

"You have, little demon, but this isn't about you. It's about the rest of this world. Even our gambit in public to protect you didn't keep you from being pummeled in class." His brow furrows and he tilts his head. "I do not get why the Prince allowed you to be paired with an opponent who would harm you, even if he is being recalcitrant."

Dank makes a weird noise, then mumbles a bunch of weird sounding words as his gloved hands run over my limbs slowly. I grit my teeth as a burning sensation spreads through my body, keeping the pained sounds from escaping in my own act of defiance. When it finally stops, I cut my gaze to the big guy and shrug.

"The others seemed to think he didn't have a choice. It may have been arranged before class began."

"If that's true… this is only the beginning, Master Kit." Dank's voice is soft as he continues working, not looking at me as he adds, "It means you have bigger enemies than jealous students and you are in more danger than you realize."

Well, isn't that just peachy news to get on a Friday morning?

Lose Control

sälem

My radar was up when Slash dropped Kit Kat off at Lit class. My roomie was moving stiffly, and our group chat was quiet all morning, so I knew something had to have gone down in Arms & Battle. It's irritating as fuck that people refuse to keep us all up-to-date when things go down, but I also know how our two leaders react to deviations from their plans. They go into duck-and-cover mode, sweeping things under the rug until they have a firm grasp on what happened and how to fix it. That comes from living in the two most contentious royal lines with the two nastiest patriarchs, I know, but it frustrates the hell out of me.

Their version of damage control leaves everyone around them swimming in uncertainty.

"What happened, little dude?" I ask as Kit lowers himself into the chair next to me. His eyes dart around, as if already used to assessing what ears might be in the vicinity before he speaks. Shoulders slumped, he opens the bag to let Dottie scamper out and perch on my shoulder, an action that makes my panda practically cheese in satisfaction. Trusting someone with your familiar is a much bigger deal than Kit realizes.

He chews on his lower lip, wincing when it splits open the freshly closed tear. His tongue darts out to catch the droplets of blood and my heart damn near stops. "Arms class was rougher than anticipated."

No shit.

"I see that," I murmur as I reach over to swipe my thumb over his chin to catch another blood drop. Grinning at him purposefully, I suck that digit into my mouth, but my cheeky gesture ends there when the taste explodes on my tongue. Before I even compute what's happening, my skin fades to the black and white of my demon and my tail escapes. I know without looking that it's fluffy as hell and whipping about at my feet.

"Salem!" Kit whispers in surprise, his hand landing on my arm to grip my bicep. "What the hell?!"

"Holy fuck, Salem," Zavida adds as he walks up to us with his stuff. "Why are you—"

I grit my teeth, trying to reason with both the demon *and* the panda inside of me. My control has been solid since middle school due to our sadistic as fuck Hybrid Health & Safety teacher, so this is much more shocking than if Jas or Slash were doing it. The bigger, apex predators and mythicals have a much harder time with shifting and emotion, much like the heavily powered magic or demonic hybrids do with their powers. "I…"

Kit frowns, his eyes softening as he watches me struggling. "Did I do something wrong? I seem to be doing that a lot today. Frustrating people even when I'm actually trying to follow along."

Shit. Shit. Shit.

"Kit Kat, you definitely didn't do anything *wrong*. My panda is… having a moment." I give him a crooked smile, trying to mitigate my unusual display of public predatory behaviour. "Tell Zav and me what happened since it's obvious no one else deigned to do so."

He presses his lips together for a second, then looks at the kitsune, then back to me. "Um, okay. But… tell me if I'm making something worse, got it? I'm too damn tired to play games with people."

"There's the spark," Zavida says quietly. His shy smile makes me snort a laugh, then cover it up when the guy we're all obsessing over looks confused.

"You're both being really fucking weird," Kit mutters. "It's making my hackles stand up, so knock it off."

Waving my hand for him to continue, I beg my aroused as hell bear and demon to fuck off so I can focus.

He sighs, running his hand over his hair. "When Prince Ballsack got to class, he was definitely off. He assigned magic duels. Once he paired people, it was obvious he'd been instructed to keep the caliphate apart, and to give me an OP partner. Some dick named Furon that I have no idea how I eventually beat. I was kind of banged up, and Anton was upset. He contacted Jasper, I guess, so that when Slash showed up to escort me, he took me to my room and Dr. D came to patch me up privately."

My inner fuckers lose their grip at that point and it's all I can do *not* totally Hulk out in the half-filled classroom. Eyes flashing with the struggle, I look at Zav to see him pushing through his tails with sharp little fangs poking out of his mouth.

I'll be damned; even the submissive guy is ready to rumble.

"Kit, why didn't Slash simply take you to the office? It was closer."

The unemerged demon's eyes dart between the two of us and I *feel* his anxiety spiking. His finger spins his ring quickly, a sure indication that he's having as much trouble controlling the demons in his head as we are the supernatural ones in our bodies. "Look, I don't want people to see me run for a doctor every time someone gets a lick in, okay? They already think I'm weak. They think I'm your… shared boy toy. If I don't show backbone when it's rough, I'll end up in a room with bad intentions and no Jasper to help me escape this time."

"He's not wrong, Salem," Zavida murmurs. "Hell is enormous, and Discordia is rumored to be full of hidden spots, portals, and passageways we don't have a handle on yet. He has to be seen getting tougher as people accept our public claiming and induction of him, or they will continue to come for him—even if it's for nothing more than the clout."

I frown. The kitsune is definitely the expert on that, so I can't argue. He's the smallest and least over-powered of our caliphate—or was until Kit Kat. He and X have been targeted in the past, and they both had to show the rich assholes in our schools that they would give as good as they got, if not worse. "You're right; I just…"

Kit ducks his head, muttering, "It hurts my fucking soul to admit this, so don't get used to it, but I don't think Jasper is to blame this time."

My jaw drops and I burst into laughter, something that helps calm my raging emotions a bit. "Holy fuckbuckets, KK. I should hop upstairs and buy one of those human lottery tickets, then a jacket."

"A jacket?" His brows furrow as he tilts his head and looks at me in confusion.

"I'm pretty sure it's going to be a really cold day today in our slice of paradise." His amused grin as he gets my drift makes my chest do that weird flutter I get when my souffles come out perfect, and my bear puffs up inside.

I want him to make that face all the time—it's my new obsession.

LIT AND INTRO TO FAE BOTH GO BY WITH LITTLE ISSUE. ORIEL, ANTON, AND Slash have Fae with us, so the gang's almost all here when we close up our stuff to head out for the day. X has class for the next two hours, but Jasper will meet us back at the dorm to wait until dinner. Normally, on Friday night Kit would get sent to the Hacker Collective with Zavida, but since they've aced all our stress relief activities, that's off the table. The kid's looking even rougher now than he did earlier, and I suppose his supe healing is really taking it out of him. Dr. D probably did as little as possible to hide the magical signature of someone else's healing, especially since Kit didn't want anyone to know he'd seen a physician.

"Come on, little lady," I say to Dottie as I stand up and stretch. She chitters happily, and Kit nods as if to say it's fine if the kinkajou catches a ride on me. "Where are we headed, guys?"

Oriel looks thoughtful for a moment, his glittering eyes skating around the small, floral scented classroom full of vegetation. "I think we should walk around for a minute and review the stuff in here."

"Why?" Slash asks as he assesses our environment.

The crow shifter rolls his eyes, waiting for someone else to answer. No one does, so he gives in. "Because this flora is both from Hell and Faerie—both common and uncommon things Kit could run into during classes, the Games, and even at the stupid dance. I'd like to test whether he's going to react to any of it so we can make a list of his reactions to them, both adverse and affinities. Even knowing something is neutral will help us narrow down possible threats or weapons."

"Could lead us to his possible demon or hybrid species, too," Zav adds as his fingers fly over his tablet screen. He's likely building a list for later so he can construct something we can all keep on our devices to have close by at any time. "This is a really good idea, O."

I blink as my face turns bright red. They all stare at me and I mutter, "I've been simply exposing him to things in the food without considering the risks. We already have some things we can add to this database or whatever."

Kit blinks then grins. "Crunkleberries are good and make me a little high. I did okay with beast meat, bat wings, chasm worm, and the root veggies. Oh, that cow, too."

Nodding at his assessment, I add, "Also our potatoes, fear fish, pomegranates, Cantu berries, and bat berries. That's all good so far."

"Kit Kat, have you run into anything yet that *didn't* work?" Oriel says curiously. "Because this definitely leads to most demon types in your blood, but gives us nothing to rule out."

He shakes his head. "Other than deviant demons trying to assault me, the Headmaster, and your Pissy Prince? Nope."

"Put that he's allergic to assholes, then, Zav," O says with a smirk. Kit holds his fist up, bumping with him happily. "Okay, then we need to get this done so we don't leave His Highness waiting."

I offer my arm to the small dude and he takes it—something he wouldn't have done even days ago unless he absolutely had to. It makes my panda puff up again, and I feel the dirty looks hitting my back as I lead Kit to the left side of the indoor botanical garden. "This pretty-smelling stuff is Faeberry. They use it to make liquor that will knock your shoes off."

He leans in to sniff it, then pulls away with a look of delight. "That shit smells amazing and I've never really… drank… but I might give it a try someday when…"

The sentence trails and Oriel steps up to Kit's other side to take his hand. "When you feel safe enough to consume it. I get it, Kit Kat."

Damn, that dude is perceptive.

"Yeah. There were intoxicants involved in the incident, so I haven't been able to let go like that again since." He ducks his head and I look at Oriel to get us moving to the next plant. When he sniffs the Crawling Thorn Briar, he pulls back to make a face. "Wow, that's pungent. What is it?"

"It's a sentient crawling briar patch that resides in the Midnight Court. They use it for a lot of things from food to catching trespassers. Does it hurt you or make you uncomfortable?"

"Nope, it just *feels* like I should respect its boundaries—and it stinks."

Zavida looks up. "If you were unable to be near Crawling Thorn Briar, you'd be in the lupine family, non-Fae related, or the Cubi family. They all have issues with it, though there could be more I haven't memorized yet."

"That helps," Slash says as he points to the huge Bone Tree in the corner. "Try this one."

Of course he'd pick that—it can sense royal and mythical blood.

Black Horse and The Cherry Tree

kät/kit

I don't know why everyone is looking at me like I hold the secrets to the Universe all of the sudden. It makes me squirm and I scowl as I hold onto Oriel and Salem to keep myself grounded. "What? What the hell is so special about that gnarly tree thing?"

"It has… powers," Zav says quietly. His green eyes are bright under his thick frames and I tilt my head.

"What kind of powers?"

Slash gives me a smug, toothy grin. "It detects those of higher blood lines than simple demons or regular supernaturals."

Oh. Well that explains why they are practically drooling.

"Fuck that. I'm not going anywhere near that thing," I say firmly, shaking my head. "I'm a regular old foster kid who thought they were human. That bony looking soothsayer plant has nothing for me."

"Kit…" Oriel says softly, his hand landing on top of mine on his bicep. His dark, intelligent eyes find mine and he smiles gently. "No matter what the Bone Tree says, you're already part of our caliphate. It won't change anything."

I frown harder, mumbling, "Stop reading me, you son of a bitch."

Salem chuckles and squeezes my arm to his side. "C'mon, Kit Kat. It's a lark. We've all done it, though obviously, as kids we didn't quite get that the result was a foregone conclusion."

"There's no upside to it," I reply stubbornly. "If it says I'm truly a peasant, it gives Prince Dingleberry another excuse to look down his perfect nose at me. And the opposite holds true, too. In some weird-ass quirk of Fate, if it says I'm special somehow, then it will either be a secret we have to keep or something we have to tell, which will make me even more appealing to people who want to take me down."

Anton finally speaks, his expression thoughtful. "He's right about that. Should we risk the knowledge? There are downsides on both ends of the equation."

"See?" I shake my head. "No way I'm touching that thing."

The shark shifter moves closer until Oriel and Salem let go of me, leaving me to look up at the hulking general defiantly. He sighs, rolling his eyes upward then back to me. I suppose he's frustrated that I'm going to make him elucidate in front of everyone else, but I don't feel bad about it. "Little demon, this is something you will find out whether it is convenient or not. It would be prudent to know *now* and have time to strategize around the answer. The ensuing irritations will be manageable, whereas finding out in the middle of a battle would be less so."

Okay, now *I see the value of his suggestion to feel up the magic tree.*

"Fine." I clench my fists as anxiety races through me. This is a lot of pressure for a day already filled with bullshit and pain. I'm regretting my agreement and I haven't even stepped a millimeter closer to their stupid soothsayer tree.

"I will escort you; do not be afraid."

Glaring at Slash as I take his arm, I grumble, "I'm not *afraid* of your damn psychic bush. I'm concerned about the ramifications of its fucking prediction. There's a big difference."

He chuckles, the sound deep and soothing as he slowly walks me over to the stupid thing. It's not even impressive; in fact, it looks like some cheap overseas knock-off in a craft store Halloween collection. But as we approach, I can *feel the* power radiating from it—this damn thing practically assaults you with its presence so you know it's important.

"Is this rare? Like, do these things grow everywhere in Hell?"

Slash shakes his head. "They are rare and difficult to cultivate outside of the wild. Professor Cedar likely used Fae magic to assist with this one. There are thousands of Bone Trees hidden around Hell, Faerie, the Mounts, and on Earth. They have been used for millennia to help identify special supes, but their locations are kept secret by the Society to prevent mass pilgrimages to their locations. It might cause them to go extinct."

"Would it work on humans?" I ask curiously, trying not to get even more nervous as we stand in front of the magic tree.

Oriel snickers, giving me an amused look. "Over the many years, a few have stumbled upon greatness by finding one. They all have legends associated with them—you definitely know the ones who clumsily bumped the wrong tree and went on to be royals and great people because they were told they should be."

"I'm going to leave that list for later, thanks. I really need to stop asking these kinds of questions when I'm not ready to have my world shattered again." The demons waiting patiently for me to get my shit together and touch a branch laugh, though the longer I stall, the more tense the room gets. "You guys need to calm down, though, or I'll never be able to make myself do this. I don't know if it's that magic of the caliphate thingy or what, but your emotions are kind of crushing me."

Zavida's tails pop out and his face turns bright red before he hides behind them. That makes Anton and O smirk, then it spreads to Salem. A swift change in the vibe in the classroom skates over my skin and I shiver. This shit is weird and there's way too much of it happening at once for me to handle it.

"Okay, here it goes," I mutter as I let go of the big guy and stand directly in front of the weird, gnarled tree. Reaching out, I touch a branch lightly, waiting for something to happen. I lick my lips nervously, waiting. "What is it supposed to do? Am I doing it—"

A blast of bright light fills the room, and it feels like I'm being zapped with a million volts of electricity by this damn thing. I can hear the guys yelling, but something seems to be preventing me from moving and them from getting near me.

Whatever is going on… it can't be good.

My eyes open to five faces peering down at me from a *much* too close distance and I scream. My brain immediately registers how girly it was and I flail a bit to get them to back off. It doesn't matter that they're all handsome as fuck and look worried. What matters is that I'm flat on my back on the ground, awakening from something that definitely knocked me out. Panic grips me and all that helpful logic flees as my breathing increases to short pants and my chest tightens.

Damn, damn, damn… I'm slipping.

It's a cruel reality that I can be aware that I'm about to have a flashback and lose my shit, but not be able to stop it once I'm aware. That only happens when my vision is already tunneling and I'm too far to consciously put the brakes on. Pulling my arms into my chest, I hug myself tightly and rock back and forth as tears fall from my eyes. The images are coming; I know it to the marrow of my bones.

My jaw locks as the fast, black and white movie of my assault comes back to me in abrupt flashes of pain and helplessness. The heat of his breath, the pinch of his fingers, the sound of the ripped fabric and the smell… the smell of stale beer, sweat, and someone's stinky Swisher Sweets in the backroom of the loft. I squeeze my eyes closed and grit my teeth harder so I don't make a sound—no, he won't get my pleas for help or my outraged attacks on his pathetic technique that lead to the beat down afterward.

Goddamn it, why can't I ever get this shit to go away and stay gone?

"Kit."

A soft voice invades the fog in my mind and I try to follow it back out of the hole. The memory of the iron grasp and heavy weight on me push the sound away, and I continue fighting the insistent tug of my trauma.

"Kit Kat."

The next voice is just as soft, but a warm hand lands on my shoulder. I'm surprised when I don't jerk away with a wail; that happened even when my shrink tried hypnotherapy and the purveyor touched me. In fact, I literally scrambled into a corner and hid. But this touch feels familiar… and safe, unlike the imagery in my mind.

"Little demon."

Another hand, followed by more voices and more gentle anchors placed carefully on my arms, until I can breathe again. My eyes pry open and the blood racing through my veins slows just a tiny bit as the sparkling sensation in my limbs fades.

"Holy shit… sorry," I croak, feeling awful about yet again forcing these guys to clean me up when I'm a fucking mess.

"Do not apologize. It is not voluntary," Slash says in annoyance. "We are a team."

"He's right," Zavida whispers. I turn my head just a tiny bit to see him peeking out from his tails as his hand covers the fingers on my right hand. "You are one of us."

Somehow, that's more comforting than I would have imagined.

"Am I a freak or just plain old Kit?" My voice is still rusty from the clenching of my throat and silent screaming.

"We don't know," Oriel admits as he lifts his hand to brush hairs off of my face. "No one has *ever* seen that shit happen before. Zav's been searching the demon and supe nets since you blacked out.'

"Just fucking great," I mutter angrily. "I'm a *super freak* then. You jackasses better not tell anyone about this shit."

"We have to tell Xerxes and the Prince," Anton says reluctantly. "You know that, KK."

The urge to smash my fists into my eyes and scream is huge, but I need to get myself off of this floor before it triggers something again. "Let me up, guys."

They all move like lightning, sitting on the ground in the small semi-circle around me with concerned expressions. Slash and Salem look absolutely ridiculous here, and it makes the edge of my mouth quirk a tiny bit as I slowly rise to a sitting position. Oriel tilts his head in the avian manner, and I smile as I notice Anton doing the same. Zav is engulfed in his tails still, so it's hard to read him but the sight of them all makes me feel funny in multiple places.

I am suddenly very aware of how attached I've grown to these guys and this life, despite its challenges.

"Okay," I sigh as I look at them pleadingly. "But *no one* else, not even Dank. I'm not ready to have even more reasons for random people to come after me. I think we've given them enough to be pissed about as it is."

"Cross my heart, Kit Kat," Salem says with a smile. "But um… do *you* remember anything from when you touched the tree?"

Frowning, I shrug. "I've got a lot of not-so-great things floating around in my skull right now. Maybe… if we go back to the room and give me time to push out… the non-related things?"

That makes Oriel scowl as he nods. "We can do that, Kit. But you realize we'll have to tell Jas and X while we're there? They're definitely blowing up our phones and none of us have answered yet."

That's absolutely fucking terrible news—the Prince is going to be angry as hell.

"Okay," I finally say. "You guys are going to have to help me up, though, because the stuff Dank fixed is probably—"

Before I can finish, they're on their feet and the big shark shifter bends down to heft me over his shoulder. I smack the muscles of his back, protesting this method the only way I can when I'm too stunned to speak. Oriel winks at me, and even Zav looks pleased as Slash ascends the steps of the hall with me slung over his back like a sack of potatoes.

"Guys, no… my…"

Salem chuckles, grabbing my bag and reaching up to pet Dottie as she waves at me from his shoulder. "We got it, KK. Just enjoy the ferry service."

If huge demons don't quit trying to carry me places, I'm going to lose my fucking mind, guaranteed.

Build Me Up Buttercup

When Slash stomped in with Kit slung over his shoulder, my heart skipped a fucking beat. I looked to Anton immediately knowing that his expression would help fight off the panic of seeing our new member being carted like a sack of laundry.

Thank fuck his face told me everything was okay—mostly.

Once everyone settled in, they told the outlandish tale of Kit and the Bone Tree, and now... well, now everyone is throwing out theories about the odd reaction of the damn thing. I figure whatever it means will become clear, eventually, so I'm focused on how uncomfortable Kit looks as people are debating who or what he is. I've been there, and it's no fun.Pressing my lips together, I stand up and hold my hands out.

"Wait."

All eyes fly to me and I arch a brow. "This is definitely strange, I agree, but you guys are making KitKat shrink to a damn ball over there. How did you miss that?"

The guy flushes as I call attention to him sitting with his knees up and his chin on them, the tiny kinkajou perched on his head like a furry hat. It's like he's made to do the cutest fucking things possible without even trying and I have no idea how to react beyond wanting to just snuggle him until he feels safe. Anton gives me a fond look and I shrug slightly, not wanting to draw attention to how squishy I'm feeling.

"He's fine," Jasper says with an eye roll. "No one was being mean or insulting. Stop being dramatic, X."

Zav pinches his leg, making the Prince yelp and look down with a narrowed gaze. I grin when the kitsune hides in his tails again, but doesn't apologize. "We don't *want* to make Kit uncomfortable, especially after he had an attack recently, right?"

The dragon grumbles something, and I take that as my cue to steer the conversation away from the rampant speculation for a bit. "I think we should deal with our outfits for this Devil's Night deal. It's Friday night, we don't have classes until Monday, and I have work to do."

"That's a great idea, love," Annie says. He rolls to his feet, looking at Slash. "Perhaps we should order some food while X measures Kit?"

A panicked expression floods his face and Kit seems to get even smaller in the huge chair. "N-n-no, I think I'll be fine in my—"

"You will not be fine in your uni, KK," Salem says gently. "It's fancy and we all have to deal with that."

"But I *will* take you to your room to do the measuring. You won't even need to take off more than your jacket, I promise. I'm very good at this shit." I give him a reassuring look, hoping he agrees. He's gotten comfortable enough with Oriel, Slash, and Salem to allow touch, and for some reason, I desperately want to be included.

Especially since Annie kissed him *in fucking Arms class and I'm jelly he got there first.*

Kit licks his lips, looking around for a moment, then uncurls his limbs. "Okay. If we can go somewhere more private and I can stay... dressed. It's fine."

Breathing a sigh of relief, I smile brightly and gesture to the closed door.

"Then off we go. We'll leave the nutrition to the rest of these fools while I get the first step in designing your perfect fit checked off."

The uncertain look in his eyes worries me, but I know I can make him feel safe—after all, I know how it feels to be uncomfortable in your own skin.

"So, I don't need to touch you much physically," I say as I carefully measure around his spread arms. Once Kit was able to stand still without looking like he was going to puke, I had him assume the position so I'd have access to the important measurement areas. "This is your wrists, obviously."

He nods quietly as I rattle the numbers off to the voice recorder on my phone. "That's not terrible. I'm not as sensitive when it's... pretty normal areas. I get less calm when it's... personal parts."

I snort, giving him a wry look. "You can say you're going to panic when I get near your junk, man."

His eyes widen and he shakes his head. "Um, not just... there. Inner legs, rear, chest... I have reasons, but I'll do my best not to have an episode."

Fuck this poor kid is breaking my heart—what the hell did that slimy human do to him?

"Okay, I'll just be slow, gentle, and try to narrate as I go, regardless of where I am. Does that help?"

"Yes," he breathes shakily. Dottie is sitting close, watching him with intelligent eyes as he struggles with his inner turmoil.

"Arms and shoulders next. I'm going to walk around you while I do it." I hum under my breath, hoping to ease his tension while I get the most slight measurements I've ever taken for someone in our group. Once I repeat them all for the phone, I face Kit with an arched brow. "Based on your frame I have a lot of options. Are you sure you want to trust me to do... whatever I want?"

He'd said that after we got into the room and I was shocked. Only Annie lets me do whatever; the other guys always guide me if I get to design anything for them. Since their families often make deals about their appearances, it's not frequent or anything, but I enjoy dressing us as a caliphate. Kit, however, just gave me carte blanche without batting a lash, and that's almost better than his comfort with touch with the others.

"I'm sure. You have a really interesting flair, and everything you wear is awesome," he looks at me as I kneel down, preparing to do the seams. "So I know you'll make something great and it will look good on me."

Grinning, I hold the tape up carefully. "Outer leg first, then inner leg. I'll be very careful to touch as little as possible. Are you ready?" He nods, swallowing hard, and I stretch the tape from his hip to his ankle. "I will, but you know that I don't... conform to traditional norms. If I get wild, will it upset you?"

His legs are trembling a little and I can smell fear on him, but he's definitely holding his ground. "Honestly? With this damn tree stuff and everything else? I'm not going to be able to avoid people looking at me angrily for something or other. Do whatever—it can't *possibly* make me less popular."

"Moving to the inseam now. Stay calm," I murmur, then look up seriously. "But there's going to be girls at this thing. You sure you're not wanting to be all 'James Bond' or sexy emo guy to lure them?"

As I call out the measurements again, he turns red and shakes his head. "No fucking way. I'm not... I'd prefer that not be a thing. So don't worry."

My lips curve up at his answer.

Couldn't have put it better myself, Kit Kat.

"Get your butts out here!"

Kit looks at me from where we're seated on the bed looking at the quick sketches I've been making. He's actually looking excited, and it makes me warm all over. Even Annie won't let me go this far, and I'm feeling tingly with anticipation. My snake is slithering around inside of me, dancing about in anticipation of getting to do things we love exactly how we love to do them.

Of all the guys, Oriel and I tend to be most influenced by the emotions of our animals more than primal desires.

"Salem sounds like he's going to barrel through the door if we don't get moving," he says with a small grin. "Thanks for... putting up with my shit, by the way."

I frown. "Kit Kat, your issues are no bigger than the ones we all have. You haven't been here long enough to see most of them, outside of Jasper's temper and Zav's need for approval. But you will, and when you do, you'll get why everyone is totally fine with accommodating you."

"How the fuck are demons better at this than humans?" he mutters. "I mean, it seems ass backwards, right?"

"It's not about species, necessarily. It's about being a goddamn asshole, and you've been surrounded by huge ones, it seems." His laugh makes my chest tighten and I have to set my tablet aside and stand up. "You're right about Salem, though. Especially because *he* thinks you're a Fae."

Kit rolls his eyes. "Hardly. I'm not delicate, pretty, colorful, *or* glittery."

"Ah, but you could and will be," I say with a wink. "Don't discount your ability to pull off the look."

The new guy ducks his head, shrugging as he gets to his feet and scoops up Dottie. "We will see. It's totally new for me—even for up there—so you're going to need to help me do all the things."

"I promise," I say as I open his door and we head into the main room. The smells lingering there are delicious and I spin to look at Jasper. "You ordered Damnation Pies? Seriously? Holy shit, Kit Kat!"

He stops on his way to his big chair, eyes wide. "What's the big deal about… pizza?"

Oriel comes over to us, grabbing Kit's hand and tugging him to his spot. "Because Damnation Pies is a demon owned shop from *your* lands and it's a goddamn trial to get them to deliver despite the fact that their owners are portal-capable demons."

"So it's… earth… ingredients?"

I stroll over with my tablet in hand, plopping down on the floor at his feet so he can see while I work. "It's *both*. And Jasper probably pulled some serious royal mojo to get those fuckers to bring it."

Kit looks around the room, his face confused. "Why?"

"Oh, for fuck's sake, shrimp. Just say 'thank you' and let Salem bring your shit over." His grumble is irritable, but there's something that sounds like regret underneath the ire.

I think he's sorry about the class bullshit; his eyes have been tracking the slow movement and how the rest of us are helping Kit get from place to place.

"Don't be pissy," Slash says as he walks over with a tray of options for Kit to try. Salem is following with one his Fae fizzy drinks he makes, and I shoot a knowing look at Annie. He shrugs, grinning back at me.

"His legs work," our leader mutters as he flops into his chair, followed by Zav carrying their food. "You're all acting like Furon crippled him."

"Dr. D said to rest."

The shark shifter doesn't have to say much more before Jasper sighs and tips his head back to look up at the ceiling in supplication. "Fuck, it makes me *insane* that even you are entranced like this."

"Ah, Jasper. The last man standing on a roof hoping the tidal wave doesn't hit him in a disaster movie. So tragically obtuse," Oriel snarks before sitting down next to Salem. "Keep holding out, man. It won't make everything harder later."

I'll be damned; the crow is always salty, but that was a direct hit. Battleship sunk.

"Fuck off, thief," he retorts.

Oriel's eyes widen and he grins. "Shit. Speaking of that…" he shoves his hand into his pocket, rummaging around and Kit stares in fascination as it expands. "…I found the perfect thing when I was… uh, doing my thing."

"Is his pocket like Mary Poppins' bag?"

I nod, watching Oriel continue to grope the big, bulging cloth. "It's this weird pocket portal he stores his temporary horde in. No one has a damn clue how the corvids hybrid demons do it. He shoves stuff in there until he finds the perfect place to put it in his room."

"I'm scared to ask what his room looks like," Kit says, still watching in fascination.

"You should be."

Kit grins at Slash, then picks up one of the Vampire Repellent Cheesy Garlic Knots to take a bite. The sound he makes should be illegal and not one person is looking at Oriel's fidgeting afterward. In fact, everyone is damn near on the edge of their chair when he wipes his mouth and looks sheepish. "This is fucking amazing. Fuck me."

The room is silent until Oriel pulls his hand out and holds up a shining platinum crown. "Ah-ha. Here it is. Would it work for the dance, X?"

Oh yeah. I forgot to mention the headwear our caliphate will have to don—that's going to get me in trouble.

This Is Not An Apology

Since the crown revelation, I decided I'm not speaking to any of them until I can calm down. I mean, what's the fucking point of all this 'we don't want to draw more attention shit' they keep spouting when they have to parade me around as their shared date with a fucking *crown* on my head? No one in the seven fucking rings of this damn place is going to miss that shit. It would be bad enough with the dudes in Discordia around, but there will be *girls* at this damn thing.

I'll admit I don't have a lot of experience with them, but that's because we suck ass at this age.

Obviously, I'm being fair by including myself in that statement, though I know I've tried like heck to figure out what the secret code is to getting them to leave me alone in the past. I didn't try to make friends or to beef with the requisite shitty female groups at any of my schools—which included both 'popular' girls and the more 'indie' girl groups. None of them wanted me, which was fine, but even the misfits used their evil powers to make sure I was miserable.

The psychology of the disenfranchised bullying the more disenfranchised is fascinating and horrible at the same time.

"I've never understood it, Dottie," I say absently as I lie on my bed reading my Intro to Supernaturals texts. "Why the fuck do the non-conformists want to form their own conforming group to shit on people? I mean, I guess it's because humans are pretty caste-oriented, and everyone wants to belong, but it's such hypocritical crap to pretend you accept everyone then actively work to keep people from your cool kids' table."

Dottie's mouth draws in and I almost think she's wrinkling her nose in distaste, but that can't be. Kinkajous can't do that, right? I don't think so, but then, Dottie's a pretty unique animal. Luckily for me, she hasn't gone bonkers about being cooped up in our room, though I did crack the window so she could scramble onto an outcropping on the dorm building to use the potty. If it hadn't worked, I would have had to find a way to keep my room from getting stinky, but Fate smiled on me for once.

The tiny rodent chitters a response that I take as agreement, and I sigh. "Discordia has assholes, but at least they're pretty obvious about it. More violent, sure, and that's fucking scary, but it's not like my old school. I'm not fending off both guys being dicks *and* the passive-aggressive shit from the girls. Though, I probably didn't help myself by not seeking out people who didn't fit those molds because of my own shit…"

I'm not being fair, and it's just as crappy as the idiots I'm grumbling about.

A loud knock on my door makes me narrow my eyes and stop flogging myself over my inability to reach out to others in the past. "What? I said to leave me alone!"

"You will eat." There's a huff and a grunt, then the sound of something being placed on the ground in front of my door. "Do not make me violate your space."

"Great," I mutter as I run my fingers over Dottie's head. "Guess that's the big guy asserting *his* boundaries."

Dottie shakes her small hand at me and I think she's trying to scold me this time. She's not wrong; I am overreacting a little, but the mixed signals are making it hard for me to know what to do. I have enough trouble reading shit as it is, but with the extreme amount of intrigue in Hell, I'm being ping-ponged back and forth every time something new and freaky happens.

There's no way to predict when these things will happen, and I can't even control my reactions to them. Adding new dimensions—girls from other schools, fancy demons, adults—is making my entire body petrify.

It would help if they'd all quit leaving shit out—intentional or not.

Setting my companion aside, I roll to my feet and trudge over to my door. I put my ear against the wood, listening for a clever demon waiting outside. When I don't hear anything, I open the door a crack, then enough to take the tray full of food from the floor. It's covered by a metal catering lid and I smile a little as I close the door. There's a black feather in the small flower bundle tied with a cord that has bells on it. Shiny *and* full of random objects? That's definitely Oriel.

I walk over to the bed and remove the lid, chuckling at the odd colored eggs and bacon-like strips shaped in a smiley face. That's Salem, and I have to remind myself that no matter how cute these morons are, I'm annoyed. Taking the plastic off the small fruit and crunchies bowl that is obviously for Dottie, I set it on the bed for her to dig in. Her happy chitters and squeaks make me smile as I examine the rest of the shit on my tray.

A small QR code... Zavida. The silverware is tied together with a sparkly edged blue plaid fabric... X. Then the cloth napkin folded into an impossible looking building... Anton.

"They're not going to give up, huh, girl?" I asked Dottie. She looks at me wide-eyed, her small hands shoving fruit into her mouth until her cheeks puff out. Laughing, I wag my finger at her this time. "Chew, woman. I don't know if Dr. D knows rodent CPR. I can't have you choking to death."

Dottie obviously has no problem with the guys, and that makes me want to reconsider my demand for space. She wouldn't let them get away with shit if they were pulling a fast one. So I'm probably overreacting, just like I thought earlier.

"Crap."

I need to eat this food, then find the guys and apologize for being such a spazz. The tension from X having to measure me, the fight earlier, and my deep seated fear of this dance becoming some Carrie-esque nightmare pushed me to accuse them of hiding something they probably forgot about.

Well, except Oriel, but I think he was... trying to help?

Damn it, I'm going to have to tell that hulking prick I'm sorry, too.

This sucks.

I WAS HUNGRY AS FUCK, AND I'LL HAVE TO THANK SLASH FOR HIS GRUFF mother-henning, too. That makes me even grumpier about this whole damn thing, but I'm not a hypocrite. I've demanded the guys behave like they had a modicum of emotional intelligence multiple times. There's no universe where I'm going to allow myself to act differently simply because it sucks. That's not who I am, nor who I want to be.

Gathering up Dottie's stuff and mine, I grab the tray and cock my head at her so she follows along, I trudge to the door with a sigh.

Time to face the music.

When I open the door, I'm surprised to see every damn one of them positioned in spots around the room. Someone switched the fucking caliphate furniture from Jasper's room to ours, making the space a bit more crowded, but leaving the chair I adore open. They look at me with expressions ranging from trepidation to concern as I march over to the kitchen, disposing of garbage then putting the dishes in the washer. No one speaks when I make my way to my chair, standing in front of it with my hands clasped nervously as Dottie climbs up to perch on the arm.

"Ahem. I…" I lick my lips and square my shoulders, looking each of them in the eye before I continue. "I'm sorry I overreacted to the stupid crown thing. Shutting you out for an honest mistake wasn't very mature of me, and that deserves an apology, especially as no one even tried to call me out on it. There were reasons—an overwhelming day, lots of new information, internalized fear of the unknown, and my issues—but those are not an excuse for behaving as poorly as I've lambasted some of you for."

Salem and Oriel grin slightly, their eyes glittering with approval, and it makes the tension seep out of my frame. When no one interrupts, I go on, "Slash, thank you for helping keep me from bad habits with food, especially with my new… requirements. I'm grumpy about it because I have trouble allowing people to help because I've been abandoned in the past. X, you're being so accommodating about my shit and taking time out to give me the right things, and I appreciate it. Zav, you're trying very hard to make up for your bullshit and I see that. Anton, you often provide rational balance during emotional times, and it's very helpful."

The guys I mentioned all dip their heads in acknowledgement and I swallow hard as I turn to Prince Fuckwit. He's definitely struggling not to smirk, which I guess is another point in his favor. "Jasper… you're a raging dick most of the time, but I sort of get why. I'm not forgiving you for the bulk of your crap because you don't deserve it, but I am sorry I was rash with this decision. And I appreciate you not making it worse when I did."

His lips curve a bit, and he stays silent for a moment, then finally says, "Apology accepted, shrimp."

I sigh, a weight lifted off of my shoulders as I collapse into my chair. "Fuck. Being an adult sucks ass, for the record."

"Ah, but you're quite skilled at it, Kit Kat," X says fondly. "I doubt any of us have *ever* had such a direct and heartfelt apology in our long lives. It's not really a demon thing to admit wrongdoing."

"Makes you weak," Jasper grunts as he looks at his tablet.

That explains a lot, but it doesn't let him off the hook.

Dottie stands taller, waving her fist at them as if to challenge that claim and I chuckle. She's not a wilting flower, even if she isn't a hulking predator. I pat her on the head before I respond to X, "Thanks. That was *years* of therapy speaking and as you said, demons aren't into that."

Slash shifts in his chair, looking at me closely. "How are the injuries from yesterday?"

Of course he's not going to say anything back in front of the rest of them.

"Doing better. Overnight, most of it seems to have healed. Is that… normal?"

The big guy nods. "It is, as far as I am aware."

"Definitely," Oriel says as he stands up and stretches. "Want a drink, KK? I'm up."

Something tells me he wasn't planning to be, but I just admitted I don't take help well and I probably will want one soon enough. Hell is fucking dehydrating, and I didn't notice until I didn't have Slash poking me every time he saw me with a water. "Yeah, that'd be nice."

"He *can* learn," Salem says playfully and I glare at him. "Don't be salty, Kit Kat. I'm teasing you because you're one of us."

My chest constricts and I'm left with my mouth hanging open as the most intense ache pulses within me. I've *never* really belonged and with one simple, throw-away remark, the panda demon just put a huge band-aid over my pain. It doesn't heal me, obviously, because that takes time, but… the balm his words put on my foster kid 'Fisher King' wound is palpable.

"Um, thanks," I mumble as I tuck myself into the chair to let that realization flow through me without a big show. "That's… cool… of you to say."

Oriel comes over, handing me both my books from my room *and* the drink with a smirk. "Thought you'd want these, too, since we're all studying and shit."

Damn him for being able to read my fucking mind somehow.

"Double thanks?" I say in a gravelly tone. I'm still recovering from the brick to the face from Salem's acceptance and the lack of protest, even from Prince Pissypants so I'm not very verbose.

"You should probably wear the crown while we work this weekend. You know, to get used to it."

My eyes whip to the damn dragon, shooting daggers his way and regretting my appreciation from earlier. "I certainly will not."

A chorus of agreement with him, followed by explanations of why it makes sense wear me down without a fight. I promised to be an adult, and I guess dumbass royal cosplay is part of that.

Doesn't mean I have to like it, though.

A Little Less Conversation

slash

The rest of Saturday and the following day were oddly calm in comparison to almost every other day this semester. Kit's well-timed belly up pacified our Prince in a manner I've not seen before, and his graceful acceptance of our courting overtures changed everything. I seriously doubt that he understands what those gestures mean, and no one is eager to explain it, but allowing us to do so has been soothing.

That's why he's walking to class with me and his little animal with a relaxed posture rather than bristling.

"Slash?"

I look down at him expectantly and he wrinkles his nose. "What, little demon?"

"Are you staying with me in this class like… forever?"

Arching a brow, I counter, "Would that upset you?"

He frowns as we amble up to the stairs of the library, quiet until he finally turns to look at me again. "I guess not. If what we all agreed to this weekend is that we can't stop people from making me a spectacle, especially with this faux dating thing, then nothing we do or say will have a noticeable effect on me being targeted. At least, not from our end. So if you want to make sure this bitch doesn't corner me again, I suppose that's more helpful than not. You know?"

The way he just talked himself into that was impressive.

"If that is your way of saying you prefer my company, it was very convoluted."

Kit grins as we ascend the steps together, shrugging. "My brain is very convoluted most of the time. It's a maze of trauma, smarts, fears, and a bazillion other things that keep me from operating at peak performance like most people."

"If you think most people—demons, humans, or supes—are operating at peak performance, you're sorely mistaken." I open the door, letting him pass as I add, "Perhaps sometimes, but more often, they are not. It is a shared condition that connects us all."

"You know, you are pretty damn good to talk to when we're alone," he says as I stab my finger into the elevator button. "I wish you wouldn't clam up every time we're around the others."

I snort, shaking my head when the doors separate and we enter. "Everyone in the caliphate has their roles. Mine does not require constant chatter, so I don't. Plus, I don't want to get used to talking that much. I'm more effective as the big, silent enforcer in the mind of the general populace."

"Well, I like when you talk more, even if I get why you're not doing it," he grumbles.

The pleasure that statement gives me is surprising, and I have to rein in my desire to find something that makes the smaller demon feel similar. Now is not the time for that sort of thing, and I can think about it after I ensure his safety in this well-protected predator's classroom.

"We will continue this discussion on the way to your Human History class. For now, we need to present a united front, yes?" I offer him my arm, my eyes full of amusement when he rolls his eyes.

Kit takes my arm and lets me guide him into the room to a seat as far from the lectern as we possibly can get. He smirks at my choice and I shrug. I'm not above keeping him far from the Cubi's reach as a front line defense. Not every strategy has to begin with aggression even if it is often the most effective way to achieve success quickly.

Hopefully, this irritating minor demoness doesn't force me to do something drastic to fulfill my duty.

THE FATES MUST HAVE BEEN SMILING ON HELL TODAY BECAUSE I DIDN'T have to intervene with Kit's class much. He was able to answer every question Lilibet threw at him—something I know was made possible by the intense studying he did this weekend. He's smart as a whip and memorizes things very quickly. If the ridiculously ill-timed Games hadn't been announced, I think our new member might have managed to catch up with his studies by mid-semester. As it is now, he's doing the best he can despite his deficiencies.

A lack of magical power and the knowledge of how to use it properly isn't just a tiny flaw, but I can give him credit for doing what he's able to.

As we walk to his Human History class, I keep my eyes peeled for anyone watching us too closely for my comfort. It's extremely suspicious that no one from administration has mentioned the demons who died in that fire, nor has there been any alert about campus safety. I know Jasper told me that *his* fire wasn't what started the blaze, and Salem confided that his Circadian rhythms were only changed for the day following the problem in the cafeteria. I believe those things, paired with a few other oddities, mean that Kit has powers manifesting that he's unaware of. I could be wrong, but I'm usually not in this regard. The hybrid demon we're protecting has accepted this world, but he hasn't quite reconciled his role in it.

"Slash, you're quiet again."

I chuckle softly, looking down at him. "You didn't seem like the type who craves constant chatter until this morning."

"I'm *not*. I just… enjoy talking to you. You're not overly excited about discovering what I am, nor are you judgmental about how slowly I'm acclimating to my new fucking reality."

That's what he thinks? He's too slow?

"Little demon, you are being too harsh with yourself. You've adjusted to a complete reset of your world with aplomb—which most beings would not be able to accomplish. Your powers and true heritage not popping up with a blinking neon billboard would be much less of an issue if Hell wasn't experiencing an upheaval of its own." He squints at me as if to ensure I'm serious and I nod. "Otherwise, we would be curious, but not anxious about it."

"Are you sure about that? I think Jasper would poke at me no matter what."

He's not wrong, but I don't need to tell him that.

"My point was that you need to give yourself as much time to deal with the changes as you have to deal with your past. Isn't that what your therapy taught you?"

He goes quiet for a second then gives me the most adorably frustrated look I've ever seen. "Stop being so damn smart all the time. You'll give me another complex."

My lips quirk as Kit pulls one of the snack bars from his bag, handing me one color-coded for my needs, then takes out one for himself, and a miniature one for the kinkajou on his shoulder. "Salem is just as bad as you, you know. These were in my bag this morning when I packed my study stuff from last night in it. He's determined to make sure you succeed in keeping me fed and shit."

Opening mine and taking a bite, I chew quickly. "He is fond of you, as are we all, and he has always provided the snacks for us. It took him a couple years to develop the right mix for our various animals, but he's very good at what he does."

The soft groan startles me and Kit flushes as he wipes his mouth. "I don't know why I love these damn berries so much, but every time I eat something made with them, it makes me sound like a porn star."

I gape at him for a second, stopping in place, and he laughs. "That was very… crass… for you."

"Maybe demons are rubbing off on me," he says with a wink and a saucy smirk. My brows furrow as he turns to walk toward the history wing with a bit of a spring in his step.

Something is off about how he responds to those berries and I want it looked into.

"Wait up," I growl, hurrying to get even with him. He's whistling a bit as he eats the rest of the bar and it makes me think my suspicion is correct. "You know I have to stay with you until I drop you at class, then Oriel will pick you up for the lunch period."

"Slaaashhhh. I know that," he says as we come to the doorway to his lecture hall. "But I have lots of energy now—which is what you guys want—and I don't want that to fade during class. Alabaster is a pain in the ass, and I want to be on my toes to spar with him."

He pulls the door open and I give him a stern look. "Kit, be cautious how much trouble you stir up when none of us are present. And keep the chat open for emergencies as you have in the past."

Dottie chitters at me, holding her fist in the air and I wait until Kit nods his agreement. Allowing him to head in, I keep watch as he chooses a seat in a corner where no one can get behind him and he can see the entire room. It calms my ire a bit that he's making certain he's safe, but I also dislike that he had this overdeveloped sense of self-preservation before he came to Hell. His extreme caution tells me how violent his past assault was, and how much we don't know about the aftermath of it.

I don't like that, either.

As I walk away from the hall, I pull my phone out, opening the chat that does not include Kit. I also dislike speaking about him behind his back, but there are things he is not ready for and my brothers and I must discuss.

Enforcer: Package delivered.

Prince: I don't think we need codes.

Thief: I disagree. Code words are always useful.

Hacker: No one is getting into your phone, Oriel.

Thief: No shit, Zav. I've got your encryption plus levels you've only dreamed of.

Hacker: Thieves are such braggarts.

Enforcer: This conversation has gone off-track.

Chef: I'll say.

Spy: Slash, why did you text? It's not to confirm you dropped Kit off.

Enforcer: Because I want Salem and Zavida to look into what species and magics might be especially sensitive to crunkleberries.

Chef: His snack bar?

Enforcer: Yes. It made him much... peppier... and slightly bawdy, which is unusual.

Thief: I miss everything good.

Prince: Bawdy?

Enforcer: Focus, all of you.

Designer: This is a lot of discussion for a research request. Perhaps you're all angry Kit has classes we are unable to monitor? If so, you're getting weird, guys.

Prince: That's it; everyone back to class.

Rolling my eyes, I shove my phone back in my pocket as I cross the quad to get to the arena. I'll see the Prince at my Weapons & Tactics session, and now that he's grumpy again, I'm not looking forward to it. The Prince gets very irritable when anyone points out that we need to give Kit breathing room, and I believe it's because Jasper doesn't know how to do that with someone he gives a shit about. He runs our caliphate by keeping tight reins on everyone, and we allow it because we're used to his gruff way of showing that he considers us important.

Being the Prince helps, too, of course.

But the little demon is never going to let Jasper wrap him in bubble wrap until he's able to defend himself. How any of us are going to convince our leader to be okay with the newest person he's hyper-focused on protecting, I don't know. Zavida is fucking him, so he doesn't balk at the possessive bent to Jasper's nature. This is a different situation entirely—for now—and if I can work out how to get the two of them to stop spitting at one another, maybe we'll all have a good time at this idiotic party in a couple of days.

It is not the Yulemas, but miracles can happen even in Hell if you try hard enough.

Oops I Did It Again

kat/kit

The next two days go smoothly, which makes me even more nervous about this ridiculous fucking dance on Saturday. Excited whispers amongst the guys disrupt every class, and it helps me fade into the background, even to the professors who hate me. Unfortunately, as grateful as I am about the ability to blend in when this big 'kick-off' event has the school buzzing, my anxiety is going nuts. Between maintaining my secret and avoiding being cornered by any number of malignant forces, it's a lot.

"Are you still with me?"

I look down at X as they work on my outfit during the long free period mid-day. We're in the center of my dorm—the new gathering area since the guys moved their chairs here—snacking on treats Salem left. He dragged the rest of them to *Triclinium* to help me be less worried as Xerxes does the final adjustments. They only have a day left to get this perfected so I'll be able to get ready on Saturday.

"I am; it's just…" My voice trails off and I fight the urge to shrug so I don't mess up his lines. "…this is very nerve-wracking. I didn't have great interactions with *any* of the students at my high school regardless of gender, and I have issues with damn near everyone here. It feels like this thing is adding more layers to the shit sandwich that is my reality."

X smacks my thigh and I'm a bit surprised when I don't react to their familiar touch. "You'll be *fine*, Kit Kat. I guarantee no one here will screw with you now that we've established the dating thing. Admittedly, it causes other problems, but that's better than ones that lead to injury."

I arch a brow at them. "X, I get that you guys go to gender-specific schools for your entire education, so I'm going to explain this like I would to a kid. Girls will be here."

"Yes."

"This college is packed with rich, eligible, sex-starved idiot males who range from hetero to the 'A' in the rainbow."

They nod, pausing to look at me. "Duh."

"And they have the same?"

"I feel like we're going somewhere, but it's mostly just stating facts." They wink at me, then fill their mouth with pins again.

"X, for fuck's sake. Demons crave power and infamy, which comes with money and titles. This place is chock full of that, but at the top of the goddamn heap is *our caliphate*." Their answer is muffled by the pins, but I'm fairly certain it would infuriate me. "None of you jackasses are on the market now *because of me*. That means every single female presenting demon who comes to this thing with delusions of grandeur is going to want to *murder* me."

They blink, then spit out the pins in a loud 'ptooey.' I chuckle as it finally hits them that the dance will be even more precarious than the school is. "Well, shit, KK."

"*That's* why I've been getting increasingly freaked out as we get closer. Paired with my outfit, and all the other crapola? I feel like we're going to be surrounded by hungry predators looking to shove me out of their way with extreme prejudice."

Xerxes sits back on their haunches, their rainbow detailed uniform skirt splayed around them in a graceful cloud. "Honestly, that's probably better than them groping and pawing at you—and us. The combo events in secondary and middle grades were quite uncomfortable for me."

"Because you're gay? I thought demons—"

They laugh, shaking their head and my skin heats as golden curls fall over their brow making them look even more gorgeous. "I'm not *gay*, Kit Kat. I fall somewhere around demi and pan, but I let people use the wrong terminology for specifically this reason. The females being single-minded about sexuality despite all evidence to the contrary in their own schools means I have far fewer people pawing at me because I'm an 'easy in' to the caliphate."

The thought of someone using or pawing at them without their consent makes my blood boil.

Clenching my fists tightly, I grind out, "So… none of you are gay? All of you are? I feel… ill-prepared for how I am supposed to actually *behave* at this thing."

X tsks softly. "That is not entirely my truth to share, Kit Kat, but you should feel comfortable in assuming there's a fairly thorough rainbow representation amongst our caliphate. I'm sure you've gleaned that knowledge on your own. But none of us are like the extremist idiots from any of the realms who act as though there's only one pairing that should exist."

"Duh," I mumble as my face gets redder. I don't know why I'm so worried about the girls trying to get in their pants, nor why I want so much info on their sexual preferences.

Dudes here think I'm a convenient sex toy—so the whispers say when the guys aren't around to stop them—so it shouldn't matter, right?

But it *does* matter to me and I'm baffled as to why. It might be because these demons are my lifeline at Discordia and if they get distracted by courtship, my shit will take a backseat. Yes, that definitely is the problem; I'm worried I will become more of a burden if they find suitable girls to lavish attention on. I want to wrap my arms around myself as I frown, needing the comfort of making myself smaller as emotions rocket through me. I can't, though, so my eyes skate over to my kinkajou.

It only takes a moment for her to scamper over, climb up my body and perch on my shoulder where she can hug my face. That soothes me, and I close my eyes as the touch of my support animal helps me calm before the anxiety ramps up too high to manage.

"Kit Kat, I can sense that," X murmurs as they pin hems. "What's got you freaked out again?"

If only I could tell them I'm falling victim to my own idiotic agreement, but I can't—keeping my secret is too important to admit how fond I am of these dipshits.

THE KNOCK ON THE DOOR STARTLES ME AND I GIVE XERXES A PANICKED look. "Oh, damn, it's Oriel."

"Don't want anyone but me to know what we have planned, hmm?" They give me a smug smirk when I nod shyly. "You look fabulous and I don't blame you. My genius is simply *made* for your frame, man. You might even look better than me."

"Uh, I highly doubt that," I reply as I watch them pick up all the pins and things so I can scamper to the bedroom to get my mostly complete outfit off in private. "Keep him busy, please?"

X grins before I slam the door, and I breathe a sigh of relief. It's been hard enough to keep myself covered in ways that shroud my smashed boobs, but Oriel will figure it out in thirty seconds. Xerxes isn't looking, so he hasn't noticed, especially because he uses magic in his measuring. But if I know the sharp-eyed crow hybrid, he won't miss a single detail. I'll be exposed and I need to prevent that from happening.

Of course, I say that given the gamble I'm already taking with this party, but no one ever accused me of being too logical.

"Kit Kat, hurry up! We have to get to Weapons before his Royal Dickhole-ness gets there."

Oriel's voice spurs me into movement, and I carefully strip off my dance duds, leaving them on my bed for X to hide once I leave. That means I'll have to help cover for the cobra shifter if he ends up being late to Jasper's class, too. Pulling on my normal uniform with jerky movement, I look around until I find my shoes. Once my boots are on, I walk over to the mirror and ruffle my growing hair, realizing I'm going to need to get it cut before it spoils my disguise.

Damnit. Too many things at once.

"It's fine, Kit. Just grab your bag and your kinkajou, then head for class. Maybe you'll get to smack someone around so you can vent your nervous energy." I should only be so lucky, but Jasper hasn't made us sit for class since the one time, so maybe it will be fine.

Blowing out a slow breath, I walk to the door, giving X a surreptitious thumbs up as I head for my messenger bag. "Okay, Dottie girl, we gotta go see the pissiest dragon we've met so far. Are you ready?"

She chitters happily, scampering over to tuck into my bag for the ride. I've noticed she likes to ride inside right after she eats a lot. I don't blame her because I like to loll in comfort when I've stuffed myself, too.

"How is the whole sewing-outfit-dance thing coming?" Oriel asks as he watches Xerxes cleaning up the mess we left. "Is it okay? I think our stuff is being delivered Friday night."

"Of course it is, you spoiled jackwad," I say fondly as I bump his shoulder. "All of you, except X, are just being handed your shit."

The crow shifter gives me a pointed look. "What exactly are you doing besides posing for them to measure?"

X stands, brushing off their knees and shaking a finger at O. "Kit is helping with design choices and it's lovely to work with him. He's very creative."

I'm not sure I'd phrase my occasional remarks about color or cut as collaboration, but if X thinks so…

"Well, well," Oriel says as he opens the door to our room. "That's very interesting. I look forward to finding out what you have come up with."

He may not say that when he sees it, but I'm not touching that with a ten foot pole. Instead, I nod and follow him to the elevator, hopping on. "You don't have long to wait, nor do any of the other dudes I'm supposed to be escorted by."

"That's the first time you've phrased it that way. Did Xerxes say something that is making you concerned about the dance—other than our multitudinous enemies, of course."

Me and my big fat mouth.

"We talked about the guests attending from the other colleges. I'm worried about the mass amount of people, especially…"

When I trail off, he grins at me like a fool until the elevator dings to announce the bottom floor. As we step out and head out through the lobby of the dorm, I notice that he's looking especially smug again. I frown at my feet, keeping my eyes off of him until he finally speaks. "Oh, you're worried about the bloody girls, eh?"

"Don't be an ass."

Oriel chuckles, and I elbow him as I pass through the front door, heading for the arena. "It's hard not to be when you're being this silly. How could you think we're going to abandon you for some random tail fluttering in from afar?"

I blink, unsure how to respond to that ridiculously accurate assessment. "I… That's not why it worries me!"

"Sure, KK. Whatever you say."

My fists clench at my side and I scowl as I stomp across the quad with the pleased bird demon. "I do say. You know I have anxiety and lots of people I don't know will trigger that. It's especially bad when you add the social pressure of some stupid dance, who knows what bigwig fuckheads will show up, and now I have to wonder if I'll get left like a purse in the club."

He snorts, shaking his head. "First of all, X would never let anyone take a purse to a club, but if we did, you would be much more important than an accessory. That's your damage talking, bud."

Stupid bird is right, but I don't want to tell him that.

"Well, excuse me if my experience with groups of dudes being flooded with opportunities to drink and get wild—especially in Hell—makes me think otherwise." I sniff as we enter the double doors to the arena, giving him a suspicious look. "I don't want to be cornered and have no one around to help this time."

"Oh, *that* will never happen again, Kit Kat. I can promise you."

Sure, but people in my life don't have great track records with promise-keeping.

I Put A Spell On You

Jasper

I don't trust this fucking 'Samhain ball' as far as I can chuck someone. The announcement last week, so close to the beginning of the semester and the unveiling of the first Games in centuries, is entirely suspect. I'm on edge, and my dragon is whirling beneath the surface of my humanoid skin, ready to strike out the moment someone challenges us.

That's never optimal, but I suppose the amount of danger inherent in this damn event requires it.

The marble of the lobby of Canto IV is a cold contrast to my simmering irritation as I stand sentinel. My claws, out despite my human guise, tap an impatient rhythm against my thigh. Two weeks was all we had to prepare for this blasted Samhain Ball. It was barely enough time to get clothing, much less assess all the negatives of having two other schools, Hell's elite, and the competitively motivated students here in one venue. The direction was for it to be woven into our already chaotic schedules like an afterthought. Yet here this trial looms, significant as any battle, on the horizon tonight.

My gaze sweeps across the opulent space, its grandeur lost on me as usual. Discordia University spares no expense on presentation, but even the gilded trimmings can't pull my thoughts from the Caliphate Games—a tournament resurrected from dusty annals of history, now thrust upon us. The last winners rule Hell, their lineage stamped on each of us in this caliphate—save for Kit.

Our families were the last victors, bound by their idea to band together, and they started the largest war in Hell's long history to take the throne afterward.

We were ready for a war eventually—all my brothers and I—but not this soon. Even watching others meet and leave for the dance in laughing groups, I sense their nerves beneath the surface, the weighty expectations of performing for those in charge looming. It's worse for us, of course, because we're not just students; we're heirs to thrones.

Kit is a vulnerability we can't afford. Both inside and outside these walls, enemies abound—the mere thought of Bamford Academy and Brimstone Academy joining us tonight tightens my jaw. Our deep desire to shield Kit from them all gnaws at me. Protecting what is mine is a flame that never wanes, flaring up with every tick of the clock that passes without them descending those cursed stairs.

I am the Prince of Hell, and no one is allowed to cross me, especially with those I have claimed as mine own.

"Late," I growl to no one, tail twitching beneath the fabric of my suit. I'm dressed to kill or be killed, whichever comes first. My bespoke jet black tux with tails and a vest have the royal crest of the demon line of wrath hidden in them, and I have allowed my spikes and tails to show in the most threatening way possible. It's my visual concession to the threats waiting for us in the ballroom.

The stakes are higher than ever, and as I hear footsteps approaching, my heart concedes to battle-readiness over disdain for punctuality. Tonight, we must be formidable for Kit, for the caliphate, for whatever hellish curveballs this celebration throws our way.

Ding.

Polished shoes clatter against the marble, announcing their arrival before I even glimpse them. Slash looms into view first, an imposing monolith in his tailored darkness, the sleek lines of his suit sharpening his broad-shouldered silhouette. His dorsal fin, a defiant crest of shark hybrid identity, protrudes through the fabric—a statement of power in itself. The air around him feels charged, as if the lobby has shrunk in response to his enormous size being present.

"Finally," I mutter, my impatience a coiled serpent in my stomach. The corner of Slash's mouth twitches in what might be amusement—or a warning. He's not one for expressing emotions like some others in our group.

"We've got this, Prince," he grumbles, his voice a low rumble that echoes in my chest. "Our little demon will end the evening safe and sound."

How he is so certain, I don't fucking know.

Beside him, Zavida is a stark contrast—his lithe form wrapped in ethereal white, the metallic orange of his bow tie a flicker of wildfire. My Kitsuné's nervous energy is palpable, tails twitching with restless flames licking at their tips. When I loop an arm around him, his tension eases ever so slightly, a subtle surrender to my possessive display. He's dressed in flame colors from head-to-toe—red shirt, white vest with the line of envy crests stitched into it, and white shoes that all compliment his bright, fiery red hair, and black nerdy glasses.

"Remember, we're showing unity—for Kit," Zavida whispers, eyes flickering behind thick lenses. I release him, nodding once, though my scowl deepens at the reminder. "Temper your… natural tendencies so people do not disbelieve our gambit, Sir."

"Unity with an unemerged human," I echo, my voice laced with sarcasm. "What a novel concept for the Prince of Hell." Zav and Slash give me a dirty look and I roll my eyes. "Yes, yes, I know. Be kinder."

The elevator dings again, and Salem ambles out, his white hair tipped with black like the panda inside of him. He's a vision of monochrome elegance, the black and white of his attire mirroring his dual nature. As he knocks back an energy potion with practiced ease, my lips twitch despite myself. This is more dressed up than I've seen him in so long I can't even remember; he wore jeans and a hoodie to our secondary school graduation.

"Trying not to fall asleep on your feet, Salem?" I smirk as he pulls another out of pocket. I didn't even think about how hard this would be on him, but I'm glad he did.

"Shut it, Prince Prickface," he retorts. There's no heat in it, only the warm glow of camaraderie, and his obvious favor of Kit's nicknames for me. "Just making sure I'm awake the entire time. KitKat remembered when we got back to the room last night after dinner."

Sigh. Of course he did. That shrimp is always making people look bad with his conscientiousness.

Anton clears his throat, drawing my attention to the fact that he's a peacock in every sense, strutting from the elevator with a confidence that makes me roll my eyes skyward. His rainbow hair shimmers, echoing the brilliant hues of his cascading tail-feathers and matching tailed suit. He's practically glowing with pride—his demon line's signature trait—as he preens like a runway model.

"Where's Xerxes?" I can't help but probe, noting the absence of his other half. They've been glued at the hip since early school, and it's strange for them not to enter together.

Anton simply arches one perfectly sculpted eyebrow, amusement written all over his features. "He'll make an entrance, as always. He just wanted to come with Kit this time since he was designing their attire."

I snort, shaking my head. "I should've guessed. He loves to be the center of attention."

They both shuffle nervously, their excitement a tangible pulse in the air. I can't fault them; even I'm curious about what Xerxes has concocted for tonight's spectacle. I can't focus on it too much, though, because I have to remain vigilant about the rest of this crap.

I'll let the others handle fawning over our newest member tonight.

"Be careful what you eat or drink," I say. "We have to keep our wits—especially with anything surrounding Kit."

The crowns atop each of our heads feel heavier with the weight of responsibility, but they are our silent oaths to each other more than our families. Zavida is right about staying united; we not only have to survive this evening but also the far more risky Games in the next few months.

My brooding is interrupted by the lift arriving again. The doors slide open, and framed by the silver archway, stand Xerxes and Kit—an image of duality so stark it snatches the breath from my chest.

What the fuck is happening to me right now?

"Damn," I murmur under my breath as they step forward, arm in arm, a vision of contrasts bound together. I swallow hard, clenching every part of my body in an effort not to show a visceral reaction to the image in front of me.

Xerxes dazzles like the sun itself, gold upon gold, their attire shimmering with every subtle movement. Their cobra scale patches catch the light, adding an otherworldly gleam to the already imposing presence of our fashionable brother. They're wearing a short golden jacket over a light shirt, with a swishy gold skirt that mimics the style of their uniform skirt. Embellishments at the neck of their open shirt as a collar and cuffs on their wrists bear shining crests of the demon Lust line, perfectly accentuate the metallic thigh high fishnets and glam gold knee-high boots.

But they didn't stop there—no, X wasn't satisfied with their own glitz being the limit.

They made Kit the shadow to their shine, cloaked in black and deep burgundy. X obviously trimmed and colored the new guy's undercut to make sure it matched perfectly. The understated elegance of his short suit jacket with the skirt that matches X's in a jet black with burgundy fishnets crawling up his legs. The unemerged demon has on black patent leather knee-high, heeled combat boots to make him almost as tall as the willowy Xerxes, and he's made up with a more subtle flair than my fluid brother. The caliphate crest on his collar winks at me, and I have to grit my teeth as my dragon snarls with happiness.

As they approach, our group is momentarily spellbound, caught in the gravity of their spectacle. I have no idea what to say—too affected by the imagery to do more than scowl in irritation.

"Stunning," Zavida whispers, his voice tinged with an awe usually reserved for celestial events. "You both look amazing. But you're—"

"Late," I growl, though the sharpness of my tone is blunted by the undeniable artistry before us. A glance at the ostentatious clock confirms we are indeed behind schedule, and my impatience flares anew. "We should've been there ten minutes ago."

"Ease up, Jasper," Slash says, his deep voice resonating like a bass string plucked in warning. "Better to arrive in style than rush and miss the moment."

"I was going to say missing *Oriel,*" Zavida chides as he elbows me. "Where is he?"

"Right here."

I blink, cursing internally as I note the crow hybrid standing in the shadows just outside the elevator. The damn thief snuck in while we were all star-struck by the glitterati, and though I should be glad he managed it, I'm more annoyed than I am grateful.

Oriel steps forward, a Gothic black and purple suit ensemble covering his lithe, muscled frame. His dark eyes sparkle with amusement at fooling me, but he's unaware he's fooled himself. His piercings are all gleaming with care, even the large greed demon line crest in his ear, and his tattoos are showing via the half-buttoned shirt has on. Fingers full of big rings and eyeliner sharp as his raven colored wings, he's the emo demon the girls from Brimstone will drool over.

And he'll hate it, which makes me inordinately happy.

Kit's eyes widen as he tries to play off his flushed face, nodding at our crowns. They are each unique to our demon lines, unlike his. "Why are they all different?" he asks, tilting his head, curiosity bright in his gaze.

"Each crown signifies our lineage," Oriel explains quickly, tucking a strand of black feathered hair behind his ear. "We'll delve into the histories later. Yours marks you as one of us, but it won't draw unwanted questions."

The shrimp looks unconvinced, but as Slash extends his arm in a gesture of protection, Kit accepts it without question. We all shuffle into a formation that surrounds Kit without smothering him, a protective barrier ready to weather any storm. He sighs, but once Salem hands him the tiny rodent he must have been holding under his jacket, that stops.

"Thanks, Salem," he murmurs, placing the thing on his shoulder. "I needed her."

"Don't forget why we're here," I remind them sharply, my eyes scanning each face. "It's not just about the ball. We've got Lucian to watch out for, and those vultures from the Games."

"Indeed," Anton agrees, adjusting his rainbow plumage with a flourish. "But I'm not about to let threats to overshadow the night. We can be vigilant and enjoy ourselves."

X beams brightly and I groan as I foresee dancing in my future.

"Enjoyment comes second to safety," I counter, as I lead the way out the door of our dorm.

Together we head toward the *Triclinium*, the grandeur of the underground ballroom waiting to be discovered by Kit when we arrive. It's another hidden facet of our world he's yet to explore, and for some reason, I'm looking forward to seeing him experience it.

How very odd.

Cello Suite No. 1 in G Major

The moment we step into the underground ballroom, I'm hit by the sheer opulence. Fiery-colored crystal chandeliers dangle like frozen flames from the vaulted ceiling, casting dancing shadows over the walls, which are etched with ancient runes that seem to pulse with a life of their own. Tables draped in black velvet line the edges of the room, each one groaning under the weight of golden candelabras and exotic flowers that hiss and steam, giving off an eerie light.

I tighten my grip on Slash's arm as the finely dressed demon males from Discordia strut around downstairs, their suits tailored to stress powerful shoulders and devilish grins. They're nothing compared to the royal-looking adults, who converse in hushed tones in corners around the room, their eyes glinting with power and secrets. Their attire is a dizzying array of silks and brocades, jewels winking from every conceivable place.

I'm going to go insane with all the fucking rich people's bullshit tonight. I just know it.

Across the room, I spy what *has* to be the Bamford Academy contingent. They wear their thrifted finery like battle armor, a variety of funky hats, suits, and dresses with daring colors and chains that scream defiance. There's a wildness to them, a sense of chaos barely contained beneath threadbare seams. They seem just as irritated as I am about the high society tinge to this party, and I wonder for a moment if I'd be able to relate to these demons better than anyone else in the room.

I won't have time to find out because their disdain pales compared to the Brimstone Academy elites. These females are a vision of every possible species of demonic beauty, each one more stunning than the last, with their gowns hugging curves that promise both pleasure and peril. They move with a grace that's almost hypnotic, their laughter tinkling like chimes in the sulfur-tinged air. Just watching them makes my pulse race as I remember the laughter of some of the queen bees from my past.

It would be best if we stay as far from those chicks as possible—both because they make me want to have an episode, but also because they might guess my secret.

"Kit, are you okay?" Slash mutters, his voice grounding me back to the present. His enormous frame is comforting and I draw in a shaky breath before I answer.

"I'm fine," I lie, swallowing hard as I take in the grandeur and the expectant looks directed our way. Our caliphate's reputation precedes us, and I can feel the weight of every scrutinizing gaze. "Or... I will be once we land somewhere."

"Everyone here is mostly bluster and bravado for attention," Jasper growls from the front, leading us down the steps with an air of entitlement that only true royalty can muster. "You are with some of the most influential demons in this room already."

"That lot from Bamford isn't a concern," Anton adds, nodding towards the scrappy group. "All bark, no bite—they've got magical constraint spells when they aren't on campus. So don't worry about them trying to cause trouble for you."

I snort, giving him an amused expression. "They are the *least* of my worries, you snob. I'd probably have more in common with them than you guys."

Slash puts his big hand over mine. "Perhaps, little demon, but we are demons. We are fine with so many things humans are not and *those* students are the people we feel should be locked up. Consider what their crimes might have been to earn that distinction."

Okay, that's probably true, though I suspect some of them simply fell afoul of the wrong rich dude.

"Watch out for the Brimstone girls, though," Zavida chimes in, his voice smooth and unreadable. "They'll come for your throat without hesitation—that's how they've been raised. Their goal is to land a well-placed husband and then rule the section of their line with an iron fist. You're an obstacle."

"Focus on just breathing, Kit," Oriel murmurs as he slips his arm through mine, joining Slash in a protective sandwich. His touch is surprisingly comforting, reminding me I'm not alone in this sea of demonic aristocracy. "You'll be fine if you don't let all of this trigger panic. Two points of contact, remember?"

"We've got you—I promise," Salem says as he looks over his shoulder at me. "Keep swimming like that silly fish you made me watch, right?"

"Right. And… thank you," I manage, trying to mimic their confidence as we continue our descent. Inside, my heart is racing, anxiety clawing at my throat with every step we take into the belly of the beast.

Hell may be my new home, but tonight, it feels more foreign than ever.

LUCIAN'S SILHOUETTE MATERIALIZES BEFORE US WITH ALL THE SUBTLETY OF A thunderclap in a silent chamber. His steaming drink wafts from the golden skull chalice like the smug smoke of his self-satisfaction. I can't help but roll my eyes at the cliche villainy he exudes, more suited for a cheesy human magic movie than the hallowed halls of Discordia.

Of course, this fuckface would make himself known.

"Ah, our esteemed royal caliphate," he coos, his voice dripping with insincerity. "Welcome to the festivities."

The air thickens with tension as my demon compatriots puff up around me, each emitting their own brand of warning—low growls, narrowed eyes, and subtle shifts into half-transformed stances that would make any sensible creature think twice. Lucian merely chuckles, amused by the display, his eyes glinting with malice beneath the ballroom's elaborate chandeliers. He knows they won't do anything in this public forum, so their fury feeds his over-inflated ego.

"Delighted to see you too, Headmaster," I say, cloaking my disdain in courteous venom. "If you'll excuse us, we have some culinary delights to attend to. I don't wish to spoil my appetite with unpleasant thoughts associated with classes."

His fake laughter follows us, but it's quickly drowned out by the encouraging snickers of my group. They enjoy when I cut people off at the knees, but I'm surprised Jasper gave me the opportunity to handle it on my own. He also likes to assert his dominance with the nasty assholes, but this time, he let me do it.

Weird shit going on at the Circle K tonight.

"Crunkleberry stuff should be right over there," Oriel points out, his attention momentarily diverted by Jasper's disapproving glance. "We should get some of your favorites and you'll feel less edgy."

"The shrimp doesn't need Fae Fizz tonight if he's eating those," Jasper warns, though X interjects with a dismissive wave.

"Let Kit Kat decide for himself what he wants. We're here to enjoy ourselves, aren't we?" the cobra hybrid retorts, shooting me a conspiratorial smirk. "He and I look fabulous, and we should be able to have anything we want."

I shoot Prince Prickface a defiant glare, feeling pumped up by X's praise. "Exactly. I'll eat or drink whatever I damn well please. You're not my dad; I don't even have a dad."

Slash's laughter rumbles in his chest, and slowly, the rest of guys turn pointed looks at the dragon prince. He sighs, throwing his arms up as he grumbles, "Don't do anything stupid we have to deal with if you get buzzed, then."

Well, that's the end of his goodwill, I guess.

"Come on, little demon. We should get you fed," Slash says firmly, leading us to the buffet while X, Anton, and Salem split off toward the bar. "Oriel, you will come as well. Zavida, stay with our prince."

The buffet is a hedonistic spread of Hellish delicacies: skewered death bird tenders crackling with flame, bowls of writhing shadow serpent pasta, and succulent slices of beast roast sizzling on heated stones. Desserts are equally extravagant; towers of pomegranate tartlets filled with lava cream, trays of frostbite fudge that chills the skin on contact, and delicate crystalline crunkle and Cantu berry confections shimmering with abyssal sugar. I'm entranced by the variety, my mouth watering at the sight of crunkleberry clusters nestled among the fiery and frozen treats.

Come to mama, tasty treats.

"Never seen anything quite like this, huh?" Oriel asks, his eyes twinkling with mischief as he plucks a crunkleberry from the pile to feed it to Dottie. She chitters happily and I smile a bit.

"Only in movies or books. And definitely not exactly like this," I admit, the spectacle erasing the earlier anxiety and replacing it with a childlike wonder.

As we fill our plates, the excitement of the Samhain Ball finally seeps into my veins, chasing away the shadows of dread. We pick out a mosaic of Hell's cuisine, then make our way to the table emblazoned with our caliphate crest, a beacon of familiarity in a room where I'm still treading water. The clinking of glass and the hum of demonic chatter serve as a soundtrack to my jitters.

"Slash, do you think Anton and X will be able to tell if this stuff is safe?" My words are barely above a whisper, betraying a vulnerability I can't fully disguise. "Poison could be on the menu, I suppose."

"Of course," Slash responds, his voice a low rumble of assurance that momentarily eases my nerves. "They are both able to test for that sort of thing to some degree without preparation."

Dottie seems to sense my unease because she detaches from her perch on my shoulder, her small paws clicking against the tabletop as she inspects our haul. When she pauses at a dish —a quivering mass of what looks like garnet jelly—she dances and waves peculiarly, catching all of our attention.

"What's she doing?" I mutter, a frown creasing my brow until the realization dawns. "Oh."

Without ceremony, Slash grabs the plate and sends it spinning into the abyss of the ballroom. There's a satisfying crash followed by indignant shouts, but he only grins, showing off a row of shark teeth. "Sorted."

"Thanks," I say, my smile genuine.

Slash's lack of pretense is refreshing, especially tonight.

The moment is interrupted when Jasper and Zavida stride over, their expressions alive with the urgency of news too tantalizing to keep. Since the

Prince rarely looks this eager unless he's giving me shit, I lean my face on my hand to let him speak without a remark.

"I'm disappointed by what's buzzing around amongst students. It's useless. But. amongst the nobles and wanna-be adults demons…" Jasper says, leaning forward with an air of conspiracy. "There's talk of what will happen after the Games this time. Most of it is cloaked in metaphors and sideways phrasing because people are afraid it might be treasonous."

"After the Games, people think a similar thing to last time will happen," I echo, my curiosity piqued despite the weight of the word. It reeks of trouble, yet the prospect stirs something in me, an ember of excitement. "I don't know how to feel about that."

"It is not something that should happen now," Zavida adds carefully. "Those who make strategy for the actual leaders in waiting placed the timing of this differently, and now that timeline could be pushed forward with little consideration for the rest of the occupants of this realm by bad actors. It will go badly if those demons can succeed."

Motherfucker. Our suspicions are being confirmed by rumors that certainly have been planted to spread to other parts of Hell at this event.

Before we can discuss it further, Anton, X, and Salem return, bearing a constellation of drinks. Dottie scampers back to my side as Anton sets down the beverages, his eyes scanning our arrangements like a general reviewing troops. He sniffs each drink, his focus intense. Relief washes over me when they pass inspection—no foul play detected in the sweet scent of Fae Fizz or the smoky haze of Shadowbrew.

"Looks like we're clear," Salem declares, and we all take our chosen drinks, the cold glasses a comfort in my clammy hands.

"Cheers, my brothers," X begins, breaking the brief silence that follows. Their gaze sweeps the group, sharp and calculating, ready for whatever game we're about to play. "Now we have to figure out how to survive the rest of this room full of crooked predators and their progeny without being scarred for eternity."

UPRISING

The chandeliers above cast an otherworldly glow over the underground ballroom, their light reflecting off the raven-black feathers in my hair. A symphony of clinks and clatters surrounds us while Dottie busies herself with the last bits of her snack.

That mischievous creature is more than a common familiar, but I haven't solved that riddle yet.

"Help me finish these, Oriel," Kit says, nudging a bowl of crunkleberries toward me. He's been popping them into his mouth like candied treats, which is making Jasper growl every once in a while. A chuckle escapes as he chews a handful, the sound almost musical amidst the hum of conversation, and it's like a breath of fresh air to see the tension ease from his shoulders.

"Careful, or you'll lose your strong sense of decorum," I tease, but there's warmth in my voice, relief washing through me at the sight of his rare, unguarded joy. His PTSD or anxiety might be triggered by the party, but I was more prepared for that than his happiness.

Xerxes leans forward then, the scales along their neck catching the light as they do. "So, about this imminent rebellion," they start, eyes flickering with a mix of curiosity and concern. "What's our strategy?"

"Why do you need a strategy?" Kit asks, his eyes curious as looks at us.

A collective shift of discomfort passes among us—this isn't the place for a discussion about our plans, not with prying ears and watchful eyes lurking behind every face. Before anyone can attempt a discreet answer, a resounding chime halts all conversation, drawing our attention to the grand staircase.

Two figures stand at the top, their presence commanding silence throughout the room. Jasper groans, the sound muffled by his palm, while Zavida's many tails become his personal shield. Kit's gaze follows mine upward, landing on the crown of jewels and demon bones dipped in precious metals that seem to pierce the very air with its sharpness.

This night just got so much worse…

"Is that…?" Kit begins, his brows knitting together as he pieces it together.

"Jasper's father," I confirm, my voice low and steady despite the fluttering in my chest. There's history there, etched into every gemstone and bone fragment adorning the man's head—a history none of us are keen to revisit.

Kit's frown deepens, a hint of concern lacing his words. "Trouble or just a headache?"

"Both," I reply, keeping my tone even as I study the man's imperious stance. "But nothing we can't handle."

"Maybe," Zavida mumbles as he hides even more. "It depends on what comes next."

Thanks, dude.

The King's voice booms through the cavernous space, a self-satisfied purr that grates on my ears. His words are a stream of grandeur and victory, painting Hell as a realm reborn through conquest and glory. I can't help but roll my eyes at the irony; the Hell I know is less about glory and more about surviving the next backstabbing scheme. Anyone who lives here knows the old traitor is just wanking himself while we all have to watch him get off on it.

Beside him, Lucian stands rigid, his discomfort palpable even from this distance. He nods along with the King's monologue, his feigned admiration so thick it could choke a lesser demon. I snicker under my breath, knowing full well the façade Lucian wears will have its own price later. The Headmaster is no fan of the King, and him having to listen to him ramble on about his achievements and glories is almost worth having to attend this stupid event.

As the King's droning finally wanes, a relieved sigh vibrates over our table. We've all endured enough of Jasper's dad's speeches to last several eternities, especially if he's full of liquor. Yet, we straighten up when he begins the roll call of honor—a parade of Hell's nobility that were his team for the last Games held in our realm. These people are his personal friends and bonded caliphate members, and he cannot brag about their prowess without giving them the shared glory because of that bond.

Sucks for him, I'm sure, because he's a raging narcissist.

"Scrums!" he bellows, and Slash's father rises from his seat, an imposing figure who looks as though he's been carved from battle itself. The eyepatch and scars are badges of his relentless pursuit of gluttony—consuming conflict as others would fine cuisine.

"General Scrum," the King acknowledges with a nod, while Slash subtly shifts in his chair, a testament to the weight of his lineage.

My gaze flickers over the crowd as the King continues, summoning the Strykers next. Salem's father, a bear of a man whose fierce lumberjack appearance belies his slothful nature, gives a gruff nod to the monarch. The tiny figure beside him, Salem's mother, seems almost comical in contrast, yet her presence is undeniable.

"Aldarics," the King calls, prompting Anton's parents to stand. They're a tapestry of pride, their attire screaming high art and higher standards. They don't glance at Anton, but then again, why would they? Recognition isn't something easily earned in their eyes.

"Zenobes," the King announces, and Xerxes' parents slink into view, their serpentine grace a shimmering display of jewels and seduction. They are the embodiment of lust, untouched by the need for parental warmth or the recognition of their offspring.

I catch Kit's scowl as the Aldarics and Zenobes return to the shadows, his sense of camaraderie flaring in silent protest.

But there's no time to dwell on the slight; the King has moved on to my family.

"Bloodstones." My heart stutters, a crow's instinct to flee rising within me. My parents stand, their dark Gothic aura a stark contrast to the surrounding opulence. Mother's sneer cuts across the room, directed at me—her disappointment made clear without a single word. Father merely stands in her shadow, as always.

No surprise there. They feel I haven't pulled a feat of heist or espionage worthy of our name yet.

"Revens," the King concludes, and instead of the expected matriarch or patriarch, a girl not much older than my caliphate steps forward. Kit's frown deepens, confusion and concern mingling in his expression. It deviates from the norm, one that hints at stories untold within the Revens' line.

"Let's hope the rest of the night unfolds with no familial fireworks," I whisper to Kit, trying to infuse some levity into the moment.

The grumbles around the table are a symphony of dread as we push back our chairs, each movement echoing our collective reluctance. X glances at Anton, a silent exchange passing between them—an agreement to endure the pleasantries before losing themselves in the doom band's mournful laments.

"We have to go kiss the rings," Jasper grunts as he looks at Slash. "A large group is better than anyone getting caught alone, I believe."

"Agreed." The shark shifter cuts his gaze to Kit, and he looks back at his Prince. "Kit is not to be alone with any of them."

"Then we should see Zavida's sister first," I murmur, and they nod with grim determination. "She's the least threatening, and it will help Kit get acclimated to the questions."

At least, I hope so.

Kit's hand is a vise around mine, his grip tightening with each step into the throng of demons and their diverse revelry. The Samhain Ball's chaos should've been a break for us, yet it feels like swimming against the current —each ripple bringing us closer to inevitable encounters with bloodlines and expectations.

We barely make it a few steps when a flock of glamazons from Brimstone intercepts us, their towering presences casting shadows over Zav and Kit. Their leader—a mass of curves and wicked smiles—fixates on Jasper, who seems torn between flattery and annoyance.

"Looking dashing as ever, Jasper," Billie purrs, her voice laced with a challenge. Billie is short for Wilhelmina von Heinrich, and her parents are part of the courts in Xerxes' line. Her dismissive glance at X makes my blood boil, but I know it's simply because she's aware they have zero interest in what she's selling.

Our smallest member's fingers constrict further around my hand, and I can sense the battle within him: engage or escape. Zav, always the most sensitive among us, retreats behind his protective tails, eyes darting nervously. I stay rooted next to Kit, ready to steer him away from conflict, while Salem positions himself as a solid barrier on his other side.

Both of us know how succubi from X's line behave when they get a target in their sights.

Anton, X, and Slash stand firm against the onslaught of the glamazons, their razor-sharp words deflecting any attempts at flirtation or seduction.

"Not tonight, ladies," Anton interjects with a wry smirk, causing the glamazons to huff in mock disappointment.

"Aw, come on boys," one of them purrs, "don't you want to make us happy?"

The other girls saunter up to each of us, their seductive smiles and flirtatious giggles filling the room. They leaned in close to Jasper and Slash, batting their eyelashes and running their fingers through their hair.

"Don't worry, boys," another says, "we can handle a little heartbreak."

Slash rolls his eyes, clearly unimpressed by their advances. "Nothing to break, unfortunately," he scoffs. "Step aside for the Prince."

The demonesses huff irritably, clearly angry they are unsuccessful in their attempts to lure us in with their skimpy dresses and pouty lips. Billie puts her hand on her hip, squinting at the group for a moment before she intervenes. "Who's your new acolyte, Jas? You know we like to hear about fresh meat."

Jasper snorts, stepping back from the succubus to get distance. "I owe you no explanation of whom I induct, Wilhelmina. Slash gave you an order, which you can take as seriously as one of my own."

"I'll bet the scrawny one doesn't even like girls," one of her groupies says, just loud enough for everyone to hear. "He's clutching the emo one and the sleepy idiot."

My hackles raise as they diss Salem. I could give a shit less about what these chicks think of me, but so far they've insulted Kit, Salem, and Zavida, plus they ignored the heir to their line. None of us should stand for this; it's tantamount to treason.

"Look, Wendy, if you could let us pass, I'd be grateful. I'm going to need a drink after your nasal bullshit," Kit says as he lets go of Salem and me. His lips quirk up as he stares the tall, rich female demon down despite the enormous chasm of difference between them. "I'm sure the rest of my caliphate will, too. You should get that looked at—you might have a deviated septum."

Holy forking shirtballs, Kit Kat.

Even Jasper looks momentarily impressed at the balls of fucking *steel* it took to basically tell Billie to fuck off into the sun, and I take a moment to even assimilate what just happened. The demoness opens her mouth, but it closes when Slash laughs. When the shark laughs, it's hard to ignore because he's normally quiet and his genuine laughter is *not*. He's damn near doubled over and soon, Jasper joins him when the girls' faces all screw up in fury.

Smirking, I give Billie and her minions a double finger gun, clicking my tongue. "Bang, bang, you're dead, ladies. *Au revoir,* and all that."

Kit gives me a tiny smile as I hold my hand out, and we all glide away from the cloud of anger left in our wake.

Hopefully, that act of rebellion won't make anything worse than it already is.

Glitter & Gold

kat/kit

The pulsing beat of dark background music throbs through the soles of my boots. The air is thick with magic and mischief, a heady scent that mingles with the rich aroma of spiced pumpkin and charred ember. Adrenaline still lingers in my veins from the earlier confrontation, but it's time to switch gears as our little entourage makes its way toward Zavida's sister, Genie Draven.

I didn't even know he had a sister before she stood up, so I can't control my anxiety about impressing her.

Chandeliers cast an eerie glow on her fox-like features, a stark contrast to the dim lighting surrounding us. Genie stands with poise, her nine tails swaying gently behind her—a clear mark of her gumiho heritage. Her eyes, though warm, hold the weight of centuries, and I sense the burden she carries representing their family tonight. Zavida said she's part gumiho and part vengeance demon, which is perfect for the house of envy. It also likely means she's just as sharp as the shy Kitsuné I know, and I have to be very careful.

"Genie," Zav greets her with a voice that barely conceals his trepidation. It's not just the familial responsibility; there's something else, a tangible discomfort that hangs between them like a veil. She looks more confident than him which might make for sibling rivalry? I don't know.

"Zavvie and his friends!" Genie's smile doesn't quite reach her eyes. The polite mask she wears is flawless, yet there are cracks if you know where to look. Her gaze flickers to Jasper, and for a fleeting moment, the temperature seems to drop. She doesn't like him at all, and I'm sure there's a good reason for it. I file that away, a weapon for later use.

"You look radiant, Duchess Evangilium," I say, drawing out the full title her brother gave me with a smirk. The pleased look on her face at my decorum earns me a sharp glance from Jasper.

That's right, Prince, squirm a bit more under your perfectly tailored suit.

"Thank you. You're all quite dashing yourselves," Genie replies, her tone even, but the tightness around her eyes betrays her concern for appearances. "But I'm afraid I am not familiar with you… has my brother and his misbegotten caliphate taken in a new member?"

Zavida's hand finds mine, his grip trembling. "They didn't come," he murmurs, almost lost amidst the hum of conversation and music. "They sent Genie instead."

Oh, I can relate to this mental breakdown. No one ever came to anything of mine, not even my hospital post-attack.

I squeeze his hand, letting go of Oriel's arm to give Zavida my full attention. "They don't know what they're missing," I assure him, hoping to bolster his spirit. His parents' absence cuts deeper than he lets on, their preoccupation with envy leaving no room for pride in their son.

"You know Mother and Father have very busy schedules monitoring all the deals, bargains, and punishments our lineage captures. Don't be a child, Zavvie."

For a second, I thought I might like this chick, but dismissing her brother's upset changes that entirely. Zav might have gone along with Jasper at the beginning, but I think it was because the Prince is the one person who cares —even in a twisted manner. "We can't dwell on those who aren't here," I say, steering the conversation back to safer waters. "We've got a night of revelry ahead, right?"

"Right," Zavida echoes, a small smile fighting its way onto his lips. It doesn't quite chase away the gloom, but it's a start.

"Nice to see you again, Genie," Salem mumbles as he joins Zav and me. "But we should get moving to greet the other royals before someone gets offended."

She doesn't even respond, simply walks away, waving at some crusty old dowager demon.

Awesome sister. Maybe it's good I don't have siblings, after all.

Weaving through the throng of elaborate outfits and sinister grins, we give Anton's and X's parents a wide berth. Their indifference during the speech was like a slap; their gaze never once landing on the pair who tried so hard to earn it. I catch a shared look between my companions—relief mirrored in their eyes when the Prince doesn't insist we pay respects to them.

"Thank fuck," I mutter under my breath, earning a chorus of silent nods.

Our respite is short-lived as we approach Oriel's parents. They stand tall and imposing, their elegant attire practically dripping with wealth and arrogance. They're the kind of demons who wear disdain like a second skin, and it clings to them, suffocating the surrounding air.

"Oriel has been doing exceptionally well," I interject with forced cheer, trying to bridge the widening chasm of silence as they stare at us. "He's made president of the Thieves Guild, you know."

Their sneers are as dismissive as their attention, unimpressed by what they deem trivialities. They turn to Jasper, their words laced with venomous certainty. "You'd do well to lean on Slash in these Games. Some... sacrifices may be necessary."

A contemptuous gaze slides over Zavida and me, lingering just long enough to stoke the embers of my anger.

Goddamnit, my social battery is quickly depleting and I'm going to have a heart attack, but I cannot let these people be such nasty motherfuckers to my guys.

Before I can retort, Anton steps in, his voice smooth as silk and twice as cunning. "Such an interesting strategy. I'm sure Slash and the Prince will consider it. We should find Salem's parents next, so they don't worry that we've forgotten them."

He guides us away before the Bloodstones respond, but we're not destined for a moment's peace, it seems.

The King's entourage stops in our path, a veritable wall of wrath as they glare at us. Jasper's father stands at the forefront, his presence domineering, backed by Slash's dad and sycophants who buzz about their leaders' latest victories. We're forced to stand witness as the King rambles on about his time in the Games without even saying 'hello' to his son.

My expression is schooled into neutrality, but it's not long before boredom catches up with me. A glance at the other guys tells me they've heard all these stories a million times before, so there's absolutely no reason to be repeating them except to hear himself talk.

"Jasper, truly, your Games cannot possibly compete—" the King begins, his voice powerful enough to drown out the music. He pauses, catching the flicker of disinterest in my eyes. My growing inability to keep my need for recharging has drawn the attention of Slash's father, who now towers over me, his snarl revealing rows of serrated teeth, his threat tangible even without words.

"Got something to say, boy?" he growls.

"Actually, yes," I answer, my voice calm. My hand dips into my pocket and retrieves a tin. I pop the lid, select a mint, and slip it into my mouth with deliberate slowness. "Would you care for one?" My offer hangs in the air, insolent yet innocent, a challenge veiled in courtesy.

Jasper's eyes go wide, his body tensing beside me, but I maintain the facade of helpfulness. To strike now, the King would have to acknowledge the slight to his second-in-command by a tiny male with no powers—tantamount to admitting a commoner can ruffle their feathers.

"Anyone else?" I continue, tilting the tin toward the crowd, each mint glinting like a tiny shield against the tension that threatens to erupt into chaos.

The King's voice cuts through the din like a serrated blade, every word dripping with contempt. "After you receive glory in the Games, I can choose the appropriate bride for you, Jasper, and you'll be free of your... current distractions."

I feel the muscles in my jaw clench as he casts a dismissive glance toward Zavida—the implication unspoken yet crystal clear. Then his gaze lands on me, scorn etched into the crags of his face. "Your little band has its uses, though. The weakling there"—he jabs a finger in my direction—"is it to keep the others satisfied, so you, my son, don't have to share?"

Excuse the everloving fuck out of me?!!

Heat floods my veins, fury a live wire beneath my skin. I'm teetering on the brink of lashing out when Jasper steps forward, his voice a low growl of defiance that still somehow carries over the crowd. "I'll choose my mate, Father. And they will come to me by Fate, not by some farcical political arrangement."

The King's eyes flash dangerously, and his mouth opens, no doubt ready to unleash a tirade. But Jasper acts swiftly, catching me off guard as he seizes my face between his hands. His lips crush against mine, igniting a storm of terror and indignation within me. For a moment, I'm paralyzed, every sense screaming at the intrusion. Yet as understanding dawns—that this is a ploy, a desperate gambit—I let the kiss continue, my mind already plotting retribution.

Tonight seems to be the night when I ignore every bit of good sense in my head in favor of emotions.

Jasper's breath is ragged when he finally pulls away, his chest heaving against mine. We're both panting, our faces inches apart, as the silence around us screams louder than any words. The others—Zavida, Salem, even Oriel— are gaping, shock rooted in their expressions. And as I glance past them, I see the back of the King's ornate garments swishing angrily as he departs with his entourage.

Now, standing here, the taste of the prince still lingering on my lips, I'm struck by a whirlwind of confusion. Twice this week, I've been kissed under false pretenses, my cover as a boy straining at the seams. My body is racing with electricity, and my heart is ready to thump out of my chest. When I feel my limbs sparkle, I look over at Oriel, my eyes wide and full of fear.

"Probably a good time to… get me somewhere…"

Like out of the public eye while I have a serious fucking episode over kissing my most annoying bully in front of the King of Hell after suggesting his general needs a goddamn mint.

Teenage Dirtbag

While the Samhain Ball swirls around us in a decadent parade of power and prestige, Kit's face is pale, his eyes wide with the terror that only comes from having one's nerves frayed to breaking. My heart lurches for him; he's stood his ground like a titan tonight, but even titans have their limits.

He certainly outshines me with his stubborn refusal to let people hurt those around him.

"We should get him out of here," I murmur to Oriel.

The crow shifter slips his arm around Kit's trembling frame. The heat generated from him and Jasper's kiss still burns in the air, as well as their brazen challenge to the King of Hell's authority. I feel the weight of every eye upon us, the whispers that will undoubtedly follow, but none of it matters. Not when Kit's well-being is on the line.

Jasper's actions were reckless, possibly dangerous, but also undeniably bold —very much like Kit himself. It takes guts to speak truth to power, more so for someone whose past haunts them like an unshakeable shadow. I glance at Kit, his fancy attire now a stark contrast to his worn-down expression, and I'm filled with an overwhelming sense of respect. Despite everything, he defended me to Genie and handled the Bloodstones with a finesse that belied his unemerged status. His bravery is astounding; his resilience, even more so.

As much as he and Jasper clash, they are more alike than either would like to admit.

"Thanks, Zav," Kit manages, his voice barely above a whisper, the gratitude in his eyes hitting me harder than any spell could. "And you, too, O."

"Anytime," I reply, trying to offer him a reassuring smile.

Slash moves ahead, broad shoulders parting the crowd like a ship's prow cleaving through dark waters. He's taking the lead, guiding us toward the edge of the ballroom, where a hidden panel waits just beyond the prying eyes of our peers.

How did he know this was even here?

"Inside," Slash says, pressing a disguised button that makes the panel slide open with a soft click. He scoops Kit up with ease, his movements gentle despite the urgency etched into his features. We slip inside, away from the cacophony of the ball, and find ourselves in a small sitting room that promises sanctuary. The walls are lined with brocade wallpaper, the settee plush and inviting—a stark contrast to the chaos we've left behind.

As Slash lays Kit down, I can't help but marvel at the foster kid who's become so much more to us than a floor mate we didn't ask for. His powers may not have emerged, but his spirit? It's as if he's conjuring courage from some inexhaustible source within him, facing off against actual demons that would make seasoned warriors balk. Still, he had the presence of mind to ask Oriel to whisk him away before he fully broke down. My admiration swells, mixed with a protective urge that has me clenching my fists.

I've never felt like I should help take care of someone before—only that I needed someone to take care of me.

"Rest now," I tell Kit softly, standing guard by his side. "We've got you."

In the quiet of the hidden room, I watch over him, feeling the echo of his anxiety like a chill in the air. If only I could do more for him…. But for now, this will have to be enough—this moment of respite, this silent vow of support. As Kit's chest rises and falls with each slow breath, I silently promise to stand by him, just as he stood up for all of us.

Kit lies still for about fifteen minutes while the rest of us give him time to recuperate. I'm fairly amazed that all my brothers are staying quiet while we watch this guy bring himself off the edge of the cliff. Even Jasper is silent as he stares into the distance, looking contemplative.

"Seriously, Slash, how did you know about this place?" Oriel's question breaks the tension that's been coiling tighter with each of Kit's shallow breaths.

Jasper's response comes from a shadowed corner, his voice low but clear. "We've memorized every nook and cranny of Discordia. Knowledge is power—even more so with hidden alcoves."

Slipping into the role of caretaker with a surprising ease, Slash gently settles at the end of the settee to watch the new demon carefully. The elaborate room, with its gilded edges and soft lighting, seems to fold around us, silencing the world beyond its secret walls. I'm actually more comfortable here than I was out there, so I will not complain in the slightest.

Maybe we all needed this break.

Kit sprawls out, limbs loose and askew, the picture of exhaustion and relief. X saunters closer, adjusting the supine guy's attire with a flourish, their eyes twinkling mischievously as they catch Kit's gaze.

"Mind your modesty, sir," they tease, earning a strained half-smile from Kit.

"You know, I haven't worried about flashing someone in ages." Kit's laugh is dry, almost a whisper. "Thanks, man."

Laughter ripples through our tight-knit group—brief, but genuine, like the flicker of a candle fighting against the dark. For a moment, I consider what the act of completing the ritual had on our relationships with Kit. It didn't change the way any of us look at one another in the past, though.

I glance over at Jasper, who stands apart from us, his jaw set, muscles tense beneath the fine threads of his formal wear. His eyes are distant, troubled even. What played out between him and Kit was far from simple rebellion; I can feel it deep in my bones.

He's getting feelings he has no idea how to deal with—I know because I've seen it before.

As Kit's breathing steadies and his color returns, he casts a wary look towards the Prince. I can see the questions swirling in his wide, uncertain eyes. Those same questions are clawing at my insides, seeking answers I'm not sure Jasper is ready to give. He struggles with adapting to such situations, and with the current chaos, it will be even more challenging to make him understand what's happening.

I know Jasper better than anyone—the way he guards his heart like his dragon hoards gold. He fought against his feelings for me once, his affection a battlefield he was determined to conquer alone. But we're past that now; our bond is complex, threaded through understanding that defies traditional labels. Our Dom/sub dynamic is just one layer of the intricate tapestry that is 'us.'

"Jasper?" Kit's voice is hesitant.

But my Prince only stares ahead, lost in a storm only he can weather. I'd help, but it will only make him bristle right now. All I can do is stand by, patient and watchful, knowing that when he's ready, the demon I love will let us in on the secret battle he's waging within.

Jasper sighs, his shoulders tense as he continues to face away from us. "Slash, will you—"

"Already on it," Slash interrupts with a knowing nod and turns to Salem. "Grab some drinks and more bites to eat. He needs energy."

Kit tries to protest, his voice barely above a murmur, "I'm not a child, you know." But the words come out soft, unconvincing, lost in the worried glances we exchange.

As if to emphasize his vulnerability, Dottie scampers over, tiny fists flailing in a silent demand as Salem stands. The kinkajou's antics draw a faint smile from Kit, a momentary flicker of amusement crossing his exhausted features.

He really has drained his battery and I'm not sure if that's from his body trying to get his magic and powers to develop fully or if it's because he keeps burning himself to bits by getting into scraps.

"Come sit with me," Anton says as he drags a chair over, sharing it with X, their shoulders touching casually as they curl together.

Oriel takes another chair and brings it closer, perching like a bird of prey, eyes sharp but caring. "KK, we want to make sure you're good to go before we leave this secret room. No one thinks you're a child."

We settle into watchful silence, our focus solely on Kit while he recovers. No one speaks of the dance left behind, the intrigue, or the power plays. We don't care—and I find that interesting as hell. This caliphate was forged in chaos, but it seems now we're bound by something stronger than duty or fear.

What a weird fucking thing to happen in the wake of all the other bullshit being thrown at us.

Salem returns, arms laden with refreshments, and Kit finally pushes himself upright. With the solemnity of a sacred ritual, he accepts the offerings, breaking bread—or rather, snacks—with Dottie, who eagerly snatches up her share.

"Sorry," Jasper grunts suddenly, his voice rough as gravel. "For... startling you."

Holy. Motherloving. Shit.

Shock etches itself across Kit's face, deep lines of disbelief at Jasper's admission. He's not wrong; Jasper Eversore never admits his errors without some sort of torture device being involved. His surprise extends to all of us and we've known the Prince for far longer.

Oriel can't resist a jab, his smirk wicked. "Anyone got a calendar? This ought to be marked as a historical event."

Salem snorts, then laughter ripples through our small gathering, a lightness that feels almost foreign amidst the night's tension. But Jasper's mood soon sours, thunderclouds brewing over his brow as he paces with a beastly grace, snarling at Oriel's gentle teasing.

"That's enough," Kit's voice cracks through the mirth, surprisingly steady. "Let him be. We've all had to face our... demons... tonight, haven't we?"

Slash gives Kit a long, measuring look. His gaze is heavy with thoughts unspoken before he says, "We should leave."

Disappointment tugs at X's lips, a fleeting shadow that reflects his wish to dance and make merry. However, Oriel nods, and Anton does as well. The thief looks at me and I agree, so he rises to his feet. "This night's been a bust, anyway. Too much drama, not enough intel."

The decision hangs between us all, eyes darting from one face to another until they land on Jasper. He pauses, considers, then nods. "Fine. Salem's room, then. Dinner away from this mess sounds much safer for everyone."

And much farther away from our shithead parents and bitchy demonesses.

In the quiet that follows, I catch Kit's eye, and there's a soft gratitude there that doesn't need voicing. He's definitely happy we're going to leave this mess, and he wouldn't have asked us to do so himself. That kid would damn near kill himself rather than ask for help, and that will eventually be a tremendous problem. However, for now, it's just something I'll be more aware of so I can help like Salem, Slash, and Oriel do.

Maybe he'll forgive me sooner if I figure out how to keep him on an even keel.

Safe and Sound

Kat/Kit

The disaster that was the dance faded once we were back at the dorm. Slash refused to let me walk—*again*—so I had to keep my face turned away from the stares of all the lookie-loos as we paraded through the throng. I have no idea if the dickhead parents we visited were watching or if they'd yeeted themselves out after being 'seen,' but I'm sure the rumor mill will take care of letting them know what happened.

I hope the boys aren't going to get their asses handed to them because I got overstimulated.

"Salem, do you have everything you need?" I ask, feeling bad as he buzzes around the kitchen in his dress clothes. "I could—"

"Nope," Oriel says with a firm head shake. "You will stay in your chair and let us handle this, Kit Kat. You've done enough standing up tonight."

My face turns bright red and I mumble to Dottie as she clings to my neck. They made me go change while no one else has, and the display of beautiful demons in perfectly tailored, but rumpled formal wear is making it very hard to concentrate. Since the incident, I haven't felt an iota of desire for *anyone*, but the sight of my caliphate does the weirdest things to my body. I feel like my skin is tingling so much that I'm going to sparkle into the air.

Zavida tilts his head, studying me with a curious look. His tails are resting beside him, a sign that he's truly comfortable at the moment even in our room. "Kit, are you okay?"

I nod, smiling weakly. "Yeah. It's hard coming down from a half-formed attack, you know? The adrenaline isn't fully spent and my body aches a bit because of the muscle freeze? I'm sure Salem's food will help me get some energy to refill the reserves."

"It will, little demon." Slash looks pleased at my answer and flutters kick up in my stomach.

Why is that praise making me feel so damn good? Fucking weird.

Jasper is sitting in his chair, still quiet as hell. I don't know what his problem is, but it makes me edgy. I'm just waiting for him to unleash a torrent of nastiness to soothe whatever shit he's got stewing in his brain. So far, it hasn't come, but I'm certain it will. He deals with emotions he can't handle by lashing out and I'm his favorite target.

"Perhaps some of us should change? My couture is going to be a *mess* after this," Xerxes says. My gaze swivels to theirs, and there's something I can't quite place in it. They have a reason for this suggestion, but it sure as fuck isn't about having to iron his fancy duds. All of them have their clothes cleaned by a service—X won't have to lift a finger.

Anton nods, leaning in to press a kiss to their head. "That's a good idea, babe. I'd like to get comfortable, and I'm sure everyone else would as well. Now that we have Salem started and KK tucked in, we can go a few at a time."

"I'm not a baby," I grumble as I sink into the blanket Oriel brought me from my room. "I can sit here while Salem cooks without all of you staring at me like a giant bug."

Slash snorts, arching a brow. "If we all go, you'll be on your feet by the time the door closes."

Damn him for being right.

"Slash is right," Salem says as he dances to the tunes in his head at the stove. The smells are delicious and my stomach rumbles, making him smirk over his shoulder at me. "Kit Kat will jump at the chance to get over here, especially if he's hungry."

"I don't snitch while you cook—that much," I protest. Dottie chitters, giving me a reproving look, and I sigh. "Okay, fine, I do, but it's because the food here is so damn good. Salem being the cook makes it even better. I don't think I've ever had food that tastes this good, truthfully."

Jasper snorts and my gaze flits back to him. I know what's coming.

"Because you have demon blood, shrimp. The delights of Hell have been missing from your diet and your body will now crave it, especially as you continue to emerge."

I'll be a redheaded step-child; he didn't insult me.

"The Prince is correct."

Slash's confirmation makes me feel a bit better; being hungry a lot as a girl in our realm is associated with things I'm *never* going to want, so knowing it's normal here helps my anxiety. Of course, I haven't done the thing you need to do for that to be possible since… the trauma.. but it's so ingrained. Girls fear what isn't even possible because of the stupid Puritanical horseshit up there. It's a tool of the fucking patriarchy, and luckily for me, it doesn't seem like Hell gives a flying fuck about that.

My eyes widen for a second as I realize I have not one single goddamn clue what various shifter or demon anatomy looks like or how they reproduce other than a vague guess about the mechanics being similar. That is very bad and I may need to have a private discussion with Dank about it. I don't foresee it being necessary anytime soon, but being ignorant isn't my jam. I want to have all the information possible so if something terrible—or not so terrible—happens, I can make smart decisions.

"Kit? Hey, Kit, did we lose you?"

I blink, looking at Oriel in confusion. Obviously, I blipped out for a minute thinking about demon sex and reproduction, which I am *not* going to admit to these jokers. "Um, yes. I spaced a little, I think. Sorry."

X gives me another one of those assessing looks and I duck into my big chair more so I don't squirm. "I think Annie and I will go first, then. Jas and Slash can follow, then Zav and O."

"Guess I'm just fucking stuck then, huh?" Salem snarks from the kitchen and I chuckle. "The chef always loses, man."

"Salem, you can go anytime once the food won't burn. I'd help, but no one will let me," I say softly. He looks less pissy as he smiles at me fondly, and I have to adjust in my seat again.

These demons are going to be the death of me.

I WAS WRONG ABOUT THE STUPID SUITS BEING THE WORST OUTCOME—SO *very* wrong.

Biting my lower lip as I wait for Salem to finish plating our dinner, I swallow hard. The guys came back from shedding their tuxes and suits pair by pair, and I haven't been able to breathe since. X and Anton have some sort of matching silk pajamas and tanks in colors that make them look statue-esque and cut like diamonds. The material flows around their bodies, clinging to lithe muscles in a way that's damn near indecent. But that's not the worst of it… oh, no.

Zavida and Jasper have ridiculously fancy PJ pants with tight tees and bare feet, looking like the very picture of the bad boy and the nerd as they lounge together. Zav is curled next to Jasper's legs while he messes with his tablet, but the fond hand that occasionally ruffles his hair is making my chest ache. The Prince loves to be a jackass to everyone, but he's not afraid to show his affection for the kitsune.

Unfortunately for me, that's not the end. Oriel, Salem, and Slash are wearing jogging pants that should be illegal to sport in public and *no fucking shirts* as they work on getting the food out. The amount of piercings, tattoos, muscles and sheer size filling that area is overwhelming and combined with everything else, I have no idea where to put my gaze. Dottie is no help, either, because she's been scampering around to get fruit treats from her faves, and giving me what I'm starting to think is a smirk when they fawn over her.

My kinkajou is taunting me, and I can't do a damn thing about it.

"Breathe, Kit," I murmur softly as my reaction to the demons surrounding me ramps my pulse. Putting a hand on my chest, I close my eyes and try to calm the random physical reactions fluttering through me like a swarm of butterflies. If I'm honest, it's not just that I haven't felt like this since the incident—no, I've never felt exactly like this. I've never felt a magnetic pull to simply devour anyone with my eyes because my insides were starving for the sight of them.

"Hey, KK, you want a soda? I swiped some from the old battle axe's stash during my Lab yesterday."

My head jerks up and I grin widely at Salem, excitement flooding my veins. "You are my favorite, buddy. I didn't realize how much I was jonesing for a Coke until you said that."

"Not satisfied with the fun drinks here, mmm?" Oriel says as he tilts his head. His expression is thoughtful, like he's digging for info, but it doesn't bother me. The crow shifter gathers information just as voraciously as he does shiny things, so I know he's not looking for something to hold against me.

"Hmm. No, I love the stuff here. But something from up there is kind of comforting when tonight had a lot of... new things, you know?"

Jasper chuckles, drawing my attention back to him and Zavida. "Meeting with the ruler of Hell and not-so-subtly inferring he can get fucked is certainly new for all of us."

"At least, in such a blatant fashion." Slash gives me one of his toothy grins from his spot next to Salem.

"He practically called me a whore, Jasper," I shoot back. "While there's absolutely nothing wrong with sex workers, I knew *he* meant it as an insult. If I'd let it go, there would be just as many problems with looking weak as there are seeming impudent."

Salem points his spatula at me, nodding. "That's true. Looking weak might have been worse, I think. Now the General and the King don't assume Kit Kat is the way to take us out."

Blushing again, I curse under my breath. The way my body refuses to ignore their compliments is infuriating and I hate it. "I can't let everyone think I'm the best way to target you all. It might be accurate, but I'd rather people wonder than prove they're right. Plus, I fucking despise bullies."

"Hear that, Prince Prickface?" Oriel calls with a snort. "He *hates* bullies, so stop being such an ass."

"As if I care what the shrimp likes or dislikes," Jasper says, smirking as he throws a dirty look at the crow. "He liked the kiss just fine, and only Annie and I have that distinct honor."

Oh. My. God.

"I..."

Before I can even find the words, they're all laughing and I'm wishing the floor would open up and swallow me whole. The guys in the kitchen stomp over with trays, and when I am able to unburrow myself enough to smell the tasty dinner, all seven sets of eyes are on me. Salem arches a brow as he hands me my soda, and Oriel matches him when he gives me the plate. I have no fucking clue what to say to either of them, so I stuff my mouth with a bite of the savory meat as fast as I can.

"He's embarrassed, you guys," Anton says softly. "Remember, both times the action was used to distract people around us. It's not like he had a choice."

Oh, right. Yes, good point. Whew.

"That's true," I squeak, then frown at myself in irritation. I don't know why I'm having such a hard time, but this is fucking stupid. Clearing my throat, I try again. "Anton is right. I didn't have an option, but... um. Neither of them made me upset like... in my past. I want to make sure you know that."

X gives me a knowing look and it makes the hairs on the back of my neck rise.

That cobra shifter knows something and it's making me jumpy as hell.

Faith

Kit burrowed into himself for the rest of the night, all of Sunday, and we all seemed to accept that he needed some time—even Jasper. My lover, however, spent that time alternating between working on their projects and eyeing the kid like he was going to disappear. I pressed him on it, but X was tight-lipped, other than to say they worried that immersion therapy would have adverse effects we might miss if we weren't careful.

I'm not sure exactly what they mean by that, but sometimes, X is too mysterious for their own good.

When I enter the *Triclinium* for lunch, I find Jasper, Oriel, and Zavida sitting with Kit at our table. No one makes a comment as I pass, though I assume they didn't give our smallest members the same grace. Dottie is hunched over a bowl of something while Kit stares at his tablet quietly, still not interacting with people despite the conversation going on around him.

"Good afternoon, my brothers," I say loudly, plopping down next to Kit. "You look cheerful."

He looks up, his eyes unsure as our gaze meets. "It's Monday, Annie."

"Yes, and despite that tragedy, we soldier on."

Jasper coughs, getting me to focus on him. "The shrimp has a point. None of us are ever chipper on Mondays and Wednesdays—especially because he's got all those solo classes. It makes it hard to focus on shit."

"I'm fine; stop worrying, Jasper."

That gets Oriel and Zavida's attention. They both frown, but O is the one who says, "You know we're not going to do that, Kit Kat. We want to keep you safe."

"I know."

I turn my head at the tone of his voice, studying his posture and affect. Despite the reassurance he gave us Saturday after the dance, he's been pulling away. I thought perhaps he needed time to process like X said, but this feels different. "Kit, what's wrong? And don't say 'nothing.' It's very obvious and none of us are fools."

Sighing, he puts his device on the table and the kinkajou scrambles over to join him. Kit looks at his hands for a moment, fiddling with the pencil before he finally looks up. "I feel like I'm a burden. You guys have to watch out for me, do things you don't want to so people don't see me as weak, and even coddle me when I have attacks. It's not fair to any of you, especially Prince Dickhead who really doesn't want me here."

Where the hell did this come from?

"That's crap," Oriel says as he leans back and crosses his arms over his chest. "No one said that. Hell, even Jasper didn't hint at it this time."

The Prince smirks and shrugs, looking pleased. "I am pleased to say I agree with him."

Kit puts his fists on the table, clenching them open and closed as he shrugs. "You didn't have to."

Narrowing my eyes, I look at the device he's been glued to since Saturday evening. When Dottie distracts our new member, I snatch it away, opening the screen to confirm my suspicions. It doesn't take me long to find the flood of notifications he's received in the past two days through email, messages, and various Underworld social media accounts. I didn't know he'd plugged into our world this deeply, but I bet Xerxes is the one who helped him. Most of it is vile and unflattering to all of us, including Jasper.

People really have a set of brass ones when they feel encouraged by a petty dictator.

"You've been dealing with this alone for days?" I ask as I pass it to O. "Why? We would have helped you back these assholes and snooty bitches off."

"What the fuck?!" O says, interrupting me as he glares around the room with dark, glittering eyes. A feather flutters to the table as he puffs up with fury. "I'll *ruin* them. Who the fuck asked these people to comment on our choices?"

Kit shrinks back for a moment, but I watch as he forces himself to sit up straight. His instinct was to back down at the outburst and I find that interesting given how much he goes toe-to-toe with Jas. "Look, I'm making all sorts of problems for you and… all I want is to go to school and get a degree. You don't have to…"

Zav shakes his head. "No, Kit. No one is coddling you. Are we concerned about your safety? Definitely."

"Maybe, but—"

"Shrimp."

We all stop to look at the Prince. He's scowling, which isn't unusual, but something in his eyes keeps me from commenting. The arrogant tilt of his head makes me worry about what's coming next. I hope he doesn't send the poor kid running for the hills again with some bullshit barbs.

"You seem determined to believe that despite being demons and royals, we do anything we don't want to. Doubting the others is easy because they are so fond of you, but hear me when I say that *I* do what I want. My caliphate would not protect you or respect your demands so consistently if I truly did not wish it. Stop feeling sorry for yourself; it's unbecoming."

The table is silent as that sinks in. I don't know if I've ever seen Jasper be quite so… conscientious of someone else's feelings in public. The guy in question licks his lips and my own tingle with the memory of kissing him in Arms class. He finally looks up, meeting Jasper's gaze steadily despite how defeated the rest of him looks.

"Even though I have a truck load of issues that cause problems?"

The snort is derisive and so is his smirk as Jasper responds. "Kit Camponella, being a demon doesn't mean we're unable to be decent beings.

You have trauma and in truth, so do all of us. If we can't find a way to mutually coexist despite that, none of us deserve to rule this realm."

Holy shit. I think Jasper's heart grew three sizes today.

ORIEL ELECTED TO JOIN US ON THE WALK TO KIT'S DEMON LINEAGE CLASS. Since the new guy started talking to us again after Jasper's statement, it's been a fairly pleasant journey to the lecture hall. The crow shifter's presence seems to make him less anxious and I realize that I missed the chatter Kit engenders this weekend. It's good to have him back, even if he's not quite to the comfort level he was at the pre-social media bash fest.

"I have to go see Dank after Lit class," Kit says suddenly.

I blink, looking at Oriel, who shrugs. "Why? Did something happen again?"

Kit shakes his head. "No. Just a follow up from the…other time. You know, to make sure everything is healing and stuff."

There's something odd about this; he's never mentioned it before.

"Okay, Kit Kat. I can take you," O says as we climb the steps. "Then we'll head back for dinner and Zav said we can do the flashcards. Last time you nailed the elder gods and devils, so this time we should do the Greeks."

The bright red flush on his cheeks tells me he's embarrassed, but I have no idea why. A last minute visit to the doc concerns me, but I'll check with X to see if they know more. Maybe he mentioned it to my lover before the dance and it got forgotten in the frenzy of the day. "You'll have to deal with Salem coming along. He won't want to leave when he hears that Kit's seeing Dr. D."

"Guys… no one is coming in that room with me. I'm awake this time."

I chuckle, giving him an amused expression. "Don't want a crowd of clowns looking down at you like last time, mmm?"

"Fuck no." Kit actually smiles at me this time and I feel my gut clench. "I'm trying hard to accept help, but I'm not letting you idiots smother me to death."

Ahhh, the spunk is back. I like it.

O turns, walking backwards up the stairs so he can look at us. "Dottie can stay with me and Salem while you visit the good doc. I solemnly swear we won't spoil her dinner."

The kinkajou chitters from her perch on Kit's shoulder and I chuckle. "We really should take Kit to meet that weirdo in the bestiary."

"Wait. What?" Our progress stops as Kit pokes me in the shoulder. "What bestiary?"

"Oh, shit, nobody told him."

I nod at Oriel as I realize the same thing. This is going to be fun as hell. "There's a bestiary out in the Wastelands. Some species of demons have better animal affinities and they send the third years to see if any attract a familiar when they visit. You, however, can bring yours for the Keeper to look at."

"Why have none of you jackasses mentioned this before?" Kit frowns as he starts moving again. "It feels important."

"Not really," Oriel replies as we head down the hall, stopping at Kit's class-room door. "It'll be fun, which you'll like, but it won't tell us anything new 'cuz you have Dottie."

Kit sighs, still looking annoyed, but jabs his finger at me. "Talk to X and figure out when we can go. Now get lost before you guys are late to shit and somehow, Prince Pricklypants blames me. We know he can't be nice to me more than once a day and lunch used that up for the week, probably."

It's fucking scary how well he knows us.

The two of us watch as he goes in, bee-lining for the back corner with his familiar, then Oriel closes the door. As we head back downstairs, the thief scratches his chin and looks at me carefully.

"Soooo… you and X, yeah?"

"Not this again. We all agreed that we like Kit." I shrug, not knowing how to explain it. "Xerxes hasn't been interested in adding to the dynamic before and neither have I. That's why, if you're going to ask."

"Mmm."

"It's not like you *ever* seemed interested in anyone beyond a hook-up, either, emo boy. Jasper and Slash have been the most actively pursued and they haven't exactly been… celibate all these years. But you're no angel. Zav and Salem are honestly the cleanest hands, I'd think."

The crow shifter smirks at me, his eyes glittering with mirth. "You know, I think our sleepy sloth might actually be the only pure one among us. He doesn't talk about it, but girls don't exactly flock to the guy who falls asleep mid-evening and prefers the kitchen to a dance floor."

"Zav wouldn't be experienced if it wasn't for Jasper. He's almost as jumpy as Kit," I shoot back.

Neither of us are being shitty about our friends, but this fake dating with someone we actually like makes it important to consider all the angles. Getting Kit to feel comfortable and safe with us is the first step to exploring that, though Jasper and I got to take short cuts. If I were to rank everyone, I'd say Oriel and Salem are closest to being able to give it go, followed by Slash. Kit's really taken to the big guy of late. But that leaves the rest of us floundering for ways to connect.

I'll get X to arrange a visit with the Keeper and we can take him together—that would be good.

"Agreed," Oriel says and I have to tune back into what he's saying. "What do you think this doctor thing is about? I don't remember him mentioning it before."

"I don't know, man. He didn't seem harmed, and even though I'm pretty sure Slash is going to *wreck* the dumbasses here who attacked KK on social media, he wasn't having a panic attack, either."

The evil smile that comes over my brother's face almost makes *me* shiver. "Then I'll be the one to deal with those girls. I'm fine with that; I can fly."

That can't be good.

Let's Talk About Sex

kät/kit

"Why are you going to see Dr. D again?" Salem asks on a yawn. "You seem like you're all better."

I smile as he scoops up Dottie, putting her on his shoulder as I get my things. Oriel is waiting patiently for us to move, but I feel the tension coming off of him at the question. He wants to know, too, but fuck if I'm going to tell them that I'm very curious about their reproduction. That seems like a statement that I can't walk back, even if I put in a context that somehow attaches to schoolwork.

Though how I'd do that, I have no goddamn clue.

"He wanted me to get checked one more time because of the… thing… and the injuries from class. I think I'm okay, too, but I'd hate to be wrong." Salem lumbers out of the row and I follow, knowing O is right behind me. "Seems like it's not a big deal to let the doctor make certain."

"True," Oriel agrees. "Since they're inching us into the training for the Games, I think making sure you're coming along well is a good plan. It's just not like the Doc to worry so much. The doc left us to figure out on our own plenty of times, then chastised us for not coming back to check shit out."

I give him an amused look as we leave the room. "Probably because you're all too stubborn to listen to him and he knows it. Dank doesn't seem like the kind of demon to waste his breath."

"Have we even asked how Kit Kat gets to call the old bastard a nickname and he barely *speaks* to us?" Salem glares at a group of demons standing by the elevator until they scatter, then holds the doors for O and me to get on. "I'm still wigged out by that."

"I didn't know that wasn't his real name. When he picked me up from the Jamesons', he told me his name was Dank. We had a fairly peaceful ride after he scared the bejesus out of them, and he dropped me off to Lucian and Jasper once we arrived. Seeing him in that office was a shock, to be honest."

Oriel scratches his chin as he watches my face. "I know you're telling the truth, but it's so damn weird, KK. He's not like that with anyone here—or anyone in Hell, as far as I know. What the hell did you guys talk about to get on his good side?"

"Just being worried about going somewhere I didn't know with a weird guy in a plague mask," I retort drily. "Nothing really but a little advice about being cautious about who I trust and that this place is a shark tank—which it is."

Notice they don't argue with that point?

"Well, it's a short jaunt to the admin building, and we'll wait outside while you get examined," Salem says firmly. "When you're done, back to eat and do the Greek review."

"Planning my entire night, I see." I arch a brow at them and Oriel has the grace to look sheepish. "I don't mind if you wait, and I definitely want to have dinner. But I might want to shower and clean up before I settle in to study. I always feel a bit slimy on days where I have Lillabet's class."

Salem shivers, nodding at me. "Don't blame you. She can't manipulate demons of our level without a *lot* of effort and prior feeding, so we're not having as much trouble. Ask Dr. D when you're in there—maybe it will get easier for you, too."

It sure as fuck can't get worse; the bitch still creeps me out.

"I'll ask him; good idea, Snoozy," I tease, bumping his shoulder as we descend the steps to cross the campus to get to admin. "I'm glad you're awake to suggest it."

"Oi, you were a pain in the ass today." Oriel gives Salem a sharp glare. "Poor KK had to stomp your foot almost flat to keep you awake."

"Look, guys. You know I can't control when it starts, and this stupid Lit class being so late is the fucking worst." He looks at the kinkajou riding on his shoulder. "Tell them Dottie."

My girl chitters and waves her tiny fists, making me grin. "I should have assigned her to honk your nose when you drifted."

"Hey, guys!"

All three of us stop joking until we see X rushing toward us. Their bright flair sticks out amongst the dreary darkness of Discordia. I'm worried they know something by the way they've been looking at me since after the dance, but I can't figure out which of my secrets Xerxes might have gleaned.

As long as he doesn't know I'm not Kit, then I can deal with the rest.

"We're taking Kit Kat for a follow up with Dr. D," Salem says. "You can come if you want. We promised we'd wait in the hall while he gets declared fit for fighting."

"You know, I didn't intend for this to be a fucking floor field trip," I mutter. The more people who join, the more uncomfortable this damn visit is going to be. I know they aren't coming into the office, but the things I want to know about and why are making me nervous enough as it is. I can't believe I'm even doing it, to be honest. Sex stuff hasn't been a blip on my radar since before the attack; I have no idea why my brain thinks I'm ready to think about it now.

Okay, I kind of do—they all make me feel things I didn't think I'd ever feel again and now I have to know what I'm getting into.

"Come on, then. Let's get this over with so we can have Purgatory Pizza tonight," Oriel says as he holds the doors for us. "I'm in the mood for it."

That sneaky asshole knows food is my new weak spot. I'm going to murder him.

"MASTER KIT! IT IS WONDERFUL TO SEE YOU UP AND LOOKING WELL," THE demon says as I come in. "What brings you to my office this evening?"

I smile, my fondness for the first person on this voyage who was kind to me is hard to hide. "I have some questions, Dank. But um…"

He simply waits, his empty eyes and burning visage looking patient somehow.

"Can you… make it so people can't 'super hear' or whatever in here?" I blurt out. My face heats and I have to jump up on the table to keep from pacing in nervousness. "I'd like *privacy.*"

The air in the room feels very tight for a moment as he nods, and I lick my lips while he walks from corner to corner muttering. When he's done, the elder demon stands in front of me again. "My bubble will keep *most* beings from being able to spy on our conversation, Master Kit. There is a small possibility of eavesdropping, but without preparation, this is the best we can do."

It will have to do; I'm not coming back with an entire cadre of assholes following next time.

"Thanks," I mumble as I clasp my hands together, hoping to quell both my discomfort and my anxiety. "So, I need to ask questions and since you're the only person who knows me…"

Dank chuckles, the sound a rough, rusty sound. "Yes, I believe I know what you mean."

My cheeks go from hot to burning at his amusement and I fight curling into myself. I know the old demon isn't being mean; this is just a very touchy subject for me based on my past. "Yes, well, because of my… past… I have a lot of problems emotionally around this topic. But… I may need to know and I can't ask anyone else without poking that bear."

"I vow to be as accurate as possible without judgment, Master Kit. That is my job and I have been doing it longer than your former country has even existed."

Another factoid I'll deal with later, it seems.

"Okay. I don't know… how demons work." Before he can respond, I hold my hand up. "I'm learning about magic and types and stuff in class. What I mean is… I don't know about their… parts."

The room is silent as a tomb for a moment, then Dank clears his throat. "I assume you mean anatomy and the process of reproduction, yes?"

"Unfortunately." I look away, knowing I have to resemble a tomato by now and my pulse is racing like the blood is going to jump out of my veins. "We don't have time for *everything*, but a little crash course would be very helpful."

"Yes, I understand, Master Kit." He shuffles to the cabinet, leaving it open as he rifles through things in it. He comes back with a flyer sized illustration that makes my eyes bug out. "Many single bloodline demons will resemble this, but it varies greatly. They will come into maturity by the time they are old enough to attend university. Maturity does mean the ability to procreate, and there are specific things that indicate potential mates."

Oh, this is… a lot.

Burying my hands in my short locks, I tug on my hair a bit to reboot my system as I stare at the diagram. "Ummm. So, what are those steps? And are hybrids different?"

The rusty laugh escapes him again, and he nods. "Indeed! Good questions, my young friend. You have not fully emerged yet, but as you do, you will rocket into maturity quickly due to age. That phase is marked by increased demon pheromone production and bodily changes that will point you in the direction of potential partners, or if you are very lucky, mates."

"Plural?" I squeak. "That's… normal?"

Dank nods. "Very, Master Kit, especially in powerful demons."

"How is that… demons haven't… 'scented' me yet? I mean, I'm around ones with animal shifter sides, too. Doesn't that make it easier to give me away?"

"It does, but not at this time." The doctor pauses, thinking for a moment before he glides over to the cabinet again as he continues. "I can assist you with that when the time comes. Being the royal physician means I can keep magical things others cannot. But as for right now, neither the full blooded demons nor the hybrids are used to human scents. They know that's what you register as currently, but very few spend enough time on the surface to recognize the different variants."

Thank fuck for that.

"What about demons who are in the sex business, like Cubi?" I ask, thinking about my least favorite professor and my genderfluid friend's line. "Would they know?"

"Their magic will sense arousal, yes. Until you fully emerge, it won't tell them much more since the Cubi are pansexually oriented by design." The flaming headed demon returns with a large bottle with an eyedropper stopper on top. A label with that damn language I can't fully understand yet looks ominous on it, but I know that Dank wouldn't hurt me. Whatever this is, he's trying to help me.

"What's that?"

"Ah, yes. This is very special, extremely hard to make, and banned from use by those who are not sanctioned by the royal houses." I blink as he opens the bottle, showing me the sparkly purple-black liquid inside. "It tastes awful, but two drops daily before bed will assist you in keeping your pheromones from drawing those around you when your maturity begins."

"It also renders reproduction impossible, no matter what hybrid or full blooded demon is involved." I open my mouth to ask, and this time the avian skull looks as if it's grinning. "And many demon species can also reproduce with both female demons and males, so that is important, Master Kit."

Holy motherforking shirtballs, I have no idea how to respond to that.

The demon continues as I go through about fifty emotions at once. "Hybrids will have special anatomy that corresponds with either their demonic nature or their animal nature. I will endeavor to look for information on the ones I believe might be of interest to you, but it will take some time. Will you be able to return occasionally?"

Licking my lips again, I feel the dryness in my throat as panic grips me. Oddly, I don't feel anxious about the *act* of sex like normal as much as my ignorance of their kind and inexperience. This is so fucking strange that it's like a fever dream. "Um, yes. I'll… figure out some excuse. Besides, it's likely someone will take a chunk out of me in some class eventually."

"I'd prefer the former, but I will send a missive when I have more for you. For now, take my bottle and I will start the process of making enough to last throughout the year."

This demon is definitely my favorite in the entire realm of Hell, and I have to stifle the urge to hug him. "Thank you, Dank. I really appreciate how kind you've been to me."

"I don't often get the chance to assist with something this important, Master Kit, nor do I encounter beings who do not immediately fear and revile me based on my appearance. You are quite special in my opinion."

He's the first person to think so and I'm going to cry if I think about that too hard.

Animal

sälem

K it came out of the doc's office looking a bit green. He was clutching a bottle, so I assumed he got medicine for whatever Dr. D thought he should have it for, but he wasn't willing to discuss it further. O and I didn't press; the poor kid was clearly processing something and Dottie abandoned us to comfort him immediately.

But now we're back in the room, and everyone else will show up once the pizza arrives. I had Oriel warn off the herd until then so Kit could go to his room to change and take a few minutes to himself without being bombarded. I don't know what Dr. D told him, but it's definitely fucking with his head and I can understand that. It's easy for hybrids like us to forget what it was like when our shit came into effect because we were prepared for it our entire childhoods. KK is dealing with all of this at once, plus his own shit.

It's normal to be overwhelmed, I think.

"I'm no good at this, you know. Kit Kat's way better," Oriel says grumpily. I recruited him to help get the room ready for our study session/dinner, and he begrudgingly agreed. It hasn't stopped him from bitching, though.

"Dude, we're giving him a second to breathe. I doubt whatever went on was serious, but we grew up knowing we'd have demon magic and shifting and all that shit. The doc has to trickle the stuff we learned as kids to him little by little. I can't imagine trying to comprehend it here from where he's from."

The dark haired crow shifter thinks about that briefly, then sighs. "True. He hasn't even seen any of us full shift yet—on either side. Hell, he hasn't seen *anyone* go total demon or total animal yet."

Oh, shit that's true.

"We should probably do that before this Games stuff ramps up, huh?" I say as I check my phone. The message from downstairs says the pizzas are here, so I forward that to Zav to handle. "I don't know if all at once is a good idea, though."

"Only one way to find out," Oriel shrugs as he sets drinks on the low table in the middle of our new hang-out spot in the living room. "Let's ask Kit himself."

"Ask me what?"

We both look at him sheepishly as he comes in dressed in the baggy sweats. After a few seconds of silence, I give in. "We realized you haven't seen *anyone* go full demon or completely shift. That's probably not good with the Games and all. Being shocked won't be good for your anxiety."

He pads over to his chair, tucking his legs under him as Dottie scampers to the arm of their chair. "You're probably right about that. I have all sorts of… ideas? But none of it is real until I see for myself."

Arching a brow, I walk over to stand in front of his chair, tilting my head. "Oriel thinks we shouldn't do it all at once. Maybe… one at a time? What would you prefer?"

Kit's eyes widen and he looks from me to Oriel then at the door. "Uhhh. All together seems like a lot. Smaller groups or one-on-one might be less jarring."

"How about now?" O says as he joins me. He flicks his hair off of his face, dark eyes watching my roommate carefully. "Salem and I could do one or the other before everyone invades. If you want, I mean."

Dottie puts her hands out, making a motion like we should scoot back as Kit just gapes. I chuckle, taking a step back from the two of them and O follows. Kit licks his lips, looking very nervous as he murmurs, "Maybe… um… show me animals first? 'Cause you can like… fully shift or half shift in both, right? So you're going to do that?"

"Do you want to see both?" I ask. "We definitely can do that. It might help ease you into the whole 'shifter' thing."

"Yeah. Okay. Um…" Kit sucks in a breath and blows it out, his face flickering between expressions until he hits resolve. "Do it halfway first then, um, whole. Just animals right now. I think I can deal with that."

"I'll go first." I step back again, shaking my limbs. "I'm pretty cuddly looking."

Kit sits his chin on his knees, nodding, and I let the panda come forward enough to expose ears, a tail, and then finally, an upright humanoid version. He gasps, putting his hand over his mouth as his eyes widen. "This is like an anime!"

At least, I think that's what he says… it's pretty muffled by his hand.

I give him a panda-human grin then nod at Oriel. "You go now, dude."

In a blink, O has shifted to his humanoid crow form—dark, feathered, sharp-eyed and with large black wings. "We can talk, by the way, but most hybrids can't in their shifted forms. In Hell, royalty or species leaders can."

"Like an alpha or something?" Kit Kat practically squeaks when he lifts his palms. "Those are the shifters who can talk?"

"Exactly," I reply. "Are you ready for the rest of the way?"

His eyes widen more, but he nods, swallowing hard. "Go ahead. I'm as ready as I can be."

Winking, I let the panda take over completely. My hands drop to the ground and my bulk gets bigger until I'm furry and muzzled. Since I'm bigger than a normal panda, I give him a second to adjust before I pad over to bump his hand with my nose lightly. "Still me, man."

"This is so *fucking weird*," Kit breathes as his fingers reach out to touch my big head. I tilt for him, hoping he'll get how much I like ear scritches in this form. Amazingly, he immediately gives me what I want and I make a satisfied sound. "Okay, go Oriel. No reason to keep me in suspense."

A squawk echoes in the room as Oriel seamlessly shifts to a crow the size of a large eagle. His feathers shine in the low light, and he slowly approaches KK from the other side until his free hands can touch the feathers. "I can be smaller, but this is easier to… you know."

"You can?" The new guy shakes his head, his hands touching both of us gently and I listen for the sound of his heartbeat to check his panic level.

Oddly, he's cool as a cucumber right now—that's a fucking great sign.

"Is it normal for shifters to be, like, bigger than the normal version of that animal?"

I nod, settling back on my haunches so he can look at me. My paws rest over my lap because having him pet my ears sent the bear into a bit of a frenzy inside. I don't want to scare him, but I'm white knuckling control. Since this has never happened to me before, I don't know how long I can maintain it. "Yep. Slash is like an enormous megalodon in the water. Truly terrifying."

My roommate unwinds his limbs, scooting to the edge of his seat to get a closer look. First, he reaches out to stroke his fingers over Oriel's wings, earning him a not-very-subtle cooing sound that makes me glare at the avian shifter. His shit is much less obvious if it's turning him on and I want to knock him on his feathered ass. "Soft. And it smells… familiar. Like… your scent is good, somehow. It makes my nose tingle, but in a good way."

Ignoring Oriel's preening, I wait until he turns to me. Kit scoots further forward, leaning in to scratch both my ears as he inhales. I grit my teeth, my eyes closing as he explores the animal form carefully. The bird may be pretty, but I'm cuddly as fuck and I know it. "You're handling this really well, KK."

"I… Well, I like animals in general. Zoos and shows… but I haven't gotten to be this close to many outside of occasional dogs or Dottie. So it's kind of cool."

If only we could show him what's really cool without—

"Well, well. Just what in the Wastelands is going on in here?"

Kit whips his head to the doorway to look at Jasper. "I…"

"Calm down, man. We thought Kit should see our forms before the damn Games," Oriel says, his sentence ending with an indignant squawk that belies his irritation.

"Sound logic, but why the secrecy?"

I look at Slash, shifting back to half-bear quickly. "Not secret. We thought of it while KK was changing, and asked him when he came out. He said we could show him animals tonight. So we did."

"Uh-huh," the Prince says as he barges in with a scowl on his face. "That seems like a decision we should have all been a part of, Salem."

Kit sits back, crossing his arms over his chest as he narrows his eyes at the dragon. "I think who I want to see shift or change or whatever and when is *my* decision, Jasper. You're the Prince of Hell, not of me."

"Technically—" Zavida starts, but quickly stops when the evil glare is turned on him. "Never mind. I'm going to deal with the pizza."

"Good choice," X says as he comes fluttering in with his books. "It's true that he's the caliphate leader, but I don't know what the gray area is for not having emerged yet. You're not fully a demon yet, so it's like there's a lot of toss-up situations."

"Stop helping him," Jasper says as he flings himself into his chair. The motion makes the floor shake a bit, and I give my best impression of a laugh in panda form.

He's definitely going to be picked last and he knows it.

"Guys, it's not a… 'favorites' thing. It was totally coincidental." Kit glances at Anton and X, then Slash, and finally, Zav and the Prince. "I have to see everyone's… everything… eventually, right?"

"Everything?" X arches a brow and the entire group laughs except for Kit, whose face pales. "That's going to be quite interesting, Kit Kat."

The embarrassment is clear on the guy's face and his eyes cut to his room, and suddenly, I get it. I know exactly what happened earlier and why he looks like he's seen a ghost now. Luckily, I'm in animal form, so my face doesn't give it away. Fondness floods me at his reaction, so I scootch my big furry butt closer and rest my chin on the chair. His fingers dig into the scruff of my neck and I make a happy sound.

"For fuck's sake," Jasper mutters. "If you let him do that, he'll be asleep before he does homework and eats. Salem, Oriel…shift."

Just like that, I'm human again and Kit's hands are in my hair. Oriel is kneeling on the other side, naked as me, but for the ink covering our skin. Kit gasps, pulling his hand back with a surprised expression. He points a finger at us, making a strangled sound then gives Jasper the angriest look I've seen on his face yet. "You *motherfucker.*"

Uh-oh.

When I look up at the guy, there's a ring of fire in his eyes that entrances me. I haven't seen this yet, but the Prince looks smug as hell. He must have known this would happen and purposely poked at Kit. "I believe that's *Prince* Motherfucker to you, mmm?"

"Not smart," Slash mutters as he trudges to the kitchen to help Zav.

"You could have warned me. I mean, I..." The guy goes from furious to calculating in an instant and I almost hold my breath as I wait to see what he's going to say. "Fine. You wanted it; you got it. Stand up and get dressed, you two."

I blink, looking at Oriel, who shrugs. We both stand, putting every damn thing on display for his eyes as we pull on our sweats. Kit's expression doesn't change the entire time, though the temperature in the room rises quite a bit. Once we've got pants on, he holds up his hand.

"That's good enough."

X snorts, putting their hand in front of their mouth to hide the amusement threatening to spill out. Kit shrugs, waiting for the others to get settled as our leader stands in front of him fuming. Zavida and Slash walk in with arms full of plated pizza, ignoring Jasper's mini-tantrum to hand them out. By the time they're done, Oriel and I are curled up in the same spots our animals chose next to Kit's chair and Dottie is munching on fruit.

"You win this round, I think," Anton remarks as he holds his slice up like he's toasting with it. "Kit-1, Jasper-0."

Considering the look on the Prince's face, I don't think that will last long.

Distractions

Since the other night, I've felt all the guys' eyes on me constantly. They were watching me before, but something about Oriel and Salem showing me their animals has intensified that. I get the distinct feeling more than just Jasper is grumpy about it, but I'm not sure how to deal with that. I'm fake dating them all, of course, but letting them show that side to me felt very intimate. I'm sure a bazillion people have seen all their animals and demons because it's normal down here. So I'm probably being super weird in holding off; I just can't help the niggling sensation that I have to be ready for it somehow.

Salem and Oriel have been nice to me from day one and it made sense to me that they went first.

Frowning at my notes for Human History, I doodle a little panda and a crow. Should I ask those two about the demon side before I move on? Is there some sort of protocol for this I don't know? It's infuriating to be immersed in this culture with only a basic understanding of how shit works.

I feel like Jane fucking Goodall in the middle of the apes. Not that the guys are apes or maybe there aren't ape shifters here, but…

A low, frustrated sound escapes me and I press my lips together quickly. Hopefully, Professor Alabaster didn't hear that. I'm on my own today because Slash had some random task he had to do for the Prince and I don't want to draw any attention to my distracted state. Alabaster loves all the eyes to stay on him; it's the demi in him, I'm told. He wants people to bask in his slightly gold glow as he expounds on how supernaturals, including demons, affected human history without them realizing it. The topic is fascinating, so usually it's not hard to focus.

But today, I'm struggling with wondering about my caliphate—especially the things Dank gave me.

I think Salem knows why I'm taking my potion medicine thingy, too. He's watched me add it to my morning drink without questioning it, but the careful avoidance of why tells me he has an idea. Luckily, I get that done before I run the terrifying shower gauntlet or get dressed in my room. No one else has witnessed me taking the draught and that keeps the curiosity down. I don't want to explain my visit to the damn doc more than what they've all assumed.

The demon anatomy pamphlet he gave me is more than a little scary, to be honest. There are variations by species, and they have… extras. I barely saw the one human dick before my incident and I certainly haven't sought out more examples so I have the internet to back up my knowledge. I'm not uneducated obviously, but there's always a difference between 'book learning' and practical experience. If I choose to… do anything… I'd be just as useless with one of those as I am with this shit.

It'd be more predictable, though; no knots, bumps, hooks, or odd variations to confuse the fuck out of me.

Putting my fingers on my temples, I rub lightly as I try to push demon cock out of my head to rejoin the lecture on Roman times. I'm interested in the fact that Hannibal's army had shifter elephants in it which explains their abilities that seemed out of the norm for the time; however, I can't stop the light panicking inside of me about this whole 'sex' issue. I know Dank said it will become more insistent when my powers do whatever, and that's frightening as well.

I haven't given a single shit about hot guys or girls or anything in that realm since the incident. It's like that part of me shriveled up and died. But… Being here, I noticed how gorgeous my new floormates were immediately.

My eyes find them to look even when I'm pissed and want to avoid them. I have odd physical reactions when they get close and for the first time in years, I'm not completely losing my shit when people touch me.

When some of them touch me, at least.

Maybe I'm healing? I don't know and I definitely do not have access to a professional to work that shit out so I have to do it myself. That's why I'm so obsessed right now; I don't have anyone to untangle this web with. Dank is a good doctor, but I'm not sure he's able to do the shrink thing. I suppose I can ask when I visit this Friday. He has something about avian and bear shifters for me, which is another pressure point. Demon dicks were enough for one week—though, I don't want to turn away his help.

"Mr. Camponella."

I look up, praying to whatever the fuck you pray to if you're a demon-possibly-something-else-hybrid to spare me. "Yes, Professor Alabaster?"

"Can you speak to what you learned about this period in your actual human school? I think it would be amusing to compare it with reality."

Oh, gross. I know why he's asking this; he wants to make me look stupid.

"Um, humans love to talk about the Greeks and Romans because it inter-twines with their Judeo-Christian mythos in some ways. Schools teach mythology, but compared to what I'm learning in Headmaster Darkstar's class, it's very watered down due to their lack of knowledge about us. They attribute polytheistic cultures as lower intelligence in a sideways fashion, and it's always through assuming people in the past were ignorant of things we know now."

Man, I hope to hell that's enough for him. I really don't want to become some sort of 'human expert' for shitty demons who hate us—and most of them do. Their bias makes sense when you realize they've been relegated to one specific view by the majority of humans due to organized religion, but it's a pain in the ass to fight off. Having to justify our species dumbassery is simply not my idea of a good time.

"Very true, Mr. Camponella. As you all heard, they're working with very slim information on the world and its development up there, which is why they are so easy to fool and manipulate."

Awesome. Thanks for putting that in their heads, teach.

THE REST OF THE DAY GOES FAIRLY SMOOTHLY AS JASPER DOESN'T JOIN US for lunch, and I have X, Oriel, and Salem to contend with. X is a bit less sparkly at lunch and I curse internally because I don't know if it's this damn 'show me your animal' thing or just an off day. None of them have said anything to me which I appreciate—it would feel a lot like pressure even if it wasn't intended to be. I've gotten a lot better at reading body language and emotional cues during the past few weeks, so I'm seeing things they don't expect me to.

Not that I'm an expert by any stretch; I still struggle with being confident about what I see.

After Dark Lit is over, Dottie and I follow Salem and O toward our dorm. It's comfortably quiet when I can't stand it anymore. Taking a deep breath, I look at Oriel seriously. "Are the others jealous about me seeing your animals? I think it's making things weird and I don't want that. But also… I don't know if just getting it out of the way is the best idea ever. I don't know what I want to do, but I know it's not hurt or upset anyone so… Give it up."

The crow shifter looks startled, then smiles at me wryly. "It's about time you asked, KK."

"Yeah, I've been waiting for this," Salem adds.

"Damn you both," I grumble irritably. "The tension is killing me. Tell me what to do to fix this."

A short bark of laughter escapes my roommate. "You can't *fix* it, Kit Kat. The animal parts of us behave like… well, like you'd expect. They're often possessive and snarly, especially when paired with our demon half. It makes us competitive, growly, and now, pouty because the animalistic parts believe you're showing favor. It'll lessen once you move on to the next person."

"What if I'm not ready to… move on to the next person quite yet?" I duck my head, feeling embarrassed that I have to be accommodated so much for such simple things. "I'm not, like, *scared* of anyone, but it feels really personal. So I want to be comfortable when I do it."

That statement earns me a bright grin from the gloomy bird. "Personal? Does that mean that Sleepytime and I make you comfortable enough that you were okay with seeing our inner bits?"

"More importantly, does it mean you'll give the demon halves a look-see soon?" Salem tilts his head, his eyes dark and intense as he waits. "Cause I'm gonna be honest, the dude is pretty excited about that for some reason."

Oriel glares at him, and I frown. "It's a legit question. Why are you giving him the death stare?"

"Because, Kit Kat, we shouldn't pressure you," the crow shifter says as we climb the stairs to Canto IV. "Telling you all the weird shit that goes through our brains might make you feel obligated."

He's right, but I'm not going to admit that.

"I can decide for myself regardless of emotions, you know." I lick my lips, not sure if I'm ready for the demon stuff yet. But if I'm honest, I definitely know I'm closest to these two guys. "I think... I can deal with the demons next. But I don't want anyone else to get upset."

Salem looks so excited that I won't even have to keep him awake. "My favorite form, KK, is half-way between panda and demon. It's sort of... in the middle. Like a combo platter."

"There's a... middle ground?" My hand flies to my chest as Oriel holds the door open and we walk into the dorm. "Jesus fucking Christ on a tricycle, how many things am I going to have to see for you jackasses?"

"He's being an idiot," Oriel says, then pushes the elevator button. "The halfway thing he's talking about is really the half shift form of the demon with a few additions. Demon hybrids are really weird, especially shifter hybrids. Something about how we're constructed makes it easy for us to fluidly change forms."

"Oookay," I say as I reach up to stroke Dottie's head. The action calms me a little and I breathe slowly for a moment, then nod. "Alright. This is just a quirk of who you all are. It's no different, in theory, than being double jointed or having a sixth toe. Right?"

The panda shifter looks at me doubtfully. "I'm not sure having an extra toe is the same as being able to change into an animal and it's definitely not as drastic. But.... one thing that doesn't change when our bodies do, Kit Kat, is who we are."

I look at him, my expression softening a little. "I know that, man. You're a good dude—all of you are, except for Prince Assface. Though, I suspect he's just... his own worst enemy more than anything."

"Truer words," Oriel says with a rueful head shake. He reaches for my hand, waiting for me to protest before placing it on his chest. "However, you're right. Nothing here is different when I have wings. I just look different."

"Your feathers are super cool," I admit. "And Salem is very cuddly looking when he's a bear."

"Pandas aren't.."

"I know, I know. But you know what I mean."

The bell dings, and the thieving shifter gives me a smug smile as he holds the doors open. "If you think we're cool in that guise, you *really* need to see us in demon form. It's much more impressive, I promise."

I know I'm being sold right now, but I can't find it in me to care.

"Okay. Let's do this."

DEMONS

Oriel

I can't believe that actually worked. Salem and I applying just a small bit of logic to the situation got KitKat to agree to see our demons. Both parts of me are more excited than I'd prefer anyone to know lest it make me less threatening to the masses.

But they're pretty fucking giddy.

Salem is damn near vibrating as we get out of the elevator, and he bounces to their door, swiping his card to get the door open so we can enter. His grin is wicked as he waits for Kit and I to get inside, then punches a code on the door to keep anyone else from interrupting. He's definitely as enthusiastic as me, and it's fucking weird because it's not like we're getting laid. This is just a 'show-and-tell' of the so-called monsters inside our humanoid bodies, but knowing that Kit considers it important makes it feel serious.

"Locking the door?" Kit asks, looking confused. "Why? Are you afraid someone will know I saw?"

"Fuck no," I reply as I drop my bag on the floor by my usual seat. "But Salem knows that they'll sense we're changing and come barging in to interrupt because they're tools."

Kit looks at Salem for confirmation, and he nods. The panda hybrid looks a bit shy as he adds, "I don't want you to be overwhelmed since you let us talk you into it, and we know that Jasper especially won't make you feel comfortable."

"I know. He's not doing it to be mean, I don't think, but his bullshit is so damn distracting." KK lets Dottie scramble down to perch on the chair arm, then puts his bag next to it. He's serious as fuck about catching up and he never goes a night without doing homework or studying before and after dinner. It's mind-blowing, especially since he probably doesn't need to worry about his scholarship now.

Our caliphate doesn't pay for this shit and adopting him cleared that obligation, though I doubt anyone actually told the poor guy.

"Do you care if I go change first? I have an easier time feeling comfy if I'm in my 'home' clothes."

Salem and I shake our heads. I strip my jacket off and hang it over one of the stools at the island. "Absolutely not. You should do whatever makes you feel safe because… demons are a little less cuddly than animals?"

"Speak for yourself," Salem says, winking at the guy.

"Good. Okay. Then I'm going to change and when I get back you can… do it."

Watching as he heads for his room, I turn to Salem. He's coming back from the fridge with a small snack for the kinkajou, and once he gives it to her, he joins me. The jacket is tossed and his bag is plopped by Kit's chair quickly so he can run his hands through his hair. He's more energetic than usual, especially at this time of day, and I get why.

He's really falling for his roommate and I'm not sure if he totally understands that.

Of course, I'm not sure *I* understand what's happening, either, but I'm at least aware enough to know there's something going on. The path to figuring this out starts with moments like these, though, because it helps Kit integrate more fully into this world and our lives. If he can accept the animals and the demons, then perhaps in time, he can accept the men beneath all the forms.

"Fucking shit, O, what is with the poetry shit?" I mutter to myself as I grab a drink from the fridge.

Salem stops his nervous tics and looks at me. "You talking to yourself now, dude?"

I roll my eyes at him. "Everyone talks to themselves, and if they say they don't, they're lying. But yeah, I was trying to tell myself that this is a good thing. I mean, I believe that, but none of us has it… easy? You know?"

"Money-wise, maybe, but not anything else," Salem agrees. "The families suck, everyone around us is either looking to use or top us, and we've only had each other since we were kids. I get it."

Arching a brow at him, I tilt my head. "Do you? Because this feels like a 'crossing the Styx' moment. Are you ready to become important to someone other than us?"

"Dude, I hate to break it to you, but we're already important to someone besides each other. Kit Kat is ours—Jas did the ceremony and it's done. But if you mean *more* than that, yeah. I'm not nearly as clueless as people think I am." He smirks as he rakes his hands through his hair again, making it wild and spiky. "Just because I sleep a lot doesn't mean I miss shit."

Fair enough, I suppose.

"Okay. Just making sure. Cause I—well, you know."

"You what?"

We turn to see Kit coming out of his room in the black Discordia sweats he likes to lounge around in. It occurs to me that he was moved here with very little luggage and he was *very* concerned about the outfit for the ball. *Holy shit, he probably doesn't have much outside of the uniform stuff.* That makes my eyes widen, but I don't say anything. I'm not going to make the kid embarrassed by asking. No, I'll just… figure out how to resolve the problem quietly and without a fuss.

"He was saying he was excited about this. It's like a… rite of passage," Salem says lamely and I have to cover my mouth to avoid a snicker.

He's really bad at improvisation; I should remember that.

"Oh, well, I'm kind of excited, too." Kit heads for his chair, flopping into it and sighing happily. "I mean, I don't know if it'll be scary or just freaky, but

I want to know. You guys are like… the closest people to me here and… I like the thought of knowing all the parts of you."

Maybe not all of them, but eventually, Kit Kat. Eventually, you'll see everything.

"Thanks for saying that," I say softly, hoping he can see how much I mean it in my eyes. I'm a means to an end to my parents—the thief to take their place in line with the crown—and besides the guys, the rest of our line could give a shit less. They're all just waiting for me to screw up to vie for my spot. But Kit doesn't give a flying fuck about our lineage or our money or any of that shit. He just likes us even though most people shy away from Salem for being weird and snoozy and me because I'm a spy.

"Who's first?" he asks, looking at us curiously. "And should I… like, expect anything big like flames or sulfur or something?"

I snort. "Not unless we're doing magic. I'll go first this time. Sound good, Salem?"

The panda shifter nods, standing a bit away from me to give me room. I take up more space horizontally in demon form than him, so it makes sense. Taking a deep breath, I let the blackness slip through me, making my eyes glitter with dark starlight and the wings unfurl from my back as the black color and feathers cover my form. In demon form, I have wings that spread out like an enormous dark angel and feathers in specific places. The deep pitch color of my skin makes me look evil, I know, but the real attention grabber is the long devilish tail with feathered adornments at the pointed tip.

"Oh, *wow*," our new member breathes as he sits up in his chair. His eyes roam over me, moving from foot to the top of my head where the u-shaped horns sit. They're black, sharp, and have feathers at the base. "That's pretty fucking cool. Can you fly or…?"

I nod, smiling in relief when he doesn't wig out. "I can. It's a lot like you'd imagine from some paranormal sexy book, I suppose. Big wings, taking to the sky like a superhero, but cooler."

My words make him blink, then he suddenly smacks himself in the forehead. I have no idea why but he looks like he's pissed at himself as he rubs his palm down his face. "Damnit. Why didn't I think of that?"

"Think of what, KK?" Salem looks confused, unsure if he's going to make it through both of us.

His face turns bright red and he shakes his head. "Nothing. I, uh, have been noodling on something for a couple days and I might have just solved my problem. It's nothing you need to worry about."

"You sure?" I ask, studying him carefully as I fold my wings in. "If this is too much, we can—"

"Nope. No, I'm good." He waves his hand dismissively and I arch a brow when Dottie crawls up to sit on his shoulder. "Salem, you go."

The big guy looks at me and I shrug. "He says it's cool, dude."

That makes him grin happily and he steps up, rubbing his palms together. "Okay, Kit Kat, here it comes."

Kit leans forward, watching closely as Salem transitions smoothly to his demon form. He's tall, muscled and his skin is black and white from head to toe. The crazy, spiky two-toned hair gets puffier, and his eyes turn completely white right before two rounded, knobby horns emerge from his head. They're demonic versions of his panda ears, we've always said, and his long, shaved poodle-like tail whips back and forth as he continues to grin at his roommate.

"Why is your tail… like that?"

I blink, then burst into laughter as Salem makes a fish-face. He's trying to figure out what to tell KK, but he can't give him the truth without freaking him out. His demon is *way* too excited about being out in front of Kit and that *only* happens when he's feeling frisky. I haven't seen it hardly at all, but teenage boys, even demons, are idiots—which is how we all know what little secrets we're all hiding about sex. "Yeah, Salem, why *is* your tail like that?"

His narrow glare slices into me as he rumbles in a dark voice, "Why does *yours* have feathers, Oriel?"

Shit. He's got me there.

"I have a feeling there's something I don't know and I'm pretty sure I can stay in the dark about it for now," Kit mutters as he frowns at us. "You're being way too cagey for me to take this at face value."

That's fine with me—I'm not eager to discuss demon sexual practices with him quite yet, anyway. It might be a discussion that's necessary later on, but I'd bet on the humanoid side being important sooner. Fuck knows we have to be careful how much we say before it seems important; I don't want to traumatize him more than he already is.

"Wanna see anything else?" Salem says as he moves closer.

I can tell he's damn near desperate to get KK to touch him like he did with the bear. My own demon wants it, too, but again, this is so much different than him petting two animals he recognizes. "Salem…"

"No, it's okay. I sort of… it's like I feel I need to?" The guy looks confused for a moment, his brows furrowed. "Something inside of me is pushing at me since he said it. Like I'm *supposed* to make it even?"

Whoa. Even I don't know what to make of that.

Salem is undaunted, though, and moves in a blur to kneel by KK's chair so he's not so tall and intimidating. The shy smile that comes over the dude's face is enchanting, and he reaches out tentatively to brush his fingers over the black and white skin on my brother's shoulders. A low rumble echoes out of his chest, and I watch as his eyes close to enjoy the sensation.

"So soft and smooth. Can I touch the poofy?" Kit grins and I almost choke on my tongue.

"Um, no. Tails are… very personal. Not… now." I say quickly, moving closer to distract the kid when Salem pouts. "But some day, I'm sure he'd love it."

"No shit," the panda mutters as he makes an annoyed face when Kit lifts his hand to turn to me. "Poof Blocker."

"Don't be gross," I shoot back as I mimic him, kneeling on the other side of the chair. Dottie peeks out from behind Kit's face, shaking a small fist at my friend and I grin. The kinkajou knows what he just tried to pull. "Okay, Kit. You're good."

He licks his lips, his hand coming out to touch the feathers at the base of my neck. "You know, I really like how shiny these are. Your demons suit you guys as much as the animals do, I think."

"Well, uh…" I'm having trouble with words, but when his fingers move to the horns, I lose all ability to form coherent thoughts.

We may have made a tactical error doing this alone with the door locked.

Touch Me

Kat/Kit

Oriel has completely stopped talking and I worry that maybe I took it too far. He and Salem are the easiest to get along with by far; I don't want to fuck this up. My eyes cut to the black and white demon watching us, and I almost choke. He has a long pointed black tongue licking his lips as my fingertips ghost over the horns and it makes me squeak in alarm. The sound makes my brain re-engage and I cough, pretending to clear my throat. I don't want to offend him, either, but the room seems to be getting warmer and my skin is tingling.

What the hell is going on?

"Um… I… if this is bad, I can stop," I whisper. "Just… tell me."

Salem's eyes droop to a sleepy, half-lidded look as he inhales deeply. "I'm not gonna fucking complain, Kit Kat. This is the best atmosphere my room has *ever* had. It's delicious."

Swallowing hard at the husky tone, I finally look at Oriel again, waiting for him to open his eyes. When he does, there's a sparkling blackness gazing at me that somehow calms me *and* makes the tingling increase. My gut does flip-flops as he tilts his head so his face touches my arm, then rubs his cheek on my skin.

"Both our demons and our animals enjoy tactile sensations immensely. The touch receptors in our bodies become hyper-sensitive in these forms," he croaks. The dark-haired shifter sucks in a shuddering breath as I trace the shape of the horns without thinking about it. "Some things are… more pleasant than others, but… it's not a bad thing. Rather pleasurable, if I'm honest."

"If it makes you upset or afraid, you can stop, though," Salem murmurs as he moves closer, dropping to kneel on my other side again. He's just within reach again and the look on his face mesmerizes me.

It's so full of desperate need paired with concern; I don't know what to do.

So I use the hand closest to him to touch the rounded horn on his head, eliciting a dark groan that almost makes me stop. When I continue to very gently explore their vastly different textures, both of the demons scoot closer, pressing their torsos to the outside of my legs. I wait for the terror to rise up in my chest, but it doesn't. Instead, the places their bodies make contact with mine feel like hotspots for sensation. I swallow again, trying to calm the frantic beating of my heart as it tries to burst out of my chest.

"Kit—"

Oriel is interrupted by a *bang* on the door that's hard enough to rattle shit on the walls. My hands pull away as I recoil, eyes wide with fear at the intrusion. I lick my lips as I lean back in my seat, my breath heaving from both the shock at the noise and the electricity in the air from my bold actions. Dottie scrambles off the top of the chair to wrap her little arms around my neck, chittering softly as I come back to earth.

"God*damn*," Salem curses as he rocks back on his heels. His demon fades within a split second and I'm left looking at the mussed hair and beautiful ink covering his torso.

I can't even think about what's below that right now; I'm too shaken.

"It's okay, KK," Oriel whispers as his dark eyes find mine. He's humanoid again, and his expression is very soft for such a sarcastic dude. "You did really well. I'm sorry some jackhole spooked you. Just breathe, man."

I don't have words yet, so I simply nod. Being able to touch them, even as demons, and have them touching me at the same time is a huge step. I'm not… exactly sure what it's towards because… they'll find out if I try to do anything more adventurous. But I haven't been able to allow that much contact from men for years, and I know what an attack feels like—everything I felt then was totally different. It felt exciting and unknown, but not scary.

"Salem, go murder whoever the fuck decided to spoil our moment."

The crow's gravelly order is followed by an indignant squawk and he claps his hand over his mouth, his face turning red on his pale skin.

I bite my lower lip, smiling a little. Oriel being embarrassed is somewhat enchanting because he's so dark and tortured and *serious* looking, but the sound made him almost shy. My voice is small when I murmur, "Probably you guys should dress first. I mean… they'll think… and I don't want you guys to have to deal with more scorn than the fake dating stuff already…"

The derisive snort comes from the kitchen and I have to bite down on my cheek not to make the squeak again when all I see is Salem's broad, muscled back and his ridiculously perfect fucking ass cheeks. You could bounce a goddamn *dollar* coin off that shit, and I have no idea how I know, but it's got to be a peak condition image. I force myself to look up at the ceiling, away from his beauty so I don't end up looking like a damn creep, but it's not an easy feat.

"I don't care *who* it is. We all know *why* someone tried to dent the damn door and I'm not inclined to move any faster because of their damn jealousy."

What? Jealousy?

"Why-Why would they be… jealous?"

Oriel's lips quirk up at the corner and he winks at me. "Because we're hogging you all to ourselves, KK. That's enough to make every idiot on this floor get a little cranky."

"I don't think—"

The sounds of Salem's heavy footsteps heading for his room make it much easier to breathe, and Oriel chuckles. "Oh, it is, even if you're not aware of it. Just… keep the last bit between the three of us, hmm? I don't want anyone giving you a hard time after the long day. We'll make some food and study, like every day, and none of the dumbasses out there have to know anything right now."

Nodding, I look at the door worriedly. "You don't want them to know I'm such a spaz, right? I get that."

"No, I figured you'd prefer not to spend the night hearing people grouse and grumble about their turns." His eyes stare into mine as he grins. "I'm not concerned about a damn thing that happened here with Salem and I don't give a shit who knows, Kit Kat. I just didn't want you to be distracted by pouty assholes."

I have no idea what to say about something that sweet; it's completely foreign. So I give him a tiny smile, then duck my head as he rises to his feet to fetch some of Salem's clothes.

These boys are going to be the death of me; I just know it.

By the time O and Salem opened the door, Dottie and I were in the kitchen, working on the dinner prep. The little private session was only about a half hour, so it's not that we started *that* late, but there was a palpable grumpiness to the group as we ate and studied. No one asked, possibly because Oriel and my roommate actively glared at their friends anytime someone opened their mouth. I disliked having the tension ratchet up, so I begged off early, going to my room with Dottie and putting my headphones on until I fell asleep.

I feel less stressed this morning, but breakfast was not nearly as fun as usual.

Mostly, I picked at my food until it was time to leave and stayed quiet on the trip to Curse & Hexes. I'm sitting on the end seat with Salem on my left, and Anton and Slash beyond him. The huge shark shifter looks displeased, but I can't seem to care. I'm still processing what happened last night—despite it not being bad before the loud bang—and I don't have the spoons to stroke anyone's fucking animal right now.

Dottie has stayed as close as possible, riding on my shoulder rather than in the bag, and she's watching every person around me as if they're planning to kill me. I appreciate it, but it's probably not the case. The guys explained why the others are being weird, and I accept that, but I just need some time to figure out *my* shit right now.

I can only hope the shit Dank gave me and the guys' ignorance of humans will last long enough for me to slowly climb out of my head. This is all me and my damn PTSD, and I already feel like a burden—I don't want them taking on my progress bar as their own. Plus, it only works if *I* get myself through the quagmire in my brain, not someone else. I have to own and face my fears in order to conquer them. It's been a torturously slow crawl over the years, but honestly? Being at Discordia has forced me to work harder and stand on my own two feet without hiding. It might be why these assholes don't believe in therapy; if you don't have a choice, you can rise to the top or let it sweep you under.

Kat Camponella is not *going to let the tides of Hell win this battle—that I can* guarantee.

"Kit."

Blinking back to reality, I look up to see Salem giving me a patient look. The panda shifter is holding off the other two demons, trying to give me space to get up and move towards the door. "Sorry. I must have spaced out."

Anton arches a brow. "Bad spaced out?"

"Not really. Thoughtful," I say softly as I grab my stuff. He doesn't respond, so I continue up the stairs with Salem at my heels. I know the avian is going to escort me to our next class, so if he's got more to say, he'll do it then. Or not—but I can't worry about that.

Fuck I sound like such a self-centered shithead, but I want to be able to handle all this so badly.

"KK, I gotta jet for my stuff," Salem says as we leave the hall. "Anton's got you covered for Mythology, then X will grab you before lunch."

I pretend to roll my eyes at him, but really, I'm glad he's being normal because I doubt I could deal with him and Oriel being fucking weird, too. There's far too much crap floating in this pool as it is. "Thanks. Anton, are you ready to split?"

He nods, looking at Slash. "Let's roll, Kit Kat."

I follow his rainbow hair down the hall, confused when he chooses to take the big stairs rather than the elevator. It's not a hard walk, but I'm not sure why we're doing it. His gait is quick, though, so I have to speed up to get even and when I do, he sighs. I press my lips together, resisting the urge to ask him what the fuck is going on.

"Kit… I'm not angry with you. Stop emoting so hard."

His abrupt command makes me scowl. "Sure seems like it."

When we hit the bottom of the huge staircase, he sighs, turning to face me as he steps in close. Anton's hand comes up, brushing an errant hair off of my forehead before he speaks. "I'm not struggling as hard as those with predators, nor is Xerxes. But still, it's difficult because our animals' dominant designation allows us to speak in that form and think—mostly—but it doesn't make them less animalistic as a rule."

"I mean, I've been told that, but—"

Anton shakes his head, clucking his tongue. "Don't interrupt me. What I'm trying to explain is that until the animal's needs are met, we *have* to be distant so we don't crowd you. That part of our brains is screaming, but it will get louder and harder to ignore, even for demons with considerable experience and control like us."

"I swear, I'm trying; I really am."

His smile is gentle. "I know you are. Everyone knows you are. Why do you think no one said a word about the distinct smell of demon sulfur in that room last night?"

"What? What smell? You're being ridiculous," I scoff as he jerks his head at the doors and we start moving. "I didn't smell anything."

"Then it's a human to demon thing because we *all* knew you let those two jokers show you their demons. Hell, they probably know we know and they're pretending otherwise. It's all to make you more comfortable, man. No one wants to pressure you."

Great. I'm even more of a fucking problem than I thought; just what I needed to hear.

OBSERVATIONS

K it was very quiet when he walked up with X, and it puzzled me. It's been that way for several days and I haven't been able to reconcile why he's withdrawn. The atmosphere doesn't feel adversarial, though I will admit the animalistic auras of my brothers is very high. We're all on pins and needles waiting for the newest member to tap us for 'inspection,' so the air is tighter as we keep hold of our inner beasts.

That is, except for Oriel and Salem.

Those lucky assholes are perfectly normal and perhaps that's irking me a bit. I know it's got Jasper wrapped in knots, not that he'd admit it. He's been fairly true to his word that he won't be purposefully mean, but he's also quite sharp when Kit isn't around. The little demon would wince to hear his random tantrums about things like that locked door. It's irritating, but I'm far less concerned about his temper when it's only aimed at us. The caliphate is used to outbursts and odd half-apologies from the Prince.

"KK, they've got a good spread today. Come up and pick it out," Oriel says. The dark-haired guy nods at my crow brother, taking his arm as they walk away from the large table to the buffet.

My eyes narrow as I track their progress carefully. That is my job and I was pleased with completing it; I do not appreciate the bird taking away that honor. Grunting, I shift in my seat as I wait for them to return. I'll get my own meal once Kit is settled safely. Perhaps if I see a treat, I will bring that. It might erase the tiny furrow that has been living between his brows since the first revelation of animal sides.

"Something wrong, Slash?" Jasper smirks as he arches a brow at me and I grit my teeth. I will not rise to his bait because he is hoping to hook me into his bullshit.

Shrugging, I lean back in my chair as if everything is perfect. "Not at all, Prince. My morning has been most productive. I can't help but wonder *when* they will give us more information and rules for the Games, though. This feels very slow moving, and that is not how my kind prefers to operate."

Jasper nods, looking thoughtful for a moment. "I find that odd as well. I don't know if it is a sign of something worse than expected or better. They have given me various required assignments for classes I teach, and occasional irksome demands, but we're still sitting on the edge of our seats in regards to the full spectrum of events and training."

"I'm waiting to see what they'll make us wear," Xerxes says as they wave a fried veggie slice. "You know it won't be the uniforms and I'll have to make a huge stink about what I can and cannot adorn myself with."

I snort. "It must be nice to worry only about your couture."

They give me a dark look as Kit and Oriel return with their trays. "Don't be a sour puss, Slash. My identity is very important to me. You know I had to tangle with Old Raggedy Cape to make concessions for the day-to-day uniform."

"Lucian fought with you about the uniform?" I'm surprised to hear the little demon speak up, but his face is screwed up in irritation. "That jackass can't do anything without punishing someone."

X gives him a brilliant smile, looking overjoyed that Kit spoke to him. "I can handle him, KK. Don't worry about little old me. I'm just irritated that I don't know what the problem will be so I can start strategizing."

Kit ducks his head, shrugging a little as he mumbles, "I think it's bullshit that anyone has to fight him about something as basic as clothing. But I didn't attend schools with uniforms before this, so I don't know how they deal with shit. I'm not very helpful in that regard."

"What *did* the humans wear, if not uniforms? We've seen movies, of course, but it feels more realistic coming from someone who lived it, shrimp. Go ahead… regale us with your human customs."

Jasper's tone is mocking and the poor guy's face flushes, though I don't know if it's anger or embarrassment. The sparks of fiery indignance he usually has are dimmed lately, even when our grumpy leader is challenging him directly. I'm not sure what the issue is, but I don't like it. I actually enjoy his disobedience and temper; it's fun to watch him go nose-to-nose with every-one, even me.

"Don't be dense. They wore normal fucking clothes: jeans, tees, sweats, whatever. The rules were only about stupid shit like cuts or length or holes… The rules up there are all rooted in bullshit puritanism," Kit fires back as he stabs a piece of meat with his fork. "Well, that and like, logos or words that people deemed not appropriate for school."

Human coddle their young far too much; it's weird as fuck.

"What a subjective set of criteria," Jasper muses. "It doesn't matter what the style is or how professional you look—only that you follow randomly selected rules about hiding your flesh."

"I didn't say they weren't stupid. The rules are always disproportionately skewed towards making girls feel as though they're bad for existing in their bodies. But that's the whole religion-based garbage, right? It's an epidemic of idiots up there." Kit wipes his mouth, shrugging again. "At least the bad guys down here are pretty identifiable by sight."

"So you'd assume…" Jasper smirks a bit, tilting his head. "But we can't always tell by sight, even in Hell."

That earns him a snort from the little demon, who goes back to his plate. Rolling my eyes, I look over at X. "Come with me to fetch the plates, Xerxes. We're wasting precious fuel up time debating whether or not demons look evil."

I probably earned the dirty look the Prince gave me, but I'm okay with it.

THE REST OF LUNCH IS UNEVENTFUL, WHICH I'M GRATEFUL FOR. KIT HAS A free period, which he and Oriel said they were going to the library during. I have History of Warfare with Octavian, and since he's been exiled to the school to teach in his old age, I know I can skip it. He's one of my father's acolytes and his presence here is specifically to ferret out those who might be nudged into applying to be in the officer ranks of Hell's legions. It takes a certain kind of persuasiveness to convince a demon from an elite family to slough off a life of excess at court to serve in the legion, but the old trickster is good at it. His exile is mostly a cover created to make his presence palatable to the academics who work here.

They get shirty about military recruiting in their hallowed halls of education and I don't blame them.

However, my father is crafty as fuck and has the King's ear at all times. He knows how to play the game right within the rules—mostly—without over-stepping, so the King looks the other way. There's a method to this madness, of course. It's much easier to convince the court that their precious children don't have to march for every uprising, than if the military was only filled with conscripted low-level demons. That means he can laze about like an indolent old fool more often than he actually has to do anything.

Skipping won't hurt my average a bit—I've been learning the shit these kids are being taught in that class since I could walk. My graduation here is about appearances, not necessary learning. So missing this class to do a little recon on the listless demon we're all orbiting isn't really a big deal. I let him and O walk towards the library building, giving them enough space to keep myself from being noticed, then charted my path behind them.

Oriel's skill at subterfuge makes this much harder, but I'm trained in this as well.

"There's something off and I want to know what it is," I justify to myself. "It is not an invasion because I am the second-in-command verifying the well being of my caliphate."

I'm not stupid; I know that I'm going about this in a ridiculous way, but I also don't want to confront the little demon and have him shrink further into himself. In truth, I'm not even sure if Oriel and Salem see the entirety of the change in Kit. They're happy he's including them and their beasts are happy to have been introduced. That's a hell of a drug, so it might be coloring their ability to read him.

"I see it, though. He's struggling with something and doesn't want people to know."

Shaking my head as I realize how ridiculous it is for me to talk to myself as I cross the quad, I keep a close eye on my avian brother as he and Kit move through the lunch time crowds. I'm not built for stealth, but I know how to keep myself from sticking out too badly. When they pause for a moment, I find a group to get close to, hoping to distract from my bulk. They look at me oddly and I give them a fierce expression that shuts up the one loud-mouth who squawks.

Idiots. Only a bunch of absolute fools would not recognize someone from the royal caliphate.

Kit finishes tying his boot, then they move on, climbing the stairs to the library annex quickly. I keep my distance until they've been inside for at least five minutes, then peel off from my gaggle of demons. Striding toward my target, I check the surrounding area before I ascend the stairs and go inside. I'm fairly certain O wouldn't leave Kit on his own, but he does enjoy being an ass by showing up in crow form in places he shouldn't be.

"Now where would they go?" I murmur to myself as I look at the diagram of the various levels on the wall.

The main hall is busy, buzzing with students as they gather materials and settle in at tables and computers. It wouldn't be here; Kit would hate this mess. Frowning, I look again and disregard the lower floors. After his incident, he'd only go down there if he had a specific thing to find in the ancient stacks. I think they went up, but I have to Sherlock Holmes my way to their location.

"Not the magical archives—Kit wouldn't be looking that up just yet. The floors with fiction are also unlikely; they will be busy and filled with demons looking for something to occupy their free time." My eyes scan the rest of the list and I grin triumphantly. "The floor under construction that has historical and religious texts. That will be quiet and mostly deserted, plus it seems to have an area by the construction that used to be a reading alcove."

Pleased with my detective work, I head for the stairs. It's not a long climb and I can't control who is on the other side of the doors if I take the elevator. When I exit the stairwell, I should be able to see through a window to verify my targets aren't within visual range. I take them two at a time, noting I'm getting cardio in as well, which is convenient. I like efficiency, especially when it's beneficial to me.

At the doorway to the top level, I peek through the window and note that I don't see either of my targets nearby. I slip in, making sure the door shuts quietly as I recall the layout of the floor from the map. Remembering the terrain is also something I'm very good at—I've been sent on many missions in the Wastelands to test my survival skills by my Father. My navigational prowess is superb, so I didn't end up getting lost while I fetched whatever bullshit he pretended to want. It is helpful right now and I hate thinking I should be grateful to the grouchy asshole.

Slinking over to the tall shelving, I make my way towards the alcove I believe they are in carefully. The stacks provide a lot of cover, even for someone of my size. I'm able to get close enough to see them huddled against over-turned furniture, sitting on the ground as they chat. Kit looks less stressed as he leans against the chair, and O is facing him as he leans back on his hands.

"They all feel so… cold and distant," Kit says as he picks at the weave on his pants. "Every once in a while, like with the clothes thing at lunch, I see glimpses of how it was before. But it's short and then they're all closed off again. I didn't mean to upset everyone by letting you and Salem go first. You're both just… you know. You were nice from the beginning and didn't let Jasper push you to be a jerk. It made it easier somehow."

Well, fuck. That explains everything. But what do I do about it?

Hot to Go

kät/kit

The time in the library with Oriel helps ease my tension *a lot*. He's a good listener, and he lets me ramble before he steps in to gently correct the wild thoughts my brain comes up with. By the time we get up to leave for Weapons & Tactics, I feel almost normal. The ability to spill all of this shit without someone judging is very similar to therapy sessions, and I really needed to say it out loud to process it. He just smiled when I told him so, and my heart did that fluttery skip as I get Dottie and my bag.

"What fresh hell do you think we're in for today?" I ask with a rueful grin. "I can't imagine Jasper will be any less cranky."

Oriel ruffles his hair and I'm surprised when I get an urge to fix it for him. His sigh is defeated as he guides me to the elevator, then hits the button to go down. "Who knows? Jas has always been mercurial, but he's worse since you arrived. You get under his scales and he has no idea how to respond."

Tell me something I don't know, buddy.

"I know that, O, but I'm not giving him a pass when he's a dickwaffle just because he has the emotional depth of a bagel."

The crow shifter snorts, shaking his head as the ding announces the doors opening and we get out. "I love the way you phrase things, Kit Kat. It's both amusing and fearless, no matter how much that isn't how you feel inside."

This time, I'm amused. Following him to the doors, I inhale as we step outside. It's weird, but the part of Hell we're in doesn't have gross, inferno-esque air. No, it's fairly normal smelling, even though we're surrounded by lava pits and fucking Wastelands. I assume it's magic, now that I'm thinking about it, but the fact that you could mistake this place for normal if you ignored the scenery is very weird.

"That hidden fear is why I make sure I'm recklessly confident on the outside. As long as I keep the panic and anxiety shit under wraps in public, people think I'm a ballsy asshole. It's a mask, just like the one Dank wears, but less literal."

He arches a brow at me, tilting his head in the bird-like fashion. "Do you wear it with us, KK?"

I ponder that for a second, then shrug as we head across campus towards the arena. "Sometimes? I find it easier to do so when the entire group is around. It's a lot of people and I'm still getting to know everyone. Plus, Jasper's an ass, so there's that. I don't feel like I have to do it when I'm in smaller groups or one-on-one."

"That's good. I'd be upset with myself if I wasn't giving you a safe space to just be yourself." He chews on his lip ring briefly, then grins a little. "I'm used to feeling like the odd one out because I tend to hang back and watch; it's in my nature and definitely my first response to any situation."

"Gee, I never noticed."

The huge building looms over us as we approach and I shiver. I don't like this place, but we got a text saying the entire class would be held on the field today. That tidbit is why I wonder if the Prince will be in a shittier mood than at lunch, but since everyone but Slash is in this class, he didn't expound. It made me glad Oriel and I were relaxing away from the fray for the free periods, that's for sure. Not knowing what the hell is going on is one of my anxiety triggers and these damn Games with their random announcements have kept a low-level of it buzzing in my head for weeks now.

"I'm not a fan of how they're dribbling info, either," Oriel says and I give him a shocked expression.

Did he read my damn mind? I hope to hell not.

"Get out of my brain box, dude," I mutter as I enter the door at the locker room entrance. "It's weird in there and I don't need any help from you."

His laugh is soft and he winks at me. "I'm not in your head, Kit Kat, but I can see the tension ratchet up when you think about this stuff. You get stiff and uncomfortable looking. I don't know how to describe it, really, but I know when I see it."

"Okay, fine. I'm concerned about the abrupt change of plans. It hasn't worked in my favor so far—remember the bruises and shit?"

Grimacing, Oriel tugs open the locker room door and we enter. The rest of our caliphate, minus Jasper, are already there, in various states of undress. I stop short, completely bojangled mentally, and O taps my shoulder.

"C'mon, KK, we don't want to be late."

Um, yeah. Don't want to be late while staring at the naked hot dudes, Kit.

Nodding dumbly, I amble into the room, heading for my locker like a zombie. I keep my eyes on the ground as I move, hoping the heat spreading over my limbs isn't as obvious as it feels. My stomach is in knots as I open my lock, toss my things in, and grab the athletic gear quickly. Dottie is hugging me tightly and I almost chuckle—she's determined to help me stay level and this situation is a challenge. Without a word, I scurry over to the bathroom, winging a prayer to the universe that they're all covered by the time I emerge.

Once I close the door to the bathroom, I lean against it, breathing hard. "What the fuck is with me? I've never been this weird around guys, other than the fear. I don't get why they affect me so fucking much. It's becoming really inconvenient."

Dottie chitters as she scrambles to the floor, then up to stand on the sink. Her big eyes look at me in concern as I shakily pull off my uniform and fold the pieces. I wish she could talk—even in my head would be helpful at this point, but that's a pipe dream.

"You have to get your shit together, Kat," I mutter as I jerk the sweatpants up and tie them tightly. "Who knows what's going to happen in this stupid class. You can't be drooling over tattoos and muscles and all that... girly shit."

If only my body would listen to my pleas, I might have a chance of surviving without making an idiot of myself.

"EVERYONE LINE UP!"

I look around the field, noting the demons I want to avoid at costs—like Roquefort, Chilton, Hoebert, and Furon—and my hands ball into fists at my waist. Salem is on one side of me and X is on the other, while Oriel is stubbornly posted behind me. Anton and Zavida are at the other end of our group, but they, too, look suspicious as the Prince yells. I feel like the energy zipping around inside of me is almost noticeable, but I know that can't be the case. It's just my normal bullshit making me feel like every part of my body is tingling. I had to leave Dottie on the bench because I was worried that we'd be actively sparring or something.

I don't know what I'd do if she got hurt or worse; I think I'd lose my shit.

"What's going on?" Salem whispers and all the guys shrug. Apparently, Jasper didn't tell anyone what the hell is going on—again—and that doesn't bode well.

"The gentlemen coming out of the tunnel are bringing you two Games uniforms. These were assigned based on the information the college store has for you, so if something doesn't fit, you get to deal with it yourselves. You may need replacements during the training or during the trials; that will be assessed by visiting the store to present what is left of the previous uniform for inspection. If it disintegrated, you will need to note that at the time of loss."

I swallow hard, considering what the hell I'm going to do if they reveal who I really am in the middle of this bullshit. That would be *very* bad and I'm going to have trouble sleeping for days now that I've got that image planted in my skull.

"Hey, Kit Kat. You okay?" X whispers out of the side of their mouth. "I felt a spike."

Nodding quickly, I keep my eyes on the grumpy looking dragon in front of us. I don't want him to focus on me when he's in this kind of shit mood. But no, I'm *not* okay, and I don't know when I will be.

"There will be events where your normal uniform is required, as well as formal events requiring specific types of dress. You should contact home to have your family's preferred clothiers on the ready, especially since some events may not be decided until close to the occasion."

Like, is he trying *to make me have a fucking panic attack? I don't have a goddamned clothier.*

"Calm down, KK. I can do most of our stuff, but if it's tight, one of us will hit up our family tailors," X says softly.

"Mine will definitely help." Salem looks down at me with a confident smile and my blood pressure decreases slightly. "Don't get twisted. This is normal crap for our world—at least, at this level."

"Yeah, I forgot you're all rich, spoiled assholes," I mutter, trying to work some of the anxiety out by shooting a retort at them. "My bad."

"Don't be salty," Oriel says as he leans forward to wink at me. "Our spoiled asshole selves will take care of you. It's our job now."

"It absolutely is *not*," I retort stubbornly. "You guys don't own me and I'm not a dress-up Ken doll. But… Thank you for helping."

I have to add the last part because I'm grateful for their help, but I struggle with feeling like a kept pet. Being a burden to foster parents for years has made me stupidly independent and so much here is outside of my control or purview. It rankles when I can't take care of myself, and I haven't figured out a way to address the inequality in a way that suits me.

"Accepting help from people who are part of your life isn't a weakness," Anton says mildly. "You shouldn't feel bad about it."

Easy to say when none of you need help all the fucking time, man.

"I'm trying," I grit out. "Give me time to adjust. My former life is still pretty fresh."

"Would the six of you like to share with the *whole* class?"

I blink, my head swiveling to see an angry dragon striding towards us. Resisting the urge to shrink back, I stick my chin out. "No, thank you. Please excuse our rudeness, Professor."

That's about as contrite as I can be; we weren't the only ones whispering, but he picked on our caliphate.

"Mmm. I'm sure you are, freshman." Jasper's eyes flash as they cut over the rest of the guys, then he looks at the line of demons with a narrowed gaze.

"Take your Games uniforms when your name is called. These students will have theirs placed on the bench, while they run laps for the rest of class."

I groan inwardly, knowing this is our punishment, but it's also something I need. I was simply hoping not to leave this damn class aching like I'm going to keel over, but alas, it's not in the cards. I'll be dying during Supe Law afterward with Zav and Slash. The former will share my pain, but the latter will definitely remind me that I need to work on endurance anyway.

God fucking dammit.

"Get moving, gentleman!"

The others follow me as I head for the track, all of our shoulders slump as we jog to our imminent doom.

Jasper Eversore is a real cocksucker, that's for damn sure.

Beggin'

Zavida

Poor Kit is run ragged, but he's not complaining—at least, not out loud. I was surprised by Jasper's interruption and more so by his punishment. Not because it's unlike Jas to be spiteful, but more because it was definitely aimed at separating us from the rest of the group. I'll ask him later tonight, when we're alone, and hopefully, he'll clue me in. I could feel his irritation spiking along our connection while he got the Games basic uniforms out to the rest of the guys.

Jasper seems mercurial and overly emotional in his decisions, but he's rarely reacting spontaneously.

X is sticking close to him, with Oriel and Salem following closely. It's interesting how quickly those two have attached themselves to Kit when they've never given a shit about much of anyone before. Something about the kid speaks to their isolation and even if Jasper can't see it, I get the allure. The guy has spunk and despite being essentially crippled by his lack of magic, he's willing to throw himself into the ring out of spite.

"What's on your mind, Zav?" Anton murmurs as we trail behind the others.

I bite my lip for a moment, not wanting to share my concerns without speaking to Jas first. After a moment, I shrug. "I was thinking about why Jasper sent us packing for such a small, arbitrary offense. I don't think it was about giving Kit crap; it felt like he was doing it for some other reason."

"He's been suspiciously tight lipped about the various bullshit the admin is throwing at him at the last minute. I thought it was about keeping idiots from suggesting we're getting preferential treatment, but that doesn't seem to be the case."

My brain takes off on one of its frequent computory adventures, and when it stops, I grab Annie's arm. "Do you think they placed a geas on him?"

Anton sucks in a breath, looking around us before he hisses, "Don't even suggest it. I'm not saying it's impossible, but if those fuckers know *we* know, they'll alter it in some way. Fuck."

Not even Lucian could do such a thing to the Prince of Hell without consulting the King, so our families will be of no help. Sighing, I let my mind wander again, knowing it's searching for anything in my mental database that will help us deal with this new possibility.

"I can sort of understand *why* they'd do it, given Jasper's place in our caliphate, but I'm not sure why he'd allow it." The peacock shifter frowns, tilting his head as his gaze focuses on his lover and the rest of our group ahead. "Do you think he was extorted? Perhaps they threatened to do something untoward during the Games if he didn't tell the King he was cool with it."

Me. If they threatened me, it would be easy to convince our Prince to bend.

"Damn it," I mutter in irritation. "They probably used me as their bait."

"Mmmmm, perhaps." Anton's voice is full of doubt, though, and he shrugs when I look at him expectantly. "Kit is far more vulnerable than you and we've all taken some level of shine to him. He would make a much better bargaining tool until his powers emerge fully."

My brother is right; Kit is tied to all of us through the induction. It weakens us all to have him powerless and our affection for him is just as dangerous. Lucian has spies amongst the student body, so he's certainly been told we're all 'dating' the new student he thought was a punishment. I'd be willing to bet he's pissed as hell and that's why Jasper keeps having to do dumb shit in our classes with him.

"This is not a good outcome," I say as I rub my temples. "Darkstar knowing what buttons to push before we even grace the field for trials means we have to work even harder."

"Perhaps that's why the Prince pushed the limits of our strength today?"

Sweet baby Asmodeus, of course it is. Slash said Kit needed endurance training.

"I think it might have gone down more smoothly if he'd said something to that effect, though." I shake my head, looking up at the sky as I regret not pushing Jasper harder to communicate before now. "Not about the spell, I mean, just a general statement that would have told us he was using the time to train our team."

Anton is about to reply when we almost crash into Oriel and Salem. They've fallen back, letting Kit and X get farther away in order to give Annie and me time to catch up. I give the huge panda shifter a dirty look; he's solid as fuck and I bruise like a peach.

"What's the buzz back here?" O says curiously. "You two are whispering like palace servants in the staff halls."

While he might be right about that, I hold a finger up. "I should probably remind you all that Kit will give you an immense amount of shit for saying stuff like that."

The crow shifter winks at me. "Probably, but he knows I'm a work in progress."

"True dat," Salem adds as he fist bumps the avian.

When the fuck did those two get so chummy?

"Whatever you say," Annie says drily. "We were discussing why Prince Asshat is even less communicative than normal—and we think we know why."

"Oooh. Do tell, bro," Salem coos as he bats his lashes. "Did the stick in his ass shift a bit and now he's even grumpier?"

I frown at the panda, rolling my eyes. "Stop it, Salem. This is serious. We think it's possible they placed a... enchantment on him. The kind that prevents... leaks."

Anton chuckles at my attempt *not* to say the real term lest it be overhead somehow. "Exactly. Though we have no idea how to test for it other than speaking to Jas very carefully and hoping he knows how to tell us without violating it."

"Anyone know how we're going to get one of the *least* talkative and proudest dudes we know to admit he let someone put a magical leash on him?" Oriel asks. When no one answers, he groans low. "Well, that's fucking super. Another day, another obstacle, I suppose."

It seems like that's becoming the norm, not the exception—which is not good news for people headed for death matches.

WHILE THE OTHERS HEAD BACK TO THEIR ROOMS, I MAKE A BEELINE FOR THE Prince's. I know he's going to be in a *mood* when he gets here and I want to make sure he vents his frustration before the entire group gets together. Salem took O to help him with our dinner because Xerxes insisted he needed to work with Kit on the new uniforms or something. I don't think Annie believed him, but he offered to pitch in on the food to give them time.

Hopefully, Jasper doesn't return with Slash in tow; I don't want to argue about how to calm the royal sensibilities with his general.

Closing the door to his suite behind me, I get to work. First I pour a Hellfire & Brimstone bourbon in his favorite crystal rocks glass, then I set up the room quickly. Jasper enjoys the classics more than fancy shit, but I've learned when to put a little more 'oomph' into the set-up. Today is *not* one of those days; no, today will be a quick and dirty affair to help him soothe the need for control that has been stripped from him.

So I strip, folding my uniform neatly and placing it on the chair I know he'll look at to see if I've followed the rules. Walking to the side table, I place the bottle of lube within reach before I set up pillows. I have no idea whether he'll be too far into his dragon to worry about positioning or not, but it doesn't hurt to have all his preferred shit just so. Sometimes, making Jasper happy as a demon, a shifter, a Dom, *and* a person is as simple as making sure his world lines up perfectly in private because it's chaos publicly.

I look at the virtual assistant on the opposite nightstand, noting the time. He should be here soon, so I drop to the pillow by the bed, getting into the familiar position as I wait.

No, it's not humiliating to be submissive, nor does this mean I enjoy degradation.

The door swings open, banging against the wall as the fuming dragon hybrid stomps in. He pauses when he sees me, his golden eyes pinging around the room until they land on me again. A small smirk graces his lips and I have to hold back a sigh of relief. That means he's pleased by the effort and I definitely wanted that to be the case. As long as our brief tryst bleeds the rage out of his system, our group dinner will be spared his fury.

"Zavvie," he growls low and it makes my entire body shiver.

Ducking my head, I put my gaze on his shiny black shoes. "Yes, Sir."

Another pleased sound escapes his throat and this time, I know the dragon is riding him hard. The sound of his jacket hitting the armchair makes my lips curve up, and I stay still as he continues his routine. This specific set of steps will help him with the feeling of helplessness and comfort me as long as I let it. Right now, he's unbuttoning his oxford and rolling up the sleeves; I don't have to see it to know what the Prince is doing and in what order.

"You poured my drink. Good boy," he rasps and my dick jumps against my thighs.

Jasper Eversore is terrifying when he's angry, but when he praises you? You feel it from head to toe.

"Thank you, Sir," I murmur low as I keep my spine straight despite his fingers drifting over my skin as he passes. He likes to tease, even briefly, to see if he can trip me up, but I'm used to it. As long as someone doesn't come bursting in here to break my concentration, he won't succeed in getting me to fuck up my standing orders.

Jasper chuckles and I hear the glass meet the wood as he sets it down. "You get better every time, Zavvie. Now turn around and suck my cock until I can focus again."

I spin quickly, settling in before I lean in and take his giant dick in my mouth without preamble. The Prince likes to grab my head and fuck my mouth hard, which he does within seconds. His hips buck as he grunts and groans, pushing in deeply so I'm drooling as I suck and scrape him with my teeth eagerly. I listen to every sound, savoring his pleasure as my own, but also to know what will help me bring him to the edge faster.

"Goddamn, you're taking it so well today," he mutters as his fingers tighten in my hair, pulling enough to make me moan around his shaft. That vibration pleases him and so he tugs again, snarling happily when I moan more. "I'm going to fuck the living shit out of you, my foxy boy. Would you like that?"

Fuck, yes, I would, especially if he's feeling this generous.

Of course, I can't answer, so I trail my tongue along the vein on the underside of his cock in response. He grasps my head hard, thrusting a few more times until I'm drooling and breathing hard through my nose. His dick ridges with the bumps I associate with his half-shift, and the shaft in my mouth gets bigger—a sure sign it's time for him to stop unless I shift, too. When the vibration kicks in, I suck harder, licking his hot precum eagerly until he finally yanks himself away. His eyes are blazing with fire in their depths as he spins me again, positioning me on the bed.

Hopefully, this is enough to calm his dragon before we have to meet up with others—otherwise, I'm not sure what will happen.

Devil Inside

kat/kit

X pulled me along to their room insistently once we were out of the elevator. I haven't been to the room they share with Anton yet—I've only seen Zav's and Jasper's so far. I'd find that odd, except that we now gather in the dorm I share with Salem, so everyone sort of comes to me. I don't know if that was by design or not, but it really does reduce my anxiety to be in my space.

But now we're headed for X's and I don't know what I feel about that.

"Um… X? What… Why are we going to your room?"

They huff in annoyance, squeezing my hand as they tug me toward their door. Once they press their palm to the reader, the door opens to what appears to be a picture perfect, magazine-shoot ready room in contrasting metallic hues of all colors of the rainbow accenting a white and a black room. It's not shocking, given what I know about the two of them, but I'm still gaping as we head inside. The door clicks shut behind me and that brings me out of my reverie.

"Hello?" I wave my free hand at them. "I asked a question."

X lets go of me, whirling around with wide eyes as he looks around, then at me. "It's not because you're… I mean. I wasn't saying anything because it's not cool, right? But then today with the uniforms, I realized that I wasn't keeping that kind of secret. Right?"

What the fuck is he talking about?

"X? I feel like you skipped a step. I'm not sure—"

They sink their hands into their hair, groaning as they look up at the ceiling. "Hecate, help me." Their gaze comes back to me, determined but kind. "Kit, I *know*. I mean, I sort of knew when you arrived but I thought… I thought I'd be crossing a line to out you and… I'm *not*, because you *aren't*."

Fuck. Fuck. Fuck. Fuckkity. Fuck.

Panic floods my system as my chest tightens and I lick my lips. I have to keep myself from keeling over or everyone will come running and I'll have to admit it to them all. "I… I … I…"

"I'm not going to tell, Kit Kat." X reaches out, grabbing my hand again and squeezing it to bring me back. "Don't start hyperventilating. But I needed you to know I know because… I can help. I don't know *why* you're hiding who you are, but… I won't tell."

I blink, swallowing hard. "You won't?"

They smile, shrugging a little. "I'd be a big fucking hypocrite if I decided what gender you are changes the person we've gotten to know, wouldn't I?"

I guess that's true.

"Not even Anton? I don't want him to be mad at you," I croak, still coming down from what would have been a major freak out. "That's not fair of me to ask anyone; I know."

"Kit, I don't know why you're doing this and you don't have to tell me. I'd like you to want to at some point and that requires trust. You need to feel comfortable enough with us to accept our animals and demons, plus let us see the real you. That's going to be interesting for sure, but regardless, it takes time." X grins as they hold up a finger. "But with all this shit coming, you need an ally, especially when it comes to getting the proper gear. So that's me."

"Oh," I say as it sinks in. "You thought I was going to lose it every time I had to have things for certain trials or whatever the fuck they make us do, right?"

X taps their nose. "Exactly. So in the interest of *not* having you pass out from panic every time, I realized it was time to reveal my knowledge. I figured it would help you keep your balance."

"What about Anton?" I press. "Isn't he going to be angry?"

"Uh, no. I often keep non-serious, non-life altering secrets that he pries out of me eventually. It's a game we play, so he won't be mad. This one, he'll have to get out of you, though." X pauses, biting their lip impishly. "But he's awfully good at it and he sees much more than people realize. He and Oriel are so damned good at that."

I nod, taking that info as I think about Xerxes' offer. "You swear you won't tell? Because I have to take that on faith and… I'm not good at that. I'll try, though."

They hold their hand out, pinky extended. "Pinky swear. I'd do blood, 'cause that's the demon way, but I think it'd freak you out."

My brows furrow as I hook pinkies with them, and I let out a long breath. "I need to get used to demon ways, X. Find something and teach me."

They blink, then move quickly to find a small dagger. X holds it up between us, their head tilted. "You sure, Kit Kat? Blood is a big deal for us, especially attached to a promise. Are you ready for that?"

"I think so? I won't know until I try. Should I expect some… big deal?" I ask curiously. "I only know what humans show in the media… about demon deals, I mean. I don't have a clue what to expect."

"Just us touching, the tingle and mingle, then a little bit of smoke and light show, but nothing big. You'll be okay." They hold up their palm, slicing it without even flinching. "Ready?"

Nodding, I keep my mouth closed as I give him my hand again. I'm too nervous to speak until it's done; this is so beyond my comfort zone I don't even know how to express it. "Okay, do it."

X slices my skin and the knife is so sharp I barely feel the sting. They take my bloody palm in theirs and as promised, a zing of energy shoots from the point where our blood mixes. My hand, then my arm, and then the rest of my body tingles like I've been shocked. I close my eyes, letting it work through me as he whispers, "As it is said, let it be written in the flames. The bond is locked and the oath will be honored until the end. *Sermo meus sanguis meus est; sanguis meus juratus est in æternum*[1]*."*

I really hope this isn't a bad idea; I don't know if I could handle being wrong about them.

Xerxes and I spent a bit more time getting measurements and talking about the previous Games before we headed back to my dorm. They felt I should be aware that the farther into the competition we get, the more likely it will be that I'll have to confess my secret to some or all of our team. The last trials had aquatic and survival portions that would almost certainly require them to make something special for me to wear—though I'm not sure what excuses we'll have to make to have that work. I also spilled the beans about the potion Dank is making for me until I emerge; it lifted a weight off of my shoulders when X volunteered to help me get refills so I'm not always headed for the doctor.

An ally who knows my secret other than a kinkajou who can't speak might be a bigger asset than I realized.

"I don't know if you've considered this…" they trail off, looking unsure for a moment, then sigh. "But most of the guys will take this with a grain of salt, except for Jasper. He's going to lose his fucking mind, mostly because he's been adamant that you're hiding something."

"Well, he's right—which he'll love—but not about what," I reply with a rueful expression. "I'm not a goddamn spy for Lucian *or* his father. I am, however, keeping a monster secret that's tripping his radar. I don't imagine he'll be easy to get acceptance from."

X wrinkles their nose. "Not for the reason you think, but yes, he's going to feel betrayed. Jasper is an odd mix of strategic logic and damaged heart. He'll know *why* you did it, but will struggle with feeling like he's been made a fool of. It won't matter that you had very solid reasons for doing this."

My laugh is dry as I nod. "Yeah, that's what I figured. But I *can't* tell him when he's barely tolerating me as a guy; if he changes his tune suddenly, it will become obvious that there's a reason. I don't want the rest of these jackasses at Discordia looking too closely at me until my powers emerge or whatever. Dank says that's for the best."

And I'm trusting the kindly old demon with my safety, so I hope to shit he's right.

"It makes a lot more sense now that you've sort of befriended him, you know."

I arch a brow at X as we walk to his door. "Why's that?"

"I don't know for sure, but I've heard that demons with his skills and experience are asked to forego relationships to ensure they are solely dedicated to the royal family they serve. He probably always wanted a daughter and you've… I don't know… activated that in him?"

"You think? Hell, I've never been able to get *any* of the stupid fosters to see me like one of their family members. I have no clue how I'd manage getting an ancient skull-head demon to do so." I duck my head, rubbing my hand on my chest as a fluttery feeling lodges there.

Of course, I doubt any of them could get warm fuzzy feelings about a guy with a fiery skullhead, either, so it was probably my fault we didn't connect.

"Aw, that's cute, Kit Kat! You're happy the crusty old sawbones likes you." X beams, reaching out to ruffle my hair and I'm surprised when it doesn't bother me.

Pulling back with a wry look, I scold them. "You can't do things that will tip anyone off that our relationship has changed suddenly. They'll notice and ask why. Get it together, man."

"Ugh, this is going to be so insanely hard," they grumble as we shut the door behind us. "I won't spill just because I know, but knowing and having the b-a-r-g-a-i-n will make me feel a kinship I can't express." The cobra shifter hisses in annoyance as we approach my dorm, waiting until I push my finger on the scanner to enter.

Somehow, they're even more adorable when they're pouting.

My skin heats in response, making me speed up my gait as I head for my room to change. "Wait here with the others, X, and I'll change for dinner."

"Kit Kat, wait—"

Oriel's voice almost makes me pause, but I know I have to be alone for a minute to calm myself. This was a *lot* of emotion and pent-up panic at once; I might feel okay with the pact now, but the danger it poses will catch up to me. My brain is racing with possibilities and I have to breathe for a few minutes before I can interact with the rest of the guys. Dottie scrambles up to my feet as I go in my room, managing to follow before I shut the door behind me.

Leaning against it, I close my eyes and suck in a long, deep breath then hold it. As my muscles relax one by one, I let it out slowly, using the quiet to gather the roiling emotions inside of me. I hoped to avoid admitting my secret to anyone, but I knew somewhere inside of me that it wasn't likely to stay hidden forever. I even considered telling O and Salem after they showed me their demons, but I resisted because the longer I'm here without a problem, the harder it will be for anyone to claim I caused a problem. If they can't say I'm a problem, they can't ship me off to Miss Mean Girl Demon Prep or whatever simply because I don't have a dick.

Gender segregated schools are such archaic bullshit, anyway.

"Just breathe, Kit," I murmur to myself as my heart rate finally starts to fall.

Dottie climbs up my legs, making her way to my shoulder so she can hug my neck tightly. I reach up to pet her head, smiling as the calm washes over me. The little animal is perfect for me and despite the way she fell into my lap, I refuse to question it. I never would have gotten through this first month without her help.

Hopefully, she continues to keep me just sane enough to get my demon side so I can survive even longer.

---

1. My word is my blood; my blood is my oath, forever.

Smile

Dinner after the weird Weapons class was surprisingly uneventful, and we all dove into studies along with Kit. Oriel and Salem eagerly helped him quiz ancient history facts and creature types at the end, which seemed to ease the new guy's anxiety a little with each correct answer. He really built a lot of his self-worth into his academic performance—possibly too much, though I'm hardly one to judge. My family doesn't approve of my artsy endeavors and the amount of control I need in my efforts and life to make up for it are hardly what Kit's kind would call 'healthy coping mechanisms.'

Yes, I've been reading up on their psychology shit in my spare time to figure out how best to help him; it's not a big deal.

While that time was uneventful, the next day also felt like it was fairly calm, too. Admittedly, I don't have shit with Kit on Monday and Wednesday, so I barely see him until dinner and study time. He's so serious during that time, helping Salem cook and working on both current assignments and catch-up that it's hard to get in time for anything else. That is, unless someone like Jasper causes a fucking issue and then we spend an inordinate amount of time untangling his mess.

Today, though, is one of the two week days where I have a chance to get closer to our new member. Despite X playing our hidden secrets games, I'm focused on gleaning whatever moments I can with Kit so he feels comfortable enough to ask to see one of my shifts. My bird and my demon are pretty insistent about it, as I imagine the others' inner beings are, too. I suspect he's seen Oriel and Salem's demons because they have this very smug, settled air about them.

The fuckers aren't saying anything, though, just like Xerxes isn't giving me hints about his newest mystery I need to solve.

Sighing as I exit our shared room, I scratch the back of my neck. When I'm restless, my bird likes to bring my feathers just under my skin, making it itch like crazy with little relief. I've been sitting on that for days now, white knuckling the irritation under my calm guise. I prefer *not* to show anger outwardly unless necessary, and that has kept me safe from my mother. She's the tyrant in my family, and the Aldaric matriarch's rage phases are well known within the royal court. My research project suggests humans would call her bi-polar, and I'm inclined to agree.

"What's wrong, babe?" X asks as they leave our dorm and join me by the elevator.

I shake my head. They don't need to hear my musings about my mother every time my past rears its head. My pride won't allow me to be that weak or vulnerable constantly and it's absolutely an inherited trait of our demon line. "Nothing. I got lost in thought as I so often do."

Xerxes squints, his head rearing back a bit, then bobbing in that very cobra-esque manner that tells me they don't believe me. Their thinking posture is directly linked to their animal and it's a tell anytime they're studying you if you know to look for it. "Annie, you're a terrible poker player. Why do you always think you can fool me? That's your 'my family sucks ass' face and I certainly know what it looks like."

Damn it, that works both ways, I guess.

"Yes, I was thinking about Anastasia." My expression sours and I wave my hand. "But I'd prefer not to. Aegon is no better, but at least he's simply neglectful and distant. That is easier to handle."

"It does more damage than you think."

My eyes snap to Kit as he and Salem leave their room to join us. The kinkajou is perched on his shoulder, looking at me as if it can read my thoughts. Obviously, it can't, nor can it talk to Kit Kat, so I'm probably safe to recognize that his hair is getting a little longer and flops adorably in his eyes. Blinking as I turn back to the elevator, I shrug. "I'm very accustomed to that particular facet of my childhood. It's not a concern anymore. I expect him to fail and he never disappoints."

"Yikes," Kit mutters. "Talk about avoiding your issues, man. That shit will eat you alive; I know it for sure."

"Demons have excellent compartmentalization skills," I reply nonchalantly. "Ask X. They know what I mean. Hell, even Salem does."

Salem groans, and I imagine his big frame wilting as I bring him into the crossfire. "Ugh, Anton, it's fucking seven a.m. Could you not?"

Xerxes saves the panda by interjecting, "We do, KK. It's part of the divide in our minds with the demons and shifters for us, I think. I suppose that seems weird to you because of all the head shrinking, but Annie is telling the truth."

"Mostly," Salem mutters. "Not that *seven a.m.* is the time to start some bottom of the pits discussion about demon psychology. It's a goddamn travesty to do this shit before we eat."

"Salem, it's always a little before you eat," I shoot back. "When can I broach anything with that kind of schedule?"

Kit snorts, and I turn to see him covering his mouth with his hand. The look on his face is joyfully amused and I feel the preening bird inside of me react to causing his mirth. "He's not wrong. You really do eat and sleep a lot."

"I'm a *panda*, assholes. That's like ninety percent of their life, minimum."

"*Guys.*" We all look at Zavida as he walks down the hall with Slash and Jasper behind him. "We don't want anyone overhearing this, even from the elevator. Unity, right?"

I roll my eyes at the kitsune. "Zav, we're just bickering like friends. No one will think I actually have a problem with Salem's natural behavior other than having to keep his ass awake in class."

"Even so, be more cautious. Though, I approve of whatever you did to make the shrimp look happy to be tagging along with us. That will sell our deception if we can do it more often."

We probably could if you'd quit pissing him off, you dickbag.

But I don't say that, only nod, and the elevator doors open to take us down for breakfast.

Today's goal is to repeat whatever I did to make Kit smile—mission accepted.

"OUR GRACIOUS ADMINISTRATION HAS ASSIGNED NEW TASKS FOR YOU TO work on for your Games trials. The curses, spells, and hexes on this sheet have been deemed *essential* to your survival. Before you ask, *no*, I don't have the slightest inkling why they are highlighting these incantations."

Wormwood gives us all an imperious look as he shoves the printed copies at a demon in the first row. I don't know the guy, but I absolutely get why he's scuttling up the rows to get away from our professor. The mage/dhmapir's temperament is notoriously unpredictable and he doesn't look happy in the slightest. When the dude finally gets to the back row, the sheets make their way from guy to guy until they reach me.

I'm interested in knowing why this is printed rather than being sent electronically—as most things at Discordia are.

I take the remaining copies and pull one loose, passing the rest to Kit. My brows furrow as I look over the tiny print that covers both sides of the paper. "Motherfucker... this is—"

"Insane," Kit whispers as he gapes at it. "I can't do *any* magic, much less learn hundreds of these things before the random day they announce the start of this thing."

The tension in his frame is palpable and I drop one hand from my copy, placing it on his arm. "We'll be okay, Kit Kat. All things in time, right?"

"But we don't *have* time!" he hisses.

Since he didn't pull away, my bird preens again and I have to focus my eyes on the lengthy list of magic. I don't see anything particularly offensive on the front of the page, but that doesn't mean anything. There has to be a reason why Wormwood did it this way, and I need to figure out why.

"Anton. The back. In the middle."

As usual, Slash is a demon of few words, but they're important. I flip the paper, scanning the list there until my eyes widen. Smack dab in the center, there are at least ten forbidden incantations. "Holy shit."

"What? What's going on?" Kit asks as he peers at the backside of his list. "I know I'm behind, but you guys can't hold back like this."

"Settle, KK," Salem says as he leans forward, peeking around Slash's bulk. "Anton will explain. He's better at this shit than us big dudes."

I roll my eyes at him, then turn back to the panicking new kid. "This list is mostly inane, but several of the spells on the back are classified by the crown as forbidden. I know that sounds weird because we're demons."

Kit snorts softly, leaning into my arm to look where I'm pointing on my paper. "Why are they forbidden?"

"Because they're difficult to accomplish, require a *lot* of power, and helped the current royals win the Games and the following war."

Slash grunts, shifting in the chair with a disgruntled look. "Several of the court royals used them. My father is more… aggressive with his magic—up close and personal. He and the King were not so subtle in their actions in those events. Spells like this are intended for less physical demons."

"So the other family heads, then?" Kit asks as he frowns. "Your parents, Anton?"

"Surely my mother. Probably X's father. Salem's parents would have been somewhere in between. Zav's would have been focused on other things. Definitely Oriel's folks," I respond slowly. "But given that it was not chronicled—purposefully—it would take someone with very intimate knowledge of the coup to put these here."

Like Lucian fucking Darkstar.

"What happens if people use them?"

I look at the nervous looking guy, squeezing his arm again. "It's basically treason, but who the fuck knows what the King would do. His moods are mercurial and he hasn't had anyone stupid enough to challenge the court in centuries."

"My father would kill them after many, many, *many* years of torture." Slash doesn't elaborate, but I have no desire to ask him to. "And they would feed the pieces to the beasts in the Wastelands."

"Well, that's not terrifying," Kit grumbles. "Thanks, big guy. I feel much better now."

Slash gives him a toothy grin and surprisingly, it doesn't seem to upset the kid. In fact, he looks pleased as hell and I have no idea why. Filing that away for future analysis, I pinch the bridge of my nose and sigh. "I don't know what their game is, but we can assume we know who is behind shoving this shit into the curriculum."

"That dickhead," Salem mutters. "As if death games aren't bad enough, he's going to have all the wanna-be competitors using this shit to come at us. You know that's why those spells are on here."

Nodding, I turn to Slash. "You need to figure out how to counteract this shit. The only two people who can ask those questions without raising suspicion are you and Jasper."

"He cannot."

Kit looks at the shark shifter curiously. "Why?"

"Besides pissing his dad off at the ball, Jasper has never been known to accept his father's advice or pay attention to his stories. It will raise eyebrows." I give the kid a little smirk and he flushes bright red when he realizes he was part of that little issue.

"It was good for him. Do not be worried."

"How was that good for him, Slash?" Kit Kat says softly. "It felt good at the time and I think Jasper was happy to stick a fork in the King, but now… It's hampering our ability to gather information. Or, that's what it sounds like to me."

Salem chuckles, shaking his head. "That may be true, but I bet Prince Pissy-pants hasn't enjoyed a party that much in *years*."

I can't dispute that, but I'm not sure if it was worth it yet. Only time will tell.

Bad News

After the revelation in Curses & Hexes, I went to Mythology with Anton, Zav and X. Luckily, the Headmaster was too busy smirking about the shit that was announced in Curses to bother my caliphate. He started the unit on the Egyptians and the creatures that are tied to their mythos, dimming the room for a long ass slideshow that definitely would have put Salem to sleep. I ate it up because I've always loved this topic and without him taking aim at me, it was easy to get lost in the new spin on this culture. The guys let me soak it up, taking notes and occasionally whispering questions, which calmed me a great deal.

Jasper didn't show for lunch—a bad sign in my opinion—and we filled Oriel in on the magic bullshit from the early classes. As is becoming our habit, Oriel and I headed for the library to have quiet time so I can balance myself by getting lost in books and studying. It's been my escape for a long time and his willingness to let me silently hyper-focus on it rather than talk all the time is more helpful than I can express.

But all good things come to an end, and we're on our way to the arena for Weapons class again. Since the Prince was absent at lunch, I assume this is going to be a shitshow—again. Whatever Darkstar is hoping to achieve in these Games is being very quietly woven into the pre-Games curricula and the physical classes are taking the brunt of that agenda. I don't think the dragon will be in a good mood and I'm ready for it.

I think.

"You okay, KK? You've been super quiet, which I get because of the 'forbidden spells' thing, but…"

I blink, jerking back to reality at O's low voice. "Um, yes. I mean, yes, I was quiet because I'm processing the spells shit, but also, I'm okay. As much as I can be knowing that people in these stupid games will be using spells intended to kill on the spot or cause such insurmountable pain that even demons commit suicide if hit with them. That's a pretty big deal."

"So…" Oriel sighs as he runs his fingers through his beautiful, shiny black hair. "The deal with those spells is the caster has to be strong enough to support the magic. That's true of all magic, right? If the person trying to use the spell isn't strong enough magically, it's a bit like a tiny person trying to lift a huge barbell. Are there people skilled enough to use them outside of our caliphate? Probably. But not as many as making them part of the training would indicate."

My eyes narrow as I squint curiously. "Are you saying a lot of demons here will *try* to use them, but like, fizzle out or something?"

He nods, looking serious. "Very likely. This isn't a human movie; everyone who is magically gifted isn't equal. They can't just use any incantation they read without fail. Plus, magic follows intent as well, and to be honest, a bunch of these clowns won't have the needed intent those big spells require."

"They don't want to kill or torture, so it won't work right? Is that what you mean?" I ask as we head across the main quad.

"Yep. They might *think* they want to because it's what's expected, but magic is more complex than that. It's intuitive and very personal; someone doing it because they think they *have* to is less likely to be successful."

Well, that's somewhat comforting. I still need magic training, though.

"What do we do about me not having any magic? How can we… goose it or whatever?"

His chuckle rumbles over me even from the short distance between us. "We can't force it, Kit Kat. That's not how it works. But we can practice the physical and mental process with you privately—Slash would be your guy for that. Magic Battles is what he *lives* for."

"Damn it. That's what everyone says," I pout as I kick at an invisible rock in my path. "I don't want to ask him. He's still being weird from this weekend."

Oriel smacks my arm lightly. "Don't be a chicken shit, KK. The big guy never turns down a chance to kick someone's ass in the ring, but also, he's fond of you."

He is?

"Don't look so surprised. Slash's love language is being a bossy dick about the shit you need to do. Do you know how often that idiot tells me to clean my nest? I mean, I know I need to, but my crow prefers a hoard." Oriel shrugs and winks at me. "Sometimes, I listen; sometimes, I don't."

I don't know what to make of that statement, so I duck my head, looking at the dark cobblestones as we make our way to the arena. It's hard for me to accept that anyone likes me, much less is watching out for me because they want to. Having people pretend to do it because they've been instructed to —that's normal. But choosing to is something totally different. I have no idea how to feel about it nor what I'm going to do about approaching the huge demon.

"Oh, man, now I made it awkward. Shit."

Feeling the heat on my face, I look up at Oriel with a shrug. "Well, I'm just a fucking mess all the time, man. I don't know how to take compliments or praise well, much less accept that people give a shit. I'm working on it; I swear."

"You don't have to apologize or make excuses, KK. Most of us have wised up to your quirks and we know how to let you have the space you need to work through unfamiliar emotions." Oriel winks at me and I mutter something incomprehensible, making him laugh. "Man, you're an awkward little turnip when you get shy. It's fantastic."

Great. Awkward turnip is exactly what I was aiming for with these guys. Awesome.

"LISTEN UP, WASTES OF SPACE!"

Salem shifts next to me, looking remarkably awake for four in the afternoon. He shoots a look at Oriel and I watch as that gesture moves down the line of the guys until it stops at Zav.

That's a bad sign.

"Today, we're going to enchant our weapons with *basic* spells to increase their strength. This is a precursor to actual magic battles, so you want to ensure that you're using this time to get your feet under you if you are not used to this kind of fighting." Jasper's eyes are dark as they bore into me, and I swallow hard. "It will only get more demanding and more dangerous from today forward."

"Fuck, fuck, fuck," I mutter softly as my body tenses up. I'm the only one in this room without a lick of magic and now they're all going to know. It will make my life a bazillion times more dangerous than it was prior to this class. If anyone suspected before, it was a rumor that remained unconfirmed since the guys stay with me nearly every second of every day.

"Kit Kat, it's going to be okay," Salem mutters under his breath. "We knew this day would come and we've got a plan."

My eyes widen, and I whirl around to look at Oriel. "You have a plan?"

His dark eyes glitter with that mischievous intelligence I associate with his crow. "We do. Anton came up with it. Slash isn't sure it will work, but he's only used to up-close-and-personal magic battling. Those of us who are made for stealth or long range attacks have different ideas about how to 'fake it 'till you make it' in this aspect."

Licking my lips, I take a slow, deep breath, nodding once I can move again. "Okay. What do I have to do?"

Xerxes peeks around the avian shifter. "First, you pick a weapon, KK. Once you do, come see Annie and me. We're step one in this gambit."

"Do you have something to share with the class?" Jasper's voice is booming as he interrupts our discussion and I shake my head quickly. We don't need him flipping out on me and I have no clue if the guys told him about this so-called 'plan.'

"No."

His brow raises when I don't add a snarky comment, but he recovers quickly. "Fine. Then all of you head for the practice armory and select a weapon you feel most comfortable with. For this assignment, there are *only* blunted and tipped weapons available. If I catch anyone circumventing that precaution like before, you will fail this class for the semester and be unable to continue the Games prep in an official setting."

Wow. He means business; that means he suspects something will go very wrong.

"It will be okay," Salem says as he nudges me toward the armory area. "Just pick what feels the most comfortable, Kit Kat. Focus on the now, not what might happen."

I snort as I look at the rack of shit I can't identify, passing that up as too advanced for me. Oriel nods sagely, but he grabs a gnarly looking bladed thing that looks remarkably like a Klingon bat'leth. "You are a complete nerd, " I mutter to myself as I wait for Salem to grab a long wooden staff thing that might be a demon-sized bo.

"What did you say?" Anton asks as he gestures for me to continue looking with him as the other two peel off.

"Nothing," I reply as we head into more familiar looking territory. I don't think I have the arm strength for a mace by any stretch, but they're cool as fuck looking. "I was just grumbling."

X gives me one of their bright smiles. "No need to grumble, Kit Kat. There's plenty of choices."

Yeah, for people capable of handling these damn things or imbuing them with magic—I'm royally fucked on both counts.

"It's intimidating when you're smaller like us," Zavida says as he comes up behind me.

Noting Anton picking up a large bow and quiver, I sigh. "It's not entirely size, Zav, and you know it."

He nods, guiding me me further down the line of weaponry. "I do. However, size and strength and even magic are never a match for brain power, even in Hell. Jasper protects me because he wants to, but if I had to, I could outwit people who came after me. Letting him feel as though he's keeping me safe is part of our dynamic."

I know what he means by that and the images make my stomach tighten.

"I, uh…" I feel the flush creeping up and curse under my breath. I've never in my life spent more time blushing like a regency socialite until I got here and had to deal with these assholes. I fucking hate it, but I know it's because they affect me more than anyone ever has before. "Um, well. That's… comforting to know?"

Zavida winks at me, then gives me a shy smile. "I know I'm still earning trust, but I think honesty is probably the only way to get it. Sometimes, that might be a little much because I'm not good with shades of gray."

"I get that," I respond earnestly. "People are a pain in my ass to figure out sometimes."

He chuckles, nodding at Xerxes holding up two handfuls of what look a lot like throwing stars but in an odd symbol-shape I don't recognize. "See? X loves to use magically enhanced talons. That doesn't require a lot of physical strength—though endurance is a thing—and like you, they don't want to engage in close range combat."

I frown, tilting my head. "But I'm good at close range fighting."

Zavida shakes his head. "You're good in this setting where people aren't allowed to fight full-tilt dirty. We won't know how your skill matches with your PTSD and anxiety in the real setting until it happens, Kit. We have to develop some long range options."

Fuck, he's right.

Sighing, I look at the remaining weapons again. "Well, I'm going with the throwing knives then. Light and in multiples to give me at least twenty-one feet to have other options, if someone has a short range projectile weapon."

"Kit, that statistic only applies when demons *aren't* using magic to enhance their weapons," Zav whispers. "You gotta ditch *everything* you know from the humans about fighting. Demons and hybrids have options you never dreamed of. Start from the beginning and assume anything in the universe is possible."

Before I got here, I would have loved to hear that phrase; now it makes my ass clench.

Desperate Measures

I don't like this one fucking bit.

My lunchtime routine was disrupted by that slimy little shit, Beccarus, who came to my office as I was leaving for the *Triclinium* to join my caliphate. He stood there looking smarmy and pleased with himself as if being associated with Darkstar somehow made him more than a lesser demon I could crush with one hand. When I finished reading, he held up a hand, daring to stop me from speaking to inform me that the contents of the missive were non-negotiable.

The instructions called for me to stay in my office and prepare for this new lesson, which means I'm hungry as fuck and four times as angry. But I'm doing the best I can not to let it seep through when I'm dealing with my brothers, especially the newest one that I promised to be less mean to. It's difficult not to wield my fury like a weapon when everything I've ever learned in my life has taught me that's an acceptable way to burn off the fire in my gut. Emotions like this make my dragon yearn for the sky and destruction, something I could give into at home, but not at Discordia.

Now that everyone has their goddamn weapons, my dragon is even more disgruntled as I look out at the class. I can feel the burning in my eyes that tells me he's struggling with my demon for control. I can't let him have it because not only is my dragon form *not* compatible with a classroom setting, he also hates damn near everyone in this realm other than my caliphate. Since the shrimp hasn't met him yet, I have no idea how that will go and I sure as fuck don't want it to be a public affair.

"Jasper?"

My frustrated musings are interrupted and I whirl around to roar, but I see Zavvie standing there giving me an understanding expression. Trusting my caliphate to protect me, I give the students my back and look at my kitsune. "I don't want to do this. It's going to go badly."

Zav rakes his hands through his messy red hair, nodding. "I know. But… it's clear you don't have a choice. So do what you have to and we will do what we can to mitigate it."

The anger of my shifter flows through me as I tip my head up to the sky and gather myself. When I bring my gaze back to Zavvie, I wink, then growl, "Get back in line. We have shit to do!"

He knows I'm playing a role more often than not, so he won't take my ire poorly.

I watch as he scurries back to the cluster of demons surrounding Kit, waiting for them to get settled before I stride across the front of our practice area. "We will start by warming up with your chosen weapon. The list of groups is on the board over there. I want you all in your groups within two minutes or you'll be running laps with the weapon you picked. For some of you, that's going to suck."

A chorus of groans echoes through the air and I grin, feeling the vicious pleasure of my beast at their pain. It takes away from the gnawing irritation I feel about having to follow orders given by an idiot like Lucian or the fact that this exercise was designed to cause problems. The groups were assigned via the administration and it was clear they purposefully put demons who would naturally be in competition with one another together for their fights. It's not just Kit who is in danger; no, my other brothers will be pitted against people they shouldn't be.

"Get moving!" I bark as they all grumble at the assignment board. "I said *two minutes.* None of you will survive the Games if you cannot follow simple instructions."

There's a flurry of movement as the forty plus demons scramble to get organized and I use that time to try to calm myself again. Everything about these Games is being done in a way that is twisted; it's almost like they want to knock contestants out prior to the start. Obviously, my caliphate is in their sights, if that's true, because we're the most powerful demons in this fucking school.

Except for the shrimp—he makes us more vulnerable.

My gaze flicks to the group he's in immediately, and the calm I've been trying to attain flies out the window. Of course the rumors made their way to one of Lucian's goddamned spies, so he has both Roquefort *and* Furon in his group. Luckily, he also has Anton, which makes my anxiety a bit less. Anton and Xerxes seem less intimidating than much of our caliphate because they are built in a slender, lean frame because of their animals. However, their ties with magic are almost as strong as mine because they are descended from Lust and Pride. The demons in those lines are powerful with their ability to enchant and mesmerize, especially those from their court. The last demon in that pod is some idiot from a lower house in Wrath, and though I *should* know him, I have no idea.

"This starting battle will be a three-minute free-for-all where *no magic* should be used to enhance your weapons. We are simply getting you ready to duel, though I'd discourage not giving it your best efforts. Everything in this class is evaluated and I will be watching to see if any of you are slacking."

Clicking the button on my phone, I sound the call for them to begin. There's a slight pause before the noise of metal and wood paired with grunts and snarls fills the air. All of the six person circles are engaged in the melee, and I have to walk around each of them to keep abreast of what's going on. I wish I could half shift and fly; it would give me a better view of the crowd. Unfortunately, my dragon is far too edgy to let him have even an ounce more of control.

Hopefully, I can keep him from blasting someone when the real challenge begins.

"AYMON, BACK OFF! HE'S OUT FOR THIS ROUND!"

Rubbing my temples, I wait until the moron from Slash's line finally backs up and lets the smaller fear demon get up. I've been holding off on the magically assisted portion of this class as long as possible, but I don't have an option. It has to start soon or I'll be in violation of the edict. The problem is that these assholes have been going at it like they're trying to murder or maim people even without that enhancement, so I know I'll have to call for infirmary transports when the assists begin.

Most of my brothers will do fine, but Kit and Zavvie will struggle.

"Okay, break," I call out. "Time to hydrate and prepare your weapons for magical battle."

Oriel and Salem both whip their heads around to glare at me, but I can't do anything about this fucking bullshit. I didn't choose it and I'm not in a position to defy Lucian's direct, *written* commands at this moment. Being here as both a teacher *and* a caliphate leader is tenuous—if he believes I'm interfering with the flow of instruction, he can rightfully petition my father to remove me. That would be disastrous, and I have to dance along the wire very cautiously.

The clanging of weapons finally ends and I watch the various demons move to the sidelines to get whatever refreshment they bring for themselves. There's water, of course, but some species need other things to regenerate their energy and I have to give them time to do so. Demons are sneaky dicks, but we have specific unspoken rules we follow when we're not engaged in true combat. One of those is that each species must be respected for their particular needs—even if it's gross.

Pit demons are not fun to watch, but they typically move out of sight for their bullshit.

My eyes dart to a group of Cubi huddled around something and I roll my eyes. They might be fun to watch when it's not so public, but I'm in no mood for feeding porn today. Growling under my breath, I stomp over to my caliphate to see what they're doing during this short respite from battle. I just want to know what their plan is; it's not like I'm concerned about anyone or anything.

"Anton, are you good, man?"

Salem tilts his head at the bird shifter, and he gets a smirk as he lifts his head from where he and X are huddled away from prying eyes. They're obviously exchanging energy as their lines require, but I'm sure they're feeding off the excess emotions in the air from that group I just walked away from. "We're good, dude. What about you?"

The panda is sitting with Kit on a bench, passing a water bottle to him as they unwrap some of his special color-coded bars. "We're doing pretty good. KK is a little beat-up, but nothing Dank worthy."

"I'm okay. The stuff Salem gave me is helping, I think," the shrimp says. He's slouched down as he takes a bite of the snack, but I don't see anything that looks like a bad injury from here.

That will change quickly, unfortunately.

"I hope you have a plan." They all look at me, even Kit, and I cross my arms over my chest. "No one can know."

Oriel rolls his eyes, scoffing at my statement. "Duh, Jas. We didn't get summoned yesterday."

"You could have prevented this ridiculous situation," Salem says as he yawns. "You're the professor, man."

I close my eyes, counting to ten in my head before I answer. How does he not realize I had zero control over this bullshit? I'm doing my best to not make the shrimp crazy—most of the time. I haven't been nearly as rough as I was before, so I'm keeping my word. Why would I purposefully allow this disastrous lesson plan if that's the case? When I'm calm enough to answer him, my eyes burn with the fire of my dragon. "Do I look like someone who is pleased with this turn of events?"

Anton and X step closer, obviously finished with their power gathering. The avian shifter tilts his head, studying me for a moment. "You do not. I realize you may not be able to say more, but I feel confident in my assessment."

A sigh escapes his partner and Xerxes gives me a look tinged with sympathy. "No one likes to be muzzled, guys—particularly a dragon."

"I think we have it covered," Kit says as he stands up. "Whatever happens, I'll survive. I'm sort of like a cockroach in a nuclear fallout that way."

"Nonsense," X says as they pat the shrimp's head. "You are not a disgusting roach, Kit Kat. Stop knocking yourself."

The chorus of agreement doesn't surprise me, but I am a little shocked to see Zavvie reach out to pat Kit's shoulder lightly. He doesn't get re-buffed and I can *feel* the little surge of pleasure that goes through my kitsune when he's included.

This guy has completely entranced my entire caliphate and I have no idea what's going to happen when fake dating turns to real dating.

Nodding at them, I walk away to check on the other groups. They seem to be dicking around, so I sound the alarm again from my phone. The gnawing in my gut increases as I catch the hungry look in the eyes of the more aggressive demon types in the class. I'm not going to be able to do this without having a better vantage point; I just won't. I step onto a bench, towering over them as I let my dragon loose *just* enough to unfurl my enormous wings. That starts whispering like a wildfire across the sidelines, but I ignore it to push into the air and hover above.

"Get into your groups and stand at the ready. Your weapon should be ready!"

As they all scramble at the sight of my flashing eyes and rumbling snarl, I scan the crowd to locate all of my brothers. They're standing firm in their sections, even the shrimp. His shoulders are squared and he has his projectiles nestled in his hands as he stares at the demons who will be coming for him.

Here we go…

Head Like A Hole

kat/kit

I know that the Fae guy and that fuckwit Roquefort are definitely problems. At least that narrows my question marks down to three—not that it will help me if they have secret alliances with any of the random enemies I've made or are jealous of my affiliation with my guys. Well, not *my* guys, but…

For fuck's sake, Kat, focus!

That reminder comes a split second before my body moves on its own, ducking under the blast of orange magic that is headed right for my face. I didn't see who launched it, but they weren't playing around. If my instincts hadn't kicked in despite my distraction, I would have been out for the count within seconds. Or, I assume so, since there's a chorus of chuckles emanating from the demons in my immediate area. I don't have to wonder if all of my group dislike me now; it's plainly obvious they all want to see me go down, even if I don't get up.

"Fucking fabulous," I mutter low, as I sharpen my focus, dancing around our space on light feet. Avoiding the bad folks in my previous life helps me, but I can't be certain these fuckers won't break the rules of engagement and enhance their own bodies, not just their weapons. Demons operate on very specific wording and as far as I can remember, Jasper's orders did *not* include a ban on self-enhancement.

I'm sure that was on purpose because that dick knows exactly what he's saying at all goddamned times.

"Have something to say, dead demon walking?" Roquefort taunts as he watches me with a sinister grin. "I'm sure we can repeat your last words to your little harem when you're gone."

Sighing in annoyance, I eyeball one of the unknown demons. Furon will go for Roquefort while he's distracted. These other three dudes don't seem to be powerful or connected, because I've never seen them with anyone who worries me. That's a guess, of course, but my time so far at Discordia has suggested that the most imminent threats aren't satisfied unless they make themselves known.

I could do without the comical villain bragging, though. It's super cliched, and I want to vomit every time.

"No answer? Not surprise since you're such a tiny, weak little fuck."

My temper flares and I whip my head around, eyes boring into the asshole's as I let a smirk come over my face. "Funny, your mom said just the opposite last night—over and over until her voice gave out."

A guffaw from the next group makes me grin more, and it only takes a few moments before it spreads. Roquefort's face goes red like a fucking tomato, and he stomps forward as if he's going to come for me, but that's when Furon tackles him from the side. My gambit worked, so I swallow my smug glee to look at the two demons battling on the other side of our circle, frowning when I don't see the one I need to fight. A burning sensation hits me in the shoulder and I curse under my breath as it spreads over my entire body.

Way to lose track of the goddamned enemies, Kat.

Gritting my teeth against excruciating pain, I turn around to face the medium-sized dude. I don't know his name, but he's wielding what I think is a crossbow that's surrounded by an emerald green energy. I drop into a fighting stance again, holding my tossers as I mutter the words Anton whispered to me before we split into the groups. Nothing happens, but a dark, angry feeling settles in the pit of my stomach. It makes me want to double over, especially paired with the burning in my back, but I fight it hard.

Years of fighting out-of-control emotions due to my condition take over as the sick sensation tries to wrestle its way to the forefront of my mind. It makes my veins ache and my jaw tight, but I lift my hands again to try to focus on the demon that looks way too pleased with himself. "You won't beat me this way, asshole. Whatever you did can't possibly compare with what my brain does to me on its own."

"Oh, I very much doubt that, chew toy." The guy doesn't even flinch at my retort, only stands in place looking relaxed. "Everyone knows you're useless without your body guards. That's why you're fucking them—like in a human prison movie."

Did this motherfucker just allude to me being their bitch?

Blatant misogyny and homophobia aside, *no one* owns me. Fury starts in my feet, working its way up my frame to battle with the ugly magic that wants me to abandon my circle to seek out something other than this fucking guy. I don't know what he's trying to force me to do, but he can suck my nonexistent dick if he thinks I'm going to let him get away with calling me someone's property. I suck in a deep breath, embracing the anger inside of me like I did in the cafeteria. It builds, pushing upward until it's slowly drowning out this asshole's green poison.

Unfortunately, that's not all it does. Panic sets in when I realize it's basically coating the inside of me with that dangerous emotion until it settles under my skin like a shield. This is something new and I have no idea how to control it or what to do with it. Not good doesn't really cover the amount of anxiety that causes, so I let one of the goddamn throwing weapons fly at my opponent before I lose control completely. My jaw drops when everything around me seems to slow and the damn thing turns end over end until it hits a mark I couldn't *possibly* have aimed for and accomplished on my own.

Much like a John Woo movie, my projectile moved like liquid through the air to imbed itself right in the snarky cockwaffle's eyeball—what. the. actual. fuck.

Everything snaps into place as he lets out an ear-splitting scream of pain, and misfires his stupid crossbow. Diving to the ground to make sure I don't get hit, I breathe heavily, my eyes wild as I try to figure out what in Satan's crispy goat legs just happened. There's a commotion, something that sounds like Jasper's barking orders, and other sounds that barely make it past the rushing in my ears, but all I can do is count my breaths. When I finally regain control, I notice that Furon is still fighting with Roquefort across the circle, and there are some weird looking things that might be imps surrounding my former opponent.

A hand grabs mine and I almost bite it in defense until I scent Oriel. His eyes are shining with something that might be pride—I'm not quite sure since I haven't seen it often—and he hauls me to my feet quickly. Another voice yells his name, so he winks and lets go before darting back to his group. I guess he's not supposed to do that, and I need to get my shit together again.

Okay, Kat, one down. Just don't think about it; keep swimming for shore.

My anxiety is often like drowning, and I remind myself that there's a shore when I need to push it aside. Sometimes, it works, and others, it doesn't, but the adrenaline pumping through me now is helping. I am a survivor in every sense of the word and this place, these demons—they will *not* beat me. Squaring my shoulders, I look for the two randos I identified earlier. They're still battling, one having a golden glow to his staff and the other having a red tint to his huge broadsword. I can't tell which one is powerful, but I think I'd like to go up against the staff guy more since he looks smaller. He moves again and I blink—or maybe not, because that jackass is *fast*.

"Get that loser out of his group!"

I turn to the sound of Jasper's voice, noting he's directing another set of the spooky looking beings to grab a prone body from the group X is in. My chest gets tight until I see the glamorous demon straightening their athletic gear with a quirked eyebrow as the fallen dude is moved out of their area. Xerxes barely looks like they've broken a sweat, and their hair is as perfect as when we walked in.

Fuck that pretty demon must be good; the guys weren't joking.

The whooshing sound to my left gets my attention and I curse internally when I realize I was so worried about X that I missed the sword guy finally knocking out the staff guy. That means it's time for me to move my ass or I'm going to be the one on the stretcher. I lick my lips as I consider his bigger build and think about the weight of his weapon. Being smaller and having lighter weapons will help me, but I'm not as fast as the staff guy, so it won't be enough. I need to be smarter *and* faster than him if I want to make it past this dude.

"Scared, small fry? You should be," he says as he stalks across the area where our group is fighting. "I'm going to crush you like a grape and reap the rewards of my success."

"Okay, *Game of Thrones* villain," I mumble as I look inward again. The golden glow is still inside of me, but it's not doing anything, so maybe Anton's spell is wearing off? Fuck, I wish I knew more about how anything of this shit worked before this crap started. Clearing my throat, I decide to use one of my most accessible weapons to distract the asshole—my mouth. "That threat would be a lot more worrisome if I had any idea who the fuck you are, moron. How scary is random dude number five supposed to be?"

His brows furrow for a moment, then he glares at me when he gets what I meant. That gap in understanding tells me he's not too bright and I can use that. Making him do brain work will give me time to react to whatever he's going to throw at me. "Everyone knows who Budet of Gluttony is! I'm a battling champion, as are my father and brothers."

Shrugging, I load my fingers with the throwing star thingies. "Sorry, Bidet. No one's ever mentioned you. I'd hire a new PR firm—and maybe consider not using an ass-cleaner as your fighting name? That's just me, though."

His roar cuts through the air, but it's not as loud as the asshat Prince's, so it doesn't make me flinch. I just grin, muttering the words Anton gave me over and over, hoping it will kickstart whatever I need to fight off that big ass magical sword as the dude gets closer. "I will feed your bones to the creatures in the Wastes!"

For real, is this corny line shit taught *demons or do they just naturally say dumb shit?*

My eyes track him as the bolt in my back continues to burn. It doesn't hurt as much as before, but I don't have time to deal with it. Pushing it to the place in my mind I've pushed injuries in the past, I narrow my gaze. I know I can do this, even if I don't know if I'll be able to beat Furon or Roquefort afterward. When toilet demon gets close enough that I have to dodge his blade, I move, pleading with whatever magic I should be using to fucking *do* something before I get skewered.

"Come on, come on…. Annie gave me your help…" I murmur as my opponent parries and attacks, forcing me to continue dancing away as I pray for help. "I just have to injure him enough to make sword fighting hard. It's not asking for a lot."

That's when the darkness lodged deep inside of me that I try to ignore lifts its head and smiles.

Oh, shit.

Not Gonna Die

One minute, I'm fighting with this idiot drude, and the next, it's like a shockwave hits our corner of the stadium. The blast of energy is almost visible as I rear back, looking around in shock.

Where the fuck did that come from?

Spinning on my heel, I find Jasper as he hovers in the air above us in his half-shifted form. He was already on the edge with his damn animal—I could feel it—and a big expulsion of energy like that had to have hit him hard. I'm greeted by an enormous fear demon in dragon form roaring into the stratosphere as it flies over the stadium.

"Son of a bitch," Salem says as he bounds over, ignoring the crossroads demon trying to follow behind him. "Text Slash. We need him like… yesterday."

I nod, pulling out my phone as the dark onyx dragon soars overhead looking pissed as hell. It's hard to type the message while I'm trying to keep an eye out for my other brothers *and* a fucking hacked off demon dragon with the powers of Hell's throne behind him. Suddenly, my eyes widen and I look at the panda shifter in a panic. "Fuck. Where's Kit Kat?"

He blanches, his skin going even paler and within seconds, he's shifted to his demon. "I don't know, but I'm going after him. What the fuck *was* that, anyway?"

"No time," I say as I shake my head. "Find Kit and keep him safe. I'll locate the others. Hopefully, Slash gets his ass here quickly. If so, Anton and I might be able to fly him up as long as Jas doesn't go too high."

"This is madness," Salem mutters as he takes off into the messy crowds of demons still fighting.

His statement is accurate, since Jasper's transformation *should* have calmed this place down and made everyone duck and cover. They're not, though. No, every single demon here seems to be fighting harder and more vehemently than before. If we don't get this under control, this practice exercise might actually lead to deaths. Taking a deep breath, I grasp my blade and head into the crowd Salem came from to find Zav and Anton.

I don't know what Lucian intended to happen at this damn rehearsal, but I bet it wasn't this.

"Move out of my way!" I growl into the throng. I don't normally raise my voice, nor am I typically the aggressor in our caliphate. That alone should be making some of these guys pause, but they just keep going at one another. Something is definitely off, and I'd bet one of my favorite shiny hoard items that the pulse of power fueled this frenzy.

Since no one is listening, I shift into my demon form, using the power of my shadows to slip through the melee more easily. An arctic chill comes over me and I groan to myself when I realize that Jasper is using his fear powers in the sky. His dragon is *pissed as fuck* for him to use both sides simultaneously.

But why? What is making him so damned angry?

"Oriel! Is that you? Come out of the fucking shadows, man."

Anton's voice brings me out of my musing and I hurry through the darkness to reappear as close to the sound as I can manage. My usually unruffled brother is dripping with slime from head to toe and dragging Zavida along beside him. The kitsune has some kind of injury on his leg, but together they seem to be making it through. "What the hell happened to you?"

"I do *not* want to discuss it. However, I will be dealing with that pit demon as soon as possible when the real trials start." Anton's gaze is icy as he mutters, "His ass is mine and I'm going to make him suffer for ruining my fucking shoes."

Pinching the bridge of my nose, I shake my head to clear it. Zav's limping along from some injury and Annie's worried about his fancy ass shoes. It's not surprising, just… Jasper would be losing his shit if he weren't already tearing through the sky wreaking havoc in lizard form. "Okay. I sent Salem to the other side to find Kit. I haven't seen him since that weird fucking energy thing that sent Jas over the edge."

"Did you guys notice everyone seems to be off the chain?" Zav mumbles as he squints up at me. "Demons are assholes when provoked but this seems—"

"Out of control?" I retort. "Yeah, we noticed, Zav. Just hang onto Annie. I'm going to pull you through the shadows with me and I need to focus. I don't want to lose either of you, but we can't get lost in this mess as we head for KK and Salem."

His eyes are worried, but he nods, so I put my hand on his shoulder and we meld into the world I slip through to do all my nefarious deeds. The shadows are disturbed by the extra presence, but I do my best to soothe them as we venture through the roiling crowds of snarling demons battling one another. I keep my eyes peeled for the black and white hulking figure of Salem, knowing I'll likely see that before I do the small stature of Kit.

When I finally catch a glimpse, Salem is lifting a chaos demon over his head like a human wrestler, his face full of fury like I've never seen. Kit isn't anywhere near him and panic flows through my veins. I don't know where our friend is, and the panda is tearing into someone in his search. Everything about this fucking situation is wrong and we have to get control. Otherwise, it might spread past the walls of the arena into Discordia proper and fuck only knows what will happen then.

"Going visible," I call to Zav and Anton. Once they acknowledge me, I bring us out of the dark realm into the mess surrounding us. "Salem! Salem! What the fuck is going on?"

He doesn't turn to look at us, and I let go of Anton to hurry over to the demon panda. Zav and Annie come along, both of them looking puzzled at the behavior of our ursine friend. Salem has a very slow burn temper, and in all the years we've known him, he's never been quite this over the edge. I look up at the sky, noting Jasper's dragon watching with a narrowed gaze. He's not intervening, so he must support this violence, but why?

I know his dragon is an aggressive asshole, but it's not stupid. It knows enough to understand why showing our hand is bad.

"What are we going to do? Where the hell is Slash? And for fuck's sake, *where is Kit?*" Zav says, his voice pitching up as his irritation spikes.

I don't have an answer to any of those questions, so shrug at Zavida. He's looking more tired by the moment and I'm sure the pain of whatever happened to his leg is starting to get to him. We can't stop, though, until we get our brothers under control and find the smallest of us. It's just not an option.

Anton stops in his tracks, smiling evilly. "He's here."

I don't have to ask who he means; that expression tells me that our general, the big man himself, is in the stadium. We don't need him to save us, but we do need him to help us get our leader back to logic rather than animal rage. He and Jasper have been friends since birth, and when the grouchy dragon won't even listen to Zav, Slash can usually bring him out of the red mist of his wrath.

The sound of squealing and snarling demons tells me where and I turn to see bodies flying through the air as the shark demon barrels through the crowd like a fucking bulldozer until he finally reaches us. His eyes glitter with the predatory machine that is his animal, and he assesses us before he speaks, "Where is the little demon? Who failed him?"

Okay, not what I expected him to say.

"No one, Slash. We don't have time to explain, but we gotta get Jas out of the fucking sky before he decides to really push his powers out. Don't you feel the chill?" I gesture around the arena, noting the fighting demons as well as the ones huddling on the ground in terror. "I guess the ones *not* cowering are the most powerful? Fuck if I know, but if we don't get him to calm, this will go beyond the walls."

His expression seems to war between emotions and I look over my shoulder at Annie and Zav. Slash is *never* split in his focus. He is *always* single-minded in his pursuit; he gets it from his shark. But right now? The biggest guy I know is torn, and it's weird as hell. "Fine. If you and Anton can assist with flight, I will attempt to bring the Prince back. But you will not stop until you find the little demon or you will answer to me. Understood?"

"Crystal clear, big guy," I reply. "Annie? Do your thing."

Anton lets go of the kitsune, allowing him to crumple to the ground and bury himself in his tails to form a force field around himself. Once he's safe, a burst of glittering rainbow and gold announces his transformation into the hybrid demon with golden skin, rainbow tailfeathers, and matching wings big enough to drape over several people.

"Show off."

I chuckle at Slash's remark, cocking my head at him. He's only half-shifted as the shark, no demon present, and though it's still terrifying, I'm surprised. "Just him?"

"I do not wish to antagonize his demon further. Jasper is accessing both sides of his power. I should remain in control."

Nodding, I walk closer and grab one of his arms. The dude is heavy as a humanoid, but he's twice as heavy in shark shift, more in demon, and his fucking full shark is damn near impossible to lift. "Let's move, Annie."

The peacock demon unfurls his huge, beautiful wings and I spread out mine, the two of us pushing into the sky as we hold Slash between us. It's a slight struggle, but we fly up until we're level with the dragon. He's swooping around at the back end of the stadium and once we get close enough to elevate above Jasper, I can see why. The dragon seems to have located the area with a *cloud* of negative emotions so thick it's opaque. I have no idea what the fuck is going on in there, but that's why our leader can't seem to fight off his wrath.

"Now!" I yell at Anton, and we let go of our general so he falls on top of the dragon. Jasper rears back, roaring into the sky loud enough to break glass. It doesn't phase me; we've heard him lose his shit before, even if it's usually not this bad.

This level of insanity is what Jasper takes off to burn away and none of us have ever been privy to his rage flights.

"We have to get down there," Anton yells over the dragon's snarls. "Slash can deal with him. Whatever is down there caused the pulse and they probably have Kit Kat."

I frown darkly, my crow and my demon in agreement about how that makes us feel. "Let's go. I don't care what Darkstar threatens us with—if they've hurt one of us, especially him, I will let the shadows rip their minds to shreds, Anton."

His beautiful, bird-like features turn dark in a way no one would imagine they could. "Agreed. Their deaths will be slow, painful, and show everyone on the campus what it means to defy the royal caliphate."

Grinning, I turn my body and angle my wings to dive into the misty scarlet-colored blob on the ground.

Someone is going to die on this hill, but it won't be me.

Any Other Way

kat/kit

I don't know what the unholy *Hell* is going on right now, and it's freaking me out. Unlike normal, that doesn't have me paralyzed on the ground in a panic attack. Instead, allowing the dark spot in the pit in my gut that's always been lurking to energize my body in a way I've never felt before. I'm moving like someone who knows what the shit they're doing, flinging my throwing doodads with an accuracy that's inhuman.

When they hit… I don't know what that is, but they seem to invigorate me more, giving me energy while our foes fall to the grass in agony.

"I wish I knew what is going on," I mutter to myself as I spin on my heel, finding a new target rushing towards me. Every time there's another demon headed my way, something inside me pushes and I face it without a shred of concern for my safety. It's sort of freeing not to be worried, not to fear for my life, but I also know that's not normal.

"No wonder those idiots picked a puny little shit for their concubine," the giant fully shifted demon sneers. I think he's a chaos demon because everything in his path is going crazy as he stalks toward me. Fighters trip, the ground moves, and people curse as their weapons miss the mark and hit someone else nearby. "You've been keeping your power hidden so we won't come for you."

I arch a brow. If only this dipshit knew that I have no idea what I am, much less how to control it. "I haven't been hiding anything, and that's not why. Get fucked."

My insult bounces off of him like the bodies and magic in his wake, his laughter dark and ominous. This dude is *not* going to hold to the rules of engagement, and I need to be ready for whatever he throws at me. I have no idea *how*, but my gut is screaming that I have to focus on him above all else going on around us.

I don't even know who he is in this form; he could be anyone because his demon is simply ugly as fuck.

"I've been waiting to get my claws on you, especially since it will fuck with your *boyfriends*. That is just the cherry on the sundae for me, and when I'm done, I'll be heartily rewarded."

Gripping my weapons in my palms, I realize not only does this idiot want to kill me, but he's using me for some fucking agenda against the guys. That makes the darkness spreading through me angrier and it pushes at my skin hard, making me cry out. Ugly Ass Demon Guy laughs again, stopping just within stabbing distance as his tail whips and he tosses his head like his horns are hair he wants to flip.

"You're already crying in fear—it's *delicious*."

Before I can process it mentally, I've whipped one of the throwing dagger-things at him and it embeds in the meat of his shoulder. He opens his mouth to say something stupid then I see it—the panic in his black eyes as whatever these are being infused with starts to sink into his body. A wordless scream forms on his lips and I feel the darkness' satisfaction grow inside me. It likes his pain; in fact, it hungers for it because the more contorted this Ugly Demon looks, the better I feel.

I'm not sure I like the joy that's rocketing through me at his suffering, but I'll take whatever help I can get.

"Not so smug now, are you, fuckface?" I call out as I pull another one of the weapons off the belt they're stored in. "Something got your tongue? No snarky comment?"

His visage is still twisted and he's fighting to stay up; I can tell by the tiny sway to his wide stance. Much like the others, the spot where my blade is lodged is turning black and spreading over his frame slowly. "You can't stop me. I *will* end you, scum."

Typical villain speech, but he's wrong based on what's happened to the other guys. I stand ready to launch another, my feet firm as I block the bench behind me. I won't let him get past me—that's where X is slumped, nursing a wound in their side. They'd rushed to rescue me, but instead, ended up being jumped from behind when the darkness escaped.

"You can try, asshole." I growl at the injured dude. He lets out a roar of pain, and I think for just a moment, I may have won.

But then a crowd of other demons storm to his aid and I swallow hard. They're either in full demon form or various shifts, all wielding magic as they stare me down.

I may have underestimated how much the Headmaster hates me.

"Fine. You want some, too? You can—"

My words are cut off by the sound of a fierce 'caw' and two flying bodies hitting the ground hard enough to shake it. Panic tries to claw its way past the darkness in my veins, but it pushes back, and I'm able to look at the intruders without fear.

It's Oriel and… Anton? I think? Fuck he's even more gorgeous in this guise; I almost can't even look at him. The golden haze and rainbow sparkles surrounding him are so bright that it makes him appear similar to what I've always been told angels look like.

Well, okay, maybe a pride angel, but six of one, right?

"Imagine needing seven friends to face one little freshman demon," Anton says as he quirks a brow. "How sad for you all when this gets out."

Oriel flexes his wings, spreading them like the fucking Crow from the movie and my heart skips a beat in my chest. He's a palette of dark, Gothic beauty in the half demon form and it makes it even harder to focus on the task at hand. The two of them are the perfect complement of light and dark like something out of *Good Omens*. I lick my lips, trying not to let my shock and appreciation show on my face. Fuck knows I don't need these idiots knowing how much they affect me.

"Very true, Annie." O looks at me, his eyes glittering with intelligence as he studies me, then notices what I'm standing in front of. "Oh, shit, they got X! No wonder we didn't see him anywhere."

That's when the glow around the shining peacock shifter increases and Anton lets out a screech of anger. "How *dare you*? How fucking *dare* you?!"

I arch a brow, looking at Oriel, who gives me an evil grin before saying, "Annie's biggest 'no-no' square is doing anything to upset Xerxes. He's taken assholes out for much less than wounding them."

My reply is cut off by Anton raising his hands and unleashing a blast of colorful magic big enough to level every single one of our attackers. They hit the ground like sacks of potatoes and my jaw drops. I would *never* have expected such a huge amount of power to come from the restrained, fussy demon hybrid, but he's making a weird, angry bird sound as he stomps across the field to hover over the fallen dickheads.

All he'd need is a flaming sword and he wouldn't look like a demon at all but for the delicate, filigreed horns that adorn his head—he'd look like a painting of Michael.

"Whoa," I mutter as I back up carefully.

Oriel laughs softly, then grabs my arm to lead me over to X. "We should let him do his thing, Kit Kat. It'll be pretty, but also kind of gross. You might not be ready for it."

I expect the darkness in me to lash out at the crow, but instead I feel a vibration almost like a cat's purr inside and the overwhelming urge to get closer to the avian demon. Having zero clue what to feel about that shit, I swallow hard again and look down at Xerxes to distract myself. They're bleeding a ridiculously attractive silver substance from the wound and I sheath one of my weapons so I can scrub my hand over my face. "Is there *nothing* you two do that isn't visually stunning? I mean, I look like someone regurgitated me, man. It's not fair."

X gives me a pained smile, and even that is picture perfect. I throw up my hands, grunting in irritation as Oriel bends to examine their torso. Oriel sighs, his wings folding against his back as he pulls their shirt until it rips to see better.

"Man, what did you do? No one should have been able to get this close. You're way too good."

Xerxes' lips twitch as they look at me. "Well... I sort of dived into the fray to save KK here before he went absolutely *bonkers*. I might have stayed unharmed if I knew what was going to unleash."

"I didn't do that! It wasn't me making everyone lose their shit, and I definitely didn't make this weird mist!" I give O a panicked look then hold my hands up. "Don't blame me for whatever Anton's magic did."

The crow shifter snorts as he pulls the shirt pieces aside to get a better look at X's wound. "Uh, in case you didn't notice, Annie's magic is like a Rainbow Brite cartoon. This red shit is *not* him, nor is the rage-out going on with every demon in this fucking arena. You can't see it in here, but Prince Prickface is full-on dragon balls right now."

Covering my mouth at his innuendo, I choke back a laugh. I'm not sure if it's in humor or fear, but my entire body hums at the thought of seeing that. "Oh, no. He's going to be so pissed."

"Uh, if he's the scaly serpent, that ship has sailed, Kit Kat." X gives me a commiserating expression as they wince when Oriel touches the blade lodged in their stomach. "He's going to be damn near impossible to get back to equilibrium for a couple days."

"Who's dealing with him?" I ask as worry fights with the darkness for control. "We have enough trouble without him getting sent away or whatever."

"Truth," Oriel says as he sits back on his heels. "X, we can have Dank remove this. I don't want to cause more damage doing it as battlefield triage. It might scar, and you'll come for me."

The cobra shifter hisses low, and I take it to mean they agree with the sentiment. "Leave it be."

"What do we do now? And someone answer me about Jasper, for fuck's sake." I elbow Oriel hard, my brow furrowing. "We need to get Xerxes out and check on everyone else."

"They're fine." The voice is flinty and when I look up, I see Anton. He's no longer covered in the sludge from before and he looks as regal as ever. In fact, at the moment, he looks better than any of us and I'm a little jealous again.

But I don't look to see what he did; Oriel said not to and I've had a lot of surprises today.

"How do you know?" I say softly. "I mean, we're in here and no one knows how to make it stop and—"

The peacock demon rolls his eyes, but his expression is fond. "Kit Kat, you're doing this. You can stop it. Whatever you did when my magic didn't help you… *undo it*. Focus your mind and remember when everything changed, then reverse it."

I blink, dipping my chin as I realize the darkness I allowed to escape isn't just pent-up fury from years of being neglected and abused. No, this part of me is the demon side, and it's been dormant until it was time. Like Dank said, the veil is lifting inside of me and I'm coming into the powers the guys have consistently told me I have. I didn't believe them—not entirely, anyway—but now I know they're right.

Which means the big pause in the cafeteria and the fire in the study room might have been me, too.

That rocks my world for a moment and I have to breathe very slowly to keep the panic from creeping in again. I don't think the darkness *and* my PTSD need to make friends, especially not right now. So I close my eyes and dig deep into my mind, visualizing my body. I see the bright blue of my panic and the deep onyx of the darkness filling my frame. Very carefully, I coax the colors to recede. I don't know if this soft begging will work, but if they're right and I'm making this misty fury fest, I have to try.

Please, I murmur internally. *I'm safe now. You can rest until it's time.*

Rocking a little, I keep talking to the parts of me, hoping like hell it works. Xerxes needs the doctor, and we have to find the rest of our caliphate.

Then we'll have to face the music with the administration.

PROTECTOR

slash

In the many years we've known one another, I have never seen Jasper so out of control without his father present. I have tried my usual basic tricks to coax him back to sense, but they are not working. It is time for more drastic measures to prevent him from getting banned from campus. Lucian will have a difficult time convincing the King, but if enough demons are harmed, my father will advise him that thinning the ranks that should fill our armies is ill-advised. The King will do what he always does—pretend he thought of the plan, take credit, and boast as he drags my brother home to be punished in ways that are best left unsaid.

I will not allow that to happen.

Holding on his scales tightly, I push forward up the enormous dragon until I reach its head. It takes a moment to get close enough to reach his tympanum, but once I do, I speak loudly. "Jasper, you have to get control of the dragon *and* the demon. You're flying over the stadium in a rage, and you haven't destroyed anything *yet*. Now is the time to grab the reins before their fury is not able to be contained. Your caliphate needs you."

The glass-shattering roar isn't comforting, so I take a deep breath. I cannot shift to my animal in this environment, but fuck, do I want to bite the living shit out of this stubborn asshole. Harnessing my demon tightly, I let the shark out just enough to shift my features so I have a frightening visage and rows of sharp teeth to make my point. This time, I don't use my words—no, I dart forward and bite into the dragon's flesh hard.

My teeth are sharper when I mix the two, so I'm able to catch some of the tender skin between his scales and that makes him roar and buck in pain. Pulling back with his black blood on my lips, I shot again. "Get your shit together, Prince! You are not your father. The danger you're reacting to is being handled by our brothers. We need you to calm down so you can stay here to lead."

There's a pause in his frantic attempts to shake me off, and I have to hold back a relieved sound. It means somewhere in there, Jasper is hearing my words. I can only hope he's working to soothe his wrathful sides slowly so he doesn't shift abruptly and send us tumbling to the earth like rocks. My hands grip his hide hard, waiting to see what he will do next.

Please let it be something not involving fire and brimstone.

I'm able to breathe again when the huge serpent tosses its head with a snort, making an annoyed growling sound. My old friend is getting through to his animal and I have to capitalize on it. So I pat its horns lightly, then lean in to speak. "That's it, Prince. Take us to the ground before you take full control back. We will find our brothers and ensure their safety together."

That earns me another irritated snort, but the dragon turns about, then angles its wings back to descent. As we get closer to the grass of the arena, I note the red mist Anton and Oriel charged into subsiding slowly. There are bodies of the injured strewn about amongst unmoving ones that might be dead. I have no idea what the fuck happened here before I arrived, but the decimation is sobering. We got lucky that Jasper's dragon couldn't see the field of prone demons clearly until the Prince got him to back off.

"Bring us down over by the cloud of magic. I believe we will find them there." Our descent speeds up and by the time we land with a ground shaking thud, I'm itching to find the rest of our caliphate. I can't leave Jasper, though, so I hop off and face the beast. "It's time. Come back so we can tend to the wounded and call for the medics."

His dragon blinks at me with an expression I'm fairly certain is saying 'fuck off,' but I don't relent until the enormous serpent fades to the form of the man I know. I allow my own visage to shift back, but I don't go completely human just in case I need to defend my charge. We don't know what's lurking in the dissipating mist, so I'd rather be prepared than fail at my duty.

"Fuck," Jasper pants as he puts his hands on his knees to get his bearings. "That was a rough one."

I nod, trying to wait patiently for him to clear the animal and the demon out of his mind enough to follow me into the fray. "It was very close, old friend. You need more meditation."

He gives me a dirty look, but I simply shrug. I'm not wrong, nor am I here to stroke his giant fucking ego. Being a general is, at times, about informing your leader of their inability to see a tactical error before it's made. Jasper needs to work on harnessing his extremely powerful and dominant supernatural sides more often. If he does not, he will definitely turn into his dickhead father.

"Fine. I'll… work on it." His muttered assent is all I need, so I jerk my head at the disaster zone ahead.

"We need to find them. Can you handle it?"

"Yes."

"Then let's move."

BY THE TIME WE WADE THROUGH THE CROWD OF DOWNED AND ACTIVELY fighting demons, I'm ready to rip something to pieces myself. I was keeping my distress harnessed to help get Jasper back to equilibrium, but my anger is rising. Darkstar orchestrated this mess, even if he didn't predict the outlandish outcome correctly, and I want to make a slow fucking meal of him.

But I can't and it chafes hard enough to earn him a permanent spot on my 'to eat' list in the future.

"There they are! I see the shrimp," Jasper says and I'm surprised to hear the amount of relief in his voice.

My eyes follow the direction of his gesture, noting that the little demon is sitting upright. That is good; I'm not quite stable enough internally today to handle another trip to the doctor with him unconscious. Salem is standing off to the side in his bear shift, and Oriel is also perched high as the bird. They are likely healing from whatever injuries they had, so my eyes flick to the golden glow on the ground with a grunt. That's Anton and he'd never be on the filthy ground unless—

"Xerxes is injured," Jasper growls. "There's no other explanation."

The fury roils inside of me, but I clamp down on it hard. It is not the time for bleeding my anger—no, we must take control of this mess and get our brother to the doctor. "I will call for Doctor D if you alert the medics at the infirmary."

Jasper's jaw tightens, but he knows it's his responsibility to get the clean-up crew and the medical staff here. "Make certain you find out who is injured and how badly so the Doctor is prepared."

Leaving him to find his clothes and tech, I stomp over to our brothers. In my head, I'm reciting the dark alphabet backwards as I try to calm myself. My worry for Xerxes is high, but since Anton hasn't gone nuclear, they are likely going to be okay. Salem and Oriel will be fine if they've retreated to their animal forms to heal. The real clawing at my gut is for the small guy sitting on the bench looking wrung out, even from here.

I need to make sure that the little demon is not more injured than he seems from here; it's essential.

"Tell me what happened immediately," I demand when I'm close enough that they can all hear me.

Kit looks up at me and my entire body freezes in place when I see the rips and tears in his baggy uniform. There's blood on him, though I am unsure if it is his, and he looks completely drained as he hefts a long sigh. "I didn't mean to do it."

My eyes widen as I look to Anton for confirmation. He nods a little from where he's kneeling next to X, and I have to take a moment to let it sink in. Once I assimilate that information, I turn to walk over to him, sitting on the bench and putting my arm around him. He doesn't shrink away and my shark is very pleased. Looking down at his tired, confused eyes, I say, "Whether you intended to or not, we should keep that information to ourselves for now. I do not believe it is a good idea to give those who are plotting against us this kind of information."

A loud caw precedes Oriel shifting back to human form, his body looking remarkably unharmed. Kit squeaks and buries his face into my side, and I chuckle deeply. "O, please find your clothing. You're making the little demon turn into a tomato. I think."

"Sorry," the little guy says, his voice muffled by my chest. "I'll get used to it eventually; I promise."

Oriel grins and I see the wickedness glittering in his gaze, even if Kit cannot. "Oh, you will, Kit Kat, but today is not the day for that conversation."

Anton snorts, shaking his head. "Stuff it, Oriel. Not the time for that shit."

He's not wrong, but Kit is not curling smaller, so he must be okay. Otherwise, I'd smack the crow myself.

"We need to call Doctor D," I announce. "Does anyone have their phone? Mine is probably somewhere in this stadium, but reining Jasper in was not as easy as I hoped when I arrived."

A hand holds a phone up from the ground and I chuckle. Of course Xerxes is prone on the grass with a stab wound but managed to keep his phone safe. I should have known before I even asked. I lean forward and grab the device, frowning at the small size. My phone is at least twice the size of this thing; I am not a small demon.

"Give it here," Kit says and I sigh in relief. He scoots closer to me, then looks at it for a second. "How do I open it, X?"

"Code is 26866548," Xerxes says. His voice is thready and I am concerned that he is more injured than he is letting on.

I look at Anton, who frowns, and then turn back to the little demon. "Hurry. I believe our brother is misleading us about how injured he is. That will be addressed later, but it is more urgent to get the doctor here."

His eyes widen and he hurries to unlock the screen, then fumbles around until he finds the contacts. Luckily, the Doc's number is programmed in—as it is in all of our phones—so he's able to get the line ringing quickly. Pushing the speaker button, he waits for the raspy voice of the elder demon to answer and then speaks. "Dank, something bad went on at the stadium. I can't talk about it on speakerphone, but Xerxes is injured. I'm… I have issues, too, but um… yeah. Oriel and Salem shifted to help but maybe they need checking and…"

I shake my head as he babbles on for another minute, relaying everything in a high, anxious tone at light speed. He's still going when a dark green portal opens up in front of us and the masked doctor strolls out with a phone to his head. It's clear Kit has never seen him do this before, so once again, he shrinks into my side reflexively. Frowning as I feel him tremble, I pick him up and sit him on my lap so I am able to comfort him better.

"It is okay, little demon. The doctor is here and we will take care of everything in time. Do not be afraid."

His head turns and I'm worried he will jump up, but instead, he nods as he bites his lip. I pull him close and sit my chin on his head, letting him feel the safety he obviously needs as Dr. D immediately heads for Xerxes. The old demon makes an annoyed sound behind his mask, then looks at me.

"We will need to adjourn to my office. I will handle the snake if you will help Kit." The doctor looks at Anton, then at Oriel as he returns. "Bring the bear and the crow with you. One at a time, I will help you. Is the Prince secure?"

Nodding, I shift so I can stand up with the little demon in my arms. "Jasper is handling the other injured demons and the dead. His dragon is under control now, so he can find us when he has been released."

"Dottie!"

Blinking, I remember the tiny creature when Kit tugs on my collar as he yells. "Oriel, please locate the kinkajou. The portal will close behind us once we are all inside, yes?"

The plague masked doctor nods, waving his hand to magic X off the ground and heads for the shortcut to his office. Anton follows, and I bring up the rear with the little demon in my arms. He must be very worried about his stadium antics because he's shivering now, and I think perhaps he's in shock.

That is okay. I will keep him safe until our brothers and the doctor are all together—it's my duty, after all.

Comfortable

kat/kit

"I didn't know Dank could create portals," I mutter as Slash carries me through the bright magic. "I figured the one he brought me here with was… static?"

Slash's laugh is a low rumble against my face. "No, little demon. Those of his species who live to be as old and powerful as the doctor are able to do many things younger demons cannot. Dr. D has innumerable talents you are unaware of."

"It's really unfair that I'm working so hard and I'm still so fucking behind. I'll never catch up." Frowning, I quiet down and stay buried in the comforting strength of his arms as he follows the others to our destination. I should complain about not being allowed to make it on my own, or protest his wordless assumptions, but… I'm so damned wiped from whatever I did in the arena that I can't be bothered.

At least that's what I'm telling myself.

The hand on my back pats lightly. "You will be fine. Stop expecting to master everything immediately; it is not possible, even for someone as determined as you."

I sigh in frustration, then groan as it irritates my aching body. "That is very logical and also kind, but it's hard for me to accept."

"But you have accepted my ability to get you to safety, and you are uncomfortable with most contact. It follows that you can also accept my words."

My nose wrinkles and I shut up because he's right. I don't feel like arguing that point when I feel so exhausted I can't stay upright. I sense the toothy grin on his face without seeing it, and nearby, I hear Anton chuckle. I know he's worried about X, so it's good that he's finding humor in something, even if it's my hypocrisy. I can deal with the fallout later as long as everyone stops acting like we're in a funeral procession.

We're not, right? They'd tell me, wouldn't they?

Suddenly, anxiety grips me and I tense from head to toe. I don't *think* the guys would hide a potentially serious condition, but what if they're trying to appease my trauma? My mind races with the possibilities, and I bite my lip as my heart speeds up with worry. I like Xerxes *a lot*. I like *all* of them a lot. Losing anyone I've allowed into my fragile psyche even a tiny bit will destroy me—that's why I built the shell around me and have kept it solid for years. I'm not ready to be tested; I'm still healing from the last betrayal.

"Stop."

I blink, then look up to see the shark shifter giving me a stern expression. "Huh?"

He rolls his eyes briefly then stares at me again. "Stop what you are doing. You're quiet, but you are upsetting yourself. I can feel it in your pulse and the tension in your body. Whatever you are thinking, desist."

"That's *not* how anxiety works," I mutter. "I can't just... *not* think about things and be better."

Slash huffs at me as if I've insulted his ancestors. "I'm not stupid, little demon. I realize you cannot simply stop thinking about things to control it. I meant for you to stop allowing it to control *you*. Use whatever techniques you normally do, as we're arriving at the Doctor's office, but he will need to tend to Xerxes first."

Oh. Damn, I made him feel bad for not being verbose.

"Sorry, big guy," I murmur. "I'm usually better at understanding you but right now…"

The train of demons stops, including us, and I feel his muscles adjust as he finds a chair that will accommodate us as we wait. The huge shifter demon lowers us into it carefully, then looks at me seriously as I get comfortable. "It's okay. I know you did not mean anything by it. However, you are usually quite good at understanding what I say. More so than most."

"I'm kind of useless at EQ when I'm close to an episode." I shrug a little, my skin heating up as he looks at me. "It's one of the things I can't seem to regulate if I'm focused on trying not to flash back or panic."

He pauses, tilting his head for a moment, then nods. "I can adjust to that. Thank you for sharing it with me."

That's all? No one ever just… accepts my shit without questioning it.

"You don't want to ask why I can't… be normal?"

His large hand runs over my hair, mussing it a little. "No one is normal. That is an illusion people cling to in order to feel accepted by their… preferred group. And it is also how they reject those they do not wish to accept while still feeling superior."

I lift my head, looking up at Slash in surprise. "That's… pretty fucking spot on."

He gives me the trademark toothy grin and I fight the urge to duck my head. "I am quiet and I watch things. It's easier to see the full picture when you're not yammering like a chimpanzee."

Laughing softly, I give him a crooked smile in response. "You know, you also distracted me from my panic attack. I think it might have been your plan all along."

Slash shakes his head. "I would like to take credit for that, but I am not so devious. Of all of the demons in our caliphate, you will learn that I am the most straightforward. I am like…" He thinks about it for a moment, his brows furrowing. "Like the elephant in the cartoon Zavida enjoys. He made us watch it once because he likes the tiny people on the plant."

My eyes widen and I cover my hand with my mouth when the realization hits. Giggles escape and I can't stop it as I ask, "Did you just compare yourself to *Horton the elephant?*"

"Yes. He is a much larger hero who saves the little ones, yes?"

This is priceless and it might be the best thing to happen all day.

"I mean… yes…"

"Then why do you seem so amused?"

I have to pause to get myself under control so I can figure out what to say without being offensive. "Because while accurate, it's a cute kids' movie and Horton is a little goofy. So I'm surprised a very masculine demon like you would willingly compare yourself to him. I doubt it would win you points with the ladies… you know, if there were any here."

His brow furrows and he looks at me in confusion. "Why would I care about that?"

Before I can answer, Jasper comes storming into the hallway, looking like a dark storm cloud on the horizon. His eyes narrow when he sees me sitting with Slash, but he turns to look at half-dressed Oriel sitting with Panda-Salem, then stalks over to where Zav is curled up in a big chair. Despite his ragged appearance, the dragon hybrid drops to a squat to pull the kitsune's tails away from his face so he can see him.

"Zavvie… where are you hurt?"

I don't often get to see the Prince behave like he's not a psycho, so I tilt my head, watching closely. Slash leans in, his cheek next to mine as he murmurs, "Jasper is a good man. He struggles more than the rest of us because his father is… worse. But with Zavida, you see the man and not the demon he was raised to be."

"I'm going to start calling you Yoda if you don't stop that."

His chuckle tickles my back and I sense another smile. "Yoda was very small. Zavida made us watch those movies once. I liked the small furry beings best. Very direct and without guile."

Turning to look at him, I grin. "You like Ewoks? No one likes Ewoks."

"I do not care what others like or do not like. They are cute, small, and aggressive. I enjoy all of those things, so it does not matter what anyone else thinks."

"He's not lying about that."

My nose brushes Slash's as I whip my head to look at Oriel. "Oh?"

The crow shifter smirks at me. "You haven't been to his room. It's very calming, but there's a cabinet you should check out."

"Uh… I don't…"

"Not *that* kind of cabinet," Oriel chortles, then coughs, holding his ribs. "Kit Kat, I *wish* you could have seen your face! It was priceless."

"Oriel, I'm going to smash you flat."

I pat the big guy's arm lightly. "It's okay. He's being silly, and it doesn't bother me like it used to. I'm getting… used to that kind of banter."

"Really?"

Zav's voice comes from down the hallway where Jasper is still kneeling in front of him and I nod, shrugging slightly. "Yeah. I mean, for some reason, I still look like a fucking tomato and like Anton says, I'm an awkward turnip about it…. But it doesn't make me spiral or anything."

The kitsune grins for the first time since class started, his eyes shining with a magical light. "That's progress, Kit Kat."

I'm about to reply when the dragon himself turns to me with his golden eyes, his expression intense. There's a scale pattern on his neck that must mean he's struggling to keep his animal in check—likely because he's worried about Zavida and Xerxes. Jasper studies me like he's trying to ferret out how truthful I'm being and so quickly I think I imagined it, a long, forked tongue flicks the air then retreats. He grunts, then shifts in his spot. "The shrimp is being truthful. He's getting more comfortable with us."

With them, you spiky-backed jackass—you still piss me off like no other being on the planet.

"Why the hell would I waste the energy to lie right now?" I grumble and Slash chuckles behind me. "I'm so fucking worn out that I'm letting someone carry me, you dipshit That *should* be a clue as to how blown I am."

Oriel smirks, looking inordinately pleased, then turns back to the Prince. "That's a fair point, Jas. The last time he was conscious and injured, he wouldn't let anyone do that. KK is *definitely* too wiped to make shit up."

"Thanks, man," I mutter gratefully.

Something in the tone of my voice must trigger Jasper because in a flash, he's up and stalking over to where I'm sitting with a dark look on his chiseled features. He's chewing on his lip ring, which means he's thinking, and within seconds, he's squatting down to get eye level with me. I frown, unused to him being this direct without saying something snarky. "Are you injured, shrimp? Is that why you are uncharacteristically compliant?"

"Do not accuse me of mistreating him, Jasper."

I blink, tearing my eyes away from the dragon to gaze up at Slash. "You're not. And as much as it pains me to defend Prince Prickface, I don't think that's what he meant."

The shark shifter narrows his eyes then looks at our leader. "He knows what he meant."

I'm missing something important here and I don't have the foggiest clue what, but I don't want any fighting.

"Calm down, big guy. I can handle his pissypants questions, promise." Even though it's pushing my limit a little, I squeeze him with the arm I have trapped behind him. I'm surprised to get a warm, tight hug in return and for a moment, I simply revel in the security of it. No wonder people are so into this shit; if most people are as good as this guy, I see the appeal more than I used to. Though, I suppose part of it might be how big and strong he is and some primal instinct; either way, Slash hugs are fucking #goals.

A low rumble echoes in the room and I realize it's coming from the bastard himself. I loosen my grip on the demon I'm perched on, then squint at the dragon curiously. "What the fuck is your problem? I said I'm not hurt. Hell, I even defended you. How did *that* manage to piss you off?"

Jasper just glares and I'm ready for him to say something mean when the door opens. Dr. D glides out, nodding silently, and I know it's time for Zavida to go in. The Prince rises to his feet, stomping back to the smaller demon determinedly.

Looks like I've been saved by the Plague Doc yet again.

CRUSHCRUSHCRUSH

zävida

"I think we should bring the others in, too, Jas. I'm not hurt badly—not like Xerxes was." I look at the tense as hell dragon, waiting for the doc to come back from his stores in the back. "Dr. D can look at them at the same time. Salem didn't even shift and… I really think Kit is hiding an injury."

I know he is, but I don't want to say that and set Jasper off again.

His eyes narrow and he studies me for a moment, obviously warring with himself. He wants to have the doctor look at me first because he's worried, but he also knows I wouldn't say that lightly. Finally, he growls, turning to the room where Dr. D is gathering supplies. "I'm bringing in the other injured demons. You can triage them all at once."

Dr. D glides out of the storeroom, nodding. "As you wish, Your Highness. If their injuries are less severe than Xerxes, I will see them now."

"I'm pretty sure they are," I say softly. "Mine isn't all that bad, either. Just some toxins that you need to drain."

Jasper gives me a suspicious look, then heads over to the door and barks, "Get the rest of them in here. I want everyone patched up and back to their rooms to rest. We'll file the report with my father's staff once we're back to our floor."

I let out a relieved breath as he comes back over and the others slowly make their way inside. Oriel guides Salem to the next table and for the first time since the battle, he shifts. The panda looks a bit ragged, which isn't surprising since he went full rage mode on a shit ton of opponents while Kit worked to protect X. Honestly, I thought it would be worse, but being in his animal form likely helped him heal faster. He flops back on the table and O rushes to pull a sheet over his lower half before Slash walks in with Kit in his arms.

It's pretty endearing how solicitous that cantankerous crow is of the new guy; I see why he was able to worm his way in first.

"Where are Anton and X?" Kit says hoarsely as the biggest dude in our caliphate cradles him close until they reach the next table. Slash puts him down gently, and again, I marvel at how much the new guy has changed my brothers in a short time. "Is X okay?"

Dr. D heads for Kit's table immediately, and I get the distinct impression he's probably frowning under that mask. "Master Kit, you are injured and disguising it. Are you able to override your magic's instinct to cloak that weakness?"

That gets a low, dark growl out of my lover, and he stomps over to the table to join them. His voice is deceptively calm as he grits out, "You said you were not hurt. Slash confirmed it."

"I did not." Everyone turns to look at the enormous shark shifter as he crosses his arms over chest. Jasper snarls, but his second-in-command doesn't flinch. "I said not to accuse me of mistreating him, not that he was unharmed."

Pretty clever answer, if you ask me, because the Prince knows his general isn't lying.

"Since when do you parse the spirit and letter of my questions, Slash?"

A hand waves in the air as Kit vies for their attention. "Excuse me, testosterone emitters? This is why I said I wasn't injured. I mean, I don't know why it's… hidden… but I lied because the others are worse. I didn't want someone to make me jump the fucking line. I'm smaller, but I'm not stupid. And no one has answered *my* question, by the way."

"I'm doing better, KK."

The croak draws all of us to look at the curtain drawn along the back wall and I realize the doc has Xerxes behind it. They must really be fucked up if Dr. D is keeping them separate. Kit frowns, scooting like he's going to leap off of the table and Slash steps in front of him with a firm head shake.

"No."

"Move. I'm going to go see them."

"No."

The admittedly smaller guy pokes the biggest one in the chest with a scowl. "You're not my keeper. I'm getting up and you'd better not try to stop me."

Slash doesn't move and within seconds, Jasper is standing next to him, looming over Kit with a matching stern expression. "As the Prince, I forbid it."

The snort that follows that statement is full of derision. "As the actual person in control of their body, you can go straight to… *here*, Jasper Eversore. I'll get up if I want to and the two of you can glare at me until your faces get stuck that way for all I care. I want to see my *friend* who is hurt."

"KK…" X's voice is soft and everyone shuts up as they speak. "Don't fight them. I'm still re-energizing from the energy I burned up. The doc said it's better to be cut off by this curtain thing so I don't lose what I'm building back up. You can see me once I'm tip-top again; you know how I hate for people to see me as less than fab, anyway."

I don't know when all of my brothers got so damn sneaky and conscientious, but I'm going to have to take some lessons from them.

The room is quiet for a moment until the stubborn guy finally gives in. "Okay, fine. But only because you asked me, not because these clowns think they're my keepers."

Anton pokes his head out from behind the curtain, his eyes dark as he studies the dark haired guy. "Thank you for worrying about them—about everyone—but you must let the doctor see what is wrong with you. If Dr. D is correct, you need to unravel the protection as you did the other. You can do this, Kit."

His words seem to make Kit feel better, but much like in the arena, I don't think he even knows how he's doing it, much less how to stop it. He scoots back, lying down on the table again and closing his eyes. His lips move as he mutters something inaudible to himself, and I tilt my head. I think he's trying to reason with his magic—something it took me years to learn. Nothing happens at first, but after a few minutes of coaxing, a warm glow emanates from his form that turns to an inky black halo where the wound must be.

Suddenly, Kit's hand flies up to cover the spot. Dark red blood covers his fingers as he holds it and he mutters, "Aw, fuuuuck."

"This is *not* a small injury, little demon." Slash's expression is stormy, and he looks at the new guy like he's going to turn him over his knee.

What's more interesting is that Kit looks like he's trying to figure out if he likes the idea.

Finally, he glares up at the shark shifter defiantly. "I didn't say it was small."

Confounded by his own trick, Slash huffs and Jas smirks at him. When my dragon's gaze comes back to Kit, it's no longer amused. No, it's full of barely contained fury. "Kit Camponella, you lied to us. I don't care *why*, but it's unacceptable."

Even Salem winces at his tone, but I know it well. This is the dominant side of Jasper, and that means he's furious with our newest brother. It also means he's attracted to him, but I'm not going to risk his temper by suggesting that. It took a while for the Prince to admit our attraction to himself because he worried that he would fuck up the caliphate and put me in his father's sights. Kit's already placed himself on the King's shit list, so that's not a concern here. But given that it's well-known that all of us have some level of interest in the kid, Jasper would have to learn to share.

It's not in his nature, so I'm interested to see how he handles this—or fucks it up for himself entirely.

"I knew X and Salem and Zav were hurt worse," Kit protests. "And, um... well, it didn't hurt anymore, so I thought..."

"You thought what?" Slash asks. "That if you didn't think about it, it would go away?"

Kit's face turns bright red and he shrugs, then gasps in pain. "I mean... yeah? That's how I always dealt with shit that hurt in the past. I just... gritted my teeth and did the best I could until things healed. I mean, except the one time, but... *that* is not a conversation for today."

Jasper makes a strangled sound of anger, then turns to his second. "I am leaving you in charge of handling him right now. I can't... I can't even deal with that statement." His eyes cut back to Kit before he adds, "But only *I* will handle his punishment. Is that clear?"

"No one is punishing me for making decisions about *my* body," the stubborn, partially emerged dude says. "I'm a goddamned adult."

"Perhaps you should act like it and let Dr. D work on you so he can heal the others instead of arguing with us while they suffer."

Damn it, Jasper.

Kit's expression crumples for a tiny moment, then hardens as he looks away from the Prince. "Dank, I'm sorry for being a problem. I would love for you to come help me—with the fucking curtain drawn."

"Ouch," Oriel says under his breath as he sits with Salem. "Denied."

"Of course I can, Master Kit." The plague masked doctor comes over, dutifully pulling the barrier in front of Jasper and me. He doesn't seem to move to close off the other side, so Kit does not mind them watching.

"Jasper," I murmur as he stomps over to me with a dark scowl on his handsome face. "That was not your finest moment. You should apologize."

He gives me a dirty look, clearly pouting about the curtain and the brush-off. "Princes don't apologize, especially when they are *right*."

Sighing, I take his hand between mine. "I know you're worried about me, about Xerxes, about Salem, and even about Kit Kat. Not being able to control that stupid scenario has you feeling responsible for those who were hurt. And you couldn't stop it, nor keep the dragon from taking over, so it's even worse. Right?"

The Prince of Hell just keeps scowling at me like a recalcitrant child and it takes everything in me not to chuckle. His father broke him so thoroughly as a child that it's amazing he's able to fight much of the training he was programmed to follow like a good little automaton until he found our caliphate. Right now, he probably wants to lash out again, and that won't help anything. In fact, it might ruin his chances altogether and because I love him, I don't want that to happen.

People besides me need to know how fiercely devoted Jasper Eversore is to those he allows into the fortress of his heart.

"Kit is scared, Jas," I whisper to him. "This is the first time he used magic and he didn't realize it was his until it was too late. He's feeling guilty and upset about everyone being harmed. With his issues, it's not surprising that he made the decision to put everyone else first. He's probably been doing it most of his life, right?"

Jasper frowns, looking thoughtful. "But he lied—several times. Zavvie, he had an arrow embedded in his fucking shoulder and sat around waiting until he was called. He could have bled out."

I tilt my head. "He wasn't bleeding until he forced the magic to recede. I think it was… plugging it? Fuck, I don't know because we have no idea what his heritage really is. His powers are a completely blank slate, though I've *never* seen people lose their shit like they did in that exercise. And that magic blocking the wound was black… shadows, perhaps?"

"He's not from my line. You know we can tell."

Whew. I'm finally getting past his rage and spite.

"Yes, and none of us can feel that he's part of our people. What the hell does that leave?"

Jasper frowns again then looks over his shoulder as mutters, "I don't fucking know, Zavvie."

That's exactly my point.

Dream

Slash is giving me a mixture of irritated and concerned looks and I honestly have no idea what to say to him. He's definitely the type of dude who would put the wellbeing of his caliphate before his own, but somehow, it's not okay that I did it. I don't get why not, nor why Jasper was being such an asshat. I did the same thing any of them would have done for the others—in fact, it is what some of them attempted to do.

Boys are stupid and if they were left to their own devices, procreation would cease entirely.

"Kit Kat, you have to stay still while the doc examines you."

I blink, realizing that Dank will have to remove the shirt sticking to the wound. Panic sets in as I try to figure out how I'm going to kick the rest of them out when I just made a point to only block Jasper. "Ummm…"

"You're hurt, man. It's no time to be weird about who sees you. Besides, you've seen Salem and I—"

The Universe favors me for once, and Dank makes a clicking sound as he removes the mask. "Master Kit is quite uncomfortable with being undressed. He will require me to draw the curtain, and Master Slash will have to exit the space as well."

I duck my chin, not wanting to look at any of them when he saves my bacon. Thank fuck Dank did because I was floundering; however, now I feel bad. I don't want the guys to think I don't trust them to behave. The big secret I'm keeping demands that I continue to shy away from exposing bare skin whenever possible. It's just not an option until I'm able to divulge the truth to all of them.

The big guy looks frustrated as he moves to leave, so I reach out, grabbing his hand tentatively. He blinks, looking surprised, and I squeeze lightly. "This is just the past stuff, you know? It's not about you or them—don't think it's because I don't trust you guys around me."

His face lights up and he nods. "If you say it is true, I will believe it, little demon, even if your magic fooled me before. The truth is always preferable to a lie, even a kind one, with our caliphate. We have our own issues from before you arrived."

Shit. I may have triggered their bad parent trauma with my selflessness. Way to go, Kat.

"I'll remember that." I let go, giving him a small smile and the shark shifter trudges out of my sickbay. When I turn to look at Dank, I murmur, "Thank you. I didn't know how to address it."

"It is my job, Master Kit. Now, lie back and allow me to examine this wound so I can assist. You have been brave for long enough."

Leave it to the flaming skull demon to call me out without calling me out.

THE GARDEN AROUND ME IS LUSH... NOTHING IN HELL LOOKS LIKE THIS, SO I have no idea where the fuck I am. The last thing I remember is Dank starting his work to heal me and feeling very tired. I guess I passed out from the pain, though that seems pretty far-fetched for me. I might freak out and have panic attacks, but I'm fairly good at keeping my shit together when I'm injured, even without magic concealing it.

Biting my lip, I look around cautiously, not enjoying the stab of fear that being in a place I don't know brings. The world of paranormal and demonic stuff is new to me and I am not dumb enough to believe that anywhere—even a land in my mind—is safe for me to simply wander about in. There are plenty of demons at Discordia whose powers reside in dreams and nightmares, so this could be something insidious made to look friendly. That happens in nature in the human world, so it follows it sure as fuck could here.

The only sound I hear is water rushing somewhere, so I use my other senses to reach out before I move. It smells like a fragrant garden, so that doesn't help me. I'm definitely not tasting anything because that seems like a terrible plan. The ground beneath me feels like regular old grass when I touch it. All I see is some gorgeous Garden of Eden-type set-up and it makes me huff in annoyance.

No other option but to explore, I suppose.

Rising to my feet carefully, I notice that I'm in some sort of hospital garb. Dank must have disappeared the torn and bloodied activities uniform, which means I'll have to figure out how to get more. I've already lost two to that damn class, and I'm down to the last one. No way that's going to survive long enough to get through the next month, much less the year.

"Okay, Ka—iiit," I say to myself with a grimace. Normally, I use my real name when I'm talking to myself, but since I don't know whose fever dream this is, I probably shouldn't risk it. I already have a target on my back from asshole classmates and that dickface Lucian. No need to give them more ammunition.

I look around, seeing nothing but a fairytale-esque landscape close by. There has to be a point to being here, but which way do I go? It's not like a friendly woodland creature is here to—oh, damn. Dottie. I hope Salem and Oriel are keeping her calm because she's probably flipping out if I'm unconscious in the doc's office. Damn demon drama distracted me and I completely forgot to make sure she's nearby.

What a bad mama, I am. Sheesh.

Feeling like a jerk, I head towards the sound of the water since it's the only thing that stands out in this weird place. I walk through the beautiful foliage, frowning when I don't recognize a lot of the plants. I'm not a botanist or anything, but these things don't look like anything I've seen before. The smell is amazing and the colors vibrant, but they're all alien to me. Either someone has a vivid imagination, or I'm really in another realm.

"There you are!"

I blink at the sound of the voice, whipping around to trace the source. My eyes land on a perfectly set table next to a waterfall and the pool below it in alarm. That was not there a minute ago and who the fuck is this person? I can't make anything out because they're in a cloak with a full hood, revealing nothing but the delicate hands that clapped as I came into view.

Female? Maybe? The voice sounded like it, but I know better than to assume given my current disguise.

"Uh… not to be rude, but who the fuck are you and where the hell am I?"

The hooded person laughs, the sound musical as they gesture towards the empty seat at their table. "Don't be afraid, Katarina. You are not in danger here; I promise."

How the fuck does this person know who I really am?!

I arch a brow, not moving from my spot. "No shade, but isn't that what every villain looking to hollow out my body and use it for some weird ritual would say? Ted Bundy didn't tell people he was a serial killer, either."

"You're cautious—that will serve you well in the coming times," the hidden figure says. "I appreciate a healthy skepticism in women. History has not been kind to them and the future will likely be no different. However, in this one instance, the unknown is not here to harm you. Sit with me."

My eyes narrow as I weigh my options. I could run, but if this person has magic, it won't matter if they're telling the truth. They'll just reappear wherever I go, making the same request. That goes double for bad intentions, so unless I want to stand here until they get bored, I probably have to do what they ask. I don't like being boxed in, though, and my blood pressure is rising with every second. I have to breathe or I'll spiral out. I don't know what the fuck will happen if I go into an attack here, so again, my options are limited.

This is bullshit and I'm royally pissed off.

Walking over to the fancy garden table, I see that it's set with finger food and a shiny silver tea set. This is like a damn scene out of a fantasy version of Bridgerton, and I'm not having it. Kat Camponella is not Alice and I'm not eating or drinking a damn thing in foreign land. I won't even eat food I haven't seen prepared in public since the incident, so this hooded asshole can fuck right off.

"It's not going to shrink you, Kat."

I drop into the chair, glaring at the amused creeper. "Don't mess around in my mind. It's bad enough that humans did. Plus, it's rude as fuck."

The hood moves with its head as the figure shakes it. "I am not in your mind. I simply know the cultural zeitgeist of this current world well enough to guess where you would go. It's predictable, as is the tough front the women I visit have developed due to the circumstances."

"You visit lots of women in this fairyland without consent, hmm?"

They laugh again, pouring more tea in their cup. "No, not lots. I have specific people to see and when I do, it's because they are at a turning point where it is time for them to accept many new truths about the world and themselves."

"Uh, you're too late, dude. I already got tapped for a university in Hell, which I thought was as fictional as the big sky man. Then I was told that I have to be part demon, again previously fictional, and was inducted into a demon boy band. The ship to Big Change Land has already sailed for a new port."

The tea cup disappears into the hood as the person sips, and once it lowers, they sigh. "Yes, I am a bit overdue with you, but maintaining the schedule I envisioned has been difficult. Not all of you hit the mark at the right time—some are early and some are quite late. It's made my schedule quite jumbled. I adapt well, but the others… not so much. For that, I apologize."

Why do they owe me an apology? This is getting weirder by the second.

"Thanks, I guess? But I still don't get why I'm here."

Another sigh escapes as the figure pauses. Once they make a decision, they fold their hands on the table. "You are not far into your education about the greater world of the supernatural because in a quirk of Fate, machinations in Hell moved more quickly than predicted. Unsurprising, as demons are… difficult to pin down because of their natures."

"I'm still not hearing why I'm here."

"Patience, Katarina. You are young, I know… younger than the others I've seen insofar. But I must be cautious how I approach this or I will cause unintended consequences."

Fucking riddles. Who the shit is this joker?

"Okay. Go on."

"When you get deeper into the world you were not aware of, you will learn about the many governing bodies outside of Hell and their relations with their people and the other species. You will likely learn about origins, but you will not be told the most important story. That will be revealed eventually and your existence will make a great deal more sense. I cannot tell you this now, but I can say that you are not the same as the others in this school."

"Obviously not since I'm a girl," I scoff. "That's not news."

"So jaded at such a young age. It's heartbreaking, but there was no way to prevent it." The figure leans in, but all I see in the hood is a black void. "I am truly sorry that the human world caused you to be so broken, Katarina. Unfortunately, the threads of Fate require great sacrifice in order to forge the fire needed for the future, and you are one of those victims."

Great. It was my destiny to be neglected, assaulted, and abused. Super awesome for my ego, you dime store Jawa.

"Not helpful at this juncture, but the sentiment is nice. You still haven't answered my ques-

tion, and I'm hoping the guys and the demon doc who are probably losing their minds right now yank me out of this acid trip."

"The reason you're here, Kat, is for me to tell you that your abilities will not be like others where you are. You need to choose your allies wisely, and keep your secrets well hidden. You must survive this education in order to find out what you want to know—where you came from and why you are like this—but also for larger concerns."

"Oh, goody, you only visit 'chosen ones,' is that it? Well, tell the Watchers I decline. We all saw what happened to the last girl who accepted—over and over, until even death didn't keep her from peace. No thanks; I'm unavailable for world saving duties."

Hood Person laughs, the cloth around their head shaking again. "Oh, Kat. You're quite delightful, but you cannot decline Fate. It is the one true equalizer in all the realms—as it is woven, it will be so."

"Again, hard pass."

They sigh, waving their hand. "You are not ready. I will return when you have a bit more experience under your belt. Be well, be wary, and most of all, be happy, child."

THAT'S WHEN I WAKE UP, COLD AND CLAD IN A HOSPITAL GOWN, WITH SIX furious looking demons, a kinkajou, and a curious skull demon doctor peering down at me.

"Uh, hi, guys… was I out long?"

Aftermath

Jasper

When the shrimp wakes up, everyone but X is staring at him. He looks panicked as his eyes roam over us, then to the doctor. It seems like the doc gives him a tiny head shake—which is odd, but at least there's someone Kit feels safe enough to trust. It certainly isn't me, though I'm not surprised or upset by that. I haven't decided how I want to proceed with the things inside my mind in regards to him, and though Zavvie is trying to help me, I don't know how long it will take me to muddle through it all.

But he should have people to trust if only because his admissions prior to the curtain being drawn lead me to believe he never had any before in his past life.

Unfortunately, I'm perfectly aware of how isolating that is, especially if you have bad things happening to you. Until I bonded with my brothers and accepted Zavvie… I was alone. I dealt with my father's fits of wrath and subsequent efforts to regain my affections and respect through gifts and praise. He wielded his favor like a weapon and still does—something that breaks you down over time until you barely recognize who you've become. I didn't end up with Kit's neuroses, but I'm aware I have plenty of my own.

"Where did you go?" I ask gruffly.

Oriel glares at me and Salem follows suit, but I cannot treat the shrimp with kid gloves. I don't want to appear to show favoritism, nor do I want him to think he can work me as easily as he does the others. The crow shifter grunts, shaking his head in annoyance. "Don't interrogate him, Jas. He's coming out of a blackout, for fuck's sake. Let Kit Kat acclimate before you start the gulag treatment."

"How long was I out?" The shrimp squints, looking at all of us curiously. "Was I like… completely dead to the world?"

An interesting question and one that was definitely phrased to seem innocuous.

"You passed out while I was completing the healing for today," Dr. D says as he moves to peer at the kid closely. "Perhaps ten or fifteen minutes… nothing that is too concerning or I would insist you remain here for the evening."

Kit's eyes widen and he shakes his head. "No, no. I'd much rather go back to my room. It's… familiar. I'll have trouble sleeping if I'm not in a place where I feel comfortable. And where's Dottie?"

"Right here, KK," Salem says as he lifts the small rodent off the bed where he was sitting before we all hurried to the shrimp's side. The damn furry little shit chitters as it scampers up the bed to nuzzle Kit's face, making his expression turn to one of relief.

Okay, fine, I get why he and Oriel cart that thing around like a Ming vase. It's a lifeline for the kid.

"Thanks," Kit mumbles as he leans into the small arms and eager noises of the kinkajou. "She helps me regulate like a support animal and this is very… Well, today has been *a lot*."

"No shit," Slash says as he pats the covered feet with his hand lightly.

He's getting really fucking weird about this kid and his insouciance earlier makes me very suspicious. I'm going to have a private conversation with my second soon, and he'd better explain his fucking bullshit. My eyes move to Zav, and he gives me a knowing look. Just great, now he expects me to say something comforting to help the shrimp and I have no idea what that would be. Everything is quiet for a moment until I clear my throat. "I think we can get you back to your dorm so you will get the rest you need. That is, if the doc can make sure we have instructions and perhaps a note to excuse you from classes tomorrow?"

Zavvie rolls his eyes, telling me that wasn't quite what he hoped for, but he nods. "I'm sure we can, Jasper. Slash can carry him, and we'll make sure Dottie is taken care of… and Salem will help, right?"

"I definitely will. I mean, I'll set alarms and stuff so I don't forget if I get sleepy, and—"

"I'll help him keep to whatever schedule you need," Oriel interrupts. "Anton will be busy taking care of Xerxes, I assume."

"Xerxes will need to be monitored for several days, but he will make a full recovery," the doctor says as he looks at me. "The young master burned his powers too brightly to fight the madness that took over the arena— according to his account. Master Salem did the opposite—he embraced it to help defend the injured with Master Kit."

I blink, looking at Slash and Oriel for confirmation. They both nod, and I file that away for our discussion once we're in the privacy of our rooms. It seems there is much about this giant clusterfuck that I missed because my dragon took free rein. We will need to rectify that once we're not in this office and it can't wait until morning. Kit and X might not be going to their classes, but the rest of us will have to face the masses. If we don't have a singular, streamlined version of events prepared, it will be too easy for the administration to pick at us.

I refuse to give Darkstar the satisfaction of punishing any of my brothers for a perceived slight.

"Understood." I look at the shrimp, but he's busy cuddling the rat like it's the one thing keeping him sane. Sighing as I run my hand through my hair, I turn to my general again. "Slash, you will need to get him to their room since Salem will be leaning on Oriel. Zavida will come with me."

The doctor reaches for his mask, settling it back on his face before he speaks. "I will assist Master Anton with getting Master Xerxes to their room. The latter is still too weak to be moved without using a portal, I fear."

"You promise he's going to be okay, right, Dank?"

The fear in Kit's tone even hits me and my dragon growls in frustration inside. He doesn't like that at all. "He knows better than to lie to the Prince."

A rough, rusty sounding laugh comes from behind the mask. "I would not lie to any of you, especially about the welfare of one of your caliphate brothers. That bond is sacred and easily as old as I am—no one wishes to find out what happens if you betray it, not even your father, Prince Jasper."

That was a very odd thing to say, but the doc never says anything but exactly what he means.

THE PORTAL OPENS IN THE HALLWAY OF OUR FLOOR OF CANTO IV, AND I lead the group out one by one. Salem and Oriel head for the panda's room, followed by Slash with the shrimp in his arms. I don't understand why Kit lets that big, toothy demon cart him around without batting a lash. He's easily as brutal as I am, but somehow, he's wormed his way into an inner circle that seems to grow every time I turn around. Grumbling in irritation, I wave Zavvie in, then move so the doc can guide a floating X and intensely focused Anton.

"Take them to the main room. We will be able to care for them better if everyone is in the same place."

"What? No!"

Slash turns, allowing the kid to look at me in exasperation as he exclaims. "Jasper, come on. I need… space. Having everyone in our room will not give me that."

"He's not wrong," Zavvie murmurs under his breath. But he knows *why* I'm ordering this, too.

If I can see them all, I can convince my dragon they are all okay.

"Don't be ridiculous. We reconfigured that room to give everyone appropriate space, and Annie can work a little of his charm to make those who need the most rest comfortable." I cross my arms over my chest, glaring at the shrimp. "Plus, we can keep guard over the injured in one centralized location."

The shark shifters snorts, muttering, "That *could* be the reason."

"It *is* the reason, Scrum," I shoot back as I jerk my head at the doc. "Move him down the hall to the room where Oriel and Salem went. We're hunkering down until everyone is healed."

"Kill me now. Just kill me," Kit groans as he hides behind his hulking ride to the room. "I cannot survive a room full of you douches twenty-four hours a day for who the fuck knows how long."

"Some people would die for the privilege," I retort as I shoulder my way through. "Hell, they'd pay us to kill them if it got them in our room before they kicked it."

A loud sniff comes from my second's arms as the shrimp says, "I could care less about your desperate conquests, Jasper Eversore. The sun even shines on a dog's ass some days, you know?"

The rusty cough followed by a hacking wheeze signals the plague-masked doctor having a good laugh at my expense and I try not to let them all see me fume. Kit is funny, but he's terrible for keeping my brothers and the staff in line. His constant pot shots would get him killed with other demons and caliphates, yet I allow each one with little more than a sharp response and occasionally, a good verbal jab.

It's quite baffling to me, even though I recognize that my verbal sparring is meaner than a punch at times.

"Jas, you wouldn't be thrilled with a bunch of people invading your room and taking up all the oxygen."

Scratching my chin, I look at Anton curiously. "Prior to moving our meeting area, you all invaded my space constantly."

"But you *allowed* it and in fact, encouraged it for good 'order' or whatever the hell you told yourself to make it less obvious that you dislike being alone." The peacock shifter gives me a knowing look, then a shrug. "Kit Kat struggles with boundary issues and lack of private spaces and neglect from foster homes. Having everyone there for an extended time period will stress him out. If you insist on it, then at least stop being a jackass for a bit."

"You love to stick the knife in and twist, don't you Aldaric?" His grin is unrepentant and I'm about to give him a piece of my mind when the soft voice of the fallen cobra shifter prevents it.

"Don't be a jerk to him, Jasper. He protected me and Zav when his powers got out of control. Not from him, but from the juiced up opponents no one was ready for. We owe him and Salem a lot—more than you know."

Frowning as I process that statement, I lean down to look at X. "You're certain that is true? It's not an exaggeration to keep me from being angry about his lack of control?"

Anton snorts as we head into the living area of the shrimp's dorm. "Uh, no, he's sure, and so am I. I doubt you'll find anyone here who blames the kid for not knowing how to manage whatever that was. None of us even know what the hell he did; how could he know how to use it properly?"

Sighing as they hover Xerxes until he's on the couch, I nod for Dr. D to take his leave. His service has been excellent and I'd tell my father, but then I'd have to recount things I'd prefer to keep out of his purview for the moment. Besides, I'm not sure the ancient demon gives a shit what my father thinks of him; in fact, I think he much prefers being here as our physician to being at court.

I should find out why that is and what he meant by his earlier jab when I have time.

For now, I have a roomful of caliphate to wrangle into telling me what happened on that field and how we're going to prevent it from occurring again outside of the Games.

The last thing we need is to be surprised when our lives are on the line—again.

Nervous

Slash deposited me on the bed carefully, then ignored my protests as he rifled through my drawers to grab my last pair of sweats. I was relieved to note he did *not* go through my underwear drawer, so I haven't been prematurely outed to another person, but it also means I'm going commando unless I want to call for help or struggle to move on my own.

Fuck, fuck, fuckitty, fuck.

I'd try getting Dottie to help—that is, if I'm right about her understanding what the hell I say—but she's out with the others. My ears prick as vaguely intelligible phrases occasionally make it through the thick door, but none of it is enough to *really* hear what they're saying. Sighing deeply, I give in, knowing the size of this shirt is big enough to hide my meager assets without the binder. I wonder briefly what Dank did with the stuff that was battle worn and realize that even my one and only binder is now gone. That is *not* good for day-to-day and I'm going to have to speak with X about how I address that issue quietly. They'll know a way to fix it; I'm sure.

Frowning harder as I start tallying the shit I will need to deal with sooner rather than later, I curse under my breath again at Jasper's decree. If it was just Xerxes staying here, I could wait until Salem crashes from the bear's needs and chat in relative safety. But having *all* of those douchenozzles here is going to severely cramp my ability to have a private convo with the one person who knows my damn secret.

Satan's charred bungholes… I'm so goddamned screwed.

The light tap on my door lets me know I'm taking too long, so I carefully pull off the gown and get into my clean clothes. I don't know which of them did that, but it definitely means Jasper is getting impatient. The worse that gets, the more likely it is that he'll tromp on my boundaries by storming in and we'll spend the rest of the night arguing. That won't help me or them, so I clear my throat and croak, "Come in."

Oriel's dark countenance greets me, though his lips turn up in a smile when he sees me dwarfed in my baggy shit as usual. "Lookin' normal, Kit Kat. That's good to see."

Wrinkling my nose, I wave my hand a little. "Yeah, I'm a real treat for the eyes at the moment. Can you hand me my basket thingy over on the dresser? I won't feel good until I clean myself off a bit."

He arches a brow but nods, walking over to get the opaque plastic basket that all of my toiletries are in. Luckily, I had the forethought to *not* keep feminine products in it day-to-day, so he won't accidentally see my period stuff. I'm not on it now, but it should be coming soon enough. "I don't know what you need for this, but it's a bit heavy considering all the provided stuff in the bathroom."

I snort. "Why are most guys so damn dense about self-care? I know you all have styling products and shit in there, but do none of you actually do things to prevent damage to the stupid meat sack you live in?"

"Uh…" Oriel scratches his chin, then does his bird-like head tilt. "We're *demons*, KK."

This time, I look at him with the questioning expression. "Does every demon in Hell look young or…?"

He blinks, then I see his expression change to one of understanding. "You think the ones who age better like… use skin care and shit?"

"I'd almost guarantee it, dummy." Opening the box, I take out my micellar water and a washable pad, wiping the gross off my skin, then apply my moisturizer. "Honestly, I'd bet it's the same for a lot of supes because the rich ones look better, mm?"

"Holy fuck," O says, his tone similar to if I'd just told him who orchestrated the Kennedy assassination. "You have to tell everyone that X was right. It will make them feel *so* much better, KitKat."

Of fucking course Xerxes tried to tell these dingleberries and they didn't listen.

"I will," I reply as I use a few more products, then put everything back in the box. "Okay, now I feel less like I'm covered in grossness. I can go out there once I put on some deodorant."

"Your routine didn't seem this thorough last time we were all in this bathroom," he grumbles.

I shrug, not wanting to draw attention to the fact that I do most of this in the shower stall to limit the amount of time I have to look at them all half-naked. The motion makes me wince—damn shoulder wound—and Oriel rushes over to sit next to me. He looks worried, so I shake my head. "I'm okay; I forgot about the damn injury for a second. It pulled some—no need to panic, man."

The crow shifter blows out a relieved breath. "Damn, KK. You're killing me with this shit. Today was the most stressful day I've had in a long fucking time."

It's my turn to blink in confusion. "Really? Why? I mean… I get the magic thing was um… weird, but…"

Oriel gives me a crooked smile, taking my hand and lacing our fingers together. "Because, dude, usually I let all this bullshit slide off my back like I'm a duck instead of a crow. Jas and Slash get all pissy, Anton and X do their calm unaffected thing, Zav follows whatever Jas says… But Salem and me? We almost always just ride things out, only doing our parts and not letting shit affect us."

"Yeah, that tracks. What's different?"

"Man, you really *are* dense sometimes." I pull my hand back at those words and he chuckles, grabbing it to squeeze. "KK, *you* are the difference. Every-time you are in danger, it's like someone is putting my goddamn chest in a vice and I *have* to figure it out. So yeah, this damn magic thing and all the threats, and the injury paired with my brothers being hurt, too? It's made me feel like one big raw nerve. Seeing you look fairly normal makes that loosen up so I can breathe."

I have no *idea how to respond to that admission.*

Licking my lips, I stare at our hands as I consider what I'm going to say. Once I feel like I'm able to speak, I look up at him with a small smile. "I'm not used to people giving a shit, so yeah… that's kind of news to me. If I seem dense, it's because a long time ago, I built this whole system around me to protect myself from bullshit in my life. Letting people past those walls isn't easy, but I am trying."

"I know. Letting Salem and me show you our other forms showed me that." My face turns red as he continues, "But you have to know that there are people who care and doing reckless stuff is going to affect us. That's the normal you aren't used to—I get that—but you have to sort of… be aware of it?"

Oh.

"That's a very nice way to say don't have my head up my ass like Jasper." Oriel chuckles and I dip my chin. "You're asking me to allow people to help more often so those of you who *are* connecting to me don't worry as much."

"Good boy!" He says with a joyful grin.

My eyes widen as my entire body tingles and I yank my hand back as if I've been burned. What the fuck is happening to me right now? Scooting to the edge of the bed, I swallow hard then rasp, "Um, we should probably go… you know."

O looks confused, but he nods. Rolling to his feet, he takes my basket back to the dresser, then comes back, facing me. "Okay. But I'm helping you to your nest in the chair that Slash has spent the past half hour building. It's really weird, yet kind of adorable at the same time. You might have enjoyed watching that big dude as he built it."

I nod, still having trouble with my throat being tight as I push to my feet very slowly. "You're right; I'm kind of sad I missed it."

His grin is wicked. "Pretty sure X had Annie film it secretly. Ask him when you get a moment alone."

That's the rub, isn't it? I can't get a damn second alone with the slithery demon and now I need one even more.

***

Now that I'm curled up in this truly elaborate set-up Slash built, I see why Oriel found it so charming. I don't know where he got all of the extra blankets and pillows, but every part of me is warm and supported. He made sure there's a table on either side of it with food and drinks on one side and creature comforts on the other. Dottie has a little space of her own just above my head, and my feet are up as I look at the guys in their own spaces around the room.

"Thank you," I mumble, pushing my hair out of my face as I try not to panic that I'm going to let everyone down as usual. "This is really comfortable. Oriel said you did it, big guy?"

The shark shifter gives me a proud smile, nodding once. "I did."

He won't be as talkative in this environment, so I'll have to thank him again later when he'll really communicate.

"I made the food."

My eyes cut over to Salem, who's no longer the bear, and half-dressed in his university sweats again. I have to swallow hard before I respond, because these guys completely fuck up my focus when they swan about so damn undressed. "Thank you, too. I'm going to eat some as soon as my stomach settles; I promise."

His smile is bright, but I see the strain at the corners of his eyes. The amount of energy he burned during that rage fest really must have him struggling. I haven't seen Salem look so wiped out since I arrived, and that's saying a lot. "I'm always happy to feed you, KK. You know that."

I sort of do, but I have no idea how to handle that. So I pull the blankets a little higher as I smile at my roomie, then look over at the glowering Prince. "You wanted this big slumber party, so I assume you're going to…. debrief us or something?"

Multiple expressions dance over his aquiline features, but he finally settles on looking annoyed. "Unfortunately, I was *indisposed* during the big event, so I require information from all of you. I need to know how people were injured, what exactly you did, and what I might need to spin tomorrow morning."

"Indisposed is a fancy way of saying your dragon went apeshit and you couldn't stop it, right?" I arch my brow at him as the corner of my lips curls up.

Jasper inhales deeply, then gives his second a sharp look. Slash shrugs, and glaring at the others doesn't help his cause. In fact, all of them seem to be on my side, which makes the butterflies in my stomach dance again in happiness. "Yes. Fine. That's what it means. The rage burst tapped into the emotions my dragon often struggles with due to my own issues."

"It's a Devil's Night miracle," Zav mutters and I have to smother a giggle.

Yes, Zavida, yes, it is.

Stuck in the Middle with You

Xerxes

I feel like a wrung-out dish rag—and that's being kind. Whatever the fuck Kit Kat did in the arena was powerful enough that trying to counter the effects while battling totally blasted my reserves. I don't think anything like this has happened since I was a hatchling; my powers are typically far beyond the scope of my peers.

And she doesn't even know the extent of her abilities yet, which is terrifying and hot at the same time.

I've started referring to KK in the feminine in my brain to help myself adjust to my confirmed suspicions. It's partially because I know she'll have to spill the beans to everyone eventually and partially because I haven't been interested in a femme-presenting being so far. In fact, Annie's the only one I've ever given a shit about, so despite everyone assuming I'm gay, I've always suspected I was more demi than anything else. But I hate labels that aren't on clothing, so I often allow people to choke on their own misconceptions rather than correct them.

Educating people isn't my fucking job, and I'm not giving away emotional labor for free. Unlike Kit, I haven't been forced to spend a great deal of my life explaining how I work in order to get what I need. That shit is exhausting and I don't blame her for putting up walls a million miles high to keep assholes out. My brothers have always accepted me for exactly who and how I am, without question, so I've been lucky in that respect. My family is a different story, but I stopped giving a shit about their bullshit a long time ago unless it directly impacted me.

Annie has a similar relationship to his bio donors, and we're aligned in that respect.

Attraction to KK, though? That's a different story altogether. He definitely believes he's one thing, and this is going to rock him a bit. I feel bad not telling him, but it's *not* my story to share and I won't push Kit into doing so before she's ready. I will subtly nudge my love to open up to her, though, and perhaps she will do the same. Playing matchmaker is one of my fortes, despite not practicing the skill often because I worry about abusing my powers. I don't like allowing the Lust lineage to cross lines I believe should be negotiated before they're crossed.

Licking my lips, I wait for my new secret obsession to continue her tale after besting Jasper in a verbal spar about his lack of control in the arena. She looks worried, so I give her an encouraging smile, weak as it may be. The expression she gives me is grateful, and my chest tightens.

Damn, I like when she looks at me like that.

"Okay. Jasper was off-the-rails; we're in agreement." Kit pauses and winks at the growly Prince, which only makes his scowl deeper. "The group was split up across the field by the opponent list, and on the far right, my group was closest to Salem's and X's. Annie was on the other side and Oriel was toward the middle with Zavida."

"That sounds accurate," Annie muses. "Being all the way at the other end made me concerned about the reach of the spell, but we didn't have options. That much was obvious in your tone, Jas."

The dragon nods sharply. "I could not deviate; that is true."

Another fucking geas, it seems. Darkstar needs to be tortured until he cries like a baby.

Kit sucks in a breath, then lets it out slowly. "I was doing the best I could against the idiots using magic. But it amped up as the battle went on, so I did what Anton told me to. That felt like it… fizzled out? And the more I tried, the harder it got to keep up with the fuckers coming for me. They definitely weren't treating this as training and their bullshit trash talk confirmed it."

"What. Did. They. Say?" Oriel snarls as he and Salem come back from refilling the drinks.

Even Jasper gives him a surprised look, and I grin to myself. Kit Kat has even the most lackadaisical of my caliphate up in arms at the merest slight; I'm going to enjoy watching these emotionally stunted royals figure out how the fuck to deal with their shit without fucking this up.

"Stupid shit about why you guys picked me as your 'boyfriend' and how excited the dumbass was to fuck me up." Kit rolls his eyes and leans back in his chair when the room fills with growls. "It's what every dumbass motherfucker says when they come for me, by the way, and very much like what human asswipes say when they're about to violate you in some way. I'm definitely used to that attitude, but this shithead seemed to also think he'd get rewarded for ending me. Very Bond villain monologue stuff."

Jasper's eyes flash with his dragon and for a second, I hold my breath. That's never a good sign and the Prince already lost his grip once today. I clear my throat, hoping to distract his animal. "You think he meant Lucian?"

She almost shrugs, but seems to remember at the last second that she has an injured shoulder. "I mean, I guess? I was so… overwrought that he didn't get a chance to elaborate. I sort of… threw the knife things and then…"

"Then what?" Slash asks, his expression unreadable. "What happened next, little demon?"

Swallowing hard, Kit pauses before answering. "Well, they hit him with more accuracy than I expected and… I don't know. His eyes got scared as whatever magic they were infused with took hold. He was definitely screaming in agony and the more he did, the happier this part of me got."

We're all quiet as that sinks in, but only Salem is brave enough to ask, "What part? What do you mean, Kit Kat? Is this a new thing?"

"I…" Her head dips and the kinkajou moves from its post above Kit's head to snuggle into her neck. That seems to help and when she finally looks up, there's a guilty expression on her features. "I've had a darkness in me since I was young. There's this small piece of me that was *always* angry about my life and how everyone—the system and the adults—treated me. Until the incident, I mostly squashed it because human kids are taught that kind of anger is a bad thing. Admitting to it would definitely keep you in group homes, not foster placements. Both suck, but the former is much worse."

Oriel walks over, kneeling next to her chair as he shakes his head. "Humans are dumb, KK. Anger is healthy; it's how you deal with it that's good or bad."

"Well, I know that *now*. All the damned therapy after the… thing… taught me the difference. But I also struggled with that fury and white-hot rage a *lot* more once I was violated. It was a louder voice in my mind, and a darker joy in my gut when I saw people get what I felt they deserved. The sense of justice and vengeance was so deep that it worried me. I kept my big yap shut to the therapists and learned to shove it as deep as I could—until today."

Slash grunts, crossing his arms over his chest before his toothy grin spreads. "Your demon."

Glad I'm not the one who said it.

Kit's eyes widen as she looks at each of us in turn, seeking confirmation of her simple declaration. "Seriously? I'm not secretly a psychopath?"

Jasper bursts out laughing, earning himself a haughty glare. It doesn't bother him, though, because he knows something she doesn't and it's making *his* petty side happy. "Shrimp, you're no more a psychopath than I'm a pretty princess."

Now everyone is laughing and Kit is burrowing further into her blankets with a bright red face, so I step in. "All jokes aside, Kit Kat—Jasper's right. Your basic knowledge of things from therapy probably made you do internet research and well, you just assumed incorrectly because you didn't have all the information possible."

Zavida finally pops out from behind his tails at the Prince's feet, nodding eagerly. "Guaranteed, X. The human internet is *stuffed* with bullshit about psychology that is referencing very common supernatural behaviors. It's why they try to gather up lost ones of the different species and drop them in enclaves so they don't get misdiagnosed and imprisoned like the *X-Men*."

"Ohhhhh," Kit says, understanding filling her gaze. "I mean, that's probably not *all* of the bad people up there, but that definitely makes some shit make sense."

Zavida smiles shyly. "You'd be amazed how many exceptional or evil humans weren't humans at all. Between the Society and all the leaders of various realms, things are kept as tightly guarded as possible. But shit slips and then… a lot of retconning has to happen to provide logical excuses for them."

She holds her hand before he can continue. "Okay, okay. Not yet. I have to take things a little bit at a time, Zav. I'm already reeling from the new spin on mythology, this place's existence, and now I have magic. I mean… I really can't take more world rocking at the moment."

There's an odd glint to her eyes as she looks at each of us in turn and I wonder what's behind that. Are our real personalities versus the images we project also causing her to have dissonance? Perhaps so, but she has to get to know the real us for a multitude of reasons. That, I can't soften for our new member, as it will build trust over time. Kit will have to process that on her own, unfortunately.

But that doesn't seem like everything and I can't put my finger on it—yet.

"Okay. So this 'darkness' has always been your demon trying to communicate with you, but you didn't know it. What else, shrimp? What happened when the demon was able to wrest control?"

"I'm getting there, Jasper. Calm down," she snaps. He frowns, then Kit sighs. "Sorry. You asked like a normal person, but that tidbit you guys just dropped is making my anxiety spike. I shouldn't have been shitty."

"Holy fuck, that's both of them. It really *is a Satanic* miracle," Oriel mutters.

"Not helpful," I chide the crow shifter weakly. "Don't ruffle their feathers or they'll start taking chunks out of each other again."

Dottie moves from Kit's neck, shaking a tiny fist and chittering loudly. That makes O chuckle and he holds up his hands defensively. "Okay, bitty brawler. I get it. Don't tease him right now. Message received."

"I cannot *believe* you guys talk to that rat," Jasper grumbles. "It's insane."

Zavida clears his throat, his face pained as he looks up at the Prince. "Not really, Jas. Familiars are very intelligent; they often have the ability to understand their companion perfectly. It's possible being in the caliphate means that extends to us as well. I'd have to do more research but…"

Kit curses under her breath, then mutters, "I *knew* she could understand me! I thought I was nuts at first."

"You might be, but not for that reason," Zavida says with a tiny grin.

I really enjoy how she brings everyone in our family out of their shells; it's refreshing as fuck.

"Bad Zavvie!" she scolds and a low, dark growl echoes in the room. The emerging demon whips her head to follow the sound and frowns at Jasper. "What the fuck is your problem now? Even X said we were doing well, and now you want to spoil it?"

Jasper's dragon flashes in his eyes as he drops a hand to the kitsune's head and ruffles his messy hair. "You do not get to call him that, nor scold him. That is *not* your place, shrimp."

I blink, realizing Kit knows fuck all about BDSM roles and definitely not as they work between demons like us. Jas is going to rip her a new asshole because she inadvertently crossed a major boundary. Before he can pounce, I cut in. "KK, you know how some of us share your nickname?"

"Yeah, but Salem bitched at first."

Salem coughs and has to cover his mouth, so I continue helping. "Well, there's a reason why our animals or demons don't like that concept. It might be a bit much for you at the moment, but it's pretty unnatural for such a moniker to be shared. They prefer their own personal term of endearment, so to speak."

Her eyes narrow and she squints at Slash. "Is that why you always call me 'little demon?' That's yours?"

He nods then cocks his chin at Jasper. "He uses shrimp."

"Huh. So you two suck at sharing and the others have evolved? That tracks."

Jasper growls again, and this time, Annie jumps in. "No, their animals are the bigger predators and therefore prone to being... demanding. It's very likely everyone will find their own eventually and Salem will feel much better. But the point here is that the name you used is very personal for the Prince for a multitude of reasons that you may learn some other time."

"Not fucking likely," Jasper mutters.

"Maybe."

Everyone but Kit looks at Zavida in surprise and his face flames immediately, sending him back into his tails fast enough to be a red blur of motion.

I'll be damned twice now—even the most submissive dude in our group just defied the Prince for the girl who has no idea what she's gotten herself into.

This is going to be so very, very fun to watch unfold.

Trustfall

kat/kit

The rest of the night went awkwardly, to say the least. I did my best to describe what happened to me in the arena step by step—as best I could. Salem and the others filled in their accounts of the magic in the air increasing their rage, making the worry and fear inside of them explode in powerful reactions. X and Zav were spared because of their injuries, and Slash swears he wasn't any more angry than normal. Jasper had already lost his shit, but he admitted that perhaps it helped his dragon stay in control longer.

By the time we bedded down, I was so exhausted I could barely keep my eyes open. Oriel and Salem curled up by my legs instead of their chairs, making Jasper get even grumpier as he finally shut off the lights. I honestly didn't get all the weird looks and growls being traded around me, but boys are fucking weird.

If they've got something shoved up their asses, it's not my responsibility to help pull it out.

However, the way they're all violently getting ready in the bathroom this morning tells me I was right. Jasper is brushing his teeth like he's going to scrub off the enamel. Oriel and Salem have been jerkily fussing with the gel in their hair for much longer than normal. Slash is quieter than ever, but he's flashing his teeth occasionally as he looks in the mirror. Poor Zavida keeps ducking in and out of his tails as he does his morning self-care, while Anton is grunting in irritation as he helps Xerxes get cleaned up and pretty. The wings on X's eyeliner are T. Swift sharp for certain.

Clearing my throat, I look around as I step out of my stall. I have my remaining uniform on, but it's messier than usual because I refuse to tighten anything against the healing wound. "So… what's the plan for today?"

Seven heads whip around to pin me with their gaze and the intensity makes me back up a bit. Salem's face lightens as he smiles at me, his gorgeous torso on display all the way down to a very defined pelvic V above his pants. "There you are, Kit Kat. I thought you'd drowned for a second."

Ha, ha. I was hoping you assholes would get dressed so my tongue wouldn't feel too big for my fucking mouth, but here we are.

"It's harder to get my shit on with the shoulder." Plus, I had to use the ACE bandage I swiped from our medicine cabinet to bind myself until I can get X alone to chat. "Don't fuss at me."

A snort makes me turn to look at Jasper and I swallow hard as my eyes take in his broad shoulders, muscled back and the dragon spikes he always wears. He looks dangerous as fuck, even half-naked. But despite my mixed feelings about the spicy Prince, my whole body feels hot when he finally looks at me. "Someone has to. You take far too many risks, even when they're with good intentions, and you don't seem the least bit concerned with the fact that someone is actively instructing people to kill you."

"Of course he's concerned."

My eyes swing to Slash when he speaks, and my mouth gets dry. The enormous shark shifter is using some kind of moisturizer on his thick biceps and boy, does it make my stomach flutter to watch. I push out a slow breath, hoping to calm myself before I speak. I'd prefer my voice not come out like Minnie fucking Mouse, and I'm not sure it won't right now.

Anton saves me as he leads X to a bench to sit down. "You're both right. Kit cares, but he's unable to let any of us be harmed. That's part of the caliphate bond and you all know it."

"Yes," Jasper grits out as he turns back to the mirror. "But he keeps getting hurt, which defies coincidence. He's not being cautious enough and that has to change."

"Kit is right here, and he does *not* like being talked about as if he isn't." I cross my arms over my chest as I finally find my voice. "I'm doing the best I can with shall we say… *limited resources*… in comparison to the people threatening me. You guys keep coming up with plans, but then Lucian or whoever the fuck, does something to put me right back in the hot seat. Stop blaming me for shit outside of my control."

Xerxes gives me a thumbs up, and I dip my chin, oddly pleased that he agrees with me. "It's true. We have *got* to find out what the hell that dick is up to. It probably has something to do with his journey to the surface before the ball."

Everyone is quiet for a moment as his statement sinks in, then the Prince nods. He spins to face us, his expression one of grim determination. "Xerxes is correct. However, it will take some time to arrange for an expedition to look into it. I'll send word to my father that I require passes today."

Passes? What the hell for?

My heart rate speeds a bit at the knowledge that the King will know anything about our efforts. I'm definitely not his favorite person now, and the guys—including his son—don't seem to be in his favor often, either. Maybe this isn't a good idea. Licking my lips, I raise my hand and Oriel chuckles until I yank it down. "Are we sure bringing him into our business is a good plan?"

"Absolutely not," Jasper says with a smirk. "But I've spent most of my life finding ways to induce my father to grant his permission for things without telling him the real reason I'm doing them. I will make sure he doesn't suspect our true aims."

Slash nods. "That is accurate."

"I hate to mention it, but our first class this morning is Arms," Anton cuts in. "While Zavida may be okay to participate, I don't think X or Kit should go. We need a reason to keep them out and someone to escort them, just in case."

"We can go for a check-up with Dank," I offer, eager to get Xerxes alone so I can talk to him about things I don't want the others to know about.

"Mythology is useless to me. I am all too aware of the history of Hell,"

Slash replies. "My free time is afterward, so I will take them to visit the doctor."

Perfect. Slash will keep his distance if I ask, so I can talk to Xerxes on the way.

Jasper scratches his chin, then nods. "Acceptable. You will keep everyone but the doc away from them, then take X to Human History, where Oriel can take over. Kit will stay with you until we meet for lunch in the Triclinium."

The shark shifter grins broadly and I breathe a sigh of relief. He, Salem, and Oriel are the easiest to be with when there's no classes involved. I'm getting there with Xerxes and Anton, but I'm still nervous as hell with Zav. Jasper is a whole different enchilada and I don't want to stay with him solo until I feel more secure in his support.

"Okay," I murmur. "I can deal with that."

"You looked like you wanted to run like a rabbit in there," X says as we walk down the hall to the elevator on our floor.

We all finished dressing and got our shit together, the rest of them leaving for the arena before they ended up being late for class. Breakfast was a round of packable treats from Salem, and I swallow the bite of my special granola bar before I answer the cobra shifter. "I get… nervous in there. It's not an atmosphere I'm used to, *obviously*."

They grin a bit, tilting their head as they study me. Slash is standing a few feet back, giving us the distance X asked him for. "I'll bet it's not. Lots of pretty guys running around half-naked is definitely out of your wheelhouse."

I roll my eyes at them. "As if I care about that. You know I have issues. It was just very combative in there this morning."

"Bullshit." X shakes their head, their eyes knowing. "My gifts are in this arena, Kit Kat. You can't fool me, even if you're trying to fool yourself."

Sucking in a deep breath, I shake my head, not looking at them. "I don't have the ability to analyze that statement, X. It's… I'm not there, and I honestly don't understand the things you're referring to well enough to respond. Plus, with all the weird shit happening to me with this… demon thing? Hell if I know what's what."

They pause as the door to the elevator opens, following me in then holding the door for Slash. "Fair enough. You had a huge fucking burst in the arena and none of us really know what it means. Even Jasper is puzzled by the mix of powers your demon presented. It's not... directly representative of anything common."

"I do not believe that is the extent." We both look at Slash, who just arches a brow. "you are holding back, little demon. There is something you did not reveal."

Xerxes looks at me curiously. "Is he right, KK? If so, you can tell us now and we won't rat you out to Prince Prickface."

"I don't know..."

The shark shifter grunts, then eyes me. "Your secrets are not mine to tell."

I might be stupid, but I actually believe him.

"C'mon, Kit Kat. What did you leave out last night?"

The door dings and Slash holds it open for us, then falls in line on my other side as we slowly walk out of the building. Once we're in the open air, I feel safer, though I'm not sure why. "I think I had an incident... before this. But I'm not sure because no one's ever mentioned this sort of thing so far, and I don't know enough about all this shit to be sure."

Xerxes bumps my good shoulder with theirs. "Tell us, Kit Kat. We might not know, either, but it will help us try to figure out what you are. Or I think it will, but I won't know until you tell us."

"X is correct," Slash says firmly. "More knowledge can only help."

Clasping my hands together, I consider their words. I never trust people with all the information; if you don't have anything held back, it puts you at risk. You have to have things just for you that no one can take away. My trauma screams in my head, trying desperately to convince me that I shouldn't share this with the two of them. I fight with myself internally, warring between wanting people to lean on for once and fear needing them at the same time.

Sweet baby Cerberus, I'm a goddamn mess.

"If you don't want—"

I shake my head at X, pushing all my fears down into my feet so I can speak. "No, I want to. It's just really hard to fight the voices."

"I would eat them if I could."

Blinking for a second as my brain halts in place, I burst out laughing at Slash's statement. Suddenly, the conflict in my head seems silly; after all, someone who would consume my internal voices if they could wouldn't willingly hurt me.

Xerxes chuckles as I work through that thought process. "Leave it to the big guy to put it as simply as possible."

"Don't be mean," I chide them as I get control of my mirth. "It was simple, but extremely clarifying, and that's all it needed to be."

My answer is a big, toothy grin from the shark shifter. He gets that his words struck a chord inside of me and he's giving me time to reconcile it. X is supportive, too, but in a very different way than the huge enforcer. Their opposing styles are surprisingly complementary, much like the dark cleverness of Oriel and the happy ease of Salem.

Taking a deep breath as we cross the quad, I look at them and say softly, "I'm pretty sure I stopped time in the cafeteria the other day. I mean, I think I did. Is that weird?"

The looks they give are not encouraging, and my chest tightens.

I guess that's not a good sign at all.

Secret Agent Man

oriel

I'm supposed to be in Mythology, but I'm skipping out. That's not usual for me in a class that basic, and I don't give a flying fuck if Darkstar has a problem with it. He can write me up if he wants or hell, even send bullshit to my parents. I'll handle that just like I've been handling another problem quietly, because that's what I do.

Lurking in the shadows and stealing things is what crows do best, and I'm one of the best thieves in Hell.

"Now to leave this in Wormwood's office and scare the living shit out of that moron," I murmur as I skate through the shadows, moving through the building carefully so any demons in my line don't notice me.

Luckily, too much shit has happened since the classroom threat for Kit to realize that the dhampir hasn't mentioned his punishment since that fateful morning. Every day, I think it'll come up as we eat breakfast or meet for studying, but it doesn't. I'm glad for that because I don't want him to be anxious and worried, but I also know he'll get prickly as hell about people handling things for him. His push-pull with allowing us to help him is adorable to me, but I know Kit Kat would demand to take the punishment he practically asked for with his words.

Salem was suspicious of how the magical asshole worded his edict and frankly, I'm not willing to risk yet another goddamn demon trying to do something sketchy to our friend. Besides, it wasn't hard to find the pain points for the hybrid demon; Wormwood isn't very bright and he's definitely not smart about how he manages his private vices.

That's how I was able to take this concern off our plates and I'll continue to do so until it no longer works.

Pausing at the end of the hall, I watch carefully, then slip along the edges until I reach the Curses professor's door. It only takes a few seconds to pick the rudimentary lock and I grin as I shut the heavy door behind me. My eyes dart around his space, checking for added security since my last visit. I don't see any cameras or tiny eyes watching me; that means I'll have to check for magical precautions. The dhampir isn't even in the same realm of power as me, so if he has attempted to prevent me from leaving my new message, it won't work. That doesn't mean I don't enjoy being amused by his fumbling tries, though.

A tiny spot of energy vibrates from the far corner of the ceiling and I snort. "Seriously, dude? A camera cloaking spell? Lame as hell for a fucking demon professor in Hell. I can't believe he resorted to human tech thinking it would defeat me."

Shifting to the crow form, I leave my clothes behind as I fly up to the corner where the magic is emanating. Tilting my head, I study it for a moment before flapping my wings to blow it away from the device with very little effort. Another light breeze from my wings has the components of the security device disassembling and hitting the carpeted floor within moments. I caw in victory, then swoop down to shift back to my humanoid form.

"Zav is going to have a field day playing with this before I bring it back," I murmur with a smirk. I'd prefer not to involve anyone else in my subterfuge, but the techie kitsune will have this thing re-programmed and working for us before the end of the day once I ask. He'll tell Jasper, *of course*, but I was only keeping this to myself so it didn't get back to KK. Zav might actually have the stones to keep the Prickly Prince quiet, especially if we make sure he understands the stakes.

Being sent to anything referred to as 'dungeon detention' is not something we want for our brothers.

I tap into my other senses, including the deep greed that runs through my family lines. It's what makes us top tier thieves as it applies to almost anything tangible or intangible, including information. Thirsting for knowledge drives me to examine the file cabinet first, easily picking the ridiculous lock before I flip through the files until I hit what I'm looking for—Kit.

Since he's new to Hell, the file is as thin as I expected, though the gossipy notes about his relationships and speculation on his demon type shed some light on the dhampir's motives. He's obviously keeping close tabs on our little enigma and it's more than what a professor should give a shit about. Demons are nosy by nature as they love to use flaws and weak points as weapons, but this feels like it's more than that. I don't know if it's by Lucian's decree or if someone else is pulling the strings; however, knowing he's got someone pressing him for intel is useful.

I hum to myself quietly as I shuffle through the files on the rest of my caliphate, curious enough to wonder what the douchebag has to say about us. There's a lot of garbage from our previous schools,—reports, grades, demerits, etc—and again, a lot of notes that are filled with rumors and intrigue. My eyes narrow as it details incidents that have happened since we arrived that are not part of disciplinary action; he's got rats in the student body filling him in on events across the campus.

Jasper will be livid; I can't wait to share that with him eventually—thinking about it makes me giddy.

This stuff is good to add to the arsenal, so I take a few pictures with my phone, then replace everything exactly as I found it. The cabinet was mildly interesting, but there has to be more to keep my idiotic blackmail victim on the hook. I've been using bluffs up until now. That won't work forever, and this trip is meant to find physical or digital shit I can hold over the pompous fuckwit indefinitely.

Rubbing my hands together, I open the laptop on the desk. I'm not bad with tech because of my skill set, but I learned a long time ago that getting help from the truly gifted is much easier than fumbling on my own. To that end, I pull out the flash drive Zav made for me in middle school that is chock full of viruses and codes that work to unlock computer systems. Sliding it into the port, I wait for it to begin the sequences, then turn my attention to the desk itself.

"Pretty fancy looking furniture for a professor."

My magic skims over the surfaces of a design that I'm fairly certain is made by some hoity-toity name in Hell. Annie would know who made this without pause, but I'm less concerned about labels on things like furniture than him. Jewelry and such—that I know easily because I'm often asked to steal that sort of pocketable shit. Assessing value is important to price consideration; demons love to lie when your fees are based on item resale value and complexity of the job. Knowing my worth is what fills the coffers of my personal and family accounts.

A soft whirring sound tells me the hard drive for the computer is being engaged and I smile as I drop to my knees so I can check out underneath the desk. The saturated stench of sex fills my nostrils and I rear back, making a face at the obvious implications of that discovery. Wormwood is playing at being a big deal with this little fantasy and that knowledge is also quite valuable. It's fresh enough to be noticeable , but not so much that I pick up exactly which boys or professors he's managed to squeeze into that small space.

"Randy fuck is probably taking blowies for grades," I mutter as I inhale a breath of clean air then dive back under while I hold it. The space is tight and there's definitely stains on his Berber, that I wish I weren't touching, but after a minute of searching, I don't find a hidden compartment. When I pull back, I let the breath go and suck another moderately clean one in. "Damn that sucked. I need to bring a fucking mask with me if I have to come back."

I crawl out from behind his big chair, moving along the outside of the thick wooden furniture. My fingers dance over the surface as well as my powers, searching for the catch that is *bound* to be here somewhere. I know there's a spot because demons love this kind of shit, but *also*, the damn dimensions of the thing are off in comparison to my mental calculations. Even factoring in drawer spaces and hardware, I know this piece of shit is hiding a secret treasure in his seated pleasure palace.

After a few minutes of crawling around like an imp, I finally find what I'm looking for in the curvature of a flourish on the front panel. Grinning wickedly, I activate the release and sit back on my haunches when the entire front opens like I said 'sesame'. Obviously, the space for legs underneath is so tiny because of this interesting little cabinet. Scooting closer, I mutter an incantation to make certain I'm not tripping a magical security spell by touching the contents. It fizzles immediately and I snort.

What a fucking idiot. Wormwood teaches casting classes and doesn't protect even his hidden shit with magic.

"No wonder this dickwaffle is stuck teaching at a university. He's as useless as tits on a minotaur."

Smirking at my own clever insult, I examine the objects in the cabinet. There are a few jars that I assume have potions, gases, or salves in them. They aren't labeled and I'm not stupid enough to open them to find out what they contain. I can come back for this shit later when I have gear to protect myself from falling victim to whatever their intent is. I doubt they're more than shitty love potions or 'stay hard' creams, but I'm not betting everyone's safety on this fucker being a perv.

I squint at the objects on the opposite shelf, studying them with both my physical senses and mystical ones. The statue of the King seems harmless enough, but if it were strictly for ass-kissing it would be on his desktop. It's stored here for a reason, so I snap a picture of it before continuing to the next item. The crystalline sculpture is adorned with real jewels and precious metals, but I don't recognize the subject of the piece. It's very primitive and rough, so the features aren't distinct, nor is the style. This, I believe to be important, so I take more pictures that I can give to the group. The vibes emanating from it are disconcerting, which is a good indicator of trouble.

The last object is a ring, and the closer I get to it, the worse my gut clenches. It's filled with symbols I don't recognize, and the aura is not from Hell. This thing wasn't made or infused with power in this realm for sure. I don't know what it is or does, so again, I snap away for future reference. I'm not sure if any of this will turn out to be blackmail worthy, but I damn sure won't ignore shit that could bite us in the ass later. It would be irresponsible and I'm far too greedy for the knowledge to be lazy with this job.

One thing remains, and I frown as I consider how to handle it. It's a book, and to find out what is inside, I'll have to touch it. Doing so is a gamble, even with the gloves in my pocket. Much like the jars, the damn thing could have spells woven into its construction or use that will sear the presence of my magic into its core, or even harm me for not being the owner.

But no one hides a small, black book inside of a secret compartment that isn't full of shady shit.

I consider simply swiping it for a moment, but there also could be barrier spells. Magic is extremely specific, intent-driven, and able to hide when necessary in the demon world. I know that my checks could fail when the curse, hex, spell, incantation or any number of vehicles were written by someone with enough knowledge of demon magic to embed traps. That's why I disassembled the damn camera rather than just destroying it.

"This could tell me what Wormwood is up to with Kit, or even something bigger. I *can't* leave it here without knowing what's inside."

Closing my eyes, I murmur a cloaking spell, weaving the skill of my family line into its creation. This works for a great deal of my assignments, but I know it may not accomplish its intent here because I lack the typical prep on a target I would have elsewhere. Once it pops into place, I take a deep breath and grab the book, opening to the first page.

Here goes nothing…

Creep

Xerxes gapes at me, but Slash merely grunts. Neither of them stop moving towards the building where Dank's office is located as I wait for someone to say something. My anxiety spikes and Dottie chitters to get my attention so I don't fly off the rails. As we climb the stairs, X looks around carefully, then looks at me seriously.

"Kit Kat, you *definitely* can *never* say that to anyone outside of our caliphate. Not even if you're angry or scared. It's really important," they say urgently.

Frowning, I tilt my head, hoping Slash will put in his two cents. He doesn't, so I address Xerxes. "I haven't learned anything about that power so far—even in my personal studying."

"The Fates do not approve."

The shark shifter's comment makes me swallow hard. "Because that can undo their… tapestry thingy?"

X nods, then shakes their head. "No. Yes. No. Well, sort of, KK. Those with chronomancy are as rare as necromancy in every species where the skill is possible. The hags aren't fond of either power as it screws with their shit and fucks with seers. But it's so much worse if it occurs in someone with demon lineage. It's basically illegal in Hell."

Just fucking marvelous—I'm not just a fraud in this school, but the entire realm.

"Would explain why he was hidden."

Turning to look at Slash, I wrinkle my nose. "Yeah, I suppose so. Not that I give a shit about anyone who abandoned me to that bullshit for my entire life."

X grins, clapping me on the shoulder. "I don't blame you, but he means it might help us reveal your entire lineage, which will tell us what kind of supe you are. Obviously, demon is in there, but there's more." They pause for a moment, chewing their lip before adding, "I suspect you're rare in multiple ways other than what we've discussed."

Slash narrows his eyes at us, but he doesn't ask what Xerxes means. Instead, he turns to look at the students on the stairs around us and then opens the door to the building. "We will suspend this discussion until we are in the doctor's office."

I nod, following X inside and heading for the elevator. The main entrance is busy, students are heading for their classes or lounging on the furniture until their next class. There's too many of them around to feel safe, but as soon as the thought occurs to me, Slash steps closer. His big arm takes mine, tucking it into his chest as we wait for the elevator to open.

"Thanks," I murmur softly. "I didn't realize there'd be so many people in here at this time of the morning."

While I've slowly gotten used to the guys being around me en masse and even some touching, I am definitely *not* good with the rest of the student body in my space. That's probably not a bad thing, so I haven't tried to acclimate myself better. Having an automatic alarm system in place makes it harder for shitheads like Roquefort to get near me without permission.

The door opens and Slash blocks the entrance to any other students waiting, so we're alone. I open my mouth to ask X about their statement, but the big guy shakes his head. It confuses me, but he looks serious. The bell dings and we exit, heading down the hallway until we get to Dank's office. Slash lets go of me to bang his fist on it, resulting in a masked Dank opening the door carefully.

"Ah, Master Kit and Master Xerxes. Right on time."

I frown as I follow the others into his space. "We didn't have an appointment."

Removing the plague mask and setting it aside, the elder demon gives me what appears to be a smile. "That does not mean I was unaware you'd come. Please have a seat on a table—both of you. Master Slash, you will have to step out when I examine your newest inductee as before."

"Fine," he grumbles as he takes a place between two tables and crosses his arms over his chest stubbornly. "But I will remain here until it is time."

I'd swear he's pouting, but how the hell does one identify that on a shark shifter?

Xerxes moves slower than me, but they get up on the table to Slash's left and I head for the one on the right. Once we're settled, Dank gives me a weird skull-faced smile again. "Excellent. We are all in agreement, then. I will mix the things I need and return shortly."

"Thank you, Dank," I murmur gratefully.

The demon's fire flares a bit, then he dips his head and shuffles toward the back of his office. After he shuts the door to the room, I turn to my companions with an expectant expression. "Well, spill it before he comes back. I'm nervous enough after X's pleas for secrecy; I don't need to get too close to the edge."

"Breathe, little demon."

"I *am* breathing, but I want them to tell me what the hell they were talking about back in the quad." I cross my arms this time, making a stubborn face as the shark smiles.

"Okay, okay," X says as they run their hand through their hair. "You know that supes can have two-sides like us, right? The truth is that, while extremely rare, there are a few supernaturals in various realms born with three. The folks above call it *tripleskia* because the divine folks named it first. It's unheard of in Hell, but for some ancient texts."

"What the hell does that have to do with me?"

Slash grunts, rolling his eyes at me and before I can stop it, I smack his big arm. Despite the fact that I hit him, he looks pleased as shit. "Xerxes is trying to say that being here means you have some form of demon blood. Having an affinity for animals and for some of our animals leans toward shifter as your second half. But… the time thing might suggest you are the first *tripleskia* in the demon world for a very long time."

My eyes widen and I throw my hands up in frustration. "Well, that's just dandy. I mean, what better way to put an even *bigger* target on my goddamn back than being a super secret special supernatural? Fucking hell, Jasper's going to have a *field day* bossing me around if he hears this shit."

"Kit Kat, being… that… would mean you're going to be immensely powerful. It's a gift most demons would commit mass murder for," Xerxes says carefully. "Why are you so upset? Jasper won't, like, disavow you or anything."

Groaning as I lean back until I'm reclining on the table, I look up at the ceiling blankly. "X, there's so much wrong with that question that I can't even get my hands around it all."

"Start piece by piece," Slash rumbles.

I lick my lips and close my eyes so I don't have to look at either of them as I lay out my worries. "In no particular order, this worries me because of the enemies I already have—both seen and unseen. I'm just getting one set of powers and no one knows what it is or how to control it.

I possibly have a power that will definitely get me killed. I could be a rare supe, which will attract fuck knows what else and we can't seem to keep me safe already. I'm a raging mess of mental health issues without all of the aforementioned stuff, and I have to deal with constant upheaval as I learn how everything and everyone here works.

This last mess got several people injured, including me, and it's a goddamn puzzle as to how or what I did. The asshole in charge seems to be directly targeting me personally and through proxies while maybe whipping up a war. Oh, and we have to compete in public to the death trials they say they are preparing us for, but are not."

They're both staring at me; I can feel it. Sucking in a deep breath, I blow it out and continue. "Also, I just want a damn education. Jasper said we're going to surface at some point and that makes me want to hide. I'm getting used to it here and don't want to go back there. I suck at change.

And for fuck's sakes, every one of my uniforms, athletic gear, and…. special undergarments have been destroyed except what I'm wearing now. I sure as *fuck* can't run around naked or in the Games shit. It's too damn much to ask me to also be some kind of freak show, too."

"Whoaaaaaaaa…" X's voice is soft, and it immediately helps me calm a little after being so wound up. "That was a lot of shit at once, KK. Did it feel good to get it out?"

Man, this dude is good.

"Yeah, a little," I admit as I open my eyes. "Doesn't make any of it untrue, though."

Slash leans over me, looking down at me with a frown. "You cannot bottle things up like that, little demon. Your magic will eventually push them out by force. That will have serious consequences."

"The big dude is right," Xerxes agrees from their table. "It's both emotionally and magically better for you to get your pent-up emotions out. Just grab any of us and make us sit down to listen. It will be just like your therapy from the surface."

I arch a brow, rolling onto my good side to look at them. "*Any* of you, huh?"

"Not the Prince."

X and I both snicker at Slash's very blunt statement. The cobra shifter sighs, their lips curving up. "Slash is right. Maybe at some point, but not Jasper right now. He has too much baggage weighing him down to be any help. While most of us have figured out how to manage our shit, he's struggling as hard as you most days."

Making a face at them, I grumble, "No shit, Sherlock."

We're quiet for a moment until X gasps, then smacks their forehead with their palm. They look pained, then turn back to me with a cautious expression. "Of all the things you just word vomited, I think the one thing we can actually address easily is the last one, Kit Kat."

"The uniform thing? You can?"

"Of course we can," the big shifter hovering over me says with a dismissive wave. "We will take you to the bookstore after this appointment. You can replace the lost items easily."

Damn it, no I can't—at least not all *of them.*

"Flag on the play, man. I don't think I can get everything I need there and um… also, does my scholarship cover replacements? Because I'm seriously completely tapped out on the Discordia required stuff other than what I have on. All these stupid attacks have ruined everything." They both laugh at my admission and I pull back, glaring as they try to stifle their amusement. "What?"

"KK, you're one of *us* now. Don't sweat it."

I frown, confused at X's flippant response. "What does that mean?"

"It means they will provide you with anything you need without charging you. All of the caliphate's needs are met via palace accounts. You have no need to fret."

The big guy's words make me bristle a bit, and despite it being stupid to question such a boon, I can't help shaking my head, "Uh-uh. No way. I don't want to owe *anyone*, especially not Jasper *or* his shithead father."

"Don't be stubborn, little demon."

I glare at Slash, and he shrugs. X finally stops chuckling when my expression turns dark. They sigh, tilting their head as they study me. "We'll bill it as mine if it makes you feel better. No one will question me needing extra clothes. I'm easily the biggest spender on that sort of thing. That way, the King won't know a thing. Is that acceptable?"

They're really trying and I hate to continue being stubborn simply because of pride. Plus, I won't win that battle given it's Xerxes' lineage.

"Okay, fine. But, um… what about the things I *can't* get there?" I look at X pleadingly, letting my gaze drift to their chest, then back to their eyes. I need them to understand what I'm trying to say without making me out myself to Slash. I'm not ready for that yet, even though I know the longer I wait, the worse the fallout will be.

"What could you… oh. *Oh!*" The handsome demon bats their lashes at me as they catch up. "Well, that is even better. Now I have a reason to poke Prince Prickface to get our passes faster. We will go shopping *up there*."

No, no no, no… that is not what I wanted at all.

I would think of all places, Hell would be on Amazon's route. After all, their founder *has* to be a crossroads demon in disguise, right?

Disgusting

Jasper

My Arms class was incredibly subdued after the mess of the previous day. The idiots sparred without magic carefully as if they might draw out my dragon at any given moment—which is probably true. Seeing the shrimp and my other caliphate brothers injured was one the hardest things I've had to witness while keeping control of my inner beast. At home, I could have let the dragon lose his shit, flown off and destroyed stuff for a while, then come back to deal with my fury once the fire was burned out. Here, I don't have that luxury and managing my emotions without the carnage is… difficult.

Not to mention my fucking sub gives me disappointed looks anytime I lash out to relieve the pressure. Like it's my fault the target is always the mouthy shrimp who defies me at every turn?

Growling under my breath, I stalk towards the Admin building with determination filling my veins. While my second is baby-sitting the two injured members, I'm going to find out what the goddamn hell that dumbfuck Darkstar thinks he's doing with all these shitty edicts. They're causing problems for the entire program, not just my brothers. According to the email from the infirmary imps, their beds are filled with demons injured enough to miss classes until mid next week. That's before we discount the actual *dead* demons the crews burned and gathered ashes to send home to families.

I may not have been responsible for any of their deaths directly, but they occurred in my class, and I'm not fond of the hint of failure it implies. Eversores do not fail and my father will be sending a displeased missive soon enough. He doesn't care about the deaths in any emotional sense, nor do I, but our reputation is marred by the loss of control in public. It doesn't matter whether I was coerced to run the training this way, nor does it matter that it was a set-up. The King expected me to find a way to come out victorious and I did not.

His wrath will be painful and I will take all of it so the rest of my brothers aren't subjected to whatever punishment he sends along.

There are far too many demons milling about, so I let out a dark snarl. My powers ripple outward and they scatter, making a wide, clear pathway for me to storm through until I reach the double doors. Yanking them open, I stomp into the atrium and up the stairs. Darkstar's office is only three floors up and I don't trust myself to be trapped in an elevator with the dipshits fucking around in this place.

By the time I get to his floor, I'm chewing my lip ring, the irritation at the stupid politics I'm going to have to wrangle flowing in my veins like hot lava. My eyes narrow as I see Beccarus and Silvera scurrying around the outer office meekly. Compared to me they're gnats, but their connection to Lucian makes them feel powerful enough to smirk as I enter their space. I want to crush their throats with my bare hands; however, that would only exacerbate the conflict my visit will ignite.

"His Lordship does not have you on his calendar," Beccarus sneers as he pretends to stop and straighten files on his short desk. "You will not be seen today, Prince Eversore. Many apologies."

He doesn't mean that and his expression makes that very clear. I snort derisively, striding towards the closed door of the office. Silvera adds to his protests as I ignore them and yank the doors open to find Lucian fucking that predator, Lillabet, into the wood grain of his desk. I have to swallow a laugh at his ridiculous cape fluttering while his pants are around his ankles, exposing pasty flesh. His stupid long hair is sticking to his face, and he looks distinctly like I'd imagine some aging hipster human trying to recapture his youth.

Demons don't age the same, but this is definitely amusing as fuck, even with wrinkles or receding hairlines.

"This explains why I'm struggling to get this bitch removed for her sins," I drawl as I lean on the doorframe. "She's letting you and half the demons in this school plug her holes when it suits her. Pathetic."

Lucian grabs the succubus's hair and lifts her head as he continues driving into her. "Tsk, tsk, Prince. The rumors say you're far more progressive than insulting a female for their sexual prowess. I guess it's all some sort of PR move to make the royal youth seem hip."

I have no idea which dumbass statement to address first, so I laugh as I tip my head back. Darkstar isn't quite as ancient as my father, but he's older than me by enough that he thinks this kind of manipulation will work on me. As if I give one single sliver of a fuck about what a washed up old pit sucker thinks of my character. Demons like him are so far below me that I've never worried about their opinions or desires—both as royalty and as a different generation of demon.

"Satan's frilly slips, Darkstar. I knew you were dense, but *that* was special," I say with a dark grin. "Imagine thinking the Prince of Hell would be bothered by the opinions of a crusty old loser who cosplays an evil magic user from a human movie while stuck running the school for demons far more elite than you'll ever be. It's deliciously delusional and the fact that you assumed I was judging this disgusting bitch from X's line for her appetites is even better."

"I am a professor and you can't—"

My eyes flash golden with the fury of my dragon as I growl, "You will be silent, lower demon!" Lillabet's mouth closes and I watch her struggle to open it so she can spout nasty shit. "No one is talking to you, so I am not going to allow you to contribute."

Darkstar snickers but doesn't stop his revolting fucking. "Just you and I, mmm, Your Highness?"

The urge to pluck out my own eyeballs is rioting within me, but I don't let it show on my face. "My disdain for this demoness is based on her skating the rules of the school and her lineage with feeding. And if I cannot remove her through administrative means, I will find a way to handle the situation on my own. But she is not why I came to your den of filth, Darkstar."

"Oh?" he says, pounding the Cubi harder with his claws digging into her ass.

I'm never going to sleep again, for fuck's sake.

"Stop fucking with my training," I retort. "If I'm required to train inferior demons for the Games, your constant meddling will prevent me from executing that duty. Losing or maiming competitors before the first round limits the glory Discordia can achieve. You are wasting resources—both cannon fodder and potential high performers—by fucking around in the pre-trial period."

His lips curve up and I roll my eyes as Lillabet looks like she'd been making noise if I hadn't commanded her silence. I don't give a shit about whether that sound would be about pain or pleasure, though. The tale of Oriel saving the unwilling, traumatized shrimp from her clutches burns in my gut as I ignore her. Whatever Darkstar is doing is much better than she deserves for daring to come near what is mine.

My caliphate, of course.

"Prince Jasper, I cannot *fathom* what you are referring to. I have only sent instructions based on the documents received from the official Caliphate Games committee."

I suck in a deep breath, looking up to the ceiling as if I'm asking someone to help me control my temper. That's idiotic, of course, because demons don't pray nor do they ask for help from some deity above. But the gesture is as ingrained in us as it is for other supernaturals and humans, so I stare at the vaulted roof of Darkstar's office, counting in my head until I feel controlled enough to continue. When I'm able, I look at his face, still pretending Lillabet isn't there.

"I wasn't called into being yesterday, Lucian. We've reviewed all the official documents *ad nauseum*. While your interference doesn't rise to the level of Games tampering, it is very close. My visit should be a warning."

He smirks at me. "You'd have to prove it, Eversore. Are you ready to make this an imputation before the crown? If not, I'm busy, as you can plainly see."

The grunt that slips out of the demoness makes me narrow my eyes and I murmur a hex under my breath. Her skin breaks out in boils that rupture with gross fluids, yet it doesn't stop the asswipe Headmaster from continuing to fuck her. If I'm ever that desperate, I hope the *shit* someone cuts off my goddamn head and puts me out of my misery. Shuddering, I ball my fists at my side, internally grumbling that Anton's suggestion to help me drain my rage isn't working.

"You know I am not," I grit out. "But I promise I will take my vengeance if you cause my students to risk their lives for training again. The Games require that sacrifice and we have no choice, but I am unwilling to have that consequence be part of their educational time."

"I don't believe you, Prince," he taunts with a slow, dark smile. "In fact, I believe you are here for something far more interesting than simply bristling at my intervention in your classroom. Thank you for sharing that tidbit. I'll be sure to use it later on. Now… *get. out.*"

Cracking my neck, I assess the situation. My stomach is roiling at the sight of these two fuckwits and I'm getting nowhere. Lucian knows I could fuck up his world if I chose to make this more than an academic disagreement, but that would bring attention I do not want from my father and his cronies. Without escalating this, I'm wasting my breath and being creeped out at the same time.

"Fine. Enjoy your pity fuck." The corner of my mouth tips up and I release Lillabet's mouth as I push off the doorframe.

They both try to clap back, but I'm gone before they manage to think of anything to say.

Fucking losers.

HAVING WASTED MOST OF MY FREE PERIODS, I HEAD STRAIGHT FOR CANTO IV. We agreed to have lunch together in the dorm instead of the *Triclinium* to allow the shrimp and Xerxes to be comfortable. They would have to be uniformed in the communal lunch area and deal with more walking than I felt it worthy of. Accepting that request from Salem wasn't hard, and now that I've had to watch that gross display at length, I'm glad.

The anger rippling off of me scares the other freshman away as I enter our dorm and I grin to myself. Being royal *and* a dragon has benefits too numerous to name.

When I get to Salem's room, I take a deep breath like Zavvie suggested. He thinks I need to clear my emotions before I deal with everyone, especially if the shrimp will be present. I'm not sure what he thinks will change, but he asks for very little. Besides, I would like for the only family I give a shit about not to give me angry looks constantly, so I'm playing along.

 I open the door, blinking at the sight before me. Kit is in his chair and Xerxes is on his couch, but on the floor is my general and my thief, studiously painting their toenails.

What in the fucking shit is this?!

Salem is in the kitchen, cooking as usual, but I can't even covet the delicious smells coming from his efforts because I'm so shocked. "What the hell are you two assholes doing?"

Slash whips his head around, his eyes dark with anger. "I am assisting the little demon with self-care as he has an injured limb. Oriel agreed to assist X."

Oriel chuckles, his shoulders shaking as he finishes a toe. He studies the foot for a moment, then turns to look at me in exasperation. "Jas, you don't care that we're doing supposed girly shit, so stop it. I wear polish all the time, so does X. You're pissed that we're sitting below KK and X to do it, which is dumb. KK doesn't even know the demon culture stuff yet, so chill."

"What don't I know?" the shrimp asks, looking curious. "Tell me why he's got a crab in his ass again. I like knowing what makes him pissy."

I'll just bet you do, you little shit.

For the second time today, I smirk as I reply, "No one has permission to tell him and that's a royal decree." Slash's expression says he's going to murder me when he gets me alone, but the look of frustration on the new kid's face is worth it.

I'm a twisted fuck, but at least I'm trying.

OVER MY HEAD

kat/kit

J asper refused to let anyone tell me why Slash's gesture was a big deal, which pissed me off. I know it was his plan; he loves to exercise that tiny modicum of control whenever he can. I pretended that it didn't bother me until he finally left for afternoon classes, taking everyone with him because X and I were safely ensconced in the dorm room. Now that we're alone, I can breathe a little more freely.

"Thank fuck they're gone," Xerxes says as they lean back on the couch. "I appreciate the care, but I've been *dying* to get you alone, Kit Kat."

Really?

"Why?" I ask, tilting my head curiously. "Like… we already did the talking thing, right?"

They smirk, shaking their head and clicking their tongue. "Because, KK, we're not *done* talking. I got your signals in the doctor's office. We need to get you stuff to keep the girls in place, mmm?"

Wrinkling my nose, I look at my hands, heat rising on my face. "Yeah. I'm not big or anything but I need some… coverage. Where are we going to get it? How fast can we get a binder to… you know, Hell?"

"In a couple of days. I'll use the concierge service through my family tailors. Since I have your measurements from the ball outfit, it won't be a big deal. The uniforms were super easy because of that, right?"

I nod, biting my lower lip. "Can you… get a couple? I seem to be doomed to destroy everything I put on my body. I don't want to end up in the same position in a week or two."

X snickers. "You're a trouble magnet, man. I fully expect to need to monitor this shit for you until you do the big reveal." They pause for a moment, tapping their fingers on their lips. "Can I ask you a question without upsetting you?"

Doubtful when you start out like that.

"Um, you can try."

"I know you had to pretend, but why didn't you just… change up to nonbinary or trans once you were here? Why keep up the charade?"

Sighing, I roll my eyes upward as I gather my thoughts. "It felt wrong to claim an identity that wasn't mine. I mean, I don't know exactly what my… sexuality is entirely, but… I can't imagine pretending to be a marginalized identity for personal benefit. White dude isn't that, you know? No one's oppressing the thing I'm pretending to be, so it's not shitty."

There's a heavy silence for a few moments, then X makes a soft sound. I worry that I've said something wrong, so I bring my gaze to his, surprised by the soft expression I see. "You're a good person, Kat Camponella. I get why you're doing this the way you are now."

I shrug, feeling embarrassed by the unexpected praise. "I try to be. It's hard to know when I'm succeeding because I don't often let people in. You guys are probably the closest friends I've had in…. my whole life."

Saying that out loud makes me sound incredibly pitiful and I hate it.

To brush that feeling off, I continue, "I know the guys will be hurt once I admit the truth. That's a consequence I'll have to accept, but I also know that if I'm discovered, it's likely I'll be sent away. Even if I tried to hide under some other identity, whatever you guys think is important about me makes me a target. And if I'm not amongst the caliphate, my survival chances are nil. I don't know exactly what I am or how to control myself—

magically or emotionally—well enough to continually fend off shit on my own."

X grins, tilting their head. "Which is something you'd never say in front of Prince Prickface, so thank you for trusting me enough to voice it."

My face heats again and I shrug. "You didn't judge when you figured out my secret. It makes me feel comfortable expressing my doubts now."

"Good," they reply with a happy smile. Xerxes pauses briefly, looking around the room as if someone might be listening besides Dottie. A small plume of smoke emits from their fingers, crawling through the air and branching out all over like it's seeking something. "I have a question for you."

I frown, watching the smoke as it moves to the corners of the ceiling and around our living space. "One that requires you to do... whatever this is?"

X nods, humming a little as they wait. "Yep. I want to make *certain* this room isn't bugged by our spiky-backed royal. Anton and I checked our room long ago, but he's such a fucking control freak that I'm not sure if he did it to anyone else. Salem and Oriel are the hardest to manage; he might have sweet talked Zav into doing it 'for their own good' or some nonsense."

I will grind his balls beneath my boots if he does; that's an invasion of privacy.

My brow furrows when it occurs to me that as mad as I'll be if the Prince has wired the one place I feel safe, perhaps I'm guilty of doing something similarly shitty. Being here in disguise, hiding it from the guys... That *could* be construed as the same kind of slight—maybe even worse—by someone on the outside. My gut churns as I think about that, feeling like an absolute pervert as I think about all the places I'm present without their explicit consent. "Oh, no," I mutter as I wrap my arms around my knees.

The smoke disappears with a loud 'pop,' and the glamorous demon on the couch sighs in relief. "Excellent. It's a safe space—no question." X tilts their head, studying me in the avian manner I know means they're concerned. "Why do you look like you're going to barf, Kit Kat? Did I worry you with the camera thing?"

"Yes. No. I mean, yes, you did. But no, that's not why I'm..." My sentence trails off as the worry and panic filter through me, making my veins feel like they're pumping sludge. Clenching my fists so my nails bite into my palms, I breathe slowly to fight the escalating fear before I murmur, "I'm worried I'm violating all of you. The cameras made *me* feel like that and it suddenly struck me that a girl here in all the private spaces like the bathroom might be considered a similar act. It made me wonder if I'm breaching my own ethics and that feels very bad."

Xerxes blinks, then suddenly throws back their head in laughter. I frown harder, not getting the joke. I'm very serious about this and they seem to think I'm being ridiculous. When they finally stop for a moment, X shakes their head ruefully. "I'm sorry, Kat. I don't mean to make you feel worse but… that's imposing a human standard on the demon world. We're not influenced by the puritanical notion that naked bodies of any gender are some big secret. You aren't violating your own ethics because those aren't made for our world. Not one of us would give a flying fuck about another demon seeing us bare assed in humanoid, demon, or animal form."

Oh.

Licking my lips, I shove down the embarrassment that rushes to replace the panic. I probably should have *asked* before I went nuclear, but my anxiety rarely allows for that luxury. Even the improvements I've made since I arrived can't fully stop the ingrained reaction, though I'm hopeful that it might eventually. "I'm sorry for starting to wig out. But truthfully? I'm not learning enough about demon culture from you guys *or* in my classes to make up for what comes to you all naturally."

"You're right about that, KK," they muse, tapping their lips with their fingers. "Jasper forbade us from telling you that *one* piece of culture, but he didn't say we couldn't expose you to the other important things. It's a loophole I can share with the others, so we can try to get you up to speed."

"That would be very helpful. I mean, I'll probably piss people off randomly anyway, but if I realize I'm doing it, it would be better." Smiling a little, I stretch my limbs before rising to my feet. "Want a drink while I'm up? And also… I want to know your question. Plus… what the hell Jasper did about the bodies because no one ever told me."

As I walk to the kitchen slowly, X nods, so I detour to get their glass as well. Dottie follows me, chittering happily as I walk without support. I'm pretty sure that's why she looks so excited, but I can't be one hundred percent certain. When I get to the fridge, I set the glasses down and pull out the pitcher of Cantu berry juice Salem made the other night. It's not quite as tasty as crunkleberries, but I figure we don't need to be high as kites for this discussion.

"Okay, but you have to tell me if any of this is too much for you. Do you promise?"

I give Xerxes a puzzled look. "I've been pretty consistent in communicating my boundaries, I think. But yes, I promise I will tell you if I'm having trouble."

X sits up straighter, their expression sincere as they gaze at me. "I want to show you one of my… other parts. It doesn't matter which one, but your trust today is making the need to have you really *see* me is like an enormous weight on my chest. Are you ready for that? Is your trust deep enough for that?"

Whoa. No wonder they made me promise. They don't want me to say 'yes' and regret it.

The juice fills the glasses as I think about their request. Knowing my secret has them being one of the closest demons to me, and I definitely don't think they'd do anything to hurt me. Making the pact connected us on a level I don't have with anyone else, just like the proximity to Salem or Oriel's defiance of Jasper's edicts have endeared them to me with little effort. I was able to see *both* of their forms and be comfortable; why wouldn't it work with Xerxes?

"I think…" They lean forward, eyes glittering with eager excitement as I pause. "I think I'd like to see your snake first. Oriel's form is so different from a simple crow and I love animals. Seeing the animal first makes this less frightening for someone who didn't know any of this existed up until a few months ago."

Xerxes beams, jumping to their feet, then groaning when they realize they moved too fast. "Shit. That was stupid but I've been hoping you'd say 'yes' since the idea came to me while we were talking. Obviously, we've all shared that this is a big deal to show someone in private for the first time, and that's one culture-y thing you know. Letting me shift is like… a huge deal; I know."

"Please don't hurt yourself," I murmur as I grab the drinks and pad over to sit them on the table by the couch. "Anton will be upset if you re-injure yourself and Jasper will *definitely* blame me for it."

They wait until I get to my chair and settle in before they wink. "I promise I won't fuck up my healing. A simple shift is not going to set me back."

Dottie climbs up next to me, her big eyes fixed on the demon waiting for me to give them the final go ahead. I clasp my hands together on my lap, taking a deep breath to ground myself. "Come closer and do it. I want to see this part of you, X."

The room fills with light as they grin wider, then their body goes from pale skin to shiny golden scales inch by inch. Legs turn to a huge, thick pile of coils as big as my entire torso, leaving them half humanoid on top and all slither on the bottom. Xerxes' body seems to grow exponentially as the snake form crawls up their body from the waist to trunk, assimilating their arms.

A gasp echoes in the quiet dorm as it engulfs them completely, leaving the biggest fucking reptile I've ever seen looking down at me from what has to be eight feet in the air with emerald eyes that sparkle like the gemstone. Their hood fans out as far as my arms would if I were getting measured and the flick of the long, forked tongue makes my stomach clench in response.

What the hell does that *thing do? Holy Medusa's wig tape, it's as long as my leg!*

I swallow hard, my eyes drifting over the cobra to frown at the smooth underbelly. It suddenly occurs to me that I don't have a single fucking clue what the hell snakes do to procreate. Obviously, their dick isn't….

A low hiss fills the room and before I can even ask, two large, engorged penises seem to pop out of their body. "Oh, shit!"

My hands fly to my face, covering my eyes and the bright red color of my cheeks when I realize I just made the snake… happy by looking for its dick.

Of which it has two…. I am so in over my goddamned head.

Shake A Tailfeather

anton

My head jerks up and I blink when the surge of emotion slams into me like a wave crashing into the shore. Schooling my features so Slash and the rest of our Supernatural Law lecture don't know what's going on, I struggle to assimilate everything flowing into me. Xerxes shifted, and as his first mate, I can *feel* how excited he is.

Literally.

I grit my teeth to fight off whatever the hell he and Kit Kat are doing, plus the rush of jealousy from knowing I'm not there with them. X and I discussed the strange, softness we've developed for the new kid, so I'm not upset that he's exploring it. But I'd like to be *there* to join in, not sitting at this fucking desk hoping I don't smash my dick into the desk by the end.

Leaning in, I murmur to the huge shark shifter. "I'm cutting out. I think X needs me, but you can stay and get the rest of the notes, right?"

Slash eyes me suspiciously, but very few people can read me when I choose to keep my counsel. Finally, he grunts, then nods his head. "Fine. Check on the little demon for me."

Man, that guy is so far gone and I have no idea if he knows it.

"Will do," I reply as I gather my shit. Once I get it, I scurry out the back of the classroom before anyone notices. There's no way I can survive whatever vibes KK is causing in their room in public. I don't want to be a party crasher, but they'll have to accept that I can't stay away.

I frown, wondering if there's anything quick I can do to soften the intrusion for the delicate guy. Jasper's edict pissed him the fuck off; maybe I can work with that. If I'm creative, I won't be defying a caliphate order, but I'll buy myself some credit. Luckily, this damn class is right where I need to be to make my plan a reality.

Into the stacks I go.

IT ONLY TOOK ME A FEW MINUTES OF ZIPPING AROUND THE LOWER LEVELS OF the library to find what I was looking for, and I exit the building with a small smile on my lips. I'm not usually a gloomy fuck like Oriel or an angry one like Slash and Jas, but I'm not nearly as smiley as my other half. But I'm pleased with my mental gymnastics, and I think both Kit and X will be happy to see the books I'm bringing.

That is, if I don't walk in on something more interesting…

As I hurry across the quad toward Canto IV, I look inside myself to see if I'm still feeling that intensity. It's still pretty hyped up, but maybe not quite as hungry and sharp as before. I don't know what the hell that means, but I'm going to find out soon. Hopefully, my peace offering will be enough to smooth over the intrusion.

When I jog up the steps of our dorm, I realize I'm moving faster than I normally would outside of an emergency. I'm far more invested in seeing what they're getting up to than I've ever been before. Xerxes and I have discussed inviting people into our bed in the past, but neither of us was ever that into making it reality. Kit is the first dude we solidly desire, both separately and together, and I'm strangely looking forward to figuring it out.

Of course, we're not the only ones jockeying for his favor—though we're *definitely* the ones with the most experience in *healthy* same sex relationships. I'm fairly sure Zav and Jasper would have never survived their roots if they hadn't been perfectly matched in the dominant-submissive roles. I have *no* idea what the hell O and Salem get up to, and Slash has always seemed disinterested in everyone, even when Jasper lined up easy shots.

I'm not saying any of my brothers are inexperienced sexually in general; some are just pretty secretive about the people they take to their boudoirs.

This is not the direction I saw things going when we split off this morning, nor the one I assumed our caliphate would take after the Prince made his stupid decree. When he texted his pissy orders to the rest of us, I figured we'd all spend tonight with Kit and the dragon hissing at one another from their respective corners. Exhausting, but not entirely unexpected lately as they have this deep seated need to bait one another.

Pushing through the crowd in the entry, I head for the elevator and glare until the other demons leave me to the car alone. As I head up to our floor, I wonder when I'll be able to share one of my forms with the spunky dude and if he'll think it's too feminine, like my family. Raking my hand through my rainbow locks, I sigh and shake my head. This isn't the time for my well hidden insecurities; it's the time to be supportive, no matter what I find when I open the door to Salem's lair.

The ding of the elevator reaching our floor pulls me out of my intrusive thoughts, and I step out, trying to keep control of the excitement and worry zinging through me. Salem's door is closed, so it only takes a moment for me to reach the large door and stare at the keypad. Shaking my head, I punch in the code then turn the knob as if my gut isn't churning in anticipation. And what I find…

This is not *what I expected at all.*

Kit is curled up in his usual chair with Dottie sitting above his left shoulder. There's a drink beside him and… a huge fucking cobra coiled at his feet with it's head resting in his lap. He's gently running his fingers over the wide hood as the TV plays one of the human movies he loves. The scene is so surreal that I almost can't even comprehend it as I slip inside and close the door behind me.

"Anton," the dark haired dude says softly, his eyes surprised as he meets my gaze. His fingers don't stop petting the smooth reptile skin and a lazy hiss fills the silence as I watch. "Is something wrong?"

My mouth feels dry as I shake my head wordlessly. I'm having trouble processing this—not because I'm angry or upset, but because I'm *amazed*. Xerxes drips self-confidence and swagger most of the time, but they've always been sensitive about their animal. As much as my family thinks my shift is too feminine, especially because of my sexuality, theirs was furious at the manifestation of the snake.

I suppose it proves that our parents don't even conform to the most rudimentary level of loyalty to their families or spouses. Demons aren't really picky about monogamy *except* when it comes to lineage and heirs—my bird and their snake puts our ascension to heads of our houses in question, should anyone want to challenge it. They probably will eventually, but the lifespan of demons being nearly as immortal as the Fae has kept that intrigue off our doorsteps.

It won't hold forever, though, and our shitty ass parents know it.

"You look like you've seen a ghost."

Kit's murmur brings me back to reality and I lick my lips, trying to form words with my scattered thoughts. "I… X has never been comfortable with being fully shifted. I've tried… But…"

Another hiss escapes the languid reptile and Kit's lips curve into a surprisingly soft smile. "Acceptance makes hard things easier."

I nod, finally forcing myself to move closer to the pair. "I've always accepted them. Always."

"Ah, but that's because you grew up together and fell in love. I'm no one— an alien from another world with no knowledge of your pasts or heritage or any of the things everyone else brings to the equation. I don't *have* to accept them because of the rules, yet I do."

Makes perfect sense, but I don't understand what happened to make him *trust my love.*

"That's a very simple answer for a complex situation," I say as I finally get within range of X's huge coils, noting the small shivers of pleasure in their tail. "You're calmer than I would have expected, especially since…"

His face turns bright red and it confirms what I suspected—something *definitely* happened beyond just the full shift. "You mean for someone confronted with not one but *two* very interestingly pierced, giant cocks on accident?"

A bark of laughter escapes; I can't help it. This guy waffles between spitfire, anxious penguin, and filthy mouthed little shit so much that it gives me whiplash. "Yeah… that. I felt them shift and I was worried, but then I realized it wasn't bad—but I had to find out for myself anyway."

"I'm not sure why I'm so calm, honestly." His cheeks flush more and I note the color spreading down his neck. "Seeing O and Salem change didn't involve… *that*… so I wasn't ready for it. But, um, I guess I'm handling this well. I don't feel trapped without air."

You look as comfortable as someone who's always been here.

I don't say that, though, because I don't want to trigger an attack if that truth hits too close to home. Instead, I walk around X's thick body, facing Kit from the other side. Swallowing an uncertainty I rarely feel, I tilt my head as I ask, "Would you want me to… you know. I can, too."

Kit doesn't comment on *my* sudden journey to awkward penguin-land. His brows pinch for a moment like he's thinking about it and my breath catches as I wait for his response. With his hand smoothing over X's huge triangular head, the small dude looks even smaller than normal. I know it's because my mate is in their largest animal form on purpose and most humans would look tiny in comparison. If they raised up on their coils, they'd be over seven feet tall and their body easily could fit KK inside it.

Yet he's petting Xerxes like a stray cat he just took in without an ounce of anxiety to be found. It's fucking astounding, and I keep waiting for something to ruin the picture. Kit finally pushes his hair out of his eyes and looks me right in the eyes. His expression is serious and I have to push the insecurity down to my toes as he sighs.

"Yes, I would. I mean, yes, I would like to see your animal, Anton." I wait for the flush to happen, but it doesn't, making my stomach twist in a knot.

Do I not affect him like X does? Like it's obvious Jasper does and he doesn't want to admit it? Am I not… enough?

Biting my lip, I clench my fists, feeling the warring parts of me in a way that is usually reserved for the disapproval of people at my court. I'm frozen in place, unable to do anything but feel all the emotions rioting inside of me. Xerxes and I are much less internal than any of the others, so we frequently have surges that overwhelm us. It's one of the first things we bonded over as kids; while Jasper's fury externalizes as 'demon acceptable' fits of rage, our outbursts are less threatening. And unlike Zavida, we can't hide behind our cloud of tails when it's out of control.

"I mean, that is… Unless you don't want to anymore. I know X is your, uh… and I'm touching… Maybe I shouldn't be, but they said it was okay,"

Kit stammers and I *feel* his sudden rush of blue vibes in his aura. His colors are changing on a dime and it's because I'm too fucking dumbstruck to speak.

"Wait!" I blurt when his hand stops stroking X and an irritated hiss rattles from the cobra in his lap. "That's not it. Give me a moment."

The guy frowns, looking confused as fuck. I don't blame him. He's seeing more of me than *anyone* outside of Xerxes ever does. "But you're freaking out. It's like I can smell it." He sniffs delicately, looking even more puzzled afterward. "And X-snake smells super pissy now. Emotion-wise, not actual piss-wise because that's… *definitely* a line for me, which I didn't know until right now."

His jumbled nonsense makes me laugh, breaking the tension in my body as I laugh. "Okay. Good to know, but no one in our caliphate has that particular kink, in case you were wondering."

"I should make a list," he mumbles. "Lists are good. Lists make brain happy."

Uh-oh. I broke him.

"Hey," I say, snapping my fingers in front of his face. "Come back, man. I don't want you to miss this. I'm told it's quite spectacular."

His eyes widen as he looks up at me, then smirks. "Now you've done it. The anticipation is killing me. I don't know how you're going to live up to the hype."

The easy banter makes everything calmer and I note his aura mellowing out. Sighing in relief, I back up slightly, giving myself room to do this without riling up my mate. I'm pretty sure Kit saw enough of his hemis for today and my shift might get their snake antsy. "I never disappoint."

"Less talk, more bird," he says with a sly grin. "Stop edging me."

Who the fuck taught him that word? *I'm going to punch Oriel Bloodstone, for sure.*

"Dirty mouth." I don't wait for him to respond as I reach inside, allowing the peacock within to spread its wings. He's eager, champing at the bit to burst from my skin for this guy and the only other person who got that reaction is languishing in coils on the floor. My eyes close as the wave of emotions, colors, and metallic tang fill my frame until feathers sprout.

It takes mere seconds for the rainbow to cover my humanoid frame, and in a blink, my shape reforms into the largest size of my bird possible. The plumes shake on my head as clawed feet walk forward, my bird eyes narrowing in on the ultraviolet color spectrum I can see in the form. Kit and X's auras are even more vibrant, emanating emotions like miniature explosions as I stop centimeters from them. My vision darts to the happily shaking tail of my mate, transfixed by the movement, then dart back to the dude I'm shifted for.

As soon as our gazes lock, my tail pops open, fanning out as my head bobs. A soft call escapes my beak and I almost lose control of myself when I feel my feathers shaking. Kit grins a little, shaking off the shocked look on his delicate features. His free hand gestures for me to come even closer, and without questioning it, I do. Chittering makes me jerk my head up, glaring at the kinkajou as she hops around on the cushion above Kit's head.

No. Stay away, monkey rat.

I can't say that, of course, because I don't talk in this form. Half-shifted, sure, but not in the full monte. Instead, I ruffle my tailfeathers, puffing up as my feet stomp around to warn the familiar off. This is my time and she needs to fuck off before KK gets scared. I like Dottie, but I might strangle the little shit if she messes this up. Guilt fills me and I groan internally. Of course I won't hurt the damn rodent, but I *do* want her to back the fuck off.

X hisses softly, likely sensing my irritation, but they don't lift their head. It feels like they're nesting right now and it's never a good idea to fuck with a nesting cobra, especially a seven foot tall one.

"Annie, can I... touch the feathers?"

There's no way for me to vocalize just how much I want that, but I bob my head, hoping he gets it. His smile widens as I stop dancing in place to warn Dottie off and just stay within his reach. With Kit sitting, I'm tall enough for my feathers to stick up higher than his head and my beady bird eyes almost roll back into my head when his fingers smooth over the eye of one. His thumb rubs it gently, and a trilling coo of happiness escapes.

That's when it hits me just how irrevocably fucked X and I are; there's no going back now.

Talk

kät/kit

"Well, what in the fresh Hell is this shit?"

My eyes pop open at the sound of Jasper's sarcastic drawl. Every part of me is warm and cozy, and when I move slightly, I remember why.

Oh, fuck.

The sound of four men in animal shifter form curled up around me tells me it wasn't just a nice dream. Nope, it's absolutely SnakeX, PandaSalem, PeacockAnton, and CrowOriel surrounding me in the little blanket nest in front of my chair. Dottie makes a tiny yawn sound, and I grin, leaning into her small face for a second for strength. Once I feel put together, I look at the three remaining caliphate members in the doorway. Zavida looks like he might want to scurry over and hide in his tails in this pile. Slash is grinning with his chin tucked to his chest, but I can tell he's… pleased?

But Jasper looks frustrated and his eyes are full of an emotion I can't decipher. It seems like he's wrestling with something internally and I'm pretty sure no matter what I answer, it will be wrong. PandaSalem moves his fluffy head where it's resting next to Dottie, his furry cheek rubbing on me lightly. I think it's supposed to be encouragement, so I gather my courage and spunk up to reply to the grumpy ass demon prince.

"Salem said it's like a puppy pile when he came home from Fae class and Oriel agreed." Sticking my chin out, I run my fingers over the smooth snake skin that's barely left my side for hours then the feathers of the surprisingly affectionate peacock on my other side. "X was with me resting and I said they could show me their snake. Anton felt them shift and came to check on us. I said it was okay for Annie to show me, too. Do you have a problem with me doing exactly what you assholes said I need to do before the Games start?"

My words must catch the dragon by surprise because he sputters incoherently. That makes Slash and Zav laugh, and they come into the room while Jasper continues to struggle with a response. Slash immediately walks over to ruffle my hair, making me flush, and grabs the tray of drinks off of the table by my chair.

"I will refill these, little demon. You and Xerxes must stay hydrated."

That small gesture makes my chest flutter—I've never had someone worry so much about me.

SnakeXerxes hisses softly, then finally shifts their coils in what I assume is a stretch. That triggers a flurry of feathers and fur to move, and blood flows to my sleepy limbs again. Spikes of sensation tickle my body as they all stretch and wiggle in animal form. I know we need to move, especially because it's obviously dinner time since the others are back. On Fridays, that's pretty late, so we've been lazing about for a long fucking time. In fact, I'm not sure if I'll even be able to sleep tonight because our nap was that long.

"It's good that you and X were able to get so much rest," Zavida says as he plops down on the floor close to the animal pile. "The doc will be happy, I bet. I'm not sure what will come from these three skipping all their classes, though."

Unfortunately, that unbreaks Jasper's speechlessness, and he snarls, "Without telling anyone you'd be gone, I bet. Another mess I'll have to smooth over, especially if it gets to Darkstar."

Slash returns with the tray of drinks, bending a bit to let me grab mine. "If you are going to scold them, Prince, they should shift back so they can answer for their behavior. It would be pointless to discuss otherwise."

I frown at the big guy. We're comfortable and I'm not eager for a lecture. "Why would you say that? He was quiet for once!"

PandaSalem sits up, his chubby panda body adorable as he yawns and stretches his paws in the air. The birds follow suit, and finally, Xerxes slithers off of me. I frown, feeling the warmth and safety slowly ebb when they're not surrounding me. I might just get up and kick that fucking shark's ass. Wrinkling my nose, I glare at Slash, waiting for him to answer as I sit up grumpily.

"Little demon, it is never good to have serious discussions when we are not in higher cognitive function forms. We can hear and process, but the primitive urges make true complex thoughts more difficult. I do not think you want to have the conversation twice, am I correct?"

Damn him. He's absolutely right and I hate him for it.

"Fine!" I cross my arms over my chest, sighing heavily. "Go ahead and do the thing, guys."

Jasper's brow arches as all four of the other demons shift back to their humanoid forms, but he laughs when my hands fly to my eyes. "Forget something, shrimp?"

Fuming internally, I keep my hands glued over my face as I mutter, "Maybe. Someone could have warned me, though. Dickheads."

"Aw, don't be sour, Kit Kat," Salem says in his rough, 'just woke' up voice. "Our nap was the highlight of this week. I'm totally ready to cook now."

"You should have been cooking an hour ago," Zavida grumbles after his stomach burbles. "But I get why you didn't. We should probably order out so it's faster."

I don't peek—I swear—as I wait for someone to tell me when the guys are at least covered. But I am glad Zav suggested takeout, so I nod. "I think that's a good plan. I'm kind of hungry now and I bet you guys who were in class are, too."

"Do whatever, but I'm still waiting for an answer as to what was going on in here and whether I have a mess to clean up from your absences." Jasper finally stomps into the living area, throwing himself into his big chair opposite mine as his eyes flash. "You can take your damn hands off your eyes now, for fuck's sake."

I hate doing what he says, but I remove my palms to give him a dirty look. Dottie makes a loud, angry sound, scrambling down my body to shake her fist at the dragon and I smile. He's not scared of her, obviously, but I appreciate her showing up every single time the fuckhead gets nasty with me. Petting her head, I push up and lean against my armchair. "You're a prick, Jasper."

"Perhaps, but I'm the *head* prick. Someone fill me in… *now*," he growls as he leans his head back on the cushion of his chair. He rubs his temples, and I realize that he looks a bit haggard for someone who wasn't hurt in the big battle.

I also realize that he's been handling shit since it ended and I don't know if he's slept a wink—damn.

"Jas, I'm sure they emailed the professors. Right guys?" Zavida says, his eyes hopeful as his gaze darts from Salem to Anton to Oriel.

Anton nods and I almost let out a sigh of relief. That's one. Maybe we won't have to listen to the 'clean up your messes' portion of the rant. Salem and Oriel look sheepish, and I lick my lips as I avoid letting my eyes drift below their chins. Not one of the three of them put on a goddamned shirt, only sweats, and after the snuggle fest, I'm feeling far too warm to deal with *that*.

"Fuck," Jasper mutters as he closes his eyes. "Of course you two delinquents didn't bother."

Salem chuckles, winking at me as he heads for the kitchen. "I'm going to get some menus so we can decide what we're eating while he loses his shit."

"That would be wise," Slash says. When I look over at him, he's studying the group around me, including Zavida sitting just a bit outside of the circle. Before I can figure out what his problem is, he's dropped to the ground and is scooting over to us. His big hands pick up my feet and he grins toothily as he rubs them gently.

I'd complain but honestly? This level of pampering is becoming more comfortable than I'd like to admit. Perhaps I'm getting spoiled, but I can't seem to make myself tell him to stop. Anton chuckles, grabbing X's feet to join in, and when Salem returns with the menus, Oriel mimics us. Zavida frowns a bit and it makes my chest feel funny, so I jerk my chin at him with a shy smile. We're still figuring things out, but I won't let him feel excluded.

Jasper growls when his foxy lover allows me to take his pale feet in my lap, his eyes dark. "What the hell are all of you weirdos doing? Satan's burnt taint, I can't deal with this shit after today."

There it is—the opening to find out why the shit he looks like he's been run through a grain thresher.

"Maybe you could tell us what the hell crawled up your ass and died rather than taking your frustration out on me?" I say softly as I raise my eyes to his. My expression is serious and I'm approaching it like he's a rabid animal on purpose. I think we could all use a break from his ire, but I also think Jasper needs a break from himself. He needs people to listen to his shit for a few minutes, even if he's going to act like a dick later.

The Prince tilts his head, studying me as I lean against Xerxes while I'm working on Zav's right arch. His gaze darts to the kitsune, a small smile cracking as he notices the tails wrapped around the dude. "Okay, fine. You want to hear what I had to deal with while you guys fucked around?"

"Hey, wait," X says with a frown. "No one fucked anything. That should be made very clear. It was just everyone being comfy and feeling close to KK. It will happen for everyone, eventually, I'm sure. Don't act like it was some rando hookup, J."

A flutter in my chest makes me duck my head at his words, and the big guy holding my feet chuckles. His thumb runs over the sole of my foot gently and I look up at him through my lashes. "Careful, I can be ticklish."

"Yes, that must be why I feel your pulse speeding up." Slash smirks and I know my face must be getting even redder by the second.

Jasper growls. "Okay. X's clarification is noted. Are you ready for the story now or what?"

"O, Captain, my Captain," Oriel says, his voice tinged with playful sarcasm. "Regale us."

If they don't quit screwing with him, we're going to get nowhere.

"Shut up, Oriel," the Prince sighs. "So you asked about the bodies, right, shrimp?"

I nod, watching his face. "I did and no one's ever answered me."

"We're not picky about that shit in Hell. The clean-up crews came for them and then disposed of them in the Wastelands if their families didn't want to pay for them to be sent back to their homes." I blink, looking shocked, but Jasper shrugs. "Demons that are permanently killed aren't worth a damn thing and obviously, we don't believe in reincarnation. Only the wealthiest or highest tiers of demon lines give a fuck about the dead. Don't let it bother you."

My eyes move to the others and see nods all around. "Weird. But I guess it makes sense. Why would any demons actually want the bodies then? And why the Wastelands? What did the bodies look like? Was there anything odd?"

Jasper blinks, shaking his head as if to clear it at my word vomit. "Uh… in order: rituals and parts, beasts who are carrion eaters, dead, and not that I know of."

Slash laughs, winking at me. "The Prince loves to talk but I think he's unused to your inquisitive nature, little demon."

"Well, if we're all getting closer, he should get used to it."

"Hmmph." The dragon's grunt doesn't tell me anything, but I wait for him to go. "Well, after that shit, I had to deal with Darkstar and then classes and… as promised, my father."

Oh no.

"We've been cleared to go above this weekend. I tried to get him to push our permission further into the future so we'd all be top notch, but without telling him *why*, I wasn't able to convince him. So we have to go tomorrow if we want to poke around the surface for dirt on our illustrious Headmaster."

I wasn't prepared for him to say that at *all*.

"Are you sure that's wise, Jas?" Zavida whispers as he hugs his tails. "It's dangerous for us to be there at all, much less when some of us are recovering."

X snorts. "Guys, I'll be fine by tomorrow. I've been regenerating all day and I spent *hours* in my animal form. And KK's been good all day, I think. Right?"

All eyes whirl to me and I want to deny it, but I know it's true. I'm fine now and I have no good excuse for avoiding the place I ran away from to come here.

God damn it.

One Step At A Time

sälem

We spent the rest of the evening eating dinner and studying. Kit Kat was visibly shaken by the upcoming trip, and though I know my brothers wanted to discuss it until we all zonked out in our spots, he was definitely not ready for it. I suggested we watch a recent movie and Zav scrambled to go grab his laptop so we could pick something that would help us make sense of the place above the surface.

None of us besides KK have been there much—some not at all—so it was a good idea.

Slash grumbled that he would have to 'hide himself' and Jasper agreed, making Kit shake his head ruefully. He informed us all that unless we were going to a supernatural community, we would absolutely have to hide any spare parts or start a panic. Oriel looked like he wanted to ask follow-up questions, but the kid just snuggled into his chair further, pulling his blanket up, and I glared until everyone shut up.

This morning has been just as tense—he seems like he's as jittery as a StyX fiend and I'm not sure how to help him. As he pours a coffee, I arch a brow and finally give in. "Uh, Kit Kat? Do you think caffeine is… a good idea right now? You already seem set to blow at any second."

His head swivels and I swear to fuck, it's like that possessed little girl in the poorly done human movie. The absolute evil in that glance makes my poof shrivel up like a cotton ball. "I don't need baby-sitters, Salem. I'm perfectly capable of deciding what I can or cannot handle."

"Well, yes, but, um…" I rub the back of my neck, trying not to respond to this tiny dude like I would Jasper's wrath despite the similarities in their behavior. "You're just… it feels like you're practically vibrating. That's how StyX heads feel when they're running around and I don't know if it's your anxiety or being up there or worry…. I didn't want it to be worse for you."

Kit frowns, waving off the concern to ask, "What the hell is StyX? I am *never* going to learn how to be one of you guys. There just aren't enough hours in the day."

Of course that's what he would focus on.

"Premier party drug down here. Bad stuff, very addictive. Makes demons super paranoid and shaky, but also gets used to boost energy for shit like exams or sex or whatever. Not my thing, but we saw a lot of people using it in secondary school." I shrug and think about it for a moment. "We haven't here because we're not going out to parties to make noise at Discordia."

"Is that a bad thing?" Kit sips the coffee then wrinkles his nose, adding more berry sweetener to it. "Does it hurt us in the long run?"

"Probably? Anton and X would be better resources on the whole socio-political tie-in stuff. They're the ones that picked everything we attended and Jasper laid down the rules and shit. I went because I had to; that shit isn't my jam."

He tucks his chin, smiling at me for the first time since we got up. "Not mine, either. My issue was at a party, and um… I haven't been to one since. That is, except for that damn Halloween thing where Jasper's cockgobbling father got in my face."

I grin broadly as he dumps *more* Cantu berries into his coffee. "You should add some of that Dark Cow to smooth out the Hellfire beans. They're spicy as fuck."

"Could have told me before I took a drink," he mutters, stomping over to the fridge. He sighs as he pulls out the container of black dairy, then his shoulders scrunch. "I'm sorry, Salem. I'm being a pill because I *hate* the thought of going back up there."

"Even though everyone down here wants to kill you?"

His scowl is cute as he pours the creamer, then puts it away. "Not everyone. Just… mostly everyone. But yes, despite that, I was so adrift on the surface. I'm not popular here, but I *am* starting to feel like I fit for the first time in my life. So I'd prefer *not* to take steps backwards, you know?"

Walking over to Kit, I lean my hip against the counter as I look down at him. He's frowning into his mug like he's trying to figure something out. I reach out and lift his chin, smiling as his eyes meet mine. "KK, you're not going to become an outcast just because we go up there. You know we're only portaling up to root around for clues about your past and what's going on with the Games."

Something odd flashes in his gaze and his expression turns to panic. "We can't go back to where I was living—like, not at all. It wasn't where I was born, anyway, and um… I don't think I can deal with seeing those people. Please, Salem. *Please* don't let Jasper choose there."

The sudden fear radiating off him worries me, and I don't know what else to do except pull him into my arms. Hugging him tightly, I wait for the little tremors to fade before I pull back. I don't get why going back to the town he lived in before the doc snatched him up has Kit flipping out, but it's obviously a *big* trigger. The way he's breathing tells me that he's trying extremely hard not to fall into an attack and he's gripping me like he might fall off the edge if he lets go.

I like it, so I have to think of really gross things before the poof unshrivels.

"Salem?" Kit whispers as I work to get a grip on myself. "Why are you suddenly like a statue? You give good hugs and um, I was glad you gave me one. But if that's not okay, then—"

Gritting my teeth, I look up at the ceiling for help. I know there's nothing there but I *need* to keep control of myself so I don't make this panic attack worse. But when I look down at his unsure expression and the pouty bottom lip, I realize I'm definitely going to lose that battle. My arms tighten on Kit and I duck down, brushing my lips over his without so much as a word.

He squeaks and I almost pull back, but a soft sigh keeps me in place. I think the sound means he's okay with the light kiss, so I do it again, being careful not to increase the pressure unless he initiates it. Our breath mingles, warm as Kit melts into the embrace with so much trust that I can feel my heart thumping like a bass beat,

I don't want to scare him, but I definitely don't want to break away.

"Um, Salem?" he whispers almost into my mouth. "Are we… is this…"

The poor guy is *so* nervous and unsure. It makes me want to rip whoever did this to him into tiny pieces and feed them to Slash in his shark form as chum. I don't care if I have to share with my brothers as they climb on board this train one by one—I just want to help KK heal. His awkward, broken pieces call to mine in a way I've never felt before.

"I think we are, roomie. Is that okay?"

His silence makes my gut clench, but I wait as patiently as I can while he muddles through it. When he gets there, he murmurs, "I think so. I'm not panicking and… I like you, Salem. But…"

Leaning forward, I bite his lower lip gently, then pull back. "But what?"

The shiver makes me smile, but Kit's hands hold on tightly as he replies. "I… like… others, too. And I don't want to hurt—"

Oh, this problem. Luckily, it's not one at all.

"Kit Kat, you're one of us now—that means all of us. No one else is invited, but you belong with our caliphate and anything within our family is okay. Does that make sense?"

He sighs, his fingers pressing into my sides rhythmically as he thinks. I know this is hard for him on so many levels—his kind aren't often polyamorous, plus he's got buckets of trauma to boot. But I think I've gotten through to him when he raises his dark lashes enough for me to see his eyes sparkling with gold flecks that I'm pretty sure are his magic.

"You're sure that's going to fly with… whomever?"

I grin, moving my hand to brush my knuckles over his cheek. "Yep. I'm very sure, and I wouldn't lie to you. In fact, some may enjoy more… group-focused activities in the future." Kit looks like a demon being yanked to the pits, his expression full of shock and fear. I tilt my head, smirking a little as I whisper, "Like… maybe if Oriel joined our hugs sometimes?"

I feel the second he tenses, then the subsequent relaxation as his brain catches up. Kit nods a little and the flush on his face spreads as it gets redder. "I don't think I'd mind that. I mean, you know. When we're, um, alone in the room. I don't think I can… not with other people watching."

Laughing, I boop his nose playfully. "You're not ready for an audience when you hug someone? Dear me, whatever shall I do with you, you miniature prude?"

"I'm not a prude," Kit pouts, his brows drawing together in a dark frown. "But I am fucked up in so many ways I can't count them, and you're probably better off *not* tying your boat to my ramshackle dock."

Feeling saucy and a little drunk with the excitement about this conversation, I pinch his hip lightly. "Listen up, you tiny firecracker. I'll let you run the show when it comes to being comfortable and feeling safe, but I will *not* put up with you downing yourself. I know you have more self-esteem than that, so I'm going to believe that it's because this situation makes you nervous."

Kit Kat nods, brushing our noses and lips as he moves, then murmurs huskily, "There was… a lot of self-hatred I had to work through after the… thing. And um, when I reported it, that sort of ramped up from outside people, too. So it's hard not to fall back into that place, I guess."

I pull back, though I don't want to, cupping his jaw in my palm. "That motherfucker was a dirty son of a bitch and anyone who said a damn thing to you isn't worth a damn. I know you're not ready to tell that story yet and that's okay, but when you are, all of the caliphate will support you, KK, even Prince Dickhead."

"Oh no," he says and his eyes close. "We don't have to tell him about this, right? I'm just… not with the trip today, and…"

"Kit, calm down. No, we don't have to tell him."

His eyes open and he gives me a shy, grateful smile as he looks up at me. "Um, but if he's not okay, we can tell Oriel. He's approved."

My lips twist and I arch a brow. "I'm not enough already? You're breaking my heart, firecracker."

"Ugh, is that going to stick? I know you guys said a pet name for each of you, but…"

I shrug, brushing hair out of his eyes. "I kinda like it, so maybe. You definitely blow up when your fuse is lit."

He's about to respond when I hear footsteps in the hallway. It would take a shifter hearing to pick it up, but I let go, moving back reluctantly to honor his request about being discreet for a while. "Salem!"

I frown, not understanding why he's saying my name like that. "What?"

"Did you pull away because there was stomping in the hall?"

My eyes widen and I nod, grinning again. "I did. You said you wanted—"

"I heard them, too."

Hot damn. Now that's *what I call a good fucking morning.*

No Roots

I swallow hard as Salem moves away from me, shivering as my body immediately misses the heat of his pressed close. My lack of panic proves how much I've learned to trust my roommate over the past few months. I don't know what to make of that, but I definitely know it's a *huge* step in terms of healing. These dudes have been slowly conditioning me to accept physical touch—something I didn't really notice, but I realize now was to help me in ways they couldn't say out loud.

Thinking I'd bitch at them is a fair assessment.

My defense mechanisms are sharp and formidable; I needed to keep the softest parts of me away from the people who could hurt me after the incident. But Salem and some of the others are peeling them like a fucking onion, which is both exciting and dangerous. I couldn't tell him 'no', though. My body, my heart, even my brain—none of them wanted me to say that word when he asked. All I could do was consent and now my insides are this weird mess of buzzing anticipation and squishiness for the kind panda demon.

So I do what I know: deflection. "Hearing the steps is one of the power manifestations, right? That's maybe…. a shifter thing?"

His lips curve up and by the look in his eyes, I know Salem has caught on to my scheme. However, he doesn't call me out; he just nods, walking over to the cabinets and gathering some supplies from our stores. "I do, Kit Kat. Obviously, a *lot* of animals have good hearing and most have better hearing than the humans. It doesn't tell us much—yet."

"And the magic thing is confounding us for now." I frown, my elation at the small moment of connection with him fizzling. "So really, we don't know hardly anything more than when I got here."

Salem makes a huffing sound as he methodically packs up his granola bars, organizing each pile by the ribbon color before he slides them into a sealed bag. "Don't be silly, KK. We know you *might* have three things which is rare as shit, and we know that your magic is scary AF. The time thing paired with that display at the stadium gives us some clues, and so does the hearing. I bet you've had other—"

A loud pounding at the door precedes it sliding open to reveal a beaming X and Anton. Xerxes holds up two bags, their eyes dancing. "Uniforms and the casual stuff—school logoed, of course. I have plans for some other stuff I'll make for non-school fashion."

I blink, my chest tightening again as I look at the two of them. "You had to get up super early to catch the supply store without a line on a Saturday."

"Point of fact, they didn't sleep," Anton grumbles fondly. "Naps don't work well for Xerxes; they tend to fuck up their circadians."

Dipping my chin, I mutter, "Sorry, guys. That's my fault."

X snorts, and I look up to see them striding into the room without waiting for permission. "Hardly. We're grown demons and I didn't give a shit. It was very comfy, and my snake is practically docile since. Don't take on guilt that doesn't belong to you, KK."

Anton gives me a small smile, his chin tucked as his pretty eyes communicate similar happiness in his less flashy way. "You seem to be well this morning."

My eyes widen, but I clamp down on my emotions quickly. Salem chuckles as he continues preparing for our trip at the counter. I clear my throat, shrugging as if it's no big deal. "I do feel stronger. Obviously, so does X. I should probably take the stuff they've got and get dressed for the trip, right?"

Salem turns to wink at me, then looks over at the other two. "We should let Kit Kat get settled before—"

The door to the dorm flies open again, and Oriel slips in, a stack of clothing in his arms. It doesn't look new, but a sniff tells me it's not dirty. His eyes are tired, but he's smiling a little. "Morning, KK. I brought you some surface-type gear from one of my hordes. I figured you didn't have much to wear up there since you came with so little shit."

Every demon in the room looks at him with their jaws dropped like a fucking cartoon character. I frown, tilting my head as I study them then glance at the crow shifter. "Why is everyone acting like you showed up naked painted in pancake syrup?"

Oriel guffaws, the caw-like edge of it telling me that he finds this *extremely* funny. I haven't heard him do that before—I don't think? His eyes sparkle at me as he catches his breath a moment later. "Kit Kat, you're fucking ridiculous. That is *not* the 'naked in syrup' expression—I promise you, you won't be able to miss *that.*"

"Okay, Mr. Pedantry, why are they so damn shocked?" I fold my arms over my chest, giving him a stern glare.

"Because… Oriel *never* and I really mean *never in a thousand years* has given *any* of us a damn thing from one of his fucking treasure troves." X puts their hands on their face, still looking amazed. "I mean, my flabbers are fucking *ghasted*, man."

The crow furrows his brows, frowning at them darkly. "Stop it, asshole."

"Is that true?" I ask curiously. "Like never?"

"It's not as big a deal as they're making it," he grumbles as he stomps towards the kitchen area. When he gets close, he thrusts the pile at me, and I look at it. I get the feeling it's sized perfectly and probably exactly like something I'd wear. "Just go get dressed before Prince Prickface gets here."

I lick my lips, hugging the pile to my chest as X jerks their head at the door to my room. "Okay. But um, thank you, Oriel." I get the strangest urge to peck a kiss on his cheek, but there are too many people in this room. Instead, I give him a soft, grateful smile before I follow the cobra towards my room.

X opens the door, setting the bags they brought inside the door and winks. "Don't worry, Kit Kat. We're out here if you need help with anything."

"I'm pretty sure I can get dressed on my own, Xerxes."

At least, for now I can. Who knows what I'll need to keep my secret later on?

By the time I finish dressing and binding myself, I've worked myself into a bit of a frenzy. I don't know *where* Jasper plans for us to go, nor do I have any clue what kind of beings I could encounter. According to what Dank told me, his potion will mask the 'feminine' parts of my scent as I continue to gain powers, but I have no fucking clue if that will work with anything besides demons. My guys aren't big surface visitors—a fact that helps me immensely. But supernaturals who live up there?

They could be a big ass fucking problem.

Thus, I'm exiting the room looking for Dottie without pause. She comes running over from a perch on Slash's chair. Apparently, she's not only fond of birds, snakes, and bears (oh my). The shark shifter gets up as soon as she darts over to me, his eyes sharp as he makes his way to me. Large hands land on my shoulders as he looks down at me seriously, ignoring the sounds of protest behind him.

"Little demon, are you well this morning? Will this be too taxing?"

I grin a little when X makes a grumbling protest about Slash's lack of care for how they're doing. The huge demon arches a brow, waiting for me to answer as he stares at me. He's deathly focused, so I actually look inside, taking inventory of how I feel on various levels before I answer. When I'm ready, I wrinkle my nose. "Well, I don't ache or feel weak. Salem fed me, so I'm good for a little bit on that front. I'm nervous as fuck about this trip, though, so I'm full of jittery sparkles and spiky anger. Is that what you wanted to know?"

He nods, tilting his head. "It is and you were good for telling me honestly, little demon. I will make sure I'm close by to help dampen the nerves. If you need to ground, you can grab my arm. Yes?"

I'm not grabbing anyone in front of fucking people I don't know, but he doesn't need to know that.

"Okay, big guy. But the others can help, too, right?" My eyes move to the pouting demons behind him, then cut to Jasper as he scowls. "Well, except His Royal Assface. He doesn't want to be helpful, so I'll make sure I stay as far from him as possible."

Somehow, that makes him scowl even harder and I throw my hands up in frustration. Slash chuckles, shaking his head. "Do not worry. I know you have the entire caliphate to assist with protection and comfort. Except for the Prince, of course."

A dark growl comes from Jasper's direction and I narrow my gaze. "Stop being a dick and tell us where the fuck we're going."

Moving around the shark shifter with Dottie in my arms, I see that Salem has emptied his bag and is currently filling it with his supplies. The care he takes makes me smile a bit, and as if I said his name, the panda demon turns to wink at me. "Just making sure we have what we need to survive a day up in that stupid place, KK. We can eat their food and shit, but it doesn't rejuvenate us like ours does. Plus, I've got a little safety kit Annie and X brought from the doc."

They were busy AF this morning, I guess.

Oriel finally pushes through the crowd, his dark eyes dancing as he takes me in. "I knew I had the right size!"

I look down at the ripped black skinny jeans, my combat boots, and the oversized Ramones tee-shirt that came pre-punkified with a grin. My eyes move back up to his as he pulls an army jacket from fuck only knows where and hands it to me. "I was worried at first, but you did well, O. This all fits well and none of it makes me want to off myself if people see me in it."

X scampers over to look at me, handing me a tech watch in black. "Zavvie fetched this for you because we can use it to keep connected if we get separated. I know we have phones, but um… just in case, right?"

Peeping at the red-headed kitsune, I give him a grateful smile. It makes him flush and hug his tails, which seems to be making my pulse skitter now. It's so damned cute and I'm tired of pretending it isn't. "Thanks, Zav. I'm sure you guys can track me, too, which helps my anxiety a bit."

Jasper scoffs, rolling his eyes. "Yes, of course we can, shrimp. Now if you idiots are done dancing around him, we should get moving. Time moves differently there, and we don't want to keep burning portal access time."

"I asked where we're going." I cross my arms over my chest, stubbornly refusing to move until he includes me in his goddamn plans.

The Prince sighs loudly, running his hands through his raven and dark green locks in annoyance. "Fuck, you're such a pain in the spikes. *Fine.* We're going to your hometown—"

"*No!*" The shout is out of my mouth before I can stop it and six pairs of demon eyes are looking at me in confusion. Xerxes, of course, knows why I'm flipping out, but they stay quiet.

"Little demon, we should try to find—"

Shaking my head, I hold a shaking hand out. "No, we shouldn't. Where Dank picked me up is not where I was dropped off as a baby, nor are the Jamesons even *close* to my first fosters. They'll be no help at all."

Dottie looks at me, her baleful kinkajou gaze telling me that I'm wrong about whether they'll be helpful. I remember finding her rooting through their secret safe, and it makes me pause. I can't take them there until they all know; no one in that town will cover my ass, especially not my idiot foster brothers.

"Maybe we should go to the coast instead," Anton says.

I could kiss him, but again, I'm thinking about kissing a lot of people today, so I should calm the hell down. "What's on the coast?"

"Trouble," Jasper replies with a dark frown. "If you're too wimpy to go home, then we should investigate what the fuck Lucian has been doing up there; Anton's right. That means no running your mouth and starting a fucking feud, got it, shrimp?"

Now I'm like fifty times more likely to do it—but he'll find that out later.

Mr. Brightside

Jasper

If I didn't believe this was necessary, I would have chucked the idea to go to the surface as soon as the shrimp and X were hurt. Better yet, without my father being a complete asshole, I could have simply postponed it until we were ready. It might have even given the rest of my caliphate time to convince the kid to go back to his previous home so we could investigate the present back to the past.

As usual, the universe and all its meddling forces have conspired to make shit difficult.

The commotion around getting ready to leave was an annoyance—I don't get why the shrimp is easy going with some of my brothers and an incessant pain in the ass to me. I'm doing everything Zavvie suggested; I even kept my mouth firmly closed when he refused to go to his old hometown. That made my soft kitsune smile proudly, something I dislike admitting made me feel good. I know he's only trying to help smooth things over, but something about the way the shrimp fights me provokes a deep need to fight back, even about the smallest shit.

"Where are we headed?" I arch a brow at the kid's question and he huffs in irritation. "Don't be mean, Jasper. I'm obviously asking where the fuck the portal or whatever is on campus."

See? This is what I mean—I didn't even say anything.

Slash grins down at him, and I roll my eyes behind his back. My second-in-command is enigmatic on the best days, but since our new member arrived, he's become completely unpredictable. He doesn't support me without question and his attitude towards the kid is like he's adopted a fucking puppy. I told him to help make sure Kit was trained and kept healthy, not become a walking sharp-toothed nanny.

"The place where we can form the portal is in the depths of the library building, little demon. That's where we are headed."

Kit frowns, looking confused. "When Dank brought me, the car just… appeared in the middle of campus near the admin building. Lucian and Prince Pissypants were waiting for me."

I snort, hearing him but ignoring the jibe as I lead the group to our destination.

He's not wrong, but he's asking the wrong question and I'm not going to tell him.

"That's because when someone is retrieving a surface person who belongs here—for whatever reason—they can leave and return via special portals registered for doing those things," Anton says. "Obviously, you were invited to Discordia and accepted, so Dank was able to use one."

That's oversimplified, but close enough for this conversation. I keep walking towards the library with Zav next to me, his tails swishing back and forth. I don't miss that Kit didn't give the shark shifter snark about his basic response, nor did he scoff at the peacock. It's annoying as fuck that only I get the salty shit, but I'm also the one who isn't allowed to respond to it. And they coddle the fuck out of the shrimp because they didn't see how strong he was when those fuckers were attacking him—panic attack or not.

Pussies. They're all pussies and the shrimp can take more than they're letting him handle.

"Are you saying those portals are used for like… bringing people to fiddle for their soul or some shit?"

Blinking, a barking laugh escapes me and they all turn to look at me. My mirth turns to a scowl quickly as I retort, "That's just a song, shrimp. Crossroads demons definitely collect on their debts with that kind of transportation, but there are other valid reasons as well."

"I don't think I'd like those demons," Kit says. His rodent companion makes a noise in agreement, making Salem chuckle. "I mean, I get that humans and other beings make the deals, but it feels like Hell's version of a payday loan, you know? It's more usury than help."

"That's the *point*," I reply as we get to the steps. "Life isn't easy and it's rarely fair. Taking a short cut for short-term gain has to have consequences or it's all anyone would ever do. The world can't stay in balance if everyone gets everything they want or need all the time. Demons and Fae making bargains with adverse consequences help with that."

Zav clears his throat as we ascend, looking back at the others. "That much is true. Demons are less tricky than the Fae, but they also can't tell a complete lie. Even we have rules, KK."

"It's completely unfathomable that a species can't even tell a white lie," the shrimp grumbles. "How do they survive?"

"By being *very* skilled with words and intentions," X answers. "Fae are *such a pain* in the ass to deal with. Hopefully, we won't come across any on this little field trip. They're gorgeous and fabulous, but *exhausting*."

Kit sighs and I have to keep my smile to myself. "Okay, Fae are pretty but obnoxious. What else do I need to know? How will I even recognize what anyone is? Are we going to a place that has a lot of different supernaturals or just demons? I feel so unprepared for this trip, and it makes my ass twitch."

The silence that falls over the group is hysterical, but again, I keep my comments to myself. As long as the kid behaves, I promised Zavvie I would do my best to reciprocate. He hasn't stepped on my tail yet, so I'm straining to keep my word.

"Well, uh…" Oriel stammers, then finds the thread. "We don't actually know that, Kit Kat. You could smell some or feel vibes, or see something… Since your lineage is a mystery and you might have a few, it's hard to predict what mechanisms your powers will use to identify threats and friendlies."

"Great," the shrimp mutters. "So I'll probably, maybe feel, see, or smell something, but maybe nothing, but don't worry because you're all here if it goes haywire?"

"Well put, little demon."

That should have earned my general a smart ass remark, but all he gets is a nod and a long suffering sigh.

I'm going to throttle that little shit someday.

IT TOOK LONGER THAN I WOULD HAVE PREFERRED, BUT I GOT ALL OF MY brothers to help keep Kit in check while I called the portal and within a few minutes, we were stepping out of it onto terra firma in Bay City. Squinting at the bright light of the surface, I growl under my breath. The official demon portal comes out at a spot called 'Demon's Gate' in our territory of the city. I don't want to make a huge splash that will draw the attention of the Head Fuckwit up here, so I turn to the others quickly.

"Modify your appearances—all of you. I will, too, but we need to fly under the radar for as long as possible. I don't want to head straight for the Gemini complex, but if we don't keep a low profile, someone will snitch to them."

Kit's brows furrow. "The demons up here are… enemies?"

Zavida wrinkles his nose, squeezes his eyes shut, and his tails go poof, leaving the nerdy ginger looking like a common human gamer. He's wearing jeans and a tee shirt that says 'I don't care how big the room is; I cast fireball' with a set of twenty-sided dice. Without his tails, you'd never know he wasn't the owner of a fucking comic book shop. "Some are, KK. Luca Gemini is defi-nitely in the probably not column, but we're not sure about all of his fiefdom."

"His heirs are question marks," I grunt as I crack my neck then retract my spines. I'm still big and intimidating without them because I'm a goddamned dragon hybrid, but it feels like I'm missing a part of me when I go bare. The shrimp's eyes cut to me and he nods as he studies me. "What?"

"I don't think I've seen you without them yet," he murmurs in response.

Slash speaks before I can growl back, looking just as annoyed as I am when he unshifts his fin. "We all must suffer for this trip, little demon. But the Prince is correct—we know Luca and his wife are probably in cahoots with Darkstar."

"We aren't sure of who else might be helping outside of the demon commu-nity, either." Anton doesn't wear any external signs of his animal form so unlike the three of us, he doesn't have to adjust. However, he looks around carefully regardless, because his and X's images are fairly well known by demons everywhere. Their faces are flashy enough to compare to celebutantes up here.

"Okay, okay. Trust no one. I get it, guys," Kit says as he slips his kinkajou in the messenger bag. "If all that's true, we should make our way towards shops or something. Annie and X will need something to cover up their fabulousness. All of you look like you need glasses because you're squinting so much—I assume sunglasses would be helpful."

I want to argue with him; I really do. But the little shit has a point, as much as I hate to admit it.

"Fine," I say as I pull out my phone. Scrolling for a moment, I find the settings that will allow it to work on the surface. A moment later I have service, so I use an app for a supernatural ride share service. "I've called transportation. It won't be fancy, but unless we want the people we need to investigate to know we're here, this is how it needs to go."

Salem and Oriel are flanking the former human as he looks around. I nod at them, then look at the kid, hoping they understand that I'm tasking them with sticking close to him. Kit won't be upset by that, and I need to focus on getting us to the main part of Bay City without being recognized. Once we get there, we can do as he suggested then wander the main area to get a sense of what's happening in the city.

"Can someone tell me what the hell we think this… *guy* and his *wife* might be doing?" Kit looks at all of us expectantly and I realize he's being vague because he doesn't know if any of the demons walking around in the area are listening.

At least he's not dumb.

"We don't know, Kit Kat," Oriel says as he squints at the sky then back at us. He must be itching to fly off and spy in his animal form, but that's not an option for today. "But the scuttlebutt is that he was up here, in this area, before Halloween. Some kind of party is what I picked up when I did some scouting of the shitheads in the office."

I nod, my eyes darting around as I watch for familiar faces or our damn car to arrive. "It could be coincidental, but it's not likely. That *guy* has always been unhappy with current leadership and his *wife* is just as crafty. Finding like minded demons who have eyes and ears in the courts might have given them the ability to push something like the Games."

"To wipe you guys out?"

The wide, worried eyes of the small dude look at me and the oddest urge to comfort him comes over me. I frown, clenching my fists at my side as I shrug, pretending it's not a big deal. "Probably. Take us out, start a war, and ascend is how our parents got their chairs at the big tables."

"Couldn't they do that without a big fucking mess like these Games are going to be?" he asks softly. "I mean, it seems like a *lot* of work for something they could hire assassins or whatever demons have. Right?"

Slash grins toothily and I scowl at him until the sharp teeth fade. "I have assassins for breakfast, little demon. At least five since this summer, to be exact."

Kit looks at me for confirmation and I shrug again, enjoying his expression as he realizes the big guy he's cuddling up with is completely serious.

But then he shocks the shit out of me.

"Well… good. If they're coming for my family, then they deserve it. I hope you make it hurt, big guy."

That makes my general look almost giddy and the others collapse in laughter. I rub my temples, unable to process what just happened without feeling like my brain box is going to fucking explode. Luckily for me, a big SUV with dark tinted windows pulls up in front of us just in time to keep me from having to deal with any of them.

"Let's get moving. We have things to do and limited time."

Plus, I have no idea what the fuck to do with the shrimp's newfound approval of murder.

Surprise

Now that we're all piled into this weirdly assembled SUV, I've got *so* many questions. I know it's going to piss Jasper off to ask them, but I have to know what the hell is going on and I don't have the knowledge base the others do. He doesn't think about that because they're all so used to working together. But I'm not here to stroke his fucking ego or pretend I trust every damn decision he makes—I have to learn things before they put me in danger.

"How did we call for this car? How did your—"

Before I can finish, the Prince scowls at me across the limo-esque seating, holding his finger in the air. I have no idea what the hell that means, but the others all pull out their phones and start fiddling with them. I press my lips together as I get mine out, petting Dottie as I do so. She hugs my finger, helping me calm my ire at the silent shushing the asshole is giving me. It takes a moment, but X leans across, grabbing my phone with a wink.

At least they're aware that bowing to Jasper's will is making me want to lash out.

Xerxes does whatever they're all doing to my phone, then nods at Anton, who murmurs under his breath. My hearing is getting better, so I catch a bunch of Latin that means zero to me. He finally stops and nods at Jasper, who puts his finger down.

"We needed to make certain we will not be eavesdropped on," Anton says as X hands me my phone. "Our rooms, our floor, and our table in the *Triclinium* are already safe. That's one of the things Xerxes and I did as soon as we arrived in the summertime. There's also enchantments to discourage any other students from approaching them so we don't get low level spies."

Oh, wait, is that another reason Prince Prickface was mad about me being assigned their floor?

The dragon smirks, arching a brow at me. "Yes, that's why I was so suspicious when you were assigned our floor, shrimp. Lucian's flunkies and acolytes don't have a way into our areas without permission. Assigning you to our floor would circumvent the intention-based magic those two placed on our private spaces."

"You could have just fucking told me that," I grumble bitterly. "At least, once you all decided to adopt me into your little demonic cult."

Salem laughs, bumping my shoulder with his. "Don't be a salty Seymour, Kit Kat. Sometimes this dick actually has good reasons for what he does, but he's used to people following his orders. You question the fuck out of him, and we're all here for it."

Flushing at the praise, I move my gaze to the smug dragon again. "Then someone should explain the phones, this car… all the shit that you seem comfy with despite telling me you don't come to the surface much."

Jasper growls in annoyance. "That's far more shit than I'm willing to impart for a car ride."

"But—"

Oriel squeezes my knee lightly and in the tight squeeze between him and Salem, I have to hold my breath to control the shiver it causes. I don't know how these guys have managed to get such immediate responses from me without tripping any alarms, but I wish I could figure it out. Getting all squirmy and itchy is not an option in the seats—we're squeezed in tightly and facing each other. Someone will notice me having problems if I'm not careful.

"Okay. I'll take some of this one since our Prince won't deign to do his damn job." I give him an appreciative look, settling back to listen. "Zav always gets our tech first because he puts a lot of shit on the equipment that we might need someday and shit we definitely need now hardware-wise. That's what we were doing that Jas already did for himself—switching to surface service so they work up here. He used the Suber app, which is the supernatural version of a ride share company. It's safe for all kinds and the tech was set up by nerds who work for the Society. That's the big wig global council up here we talked about."

Pinching the bridge of my nose, I nod. So many things I don't know, and it's never going to end. I hate that. "I guess that's why this car is set up weirdly inside?"

"Yep," X says as they cross their ankles in the middle of the space between the rows. "There's magic and tech and all sorts of shit involved, KK. But *that's* also what Annie just did—a small, localized bubble inside the car so we can talk without the driver eavesdropping. He smells like a shifter, so he probably doesn't have more than sensitive hearing, but caution isn't unwarranted. Supernaturals on the surface are *far* more likely to have hybrid lineage than in Hell."

My brain is going to explode one of these days, I fucking swear it.

"That's a lot to take in." I blow out a breath, wrinkling my nose as I consider what else to ask. "We're going to the city center to find supplies and then ask around, right?"

Slash nods. "Correct."

"How will I know what to ask? I mean, we don't even know if I'll be able to tell who is what and—"

Oriel nudges me this time. "Breathe, Kit Kat. You're not expected to do any interrogating. That would be silly since we have no idea what you can and can't do. We'll handle that; you just keep your eyes peeled for suspicious human things. And maybe… give us a heads-up if we're doing something really stupid that would reveal our nature to them. That's a big no-no if we're not here for official reasons, obviously."

Now I have to keep their secrets, too? Son of a bitch.

My phone vibrates on my lap and I surreptitiously unlock it again, peeking at the message through my lashes as I look down. It's from X, so I have to be very careful who sees what they're saying.

Flashy: I know what you're worried about.

Kit Kat: …

Flashy: I don't know for sure, but I THINK the doc's potion will keep you covered for us and up here. We'll have to test it carefully, but I'm pretty sure it will hide what it needs to from the beings here, too.

Kit Kat: K.

I can't really answer well with O and Salem so close; that's the best I can do. X winks at me when I look up, and I nod slightly. If they're wrong, we're going to get a *lot* of attention up here when Jasper loses his fucking mind. The others will be upset or frustrated—I think—but the Prince will go right into mistrust mode because we just don't have a foundation to build on yet. I'm simply not ready to tell anyone other than X, but now that I'm meeting all of their animals and demons, I hope that will change.

Some rando revealing this up here would fuck everything up.

Though I'm not in any way religious, I wing a prayer to the universe that Dank's potion covers more than just Hell and demons. I could have asked if I had time, but this trip was hastily planned and organized, so I didn't have the chance. I wonder if the demon has a cell? I need to ask him next time I go in because I definitely want to be able to ask him shit like this on the fly.

"Kit!"

The loud voice paired with the emphasis pulls me out of my head, and I blink at the peacock shifter who said it in confusion. "What?"

"You spaced out completely and we're here."

That makes the others chuckle and Jasper gives me another one of his assface smirks. Gathering myself, I hold the bottom of my bag to make sure Dottie is comfy. "I'm sorry. There's just so much to take in and it never ends. I feel like I'm constantly being jacked into the Matrix and downloading shit."

Oriel tilts his head, studying me in the avian manner that means he's processing something. "I get that, actually. That was a fucking great metaphor."

"It really was," Zavida says as he follows Jasper out of the car. "I got it, too. And I see how that would be frustrating and scary at the same time. I don't think I understood where you're at very well until now."

"Should have started with movie references," I mutter as Anton and X get out after the kitsune. "It would have helped us find common ground much faster."

"Only some of us," O replies as he moves next, then waits for me to follow. Salem is right behind me, the two of them forming the same kind of shield Slash and Zav did around the Prince.

How exactly is the nervous red-head going to protect the Prince?

I don't get the chance to ask, though, because Jasper waves the driver off, and we're standing on a street that is full of shops, but oddly, no foot traffic. "It's a weekend and this city's pretty big—where is everyone?"

Slash looks around, his expression unsettled. "I do not like this, Prince."

"It's not an ambush," Jasper shoots back with an eye roll. "This is way too big for Lucian and his lackeys or even the Gemini to arrange. There's something else going on."

Squinting at the various shops, I find one that looks like it will be fancy enough for these rich assholes, but also have what we came for. "Okay. Let's go to that *Rigoletto Abbigliamento e Accessori di pregio*[1] place and get what we need."

"You speak Italian?" the Prince says wryly.

I smile sweetly, my tone mocking as I reply, "Nope. But if I can't pronounce the name of a place I'm pretty sure only rich fuckwads like you can afford it. Process of elimination and all."

Even Slash snickers, and I know he's concerned about our situation right now. Jasper sucks in a breath, holds it, then lets go as he glares at me. "Despite your shortcomings in the cultural arena, you happen to be right. That should do nicely, as *Rigoletto's* is run by an ancient Italian supe family descendant.

Looking pleased as fuck, I pretend his jibe didn't land and turn towards the storefront. "Then let's go get you guys some sunglasses so you quit squinting, and we'll see if the people working here have any idea why the hell this place is a ghost town on the weekend."

Jasper doesn't move, so I stride away from the group to cross the street. I'm not surprised when Salem and Oriel catch up to me quickly, taking their flanking positions again like good little soldiers. I'd be annoyed by that, except... I like them here. The two of them are my most comfortable relationships right now, and I don't feel bad when I murmur, "Being up here is really weird, you know?"

"Uh, you're telling me," Salem says as he ruffles his white locks. "Half of us can't even stay in our preferred forms in this place, KK. This is how you feel in your skin all the time? Like really?"

I know he's not being shitty, so I don't hit the panda demon with a snarky response. Instead, I reach down and take his hand. "Sometimes. I mean, here? Yeah, pretty much always. Down there? I'm getting better at not feeling so disconnected. I didn't expect that when I got there, but it's true."

He grins broadly and Oriel bumps my shoulder with his before saying, "That's good to know, Kit Kat. Even if you are having brain dump overload, you're doing a bit better. Right?"

Nodding, I head for the fancy doors of the Italian shop. "Yes, I am. With some stuff, I mean."

"Something is better than nothing, so we'll take it." Salem pulls the door open for us, then we head inside the opulent looking boutique. "Whoa."

Rolling my eyes at the leather, fur, and dark crystalline design, I mutter, "Fucking rich people."

That's when a giant motherfucking half-shifted spider comes scurrying out of the large archway at the back of the store and I almost pass out.

I'm going to murder Jasper Eversore.

---

1. Rigoletto Fine Clothing and Accessories

Take A Chance On Me

Anton

Poor Kit looks like he's going to turn on his heels and leave cartoon dust behind as he runs for the hills. I don't know if it's because he's arachnophobic, scared of something so enormous, or just having trouble coming to terms with yet another surprise. It's a toss-up, and I know exactly what's going to happen next.

"Jasper, I'm going to fucking—"

The hissed words are cut off by the giant recluse shifter coughing in a comically loud fashion. "Welcome to my humble shop, Prince of Hell and his companions. I am honored to have your unannounced visit as you prepare to attend the Apalachin."

My eyes narrow for a millisecond at the spider's carefully chosen words. He's ancient as hell—his aura is colored in such vibrant shades and so fully that it would be impossible to miss. There's no way he wasn't being extremely purposeful in the way he greeted us. I cut my gaze to X who then looks at Oriel and down the line it goes until Slash is watching the Prince.

"Signore Rigoletto, I appreciate your willingness to work with us when we appear at your doorstep without notice. Are you able to outfit us for the auspicious event with such short notice? We were certain our education would prevent us from attending, thus the lack of preparation."

Jasper's smooth handling of the situation makes the new kid blink and I have to hide a chuckle. Kit hasn't seen the side of the Prince that isn't rough and pissy as he is at school. Even at the ball, Jas didn't show the truly diplomatic capabilities he has when the seven of us are forced to attend court shit at home. He's been trained since he was tiny, like all of us, and we have the ability to switch it on and off like a lightbulb.

Unfortunately, the Prince usually has his flipped off.

The giant spider sighs and claps his hands loudly. A small but business-like raccoon shifter comes scurrying out of the back with a tablet in her small hands, stopping in front of the arachnid tailor to look at us. Her gaze is shrewd, but she smiles once she's done examining our group. "Are we outfitting the Prince's caliphate today?"

"*Sì*, Laurel. His Highness apologized for the late notice and since we accommodated the twins, I would be remiss if I denied heirs of the seven courts the same courtesy."

I arch a brow at the old shifter's words. "You dressed the Geminis for this event?"

Laurel nods, her small eyes glittering. "The Gemini family has been one of our major clients for many, many generations… going back to the old country, even. The twin heirs are quite lovely, as is their new mate and her other fated."

What the actual fuck?

Before I can express my surprise, X jumps in to save the day. "You must have been honored to dress that large a party for such an auspicious event. Perhaps while we are getting measured, you might share a little about what wonders you worked for them? Fashion is my passion, you see."

"Ah, that explains it. You are the heir to the lust lineage, no?" The spider tilts his head, skittering sideways a tiny bit as he studies my lover. "Your skill has grown since I last saw the pieces you made."

X looks like they're going to faint, and I chuckle softly as I whisper to them, "Don't let the flattery send you into spasms of joy. Bigger picture."

"Very good, young demon." The tailor squints at me and I feel as though he's trying to see into my soul. I don't know if that's for the outfit or out of curiosity, but it makes my magic prick up in response. "You are the Alaric heir, then. Logic is often in conflict with pride, but I sense you ride the line well."

"You could introduce yourself, since you seem to be adept at guessing who we are," Kit grumbles and we all stare at him in shock.

This was not the diplomacy I'd hoped for, but at least it wasn't Jasper.

A bark of laughter escapes the enormous spider, his legs moving quickly as he scurries up to the kid. "*You…* You are not a royal at all, are you? All the courage to confront my lack of manners, but none of it to believe in yourself. Tsk, tsk, young rebel. I sense many things about you—none of them surprising or bad, yet your destiny is fraught. Laurel, please escort the gossip loving heir and this young one to the back. They will go first, then the Prince and his general. After that, two at a time until we are ready to select the pieces."

"That still didn't answer my question, even if you did give me the magical version of a fortune cookie," Kit complains as the raccoon woman takes his hand.

"Oh, I *like* this one," Laurel mutters happily. "You're as fun as the twins' new mate. Let me take you and Duke Xerxes back to get measured and we'll talk all about it."

"My name is Guillermo, but you may call me Gui," the tailor says as he turns to follow his assistant and our friends. "I do not often extend that offer, but Laurel is right; you are quite amusing."

Salem leans in, whispering to me in a shocked tone. "Who had KK charming the fuck out of the ancient spider dude by calling him out on their bingo card? I sure as fuck didn't."

"I don't have the shrimp charming *anyone* on my goddamn bingo card," Jasper snorts. "We'll be lucky if he doesn't get us killed with that fucking mouth."

I'd correct him, but in this case, the pissy prince might actually be right.

Once the designers and our friends disappear into the darkness of the archway, I turn to my brothers, my expression serious. "We didn't know there was a huge event up here, right? Is this why your father would only grant us leave to come up here this weekend, Jas?"

Pinching the bridge of his nose, the prince sighs. "I don't know. Maybe? Probably. He's a sketchy asshole and if he'd gotten wind of some big fucking surface event he wasn't informed of by our representatives, he just might orchestrate our gate crashing without telling me."

"He definitely would." Slash crosses his arms over his chest, his eyes darting around the shop as if ninjas are going to leap out of the mannequins and attack. "I do not like this, but I also do not see a way for us to utilize this trip without going."

"Exactly," Oriel adds as he pulls out his phone. "We need Zav to get on this shit pronto. Right now we're skating by on X's ability to pretend, but that won't last long."

We all turn to look at the kitsune, only to find him staring at his device as his fingers fly over the screen furiously. Jasper chuckles, reaching over to ruffle his messy red hair in an unusually fond gesture. "Looks like he's on the case already."

"Great. But like… how long is this shit going to take? We packed for a short day trip. Are we going to get stuck here at some ridiculous party? Those fucking things go on for *days*," Salem grumbles. "And we'd have to be guests of the *Geminis*. I don't know about you, but I wouldn't feel safe letting Kit Kat anywhere near those dickwads, especially when it comes to food and drink."

I blink at the panda shifter. Sometimes, he's pretty sharp and it's hard to know when to expect it because of the snoozy shit. "Salem's right, though it's not just about Kit. I'm not excited by the prospect of having any of us at the mercy of those assholes. We came up here because we wanted to find out if Darkstar is arranging a coup with Luca. Nothing in their territory is safe for us."

Jasper rolls his eyes down to the floor, his hands behind his head as he paces on the expensive as fuck carpet. "None of this is going to plan, but if we don't play along, who knows when we'll be allowed to come back. But we can't trust anyone up here and we have limited time to discover any leads. We can find what we need to infiltrate, but we know nothing about the setting."

Slash sees my curious expression and shakes his head. "Let him work this out on his own, Anton. The Prince often talks himself through things when only I am present, which is why you don't recognize his process."

I snort, covering my mouth for a second as it hits me. "Is *that* why you two hole up to 'discuss' strategy alone? Jasper likes to talk to himself and you're the only one who will stay quiet while he does it?"

"I stay quiet, too," Zavida mutters as he works on his phone. "But yeah, that's why. Everyone else talks too much."

For fuck's sake, they're all insane. He can't be the only one looking at a problem before we address it.

"I say this with love, guys, but you're dumb as fuck," Oriel says before I can respond. "If we're a team in these damn Games, Jasper can't be the only one solving a problem. We have eight people who have vastly different outlooks on everything. It means we can see a lot more sides of things than other people."

The dragon whirls around, and I'm certain he's going to scream at our resident thief, but instead, he nods. "You're not wrong. I've spent too long handling every crisis myself and it's not only exhausting, but it's also not going to work when the playing field is bigger than our families and school. You all need to step up and help me strategize."

"That was easier than expected. Did someone replace Jasper with a pod person?" the crow shifter mutters. The Prince growls loudly and he grins. "Nope, it's really him. Okay, then we scheme as one. Zav, what do you have so far?"

Zavida looks up, his brows furrowed. "There's some big party/meeting/whatever for the major criminal enterprises in Bay City. They have a secret location and all the various supernaturals will likely have territories based on what organization they are part of. It's fancy, from what I can tell, so this was a good starting point. But it's also exclusive."

"He's the Prince of Hell, Zav. I'm pretty sure we can find a way in once we get there," I remind him wryly. "But the location is another piece of the puzzle we need to find. Why are they having this thing?"

"From what I can tell, it happens whenever one of the major players calls for it, but no one seems to know who and why it was called this time. At least, not in anything I've gone over yet." He pushes his glasses up, his eyes moving to Jasper. "We're definitely going into this with zero prep. That means we have to rely on powers and shit to keep everyone safe."

"Oh, crap," Salem says. "Kit Kat's only seen four of us as animals and two as demons. That's gonna be jarring if we have to… you know. Fight a bitch or something."

Jasper rolls his eyes. "I swear to fuck, if you assholes don't stop framing *every-thing* we do around making sure the shrimp doesn't get upset…"

"It's not like I asked for it, dickhead." We all turn to see Kit and X walking into the room, the latter looking furious with us for getting caught. No one speaks as the newest member strides across the floor, standing in the middle of us as he goes on. "Look, I know I've got problems and you want to help me. But we may not always be able to keep me from having an issue—not with what's coming. So stop worrying about coddling me, and *use* the fact that I'm not a known player in this world."

I'll be damned; he's spot fucking on.

Kit Camponella is a perfect weapon against the people who don't expect him.

Everybody Talks

kät/kit

The chatty raccoon lady and her arachnid boss were actually pretty fucking helpful. Neither of them commented on my wraps, nor my clearly not quite boyish frame. I got the feeling they were used to people concealing things and obligated to keep their mouths shut because of some ancient tailor/customer oath thing. Okay, I assumed that because while they talked to X and me about the fit of the suits they're going to alter, they studiously avoided asking questions that nosy humans definitely would *not* avoid. Even well meaning allies would have queried Xerxes on their non-binary presentation and my clearly female body, but not Gui or Laurel.

They were about as clinical with their craft as one could be and I could have kissed them for it.

But coming out to overhear the other guys trying to strategize around keeping me in a bubble set me off. I appreciate the care they all show me—some more than others—but they have to start expecting me to pull some weight. I haven't read enough about the past Games to know for certain, but

I know worrying about protecting me instead of the entire group will fuck everything up. At some point, they have to start treating me equally rather than just protectively. I don't want them to stop being attentive, of course, because the affection starved idiot inside me is kind of getting used to it.

Pushing that anxiety-inducing thought aside, I face the guys. "Annie's making a face that says he's thinking, so Jasper and Slash should go get measured. Laurel said they'll be able to get formal wear they have in the boutique altered, but we need to hurry if we want to arrive at this thing *before* the big secret meeting or whatever."

Jasper frowns at me, tilting his head. "Just how much did you get out of those two?"

I shrug. "I might be an awkward turnip, but I'm a good listener and X is a good talker. We were able to get a lot, I think."

The dragon and the shark look over to my partner in gossip, and they grin cheesily. "KK's quiet is a perfect foil to my gab. It makes the fishing look less…. well, fishy."

Slash flashes his teeth at me, then nods at the prince. "Come, Jasper. The little demon is correct; we need to get this done so we can infiltrate this party. It would be foolish to waste this opportunity."

Waiting for the two of them to stomp out of the room, I think about the situation we're in. The territory is unknown and filled with question marks and enemies—just like a high school party. Much like that setup—which admittedly I haven't been in since the incident—there will be areas where all the 'cliques' of different criminals and their allies plant their flags. General areas will be full of people indulging in whatever the fuck shit they have as vices at supernatural rich people events, but the small, controlled spots will be the most dangerous while likely containing the most information.

This will require a lot of very careful maneuvering if we don't know who is allied with whom in the background.

"KK, are you off in the clouds again?"

Salem's voice brings me back to reality and I shrug off the embarrassment. "I was, but only because this party feels like it's probably just an exaggerated version of parties we've been to. Or, um, maybe you've been to multiples, and I've been to much less, but…"

Anton nods, his eyes filling with understanding. "Right. Divided into mini-territories, but large open spaces with mingling and partying. The people in the open areas will be indulging and less likely to resist giving out secrets, but also probably not very high on the food chain."

"Exactly," I reply as I look at the guys seriously. "No one should go off alone for anything. That's how bad things happen."

The crow shifter is by my side in a second, his hand reaching for mine to squeeze it. I think he knows that's an issue for me, and though he's not saying anything out loud, his determination to keep me from having a flashback is obvious. "We won't, Kit Kat. I don't just mean you; no one will go off alone, right?"

They all nod, and Zavida holds up his phone, wiggling it. "Your watches and the phones have two forms of locators—tech and magic. Xerxes and Anton provided the magic, but it requires more proximity than the tech on the surface does. If anyone gets out of range for their basic spell, we'd need supplies to extend the range."

His reassurance helps a bit, but no one has to be taken far away to be assaulted and hurt; I know that very well.

"Thanks, Zav," I murmur. "But Oriel's still right; we have an even number of people and everything should be done in pairs or higher. My experience is that if someone wants to harm you, they don't need very long or even a lot of secrecy."

Xerxes nods at me. "Okay. Pairs or more when we're circulating to gather intel. We can discuss it with Jas and Slash when they switch places with Oriel and Salem. But we should probably talk about how we're going to play our presence from a social engineering standpoint."

That makes me pause because it's obviously *not* my forte. "Um, I'm not the best person to do more than throw out suggestions from movies or books. You all know how introverted I became after the thing."

I wish I could use the word; I really do. But I've never been able to stay calm afterward and I'm not starting now.

"This part isn't the prince or Slash's area of expertise, either. They can play along with shit and be smooth with diplomacy—more Jasper than Slash— but they are both reticent to connect to people, too." Anton sighs, looking to his lover for help. "What's our cover going to be?"

"Emissaries." Xerxes grins. "Jasper can simply be himself and state like a pompous ass that his father sent him as his representative. Someone will check with the Geminis and denying us entry would trip a red flag with the King, so they'll let us in. He can be impatient and demanding, neither of which are a stretch. Slash can be hulking and intimidating. It will get us in with little effort."

"He's right."

I blink as Slash and the prince come back faster than X and I did. The shark shifter is smirking as he confirms X's plan, his stern face handsome when he's being just the tiniest bit defiant to his leader. "No duh, big guy."

"Oriel, Salem, get moving," Jasper barks as he strides over to us. "I assume your jabs are in service of coming up with our plan to infiltrate?"

Xerxes winks at him. "Why, of course, my Prince. We're working hard to make use of the skills we bring to the table."

"For fuck's sake," the dragon grumbles as he looks around. Once his eyes light on a chair, he glares at the rest of us for a second, then he heads for it. "Gather 'round. I want to hear what our demonic butterflies think we should do to survive this bullshit."

It's almost like he just admitted he can't do something—but that can't be, right?

By the time Guillermo and Laurel finish measuring the guys, I'm feeling hungry and antsy. The shop is luxurious, but my stress about the plan X came up with is making my veins tickle with worry. Dottie is sitting on my lap, her tiny body pressed against my stomach as I stroke her head. My knee starts jiggling in my cross-legged pose and I hear a sigh from across the circle. I guess my tics are becoming more noticeable and the impatient prince has noticed.

Well, fuck him and his sociopathic level of calm despite the danger we're going to face.

"Someone take the shrimp out to grab food or something. There's plenty of places out there; one has to be open."

I open my mouth to protest being treated like a naughty child, but Oriel leaps to his feet quickly and holds out his hand. I suppose I could use some time away from this tense waiting room with someone who makes me feel calm. I'd prefer to fight the prince whenever possible, but doing so this time feels stupid. I'm a lot of things, but dumb isn't one of them.

"Okay." I take the dark haired demon's hand, making sure I don't smoosh Dottie as I get up. Looking down at her apologetically, I murmur, "You'll have to go in the bag for now. I think you can stay out at the party 'cause it won't have humans to gawk. For now, though, in you go."

Luckily, the kinkajou is pretty complacent when it comes to me, so she lets me slide her into my bag carefully. Once I'm ready, I nod at O. He grins as he cocks his head to the door. "Time to explore a bit. We might not find a lot but it will get some of that nervous energy out of your system, KK."

I follow Oriel out the door of the boutique, instantly relieved when I get a breath of fresh air. I'm not claustrophobic, per se, but I feel crowded when my anxiety builds up alongside anticipation. Being in the open air is probably *more* risky than staying inside, but I needed the space. Somehow, dick-face Jasper realized it before I did, and that really pisses me off.

"Stop worrying about Prince Prickface," Oriel says as he points towards the sidewalk heading to the right. "I know you're obsessing because you get this little wrinkle between your eyebrows whenever Jasper's done something to get your dander up."

My scowl is petulant; I can't help it. "How do you even know that phrase?"

"Some grumpy kid has been making us all learn about human movies. I'm sure I picked it up from there. What's a dander, anyway?" His expression is so earnest that I laugh softly, and when he reaches out his arm around me, I don't shrink away.

Progress comes in millimeters and centimeters, but it's still progress.

"Uh, it's like skin flakes that shed on animals."

Oriel recoils, giving me a disbelieving look. "Why the hell is there a phrase about getting your dead skin flakes up when you're mad? Humans are so fucking bizarre, man."

Chuckling, I shrug as he distracts me and we start walking past the store-fronts to see if anything is open. "Don't ask me; I'm not a linguist. It's just an idiom that means getting pissy. I don't have the entire history of human shit in my head, O."

"Well, it's weird." He pauses for a moment, looking at the window of an ice cream shop wistfully. "Too bad this place is closed. I'm dying to taste what it's like up here."

"Why don't you guys come up here more often? I mean, you all say you're soooo much older than me and that you and demons age differently, so I assume that means like centuries have passed up here while you grew up. Why not drop in every once in a while?"

Oriel sighs and shrugs. "Honestly? There's too fucking much going on up here *all the time*. The Society isn't fond of demons and neither are most supernaturals. We stick to Hell other than the normal worker bees who come up here to do their thing and the reps the royals send across the globe to keep their eyes on shit. Why get involved in this mess when we don't have to?"

I grin a bit. "In other words, we're fat and happy in our little bubble, so whatever happens to everyone else is not our business? How very privileged of the demon world."

"Don't go all '*vive la révolution*' on me, Kit Kat. Keeping Hell from spilling onto the surface isn't easy, either. Our families are assholes—no argument there—but they're also quite capable of fucking up shit here so much worse than it already is. We keep the demons here for the same reason the deities and the Fae try to limit how much their people cross realms. Way more power and so much potential for extinction."

Stopping in front of a pizza joint, I look at him seriously. "Seems like this trip is about finding out if some of the demons have decided they want to come out of the shadows."

Oriel nods as he squeezes my shoulders. "The announcement of the Games is a precursor to bad things in our history, KK. Jasper's right to worry, especially since Darkstar's behaving so boldly. It's more worrisome than he's letting on."

Great. We're worried about dying in trials by fire, and if we lose, the ensuing war could spread to humanity—no pressure or anything.

Somebody Told Me

sälem

Kit Kat looks much better when he strolls in with Oriel, and my panda calms down significantly. It's fucking weird that he was completely wired while they were gone; given our nature, that kind of hyperactivity is totally not a normal state. Slow and languid, that's my speed and until my brother came back with that quirky little dude, I was the farthest thing from it.

And I only barely *kissed him for like, a second.*

I watch as he plops down on the floor, pulling Dottie out of his bag to let the tiny animal rest in his lap. Oriel calmed him down completely and it made me feel even better, so I dropped to my knees and crawled over so I could sit with him. It draws a scoff from Jasper—I assume—but I don't give a hairy rat's ass what that uptight dicklicker thinks. Right now, I'm happy to scoot over next to KK and pet the kinkajou until our hosts bring out the clothes.

"Did you get some food?" I ask with a grin. "You look less hangry, so I assume you did."

Kit nods, his face bright with amusement as he cuts his eyes to the crow. "Oriel had a meat feast pizza with me and he was totally weirded out by human toppings. It was fun to see someone besides me experience odd food and make faces."

Oriel glowers a little as he comes over to join us. "These fuckers are so damn strange. It had this… spicy yet processed taste that made me wonder if the beast was made of chemicals."

"Well, there's definitely a lot of those in food up here," KK says with a shrug. "I noticed that stuff in Hell doesn't, but since you guys didn't have a frame of reference, I didn't mention it. There's more natural stuff, of course, but we didn't have time to find a non-chain spot to eat."

Jasper arches his brow as he looks at us. "Be careful, O. We have no idea what effect putting their garbage into our systems will have. If you did it all the time, it might not be a big deal, but we're not used to the poison the demons who live up here are. It could make you sick as a hellhound."

"Nice to see you worried about me getting sick on *your* food, knobhead," my roomie mutters as he plays with his familiar. "And now I'm paranoid about every new thing you give me… great."

"KK, calm down," X says as they get up from their perch on the arm of Anton's chair to come over and sit on the floor with the four of us. They smooth their palms over themselves automatically, then curse the disguise clothes. "I'm not a fan of this realm so far except for our new friends. But once we run around this party, we can head home and make a big cozy movie pile tomorrow. Sound good?"

"Ooh, I like that idea!" Kit bumps my shoulder, then Oriel's as he grins. "We can make some tasty food, too, right, Salem?"

Be still my heart.

I love that he wants to cook with me—like for real, not just because Jasper assigned it to him. Nodding, I reach down and squeeze his knee gently. "But you'll want to do your reading first, I bet. Annie brought those books…"

His eyes pop open and he claps his hand over his mouth for a second. The peacock winks at him from his chair, too fancy pants to come sit with us in his humanoid form. Jasper's frown deepens as he watches us, tilting his head curiously.

"What books?"

"Study materials," X says breezily. "You know Kit Kat is trying to catch up as fast as he can. He finishes stuff so quickly that we switch things out for him if we're closer to the library or you know… confined to the damn dorms because we got hurt in a battle."

"Ah. Well, that's helpful, Anton. Good job," the Prince says as he settles back in his seat. He looks at the shark shifter, arching his brow. "And you're going to continue working with him on training and diet? He doesn't look much bigger than before, Scrum."

Slash glares at his best friend in a way I've not seen before—ever. "Bulking up is not a rapid thing for new demons, Prince. I cannot simply dump food into his mouth until he's an appropriate weight. That is neither safe nor efficient if you want him to be like us."

Holy shit, the big guy just told Jasper to fuck all the way off in the most Slash-like way possible.

Everyone is silent, even KK, as our leader's face contorts through a range of emotions. Zav's tails pop out, making him blush and press against the prince's leg. Thank fuck, that gets Jas' attention and he looks down at the kitsune with a sigh. "Sorry, Zav. I didn't mean to make you panic. Put them away for me, mmm?"

Zavida nods, and the tails disappear as his posture calms. "I didn't mean to. Having to be careful up here is a pain in the ass."

"I can't imagine how hard it is for all the different supernaturals who live up here all the time," Kit says as he gives Zav a sympathetic look. "They're hiding such big parts of themselves all the time. It has to be exhausting as fuck."

Xerxes arches their brow and gives the dude a smirk. "Yeah, that's gotta be really tiring. Having to pretend to be something I'm not for this short time is wearing me out, especially around the people I care about."

What the hell does that even mean? X is even weirder than usual on the surface.

Kit opens his mouth, but right as he's going to speak, the raccoon lady and the giant spider come out of the back room. Laurel is pulling a tall rack with eight garment bags on it, her small features bright as she moves towards us.

"Signore Rigoletto has outdone himself," she crows. "Even some of his bespoke designs would pale in comparison to the work he has done for the royal caliphate of Hell today."

Jasper rises from his seat, responding to the decree as you'd expect a prince to do. "We are very grateful for your speed and grace, Signore."

The giant spider scurries over, his face smug as he looks down at all of us. "My gifts are many, young royal, and I am always happy to share them with those who have great destinies in the making."

I frown when X bobs their brows at KK and the guy pales a bit more than usual. They seem to be having some sort of confusing wordless conversation as my roommate hunches into himself. It makes my panda unsettled, so I scoot a little closer and drape my arm around his shoulders. "That's pretty vague yet oddly specific, man."

"As most prophecies are, heir to the Stryker line." Guillermo chuckles, gesturing for Jasper to head for the rack and take his bag. "But you are all quite important for many reasons, and I cannot divulge all of them. I can, however, say that your differences make you strong. Do not allow your lineage weaknesses to keep you from the roles you are destined to play."

"Stubbornness is not a virtue," the raccoon says as she hands the Prince his bag and points to a dressing room. "Nor is obliviousness."

Jasper gives her a surly expression he wouldn't dare shoot at the giant spider, then stomps to the door she indicated. Slash sighs heavily, shrugging at us, then gets up. "He does not mean to be offensive, Signore. The Prince has strong ties to his family line as you can tell."

"Yes, he does take after his father in ways that are less than helpful," Guillermo replies in a matter-of-fact tone. "However, I sense much diversion from the natural inclinations of his kind and his family. As his caliphate, you balance the urges quite well, I believe. Some more than others, and some less, but that is the challenge of achieving true equilibrium."

This dude speaks in riddles and I'm ready to say something dumb, I just know it.

Before I can, KK digs around in his bag, pulling out one of my snack bars with a grin. "You seem like you need a 'pick me up'. Want your Scooby snack, Salem?"

"Thanks, man," I murmur as he smiles shyly. It sort of makes my chest tighten and I have to look away as I unwrap the bar. This thing with Kit is throwing me off and I have to make sure we don't draw any attention to it until we've had time to explore it more. "You're probably right; I'm fading a bit."

"Toss those around, Kit Kat. I think we should all recharge before we call a car and head to this thing. Who knows how safe anything they serve will be?" Anton's suggestion makes everyone but Kit and Oriel mutter in agreement and I breathe an internal sigh of relief.

"Good idea, Annie," Kit says as he plucks each ribbon color out one by one and tosses them to X, Anton, and Zavida. "I'll give the grump and his BFF theirs when they come out."

"Give us what?"

We all turn to look at the growly voice behind us and within seconds, I can feel the heat traveling up KK's body. My lips twist as I hold back a chuckle; Jasper definitely looks hot as fuck doing the bad boy rebel thing. I suddenly understand the spider's mysterious bullshit from a minute ago as Kit pretends not to wiggle a bit next to me. He was trying to say that Kit's the scale balancer in the group and that means this whole fake dating thing was almost prophetic.

Kit's definitely meant for all of us and there's something bigger than that going on.

"Why are you all staring?" the Prince growls as he tugs the collar of his shirt a little. The spider shifter sighs, obviously annoyed with the dragon futzing with his precise measurements. "It's just dress clothes. Stop being ridiculous."

"Jasper, you look *fabulous*," X says as they pop to their feet. "That open mandarin collar and basic black and white motif in silk is divine. Very bad boy forced to clean-up, especially with the tattoos."

"Oh, no," Oriel groans as he stands as well. "We'd better take our bags once Slash comes out. Xerxes is going to *narrate* the runway out here."

Kit is still silent and it's getting very hard not to laugh. The poor kid is going to be mute by the time this fashion show ends, if I'm right about what Guillermo meant when he was riddling us.

The shark in question comes out dressed in black from head to foot, buttoned up and wearing a tie compared to Jasper's more casual, 'rumpled on purpose' look. It makes him look *exactly* like the enforcer he is and it's perfect. "I am pleased with my garment. Thank you."

Never one to get mushy, that's Slash.

"Damn, man. You look dangerous as hell," O says as he grabs his garment bag and hands X theirs, too. "I guess it's our turn to get pretty, mmm? KK, you and the lazy bear can go last. That seems fair since you got to go first."

"But X—"

I cut a look to Anton, glaring. "Oh, hush. You and Zav are next. Get over it."

Jasper rolls his eyes, looking at his second-in-command. "Slash, give this lovely assistant our information so she can forward the clothes we're leaving with her to inter-realm mail. She will make certain our things get back to Discordia."

"I'm not letting go of my bag *or* Dottie," Kit says, finally breaking the sexy demon spell he's been under. "You can forget it."

"Do not worry, little demon. You don't have to; I promise." Slash crosses his arms over his chest, looking a shit ton like a big bad mob guy now. "I'm certain they have something appropriate for the venue you can use."

Laurel beams as she nods. "We do. Xerxes asked while we were measuring. It's in Kit's bag. He can stock it all up and we will include the original in the package back to your realm."

Whew. Dodged a bullet there.

"Then why the fuck—"

"Shut up, Jasper," I say as he starts to growl something shitty. His expression is priceless, as I don't usually make waves, but I feel like I've been shown the ending of the play before intermission. I get why they keep smacking into one another and I know why it feels like they take one step forward, then fourteen backward.

The problem is getting our pissy Prince and the broken ex-human to realize it before they kill one another.

Puttin' on the Ritz

kăt/kĭt

I have no idea how I'm going to function at this event.

As if my anxiety about going to an unknown place full of possible bad guys wasn't enough, I'm sitting in this weird supernatural ride share thing in the middle of seven of the hottest dudes to ever live. My suit is all white with high waisted pants and an open necked shirt under a loose silk jacket. It makes me stand out—something I'm never happy about—but somehow, it looks good as hell. I haven't worn this much white in my entire life, mind you, but damn, that spider knew what he was doing. It makes me look fancy and confident even though I don't feel like that inside, and Salem told me it looked 'fuckin' awesome'.

I don't know how he noticed given what Jasper and Slash had on when they emerged, and after the others came out, I almost swallowed my goddamn tongue. Anton was in an all black brocade tux with no bow tie, his lithe form looking elegant but dangerous in the off-beat pattern. Guillermo put Xerxes in this heavily tailored, wide legged black and silver suit with big buttons, a tie at their narrow waist and a deep dip between the lapels—with no shirt. They look sexy yet gender-bending in a way that's perfect for them.

My eyes drift to the last three of the demons, swallowing hard as I try not to let their appearance make my cheeks burn. Oriel is wearing high waisted black pants with a loose black silk shirt under a midnight blue silk jacket with velour lapels. His emo look is still in place with tattoos and steel peeking out and the shine of his raven hair falling over his kohl rimmed eyes. He winks at me and I duck my chin, looking at Zavida in his brilliant red houndstooth patterned suit with a pale cadmium orange shirt tucked under the shirt jacket. His red hair seems to gleam against it, which I wouldn't have ever thought would work, so he looks like the fiery fox he is.

But Salem? The panda shifter is in a well tailored suit that's all black with satin lapels and an open shirt showing off black and white tattoos on his chest. His duotone hair is mussed perfectly like he climbed out of bed, and for some reason, the adorable raccoon assistant *insisted* he put on a pair of thick white glasses with ombre lenses that make him look delectable. He doesn't even *need* glasses, but they coordinate with the small pocket square sticking out of his jacket pocket in a way that draws everything together.

Of course, I only know all this shit because X gushed over everyone as we got into the car.

What I actually know about fashion you could fit in a thimble, which is why I'm just sitting here drooling like a dumbass as I squirm in my seat between Slash and the Prince. I'd prefer to be sitting with the others, but Jasper threw a hissy fit and I was too damned nervous to fight with him. A miracle, I know; it's just that I haven't been this unsettled without having a panic attack in… my life, I think.

"KK, you look like you're going to hurl. Is sitting next to Jasper that odious?"

I blink, shaking my head a little to clear the inappropriate hot guy thoughts out of it. Once I can focus, I look at Oriel with an amused smile. "I mean, if the shoe fits, buy it in every size, right?"

Xerxes snickers, leaning back in their seat as they smirk at me. "That's *my* motto, and lucky for you, we wear the same size. That makes it imminently easier for me to help turn you from the frumpy introvert to an elegant boyfriend to the royal caliphate."

Wrinkling my nose at them, I hunch forward to pet Dottie inside of the soft, black leather bag I have crossed over my body. Laurel and Gui said it was *'oltre l'eleganza*[1]' and I figured they knew what they were talking about. My girl seems comfortable in it, and there was enough room for her and some non-sketchy snacks, so I consented to the switch. Dottie chitters a little, her small digits grabbing mine and the calm rushes over me.

"You should be asking *me* if having the shrimp between us is off-putting," Jasper grumbles as he cocks a brow at the crow shifter. "You know he smells like fruity flowers and I hate that."

I whip my head around, glaring at the dragon indignantly. "Oh, yeah? You smell like musky citrus and vanilla and… fruity incense. It's the shower stuff, dumbass. It's scented and we all use different stuff in the morning. Complain to whoever stocks the damn bathroom, not me."

Slash leans towards me, sniffing for a second, then shrugs. "My sense of smell is best and I don't find it offensive."

"See?" I scowl at the Prince, then turn to give the shark demon a grateful smile. "Thanks, big guy."

The toothy grin makes my stomach flutter, and Salem bobs his brows at me when I turn to face forward. He lifts his arm, sniffing under it with a frown. "What do I smell like, KK? I pick whatever's there usually, so I don't pay attention."

"Citrus-y with fresh berries and leafy scents," I reply without thinking and my answer gets immediate chuckles from the guys next to me. "What? I live with him, you guys. Of course I know what he fucking smells like. Why is everyone being so weird today?"

"Because your sense of smell is getting *much* better, Kit Kat." Anton looks pleased as he crosses his arms over his chest. "The gels from the bathroom aren't heavily scented like you'd find up here—or so I'm told—but we're all drawn to things that make our animals happy. The spicy floral scents with musk make my bird feel like he's doing a happy dance inside. I assume it's the same for the others."

Salem nods. "The panda loves that one specific scent, though I don't much notice *what* it smells like as much as him enjoying it."

I narrow my eyes at them, not quite sure what I'm missing. There's something they're not telling me, especially given the smug look on X's face. "Zav smells like ginger and cinnamon."

"No, he smells like ginger, citrus, and saffron," Jasper growls, bumping my shoulder with his. "I should know; I'm naked with him *far* more often than *you*."

Just like that, my face goes red and I gawp, at a loss for what to say in response. I mean, *obviously* 'Big Bad Demon Daddy Jasper' sees Zavida naked more than me! I'm not trying to see any of them nude, despite my weird inability to take my eyes off of them when they parade around in various stages of undress. I open my mouth to say something, and yet again, not a damned thing comes out.

"Holy fuck, I actually shut the shrimp up. Someone take a fucking picture," the Prince says, his dark features breaking into an honest-to-Satan grin that lights them up beautifully.

I hate to admit it, but Jasper Eversore is stunningly handsome when he's not being an evil fuckwit.

Since I can't figure out what to say, I slam my elbow backward, hitting his ribs. He doesn't react and I frown at the carpeted floor angrily. That shithead's muscles are as hard as rocks and he barely felt my jab, which is even more annoying than his deeply amused chuckles. "You suck, Jasper, and not in a good way."

"Actually, that's not true. You see, it's Zav's job to—"

"*Oh my fucking god, shut up,*" I groan as I put my hands over my face. "I do not need to know anymore about your sex life than I've already heard."

"Plus, Zav's gonna turn into a tomato soon," Oriel says wryly. "I don't know what's redder right now—the suit, his hair, or his face."

Peeking out between my fingers, I see the poor kitsune trying to hide behind his tails as he flushes. I understand his introversion, so I move my hands to smile a little in commiseration. The Prince is enjoying the hell out of making both of us uncomfortable while everyone else is having a grand old time. He deserves a nut punch, and if I can figure out how to give him one without anyone at this party noticing, I'm definitely doing it.

We'll see who has the last laugh.

THE CAR FINALLY PULLS UP TO THIS DINGY WAREHOUSE DISTRICT AND I LOOK outside skeptically. "I don't know, guys. This feels like the prelude to one of the gritty cop shows on TV—some skeevy bad guy is going to jump out and crack us over the head before shoving us into cages."

Slash snorts, shaking his head at me. "They would not be successful, little demon. You are with some of the most fearsome demons of Hell."

I roll my eyes as we step out of the SUV. "Slash, the point is the bad guys always have shit to like… defeat the powerful humans or vampires or whatever it is. They have their 'kryptonite' item like in Superman, and then they use surprise to launch the attack. And it's *always* some sketchy, bad part of town, abandoned place like this."

"This is just a mirage," Jasper says as he pushes past me. "The magic is strong, and it's definitely the work of multiple species within the supernatural world, but it's covering the true venue. You don't have to worry about some axe murderer, shrimp. It's neutral ground."

"Just another way to lure you into complacency," I mutter as I move closer to the big guy. "You guys are used to being the top dogs down there and it's going to get us Dahmer'd if we're not careful."

X walks up and laces their arm in my free one. "C'mon, KK. Less fear, more cheer, dude. We're dressed for excess and attending a huge party full of Earth's big players. There's so much gossip to overhear and clues to sniff out. You gotta let go a little."

I've definitely heard that song before and the ending was not *something I want to repeat.*

"I'm not great at parties, for obvious reasons," I reply as I hold onto Xerxes and Slash tightly. "But I'll be damned if I'm going to let it stop us from finding out shit we need to know."

Salem walks up behind us, leaning in to murmur, "You can do it, Kit Kat. We're all here, and Xerxes is the best chit chatter of the whole crew. They'll help you."

"Ahem," Jasper coughs as he stands at the rusty door ahead of us. "If you're all done fucking around, we need to get in here and do this. We're not scheduled to be up here all fucking weekend, you know."

Slash glares at him as we approach the door. "You cannot be mean to him here, Prince. We agreed to Xerxes' plan and that involves playing up our dating status to keep up appearances. Treating the little demon poorly will spoil the plan."

I grin smugly as I follow him through the door, appreciating the reminder for the surly royal. "What he said."

Jasper growls at me, but it doesn't have the usual bite to it. He must be adjusting already, so I just continue into the big warehouse without another word. Once we're all in the center of the empty room, I look around, not understanding. There's nothing here besides us and a lot of dust, which seems marginally better than a serial killer, but not very useful.

"Be patient," Salem says as he stands close enough to feel the heat coming off his form. "Jasper knows what to do."

The Prince turns to face us, raising his hands in the air as his eyes go dark and fiery. *"Ab ignibus Orci petit hseres ad throni ingressum. Revela porta vel face consequatur.*[2]*"*

My eyes dart to all the others, then back to the Prince as scales ripple over his skin then fade away quickly. A column of fire shoots up from the floor, making me grip X and Slash in shock until the flames swirl around and form a gateway. I lick my lips as I see a vaguely glitzy background through the portal, hoping I'm going to be able to handle this.

"Okay, people. Time to step into your roles," X says as they tug me forward. "Follow the plan and don't force us to get into a battle—especially you, Kit Kat, and you, Prince Pricklypants."

I nod quietly, following along with Slash and Salem behind me.

I'd love to promise him I'll be good, but I've never been able to do that successfully, even when it would save my skin.

---

1. beyond elegance
2. From the fires of Hell, the heir to the throne demands entry. Reveal the gateway or face the consequences.

We Like To Party

Xerxes

I'm projecting more confidence than I truly feel right now, but it's needed. Not coming to the surface much leaves every one of us but KK at a disadvantage, and she's got enough shit to hide without worrying about keeping the rest of us balanced in this atmosphere. Annie and I need to handle the peopling, me more than him if possible—so the rest of them don't give away our weak points.

Yeah, I'm not real sure it's going to work, either, but if it goes to shit, we'll pivot.

Walking into the portal with my head high and my lover at my side, I look around the open space of a garden. It has paths heading in multiple directions, the scents of which give me a clue as to what might be down them. I look over at Kat, motioning for her to come closer so I can ask, "Where do you think we should go? I can smell different things and I want to see if you can suss it out, too."

"For fuck's sake, X, this is going to take——"

Salem glares at the prince. "Shut up, Jasper. They're trying to let Kit Kat get his legs under him. You know we need to do that in live situations, man."

"That one," Kat says as she scrunches up her face. "It smells like wet dogs, so I'm thinking maybe shifters?"

"Excellent, little demon."

I nod at Slash, my eyes shining with pride. "Yep. Probably not just dogs, but if there's a large pack it will overwhelm some other types of shifters. Doggies are super easy to catch the smell of."

Kat beams happily, grabbing my hand. "Okay, I think that one just beyond it smells like spices and incense… witches, maybe? Or um.. could there be genies here?"

Jasper snorts, shaking his head. "Djinn are as rare as hen's teeth and there will never be enough of them in one spot to wipe out their kind. Witches and mages are likely correct."

Well, that was nicer than normal, so maybe he's going to behave.

"Oh. That's good to know. I didn't read any stats or anything in my books." Kat tilts her head to the next path, sniffing a bit. "Um, that one might be Fae. I smell like weird florals and candy and sugary scents, plus… wine, maybe?"

"That sounds about right," Annie grins as he pats her head. "Those fuckers will have an entire Faerie garden created for their people. Since this seems to be divided by territories, I suppose that we're going to see some lavish set-ups."

Kat bites her lower lip as she focuses on the path right in front of us. "This one smells like the ocean. Aquatic shifters and magic, I'd guess?"

"Ugh, let's stay the fuck away from that," Zavida says as he shakes his head. "Outside of Slash, I'm not fond of those with water elemental powers."

I roll my eyes, sighing heavily. Everyone has their own dislikes, but we really should wander through some of the other territories before whatever huge meeting these people are having gets called. The Gemini section is the *last* place we should visit just in case Jasper has to call in a fast escape. "Good job, Kit Kat. I think we're going to go to the Fae area first because while they're tricky as fuck, they gossip better than anyone else."

Slash grunts, his lip curling. "I am not fond of the Fair folks. Perhaps you and Anton will lead while Salem and I guard the little demon." He looks down at Kat with a stern expression. "Analyze every word they say and do not answer questions without considering every angle. They will be as eager to work out bargains as demons are, but much less straightforward."

"I will do my best, but…" Kat's eyes shine for a moment as she rubs her hands together. "I cannot *wait* to meet real fairies. I mean, it's such a *thing* right now up here and none of the humans get that they're real, but *I* get to meet them!"

Fuck. For someone not that impressed by demons, I'm a little concerned about her fangirling over the Fae.

As we approach the wrought iron gates covered in Fae flora, I shoot a look at Anton. He nods, his magic stretching out to test the plants for safety. Once he gives me a thumbs-up, I pull them open to reveal a small podium like a maître-d stand in a restaurant. It looks empty until we get close, then magic sparkles in the air, and a gruesome looking male with a bloody hat and scraggly beard appears.

"Who dares to enter the realm of the Fae on this wretched plane?" The creature points clawed, gnarly fingers at us, his rheumy eyes watching my caliphate as if we're a ticking bomb on his doorstep.

The collective grumbles of the entire group are quiet, but not as contained as I would have liked. I turn to give them all a dirty look, then back to the weird ass fairy. Forcing a bright smile, I cover up the revulsion to his blood-soaked headwear as I reply. "Good evening, guardian of Faerie on the surface. My name is Xerxes, and I am part of the royal caliphate of Prince Jasper Eversore of Hell. We wish to visit your lands and see the fabulous powers of your people."

His grizzled face creases as he snaps his fingers and a large, ancient looking book appears. "None may enter without stating their name and a boon. The courts of Faerie will split the boons and remain in balance as they have been for many millennia. You must write in the book before you may visit, young royals of Hell, or you will not enter."

Of course these assholes want a goddamn secret in exchange for entry—they're such covetous fuckers.

"I am the Prince of Hell," Jasper fumes as he stomps up next to me. "Our kingdoms have mutual—"

Holding up my hand as I notice the gross dude's hat getting redder, I clear my throat. "What the Prince means to say is that we will honor the treaties between our realms by following your traditions. We simply need a moment to consider our boons, as we did not have them prepared."

"Hurry up, then. And keep the dragon on a leash lest he offend a guardian of the lands."

I turn back to my caliphate, my expression begging them *not* to make a big thing of this shit. Gesturing for them to move back a bit from the stand, I wait until we're all huddled closed before I murmur, "This is a test. You will have to offer something important, but small, in exchange for entry. The Fae are extremely concerned with balance and allowing us to come in and enjoy their spoils without paying a toll is an offensive thought. Just do what we have to so we can do what we came to, guys."

Kat frowns for a moment, then nods. "Okay. I don't like it, but somehow, that explanation helps me understand why we're playing along."

"Holy fuck," Oriel says with a smirk. "Well, if KK gets it and isn't fighting, I guess I'm in."

The rest of the group agrees, even Jasper, though the Prince is obviously unhappy about it. Sighing in relief, I walk back to the stand and hold my hand out for the quill. "I will go first… uh, I didn't catch your name."

"Delamar the Deceiver." The crusty Fae grunts as I write my name and the small truth required, waving his long fingers over it like he's checking the veracity. "You pass, Xerxes of Lust. Stand to the side while I work my way through your companions."

I'm not fond of anything I can't identify, and even less excited about a crea-ture whose name is followed by 'the deceiver', but we don't have a choice. If we want to get info from the chattiest supes in town, we need to get through this stupid test. "Go on, Annie."

Anton moves up to write his information, getting waved aside quickly for Kat to approach. I hold my breath as the bloody headed gatekeeper eyes her, but he doesn't say anything other than 'pass' before he points her towards us. After a few minutes, all of our group have been waved over except Jasper, who is very slowly filling in his name. I think he's doing it slowly to piss the thing off, and I'd like to kick him in the shin.

Fucking with the persoon who can kick you out on your ass isn't a good plan, if you really want to get inside.

"Prince Jasper of Hell… your boon has been accepted, even if you were not entirely truthful." The creature gives us a gap-toothed grin as he points at the Prince. "Delamar believes you are lying to yourself as well, so he will allow this one exception. Go forth into Faerie and do no harm, demons."

Breathing a huge sigh of relief, I lead the group to the wooden door Delamar had disguised until we all passed his test. Opening it, I walk inside to a lush, beautiful Fae meadow filled with floral scents, the sound of rushing water, and soft grass under our shoes. The sky inside this realm is light purple and there's a pink moon high in the starry sky as we clamber inside. Squinting, I look around until I see an ornate tent city in the middle of the meadow. It has four large corners, and I assume those are probably the reps from each court. All the other installations are smaller and more likely their vendors, food and drink purveyors, and other places where we can find what we want.

That is, if we can get to them without being paged to the royal tents.

"This is gorgeous," Kat says, the awe in her voice apparent. "Is this what their realm looks like? Cuz you guys got screwed, man."

Jasper snorts, shaking his head as he looks around. "This is being controlled by the Daybreak Court at the moment. Each court has their own look and feel based on their affinities, and the spring-like evening is probably the work of their aestheticians."

"At least they're Seelie," Oriel mutters. "I'm sure the feel of this place would be *much* less welcoming if Midnight or Reaping was in charge right now."

Kat slaps her hand on her face, scraping it down her features as she groans. "Fuck, there's so damn much to learn. Salem, promise me you guys aren't going to let me hang out in the dark with all this shit. I really wanted to see this, but I… um, I haven't really studied them yet."

"We will not let you look silly, little demon. Fear not."

I smile when Slash's words get a nod of appreciation. "Okay. With that out of the way, are we ready to face the pointy-eared fruitcakes?"

The two assigned to keep Kat safe flank her again, giving me a look that says they're ready. I wait for Jasper to nod as well, then Annie and I trudge across the colorful meadow filled with weird plants and flowers towards the tents. Odd little creatures zip through the air and across the blue-ish grass making KK gasp softly here and there. By the time we get to the populated zone, the sound of lively music, cooked food, and other delights wafts through the air temptingly.

"Remember, you can't eat things we haven't checked," Anton says to the group. "And definitely do not drink things, or inhale—"

"Just be fucking careful, right?" Zavida says as his tails pop out and flick behind him. "Let you and Anton check everything, even things we want to touch."

"Exactly," I reply as I let the carefully curated human visage drop amongst our fellow supernaturals in this weird traveling village. "We don't want anyone sick or dead or… chained to something they don't want to be."

"Chained to— Mother, fucker, X," Kat mutters as she grabs onto Slash's big arm. "Keep an eye on my hands, both of you. Curiosity is not going to kill *this* Kit Kat."

I grin, winking at her. I'd love to know what the secret she wrote in the book was, but it seems like a 'later' question. "Probably for the best, KK. Now, let's roam this place and see if we can find some gossip."

And hopefully, not any trouble before we get to our own territory at this damn event.

The Moon Will Sing

kat/kit

It's damn near impossible not to gape at everything going on in the Fae encampment. I know I've been in Hell for a couple months now, but outside of battles and a few weird things, it's been pretty… normal looking most of the time. This is definitely not *at all* like that because the beings here are all noticeably supernatural from head to toe. Tall, elegant looking Fae mingle with tiny pixies, grumpy goblins, dwarves, elves, and a veritable bestiary of shit in semi or non-humanoid forms as we wander through the bazaar-like area.

No one would ever believe me if I told them back home; in fact, they'd probably lock me in a padded room.

Jasper and Slash stop at a booth full of gleaming weaponry, and Salem leans in to whisper about the legendary Fae steel they're inspecting. It's deadly and gorgeous, but I follow X as they navigate to another stall with bottles full of fragrant liquids that I assume are potions. They aren't bottled like liquor or drinks, so it's an uneducated guess on my part as to their contents.

Anton pauses there with Zavida, leaving me with the others as we continue moving. The next shop is full to the brim with wild fabrics and clothing, drawing a soft squeal of excitement from Xerxes. I grin a bit at their enthusiasm despite my lack of knowledge about what is and isn't in style.

"These are *stunning*," they say as they hold up two bolts of gauzy fabric that seem to float of their own accord. "Can you *imagine* what I can do with this material? I'm thinking… formal dinners and cameras, KK."

They're pretty and the colors seem to coordinate with both their complexion and mine, so I get the gist of what X is hinting at. "Um, for what? It's, uh, very…"

"Elegant?" Xerxes hums as they tuck them under their arm. "Exactly. Now I'm going to find some more things to experiment with for when we're *not* fighting to the death. Since I'm dressing the both of us, I must have the best materials possible."

Save me from the black hole that is their version of clothes shopping, please, Universe.

Oriel grabs my elbow, leaning in to murmur, "How about we leave Salem with Xerxes while they shop and we'll head for something a bit less… girly?"

I blink at his dark eyes for a moment, mesmerized, then finally remember that I'm not supposed to be a girl. "Um, yeah. That would be great. I'm not… as into clothing as X."

"*No one* is as into clothes and shit as Xerxes is outside of the fashion world." Oriel chuckles as he leads me away, nodding at Salem as we move to another display.

The panda keeps his gaze on me for a moment, then turns to watch X as they gather up armfuls of stuff. Smiling to myself, I look up at the crow shifter curiously. "You know, we're not following the protocol you guys set. We're in twos, but Jasper told you guys twice that Slash and Salem are supposed to guard me or whatever."

"He and the big guy got be-spelled by the armory display. Hard for the asshole to complain about us breaking the rules when he's the one who decided to stay there so he can buy some obscene fucking sword or whatever."

Grinning, I nod as I turn back to the booth full of crystals and gemstones. "Are these used for spells or something?"

Oriel nods, picking up a beautiful red stone in the shape of a heart. "This one is for absorbing negative energy and promoting tranquility."

"What's it called?" I ask as I take the palm-sized piece.

"Red jasper." His smirk makes me scowl and I swat his arm. "What? It is."

Frowning, I set the stone on the display and sniff haughtily. "The very *last* thing in the universe Jasper promotes is tranquility, Oriel. For fuck's sake, he's damn near an advertisement for blood pressure medicine."

Laughing, the demon shrugs and picks up another item off the table. "I agree it doesn't seem to work with you, Kit Kat. Perhaps this would be more useful."

I blink, looking at the choker made of some kind of dark metal in the shape of spiky thorns. The combined beauty of the design and the deadliness of the points makes it hard to take my eyes off of it, especially when I get to the gleaming coffin-shaped stone in the middle. The iridescent stone looks familiar, but the only thing that comes to mind is an opal and I don't think that's what it is. "Holy fuck, O. That thing is amazing."

He winks at me as he waits for what I'm pretty sure is a dwarf to come stomping over to glare at us. "Merry meet, sir. Tell us about your creation."

The stocky red-headed man furrows his brow. "Why should I entertain a child of the Underworld and his pet?"

"Excuse me?" I blurt before I can stop. "No need to be fucking rude."

"It's not common for your kind to mingle with ours in this realm." The dwarf shrugs, tilting his head as he studies us with zero repentance. "However, if you'd like me to answer yer pet hybrid, I will. But be cautious how you receive the answer, demon. I won't be slighted on my own lands."

What the fuck? He meant Oriel was the pet?

The response makes Oriel snicker as I gape at the rude as fuck vendor. "Uh, okay, I guess. Reply to him and we'll see what happens."

"Fine. That is a collar of titanium with a kite-shaped coffin rainbow moonstone. It has been cleansed of impurities that would prevent those from our realm from wearing it and its design mimics an ancient relic the world has not seen for a millennia." The dwarf crosses his arms over his chest, looking at me pointedly. "It would cost a small fortune outside of this event, but we do not barter with money at an Apalachin."

Oriel arches his brow, taking in the odd terminology without comment. Obviously, we've stumbled into an event steeped in weird ass traditions that we're going to bump against all night. At least this mysterious jerkwad gave us information we didn't have before while he lectured us. "And, what, pray tell, would you be willing to barter for if the pet would like to obtain this well-crafted replica?"

At his question, the dwarf walks away, then comes back with a stool. Climbing onto it, the ginger creature is now tall enough to look me in the eyes directly. "If yer pet wants my vision of the Collar of the Three-Headed Beastmaster, he will have to give me a possession that he holds dear in exchange. I can scent what he is, and I know that to be a more appropriate cost than secrets or favors. Crows treasure their hoards more than most shifters—but for dragons, of course."

"I don't think so. That seems—"

Before I can finish, Oriel grins wickedly. "That's the deal? An item I hold dear from one of my hoards for this collar in its entirety? You will lift any curses or hexes you've cast on it as well?"

Well, I never would have thought to fucking ask that. I'm so screwed in this damn place.

The dwarf growls, squinting at my caliphate brother as he scratches his beard. "You drive a hard bargain, pet. Yes, I will remove all magics from the piece if your item has enough tangible value to you."

This haggling is making me nervous, but I swallow it as I watch the two of them stare at one another combatively. Finally, Oriel nods, pulling a small velvet bag out of his pocket. He takes out a shiny ruby that must be expensive, rolling it over his knuckles as he looks at the merchant. "This ruby was… *acquired* as part of my training as a child. It comes from mines far below the earth and owned by those of my name. I almost died retrieving it."

"Oriel, don't! There's no way this thing is worth something like that."

"Ahh, young denizen of the Underworld, you are wrong. Yer pet knows what he is doing; I can see it in his eyes." The dwarf clears his throat and claps his hands, nodding in satisfaction. "I accept your payment, Duke Bloodstone, and relinquish all rights to this piece and any boons associated with it. Be safe in yer travels this eve."

Turning to Oriel as he shakes his head, I grab his arm and lead him away from the booth before something else insane happens. "Oriel, he *knows* who you are. How did a random… dwarf… know who you are?"

"The register, KK. Pretending not to know was just one of their stupid games. It's part of why demons hate the fucking Fae and their realm. Too much pretense, and obsession with outsmarting one another. Now, do a little turn for me so I can put this on you."

I scowl at him, batting his hands away. "Hell no. You guys said I'm not allowed to eat or drink here like Alice in fucking Wonderland. Why in the name of Dante's seven layers would I let you put some piece of jewelry with a *name* on me?"

"Well, I definitely understand why he'd ask *that*," Xerxes says as they come up to us. Salem is carrying a pack full of crap on his back that must be the demon's purchases and for a moment, I worry about what currency X used to get that much shit.

"Kit Kat, I wouldn't give you something that was dangerous, now would I?" O says with a grin. "I'm glad you thought about it, though. That means all the damn lectures about this place sunk in."

Xerxes snatches the collar, inspecting it curiously. "In this case, I'd like Annie to concur, but I believe your rough-hewn tradesman removed all traces of his magic from it. Though, he's a fool if he thinks we'll believe it's a replica."

My eyes widen. "What?! Are you saying this is some black market lost treasure and Oriel wants me to put it on? Have you guys even *heard* of the Hope Diamond? No way, man."

"Who do you think worked the bargain that allowed that thing to remain cursed for this long?" Anton shrugs as he walks over with Zavida and another bag full of… whatever. "Demons, of course. The original curse was from a deity, but they bore easily and don't often personally maintain their decrees. Throughout most of history, the heavy lifting of keeping curses, hexes, and the like from gods or goddesses has been farmed out to demons. We enjoy it far more and gain power from being cut in."

My head is going to explode; I need to get somewhere semi-normal for a few minutes or I might lose it.

"You are overwhelming the little demon."

Slash's words make my breath whoosh out in relief and I walk over to him, looking up at the shark demon gratefully. "You are one hundred percent right about that, big guy."

"We should continue moving through here until we reach the other end, then leave." Jasper looks around as he approaches, then sighs. "I do not think it is wise to approach the courts at this time. But I do agree with Oriel—you should wear the damn thing unless Anton disagrees with X's opinion. It is not a coincidence that you and O happened on it, nor that it is a real artifact masquerading as a copy."

"You guys are fucking crazy," I mutter as Anton takes the collar from Xerxes. "There's just no way that damn thing appeared here because I happened to choose Fae territory at an event we happened to get wind of on a weekend we happened—oh."

Salem reaches out and ruffles my hair fondly, making my face turn red. "KK, that's just too much 'happened to' not to be some sort of Fate chicanery. Even demons know not to mess with those bitches; if they wanted you to have this, we should follow the outline, dude."

"Next thing I know you'll be telling me watery tarts distributing swords are a basis for government," I grumble under my breath. "I don't like this one bit."

Anton sighs as he gives me an apologetic smile. "I'm sorry, Kit Kat. It feels like the dwarf's magic is gone and whatever's in this thing… is keyed to you already. They're probably right."

Just fucking great. A bunch of old bats who can't keep track of their eyeball are dictating my fashion choices.

Who Are You?

"Here, KK. I'll put it on you since Oriel was gallant enough to buy it for you."

Despite my deep desire to refuse, I turn around for the panda. Except for Jasper, I don't think any of the guys would want me to be hurt, so if they truly believe this is meant for me, I have to suspend my disbelief for them. Trust goes two ways and I'm holding out on something big; I don't think I'm in a place where I can be judgy about this kind of shit. "Okay, but if my skin starts peeling off, someone get the damn thing off me stat. Understand?"

That gets a round of chuckles from most of them, and Salem reaches around me to slide the collar around my neck gently. There's a soft sound as it clicks closed and I wait for the universe to implode, but it doesn't. My roommate's big hands land on my shoulders and he leans in to murmur, "See? No big deal, Kit Kat. You're safe."

I want to say I don't even know what that feels like and haven't for a long time.

But instead, I nod and swallow back the anxiety trying to wriggle out of me. "Does it look stupid? I can't see it."

Jasper grunts, waving his hand. "It looks fine. Don't be dramatic, shrimp."

"Okay, now that I've satisfied you guys, can we get the fuck out of fairy land and find some other species to freak me out?" I force a small smile as I gesture around us. "This place is cool, but if we were supposed to come here to find this thing, I think our quest is over."

Slash grins at me then looks around. "I think the little demon is correct, Jasper. We should head south and wrap our path around by the far court tents, then make our way back to the entrance. Moving too quickly might tip someone off that we have something to hide."

The dragon hauls his bag onto his shoulder, nodding. "That seems like a good plan. Salem, stay beside him while Slash and I lead the group. Oriel, follow with Zav, and then X and Anton."

Everyone falls into place quickly, and I go along with it because I'm much too distracted by my new jewelry to fight with the Prince on principle. The various Fae and creatures mill around us as we pass the booths full of things I wish I could examine more thoroughly. Things in this territory are delicate and ephemeral, but also bold and dangerous looking, which I guess is because there are four very different courts in residence. I'd love to know more about that, too, but now isn't the time. I have no idea how many ears are listening as we stroll through the bazaar nonchalantly.

When we finally get to the end of the market, I feel a strong pulse beating in the stone of my collar. My hand tightens on Salem's as the panic rises in my body along with the swirling colors of power within me. Blackness and deep red prickle along the inside of my skin as if trying to get out—a sure sign that my supposed magic is trying to tell me something.

The damn necklace is too, it seems.

"Stop," I murmur to the panda demon as I tug on our joined hands. "We have to stop, Salem."

He frowns, doing as I say immediately then clearing his throat loudly to get the Prince's attention. "What's going on, Kit Kat?"

The others are crowded around me in a circle in a blink, and I shake my head as I meet their gazes. "I don't know why, but as soon as we got close to these two big tent things, both the new collar *and* my magic started going haywire. Something in this area is important… or a problem… or I don't know. It's just telling me to wait."

"Do not be afraid," Slash rumbles. He turns to face away from me, his broad back and fin blocking my view as he moves to scan the crowd. "I will make certain no one comes near you."

"Good thing you're worried about me," Jasper drawls sarcastically. His words are sharp, but with my senses heightened, I feel the concern he doesn't want to voice. The dragon is a lot of things and many of them suck, but I know he doesn't want his family harmed and now I'm included in that roster.

I know he's seen something he doesn't like when a low, frustrated growl escapes him. His posture stiffens and he speaks to us in a soft, measured tone. "Everyone stay calm and follow my lead. It appears the shrimp may be right. I have no fucking clue if this is an ambush or not, so watch your words and zip it if you aren't a thousand percent sure you've got your shit together."

The big demons move apart, revealing a group of five men and a determined looking woman walking towards us. They're a mixed group, I think, as their scents are confusing my nose, but I believe one of them has to be a dragon based on size alone. That one is walking in a manner reminiscent of Slash, so I think he might be a guard—and he looks quite unhappy. I can't tell if the anger is directed at the universe or us, but he's sticking pretty close to the very handsome man with dark hair.

"Get ready for bullshit in three… two… one…" X whispers to me as they step closer.

The angry looking bodyguard stops short as they get within a few feet, jerking his chin up at Jasper. "Prince Eversore. What a surprise to see you above the surface and on our lands."

"*Your* lands?" Jasper says, his voice full of amusement. "No matter who you serve, this ground does not belong to you, Lieutenant."

Does he know these fucking people? A little info would be great right now.

"Kaspar, don't taunt the Prince of Hell. It's gauche," the handsome man chides as he steps into the gap and holds his hand out to Jasper. "My second is as diplomatic as most dragons, Your Highness, but I am not so prickly."

"But he is," I mutter and Salem snickers beside me.

"Who was that? I *like* them," the tall woman says. Her eyes are delighted as she joins the mysterious hot guy and the praise makes my skin tingle pleasantly. "Show yourself, whichever one of you is actually honest."

Licking my lips, I look at the panda, who shrugs, then pull him along with me as I do as she asked. "It was me. I'm sort of the problem child. My name is Kit, but I'm sorry to say I'm not sure who any of you are, so you'll have to forgive me if I'm fucking up some official secret handshake or greeting."

The pretty guy laughs, turning to look at the tall blond, then the other two with an amused expression. "Don't worry, Kit. Morgana is similarly inclined to speak plainly, which is why she was excited to see who would scoff at the second most powerful demon in Hell without fear."

I shrug, my face heating as I try to ignore all the spiking power and energy inside of me clashing with my own serotonin and adrenaline. "You didn't answer my question, though. She's Morgana—thanks for that— but who are you all and how do you know Jasper?"

"Watch it, demon," the dragon says as sparks jump on his frame. "You are not a friend and speaking to the Prince of the Daybreak Court requires respect."

Now we have two *of them to swing their dicks around—there are fucking rich, royal assholes everywhere I look.*

Xerxes saves me by showing their face, all smiles and diplomacy as they steal the attention from me. "Oh, *you're* Prince Liam then. I really thought I'd recognize you; I follow all the court fashions and you're always impeccably dressed."

Morgana snorts, covering her mouth for a moment before she shakes her head. "Guess that whole 'magic will disguise us' thing works unless it's another royal pain in the ass, huh, Li?"

The tall blond hunk grins, socking the Fae prince on the shoulder. "Your brilliant plan hit a four-oh-four error, man. Sucks to be us."

"For fuck's sake," the bodyguard says as he growls. "The plan worked fine, though I suppose we should forget it now that you're all revealing it to everyone. We didn't expect another dragon to appear, especially one as powerful as Hell's royal family. Of course he can see me, and I'm well known in supernatural circles. My father and I are the face of the Daybreak army."

Oriel tilts his head, nudging my shoulder. "Looks like we accidentally foiled our plan *and* theirs."

"That's what happens when you think Jedi mind tricks are going to protect you," I say softly and the crow demon laughs. "Something always goes wrong and if you don't have a million variations on your plan, you're screwed."

"A very wise statement," Morgana replies as she grins broadly. "But truly, we mean you no harm. We did not want to draw a crowd, but that's the only reason Liam and Kaspar were disguised. I assume your… group…is also looking to fly under the radar?"

"Yes," Jasper growls. "We were hoping to make our way to the exit without fanfare so we can get to our next appointment. It's a quirk of fate that I happened to identify one of my kind and then conclude who it was."

"Perhaps we can agree to stay quiet as a mini-detente?"

The suggestion is made by the delicate looking man holding Morgana's hand. He looks shy and studious, not made for battle like the dragon or brash like the blond. I believe he's something aquatic by the smell, and the bulky blond is a shifter. That leaves the fancy pants dude next to the shy guy and everything about him screams money and arrogance. I have no idea what he is, but I know he'd piss me off.

"Agreed, siren." Slash folds his arms over his chest, his posture radiating tension as he watches the group. It's his job to keep us safe and he clearly doesn't know how he feels about this encounter yet.

"Prince?" The sparking dragon says in response.

Jasper nods. "My caliphate will stay silent about your presence if you do the same. I accept those terms."

"Excellent!" The handsome Fae prince claps his hands, looking pleased. "I am quite certain my mates and family will hold up our end of this bargain. Perhaps if it goes smoothly, you and I will have things to discuss in the future, Prince Jasper."

Shockingly, Jasper actually smiles at the dude. "That would be an interesting possibility, Prince Liam. I believe we might have a vast number of interests that intersect. Anton, the card?"

I'd almost forgotten the peacock shifter since he stayed quiet, but it was obviously for a reason. Anton walks into the divide, handing what looks to be a metal business card to the bodyguard. The angry dragon hands something back to him, and both princes puff up, looking pleased as shit.

This is such a weird fucking dance of bullshit.

I'm about to comment when something prickles at the back of my neck, then around the collar to the stone. It feels cool against my skin, and I reach up to touch it. What in the hell a temperature change means, I don't know, but I get the feeling it's not nothing. I elbow Salem in the side, leaning in to whisper very softly, "The damn collar is going nuts again. I don't think it was just these guys."

Before he can answer, a loud *crack* sounds out in the tent on the right and a *bang* echoes out of the one on the left side. My roomie's eyes widen, and he lets go of my hand, looking at Slash. The shark nods, and I squeak as Salem hauls me up onto his shoulder without preamble and takes off, running away from our caliphate at a speed I didn't know he was capable of.

"Hey!" I pound my fist on his broad back, but he doesn't respond. "Salem, don't do this. You can't run away from them with me and not be there for whatever is going on!"

"Sorry, KK," he rumbles as he darts through a throng of people starting to panic and run around. "My job is to get you to safety; you can get mad at me later."

You can bet that's exactly what I'm going to fucking do when I get out of his kung-fu grip —I hope he's wearing a cup.

You Rock My World

sälem

Kit Kat is going to be fucking furious, but as soon as I heard those noises, I knew everything was going to shit. Jasper and the guys can take care of themselves, but I wasn't going to let my new favorite person get hurt again when the hammer came down. One of the sounds was definitely a small explosion and the other didn't sound any better. Some kind of attack is hitting the royal courts of Autumn and Reaping back there, and I could give a fuck less what happens to any of them.

The traumatized guy I'm carrying like a sack of potatoes is what's important and that's why I'm running.

"I'm going to murder you if you don't find a place to land and let me down!"

Chuckling to myself at his fury, I keep my eyes peeled for just such a place. The commotion in the marketplace is getting rougher and I'm worried we're going to run afoul of some pissed off creature who will force me to fight. My demon would enjoy that far more than my panda—but we do much better in a dream space than in reality unless I'm being pumped up by Kit's weird mojo. That's a bag full of crazy I do not want to open on the surface and I'm sure he doesn't either.

"I'm working on it."

Squinting, I finally see two tents set back away from the main part of the bazaar, and I realize they're probably bathrooms. The Fae are as fancy as you can get, so I doubt they'll be gross. Just in case, I choose the one with the girly looking fairy on the side, bustling in quickly. Kit glares at me murderously when I set him on his feet, but I ignore it to go back and fiddle with the opening until it makes a clicking sound that I hope is a latch.

"Are you *kidding* me?!" he yells as I come back over to him. "I'm supposed to fight with you guys. You can't just haul me off to put me in a glass jar every time there's a hint of—"

I can't stop myself from stomping up to him and yanking him into my arms as the fear and adrenaline course through me. My grasp muffles whatever he was going to yell as I bury my face in his short hair, trying not to let my worry bleed into him. Kit is mad now, so he's not having a panic attack about the others, but once he's done taking me to task, he's going to be scared.

The past few months have taught me a lot about how his moods and his condition work, so I know I'm right.

The muffled sounds of protest get louder and I blow out a slow breath as I finally loosen my grip until I can look down at him. His expression is angry, but I see the fear sparking in his eyes. I open my mouth to comment on it, but suddenly, all I can focus on is the tongue that darts out to lick his lips.

It's not the time, but I can't seem to make myself care as I dip my head down and kiss the guy who's turned my entire world upside down. He squeaks adorably, but that only makes me growl a bit as I deepen the kiss and flick my tongue over the spot he just licked. I'm being careful, holding back the wave of pent-up need that's now pounding in my ears to make sure Kit's okay. When his lips part, I know he's not going to freak out, and I grin briefly before sliding my tongue into his mouth.

The kiss is soft, but hungry, and my arms tighten around him again as I pull him close. I love having him in my arms without worrying about it triggering something, and even though my dick is jumping like a fucking bouncy ball, I'm totally fine with kissing my roommate like this for as long he'll let me. In fact, I think doing this is definitely my new favorite thing.

"Salem, what the hell…" Kit murmurs huskily when our lips break for breath. "This is hardly the time to—"

I put my finger against his mouth with a soft smile. "You're stuck here with me until someone comes to tell me the chaos out there is over. Would you rather spend that time yelling or kissing?"

His eyes widen, and the shy expression almost does me in. I don't know how anyone could have ever hurt Kit, especially in the way I know they did. He's brave and fierce and loyal to a fault—plus, for someone who doesn't do this, he's not a bad little smoocher. "Um, I… I don't… know?"

That's a 'yes' for kissing if I ever heard one.

Grinning, I heft him up again, drawing a grumble of complaint as I carry him over to what appears to be some sort of sink. I place him on the edge, making our height difference a bit more manageable before I step closer and cup his face. "See, you say I don't know with your words, but your heartbeat and that flush on your face say 'kiss me, Salem'. Which one should I believe?"

Kit dips his chin for a second, then looks up, whispering, "The second one, I think."

My panda damn near does a fucking backflip inside of me as I lean in to take his lips again. It doesn't worry me in the slightest that Kit's a dude because I honestly barely notice people until I have feelings for them in some way. I don't care if the person I'm attracted to is another guy anymore than I care if they're a purple elephant shifter, so unlike some people, I'm rolling with what makes my entire body sing with happiness.

But the unusual hunger in my gut pushes a bit harder as our tongues slide against one another and the desire to be as close as I can is overwhelming. My hands slip down his shoulders lightly to rest on his waist, then grasp his hips as I yank him as close as possible. The warmth emanating from his frame makes my animal preen in pleasure, and I curl my toes in my shoes as I fight for control of my increasing lust.

Suddenly, loud noises not far off make me pull away, holding Kit protectively as I listen to the sounds around our haven carefully. "Shhh," I whisper. "I think I latched us in here, so hopefully, that's just people running off or fleeing or something."

"Salem, if they're fleeing, we don't know if the others are okay," Kit mumbles into my chest. "I'm worried about them. Not that… um.. I mean, not that this isn't… good."

Damn, he's so fucking awkward and cute; it's almost painful.

"KK, I know you're worried," I say as I look down at him again. "But we both know that you being out there in an unfamiliar place with unknown enemies would be distracting for the others. They'd be too concerned about you and not able to focus on kicking ass. And let me tell you, Slash is insanely good at what he does when he can focus. It's terrifying and beautiful at the same time like some kind of demonic killing machine."

"Does he really eat them?" he whispers, wrinkling his nose. "Like for real?"

I snort, my eyes dancing as I brush hair off his forehead. "Oh, totally, especially if he gets into a battle in the water. The dude is like a goddamn thresher of bloodshed in the water and a tank armed with knives on land. You haven't seen it yet, but you'll love it."

"I don't know about that."

Shaking my head, I tweak his nose. "KK, you're a *demon* inside. You aren't totally formed yet, but I *promise* you, once you are? You're going to fucking *love* carnage. It's going to make your whole body tremble with anticipation and glee. It'll make you hot as hell, guaranteed."

That makes him turn bright red. "I doubt it, Salem. I don't even know what… you know… does that normally. Not really. I sort of… shut that all off and sealed it in boxes."

Fuck that—no one should have to live without feeling pleasure.

"Well, we're going to unseal it, my delicious little morsel, I promise."

A soft laugh surprises me when he looks up at me from under his lashes with a shy grin. "Does that mean I have to say 'yes, chef' when I'm answering you now?"

My jaw damn near drops to the floor at the innuendo and all my former suaveness disappears. Blinking as my brain short circuits, I just stare at Kit wordlessly. His smile goes from shy to pleased to a wee bit wicked as he watches me fumble for any semblance of intelligence.

"Now I know how to get your attention, I guess."

Only if you want me to fuck the shit out of you on the damn kitchen counter.

But I don't say that because while we're doing well right now, I know KK isn't ready for *that* level of playful banter yet. "If you… You could… I mean, be careful with that."

Kit reaches up and puts his hands on my chest lightly, still flushed and rumpled from the make-out session. "Good to know. That you like it and that it might… make you a bit crazy, I mean. I'm not great at reading signals sometimes, but being this clear with me is really helping."

"I'll tell you anything you want, Kit Kat, but you have to be ready for the answers." My expression is serious as I squeeze his hips lightly. "I don't want to scare you off."

His eyes dart around for a second and he bites his lip, looking like he wants to say something. I wait patiently, so damn thrilled by how this is going that I'm willing to be patient as a saint if he'll open up. "Um, this might be a weird question, but…"

"Uh-huh…"

Leaning forward, he whispers, "Is your… Xerxes was a half-snake and his…"

How the fuck do I answer that *without wigging him out? Ahhhhh!*

Taking a deep breath, I think about the question he didn't actually ask for a moment then respond. "You'll find it's different than you'd expect in all three forms, and I'm not the only one. X doesn't have any… steel… there, so there's that but also… other stuff."

"Whoa…."

I have to shake my head to clear it as Kit stares off into space, obviously considering what I said *very* carefully. This little breakthrough is straining the limits of my control, but I'll be damned if I'm going to stop now. This rendezvous in the middle of the chaos outside our hiding spot is everything, and I'm going to soak up every second of it before KK realizes what he's missing out there.

"Don't worry about that right now, Kit Kat. Just be here with me and enjoy what's happening now." I smile softly, pressing forward until we're close again and brush my lips over his. "One thing at a time."

This kiss is deeper, and I feel like it's because he's trusting me to take care of him, to make sure he's safe. It makes my chest get tight as one hand comes up to cup his cheek as we explore one another. It's lazy and gentle at first, but the desire building up in me has been a slow, quiet burn that sparks to life in this secret alcove. Kit kisses me back, his fingers holding onto my shirt, and a soft growl of need escapes my mouth when I stop to breathe again. The hand on his hip tugs him closer as my cock twitches in excitement and I can't help fitting our bodies together—

What. The. Fuck.

Ripping my lips away from his, I look at him, my eyes wild with confusion as it hits me. "Holy Belphegor's hammock, KK! Did... tell me that asswipe didn't.... *he didn't hurt you there, either, did he?!*"

Fury fills my entire being and before I can stop it, my demonic guise takes over as I look at the guy I'm absolutely bonkers about in horror. If someone cut him, if that dead human walking did this, I don't care how much effort it takes, I will hunt the motherfucker down and deal with this myself.

Luckily, Kit doesn't pull away when I lose my shit, he just slaps his hands over his face and makes a weird, strangled sound. When I growl softly, waiting for a response, Kit lifts his palms, peeking through them with a very scared expression. "No... no. Salem, no. What you're thinking... no. That's not what happened."

"But... you... I..." It's hard not to be a loud, snarly asshole in this form, but I have to keep a lid on it so I don't ruin this shit. "I don't understand."

Sighing heavily, the smaller guy reaches down, taking my hand off of his hip and holding it with the other one between us. His expression is hard to read —sad, afraid, worried, and something else. "I have something I need to tell you, Salem, and if you don't want to speak to me again afterward, I wouldn't blame you."

Something tells me this is going to change everything and I don't know if I'm ready to hear it in the middle of a battleground—but I don't have a choice.

"I'm not actually a guy."

OMG ARE YOU GOING TO KILL ME?

Preorder book three here.

Join Ream to read the next season as it's being written here.

Get the bonus that follows this here.

GET A SECRET BONUS SCENE!

For another secret bonus scene that follows *Quiet Burn, click the link below, sign up for my newsletter, and get your freebie.*

Get your bonus scene here!

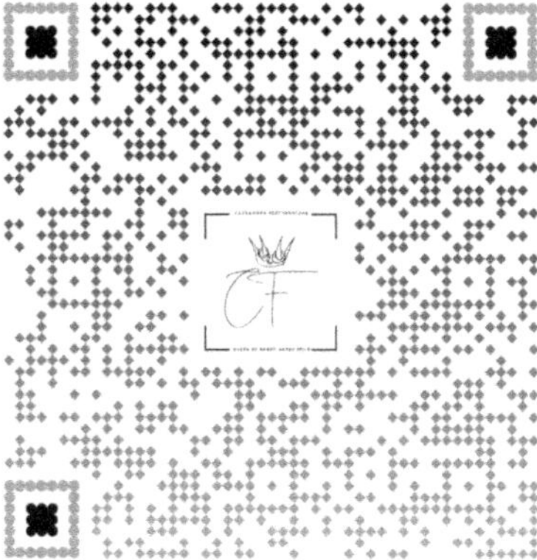

REVIEWS, PRINT, AND MERCHANDISE

If you have enjoyed this story, please review it.
It helps other readers find my work,
which helps me as an indie author.

Thank you!

Reviews are appreciated on the following platforms:

TikTok
Instagram
Facebook
Bookbub
StoryGraph
Threads
Tome
Lemon8

To purchase print copies or merchandise, go to The Worlds of Cassandra Featherstone

Some pronunciations are very basic, but my editors believe they should all have it to be uniform in style. Obviously, I know you know how to read 'Bob', but it's just weird for things not to match, 'kay?

Characters, Pets, & Creations

Katarina Camponella (kat uh REE nuh CAM POH NELL uh) foster kid living with the Jamesons; now learned to be at least part demon with some kind of magic

Nicknames: Kat, Kit, Kit Kat, little demon, shrimp, dumpling

Blake Jameson (blay-k Jay-meh-son) twin foster brother of Kat; plays football, popular kid; absolute ass; accepted to Alabama to play ball

Bryce Jameson (bry-ss Jay-meh-son) twin foster brother of Kat; plays football, popular kid; absolute ass; accepted to Alabama to play ball

Brett Jameson (Breh-TT Jay-meh-son) foster father of Kat; clueless; does whatever their mother says

Allison Jameson (al-uh-SON Jay-meh-son) foster mother of Kat; snobby; only like the prestige from having the two foster boys who play ball; disdainful of Kat

Professor Horatio Alecto (hor-ay-she-o uh-leck-to) professor at Discordia; Dean of Admissions; sends a letter to 'Kit' Camponella

Mr. Jenkins (Jeh-kinz) school guidance counselor; obviously overwhelmed and near retirement

Dottie (dah-tee) random kinkajou that shows up and is trying to break into the Jamesons bedroom floor safe; Kat finds her, and she refuses to leave; later, she's told it's a familiar

Sheriff Bob (Bahb) Useless, prejudiced town sheriff

Wilbur (will-BURR) deputy sheriff; four years older than twins; bully with a badge

Becky Sanderson (beck-ee San-der-son) town busy body

Lucian Darkstar (loo-see-en dark-stah-r) Headmaster of Discordia; sketchy AF; pit demon

Dank (DahNK) demon sent to fetch Kat; wears plague mask; aka Dr. Danckwardt

Silvera (sil VAIR UH) demon who does Lucian's bidding; fear demon

Beccarus (Beck-A-roos) toadie to Lucian; demon in Headmaster's office; chaos demon

Jasper Eversore (jas-PURR EVER-sore) Prince of Hell; leader of caliphate; dragon/demon hybrid; four years older than the others; working as teaching assistant while taking graduate classes to be with caliphate as they go to school; controlling asshole; fear demon

Nicknames: Asshole Demon, Prince Dickface, Prince Prick, Prince Prickface, Prince Cocknozzle

Scents: vanilla, musk, vetiver, bergamot, Sicilian mandarin, ylang-ylang, and honeyed neroli

Piercings: Lip, ears, tongue (both humanoid and forked dragon), Jacob's ladder and magic cross

Special equipment: stimulatingly bumpy, large as fuck dragon dick with vibration and knotting

Salem Stryker (Say-lem Str-eye-cur) Panda/demon hybrid; likes to cook; Kat's roommate; dream demon

Nicknames: Lazy Demon, Sleepy Bear,

Scents: Sicilian Lemon, Citron, Grapefruit, Bergamot**,** Green Mandarin from Italy, Juniper Berries**,** Cypress, Ylang-Ylang, Musk

Piercings: ears, navel, nipples, Apadravya

Special equipment: fluffy panda tail when aroused

Anton Aldaric (an-TOHN all-dur-icvk) peacock/demon hybrid; designer; lover of X; incubus

Nicknames: Flirty Demon, Annie

Scents: egyptian cassie, pepper flower, pink pepper, jasmine, geranium, rose, balsams, myrrh, amber

Piercings: ears, nipples, deep shaft, Reverse Prince Albert, tongue

Special equipment: cock pocket

Xerxes Zenobes (zerk-zees zee-not-bzs) cobra/demon hybrid; lover of Anton; enby; dream demon

Nicknames: Pretty Demon, X

Scents: Crushed red currants, broken twigs and blooming dahlias

Piercings: one nipple, frenum, pubic, Lorum, ears, eyebrow, nose

Special equipment: hemipenis

Oriel Bloodstone (or-ee-elle blud-stohn) crow shifter/demon hybrid; likes to steal shit; emo looking; quiet; shadow demon

Nicknames: Goth Demon, O

Scents: Clove, black pepper, rose, incense and amber

Piercings: nipples, septum, ears, eyebrow, labret, lip, magic cross, hafada

Special equipment: unknown

Zavida Draven (zah-VEE-duh reh-ven) kitsune/demon hybrid; hacker; gamer; sleeps with Jasper; very smart; chaos demon

Nicknames: Gamer Demon, Zav, Zavvie, Z

Scents: cinnamon, red pepper and saffron

Piercings: Prince Albert, nipples, tongue

Special equipment: knotting

Slash Scrum (slah-shuh) Jasper's second in command; Fireball champ; shark; demon hybrid; vengeance demon

Nicknames: Big Demon, Big Guy

Scents: amber, sandalwood, musk, rare pure Indian agarwood, pure Turkish rose, patchouli ylang-ylang and frankincense

Piercings: unknown

Special equipment: unknown

Professor Alabaster (al-UH-bas-ter) Deconstructing Human History professor; chaos demon/demi-god hybrid

Professor Kindervalt (kin-der-Walt) Demonic Languages professor; hybrid dream demon/giraffe

Professor Wormwood (werm-wood) Curses & Hexes professor; mage/dhampir hybrid

Professor Basquez (bas-Kez) Culinary Art professor; ancient; stodgy; hates cell phones; bores Salem to tears; crossroads demon

Professor Romero (rom-may-ro) Dark Lit professor; fallen demon

Professor Lilibet (lil-ih-bet) Intro to Supes professor; succubi who feeds on boys in class; jerk to girls

Bastion Queznar (bast-ee-on qwehz-nahr) greed demon in Thieves Guild; species racist; drude

Cornelius Rhodes (cor-nee-lee-us row-dz) leader of the Southern demon contingent; crossroads demon

Phelps Brewster (fell-ps brew-stir) Leader of the Midwest demon contingent; dream demon

Allegra Masterson (UH-leg-ruh Mass-tur-sun) leader of the Eastern demon contingent; pit demon; ugly as hell

Professor Salazar (SALL-uh-ZAR) Dark Magic professor; chaos demon with bent for making people nutty for his amusement

Professor Cedar (CEE-dur) Intro to Fae professor; hybrid Reaping Fae and incubus; actually a cool dude

Ivan Roquefort (ee-vahn ROH-kh-fort) demon in Kit's Waeapons class; super jackass;

King Tarron Eversore (tay-ron ev-er-soar) full nightmare demon; upset last royal rule in Hell; asshole; Jasper's father

Queen Daramah Eversore (dare-ay-mah ev-er-soar) Queen of Hell; arranged marriage; succubus; Jasper's mom; pays no attention to him or the kingdom

Professor Holmes (hole-m-zuh) Supernatural Law professor; minor crossroads/sloth demon hybrid

Magnus Chilton (mag-NUSS CHILL-ton) a drude; Zavida's family line; in Arms class

Kristian Hoebert (kriss-tee-in HOE-bert) an incubus from X's family line; in Arms class

Aesyllian Furon (AY-sill-ee-on Few-RON) hybrid Midnight Fae and vengeance demon from Jasper's family line; in Arms class

Wilhelmina 'Billie' von Henrich (will-HELL-meen-uh Bill-ee VAUGHN Highn-rick) Cubi from Xerxes' line; attends Brimstone Academy

Professor Gaius Octavian (guy-US OCK-tay-vee-un) History of Warfare professor; crossroads demon

Anastasia Aldaric (ahn-UH-stah-zia ALL-dare-ick) Anton's mother; matriarch of Pride line; thinks of him as a failure; possibly bi-polar; rage phases well known

Aegon Aldaric (AYE-gone ALL-dare-ick) Anton's father; second in command in Pride line; useless and spineless; rarely around; suspected to have married Anadstasia for political reasons; his attendent is rumored to be his lover; never around when Anton was little

Budet (boo-det) demon from Gluttony line; opponent in Weapons class

Guillermo (gee-air-moh) brown recluse spider shifter; tailor to Geminis; ancient as hell

Laurel (lah-rel)racoon shifter; assistant to Guillermo

Delamar the Deciever (day la marr) redcap at the apalachin guarding the Fae lands

Morgana LeCiel (mor-GAN-uh lih CEE-el) hybrid gargoyle/gorgon shifter; adopted my gargoyle and witch parents; educated and previously employed at Swallowtail Academy; killed her dragon fiancé Magnus; stood trial before Society and sentenced to clean up State U; has one unruly gorgon snake in her hair called Dez;

Nicknames: babe, Salaadir, M, Lass, Lady M

Slade Finn (slay-duh fihn) siren grad student who works at campus coffeehouse; meets Morgana and invites her to dinner with his pined for room mate Ignatius Briarton; son of crime lord family in Bay City

Nicknames: darling man, guppy, songbird

Ignatius Briarton (ig-NAY-shus bry-er-TON) professor and head of Witchcraft & Wizardry department; mage; womanizer; lived with Slade since they met when he was undergrad; snobby elitist; rich old family

Nicknames: Iggy, Professor

Lucas Wolfberg (loo-CUSS Wolf-berg) grandson of Wolfenberg dynasty; polar bear shifter; star hockey player for State U Bonecrushers; accused of murdering rival team member at State U rink; mates with Morgana on accident; gets poisoned; has shitty playboy/girl parents

Nicknames: Papa Bear

Prince Liam Spéirgheal (Lee-UM speej-gee-al) one of the Princes of the Daybreak Court; attending grad school for interspecies diplomacy Masters; lives in staff housing close to Morgana

Nicknames: Prince, Li

Kaspar (cass-par) storm dragon; security detail for Liam; been with family since a kid; grumpy and suspicious

Nicknames: Kas

LOCATIONS

Woodlawn High School- school where Kat goes to school

Common Grounds- coffeehouse and diner where Woodlawn moms hang out

Woodlawn Mall- where Kat goes to create her Kit persona

Short Cuts- where Kat gets her haircut for Kit persona

Raging Trends- scene kid store in the mall

Wally World- mega store in town

Discordia University- premier demon college that invites Kat to attend

Canto IV- Section of Hell Discordia is located in

State U- Supe college

Bamford Academy- reform school

Canto V- the dorm they live in

Library Enclave- Building where many lectures take place

Magic Enclave- building where magic classes occur

Triclinium- cafeteria building

Infirmary- a bad place to go for treatment

Dr. Danckwardt's Office- the elite royal doctor's clinic

Arena- where the weapons and physical classes occur; also a large meeting space

Temple/Altar- ancient space where rituals are performed

Brimstone University- female elite demon college

Wastelands- place where punishment occurs; near Discordia; desolate region where some of the lowest demons live.

Purgatory Pizza- best pizza in Hell

Rigoletto Abbigliamento e Accessori di pregio clothing store in Bay City

Bay City supe city on West Coast where they portal in

Autumn/Harvest Court one of four courts of Faerie

Midnight Court one of four courts of Faerie

Court of Reaping one of four courts of Faerie

DISCORDIA SPECIFIC-TERMS & ITEMS

Crunkleberries- used in desserts, Kit loves; they make her a little high;

Black Underworld Cow- meat eaten by demons from Hades' special cows; akin to Kobe beef here;

Meat Bag- slang for human

Beast Meat- from unidentified Hell beasts; used for food;

Bat wings- used as food like chicken wings

Fear fish- fish used for food from River Styx;

Batberry- used to make wine in Hell

Cantu berry- used in foods, desserts, and snacks

Emerge- come into supernatural powers; usually in pubescence

Society- highest Council of mixed supes from all realms who help keep their worlds a secret from humans and protect the supernaturals

Fireball (aka Magic Battles)- the sports league of Hell's schools

Chasm Worm- another meat used in foods

Hybrid- supe of mixed species

Pits- the fiery place where pit demons live and reign over the beings sent there

Faeberry- used to make wine; from Faerie; smells like sugar, strawberry, grapes, and honey;

Crawling Thorn Briar- crawling thorn patch used for both food and captivity in Faerie

Tripleskia- a supernatural with three or more supernatural sides; extremely rare.

Dark Cow Milk- milk from Black Underworld cows used for a variety of cooking and drinks

STALK CASSANDRA FEATHERSTONE IN THE DARK CORNERS OF THE WEB

JOIN MY FACEBOOK GROUP AND FOLLOW ME EVERYWHERE!

WANT MORE?

SIGN UP FOR MY BI-WEEKLY MANIFESTO FOR A FREE SERIES SAMPLER:

Join my Ream as a FREE follower or exclusive subscriber to get access to cover reveals, WIPs, Serial Stories, and personal chats from me!

Sneak Peek: Come Out & Prey

Just A Girl

Delores

Sighing, I look around my bedroom at the posters and decorations covering my walls. My obsession with pop music, musical theater, and high school rom-coms sickens my parents. They would prefer me to be into heavy metal and horror movies like the other kids my age.

Being the only child in a family as prominent as mine is difficult when you don't fit the mold. My parents—like their parents and all my friends' parents

—are apex predators. Preds rule our world, and the division between us and prey is so severe that we regulate them to a completely different echelon of society. Prey shifters are weak and beneath our lofty abilities. The ruling class of elite predator families stretches back generations, and they've evolved into a bunch of assholes who only care about succession and greed.

My animal has not manifested yet, but it will soon enough. Luckily for me, none of my friends have manifested their inner animals, either. I'm part of the in-crowd at school, and my boyfriend, Todd, is the most popular guy in my class. While he and I aren't officially engaged yet, we've talked about it enough that I know it's only a matter of time before he puts a ring on my finger. I should be on top of the world, but I can't help but feel like my life just doesn't fit me the way it's supposed to.

Every teenager wishes their life was different, but I dream of becoming an entirely different person. Not inside, mind, because I'm pretty comfortable with who I am. I don't want to be part of this legacy, this society, or even this family. They are all focused on competing to be the richest, the deadliest, or the most powerful, and I want no part of it.

I walked over to my closet and pulled out the outfit that I had chosen for my tour of Apex Academy. My mother hired her personal designers to create a custom school uniform for today and expects me to present the 'appropriate' image of the sole heir to a Council seat.

I hate having to pretend to be like them because I'm nothing like them.

Regardless, I pull on the short, pink pleated skirt, three quarter length sleeve blouse, knee socks, and Mary Janes that comprise the uniform for my exclusive private high school. Since I'm using a 'college visit' day to tour the Academy, I'm expected to represent Shifter Secondary as well.

Shifter Secondary is the most exclusive high school for unmanifested shifter teens on the East Coast. Unfortunately for me, it was not my parents' first choice for my education. They hoped I'd follow in their footsteps by choosing to force my animal to emerge early. If I had done that, I could have attended *Apex Academy Lower School.*

I didn't have the stomach to use my body in that manner at fourteen.

Their heirs followed my lead, which made my mother and father furious and their hoity-toity council colleagues angry. My closest friends, the Heathers, also refused to force their animals to emerge, as did Todd and his friends. That was the first time the adults in our circle decided I was a bad influence. After that, I had to toe the line at every turn, ensuring that I followed all the strict rules and regulations that govern the heirs to council seats.

Everywhere I went, I had to dress in a manner befitting the next Drew to sit at the table. They forced me to take dance lessons, piano lessons, diction lessons, and other more humiliating tutorials to prepare for the day that I became a true predator. In our society, teenagers have no say in how we prepare for our animals to emerge.

Your parents make all the decisions, choose your friends, choose your mates, and decide every detail of your life down to what you eat every single day. At least, that's how it is in my family, because my mother is from the old world.

She came over from Slovenia when she was incredibly young and met my father on the society fundraiser circuit. Her idea of preparing her daughter for the future involves lessons in makeup, clothing, jewelry, and on how to keep your mate satisfied. Lucille is completely unconcerned about whether I end up happy, only that I attend to my council seat and my husband's *needs*.

Once I get dressed, I grab my vintage Vuitton bag and peek at the mirror for a last check before I head downstairs. I tuck my perfectly highlighted blonde tresses behind my ears, and the smokey eye and winged liner are on point with this year's fashion trends. I apply a quick swipe of cherry red lip gloss and open my mouth, inspecting my teeth to make sure they are pearly white. Even though once I develop threatening incisors or sharp fangs, something will inevitably cover them in blood, my parents want my smile to look like a toothpaste commercial.

It's all such utter bullshit.

I take a deep breath and turn on my heel, heading for the door. I can already hear my parents yelling in a Scotch and vodka induced rage in the drawing room. It's only eleven thirty in the morning, for Hera's sake.

Lucille and Bruno don't fuck around with cocktail hour. They are nicely sauced by ten a.m. every day, without exception. I can't remember a time when my parents didn't get drunk off their asses at an event or party, much less in our 'home'. They liquor up and fight until they part for the day, and then start again once they arrive home from their daily commitments.

I brace for the barrage of criticism my mother will subject me to when I cross the threshold. Closing my eyes, I whisper words of encouragement to myself via lyrics to some of my favorite songs, desperately trying to hype myself up before she can tear me down.

"Delores! I hear you breathing at the top of the stairs, darling. Come down this instant and let your father and I inspect your presentation."

My mother's purr *sounds* friendly, but believe me, it's not. I roll my eyes as I make my way down the stairs, knowing my mother won't hesitate to send one of the staff if I don't acquiesce to her command. Most of their staff would gleefully jizz themselves with being chosen to drag me downstairs for inspection.

At this time of day, the only servant in the drawing room will be Matilda—my ex-nanny turned personal assistant—and that request would test her loyalties. As the only person in my household who has my back, I don't want to put her in that position, so I answer. "Yes, Lucille. I'm on my way."

I'm not allowed to refer to her as 'mother' because it makes her feel old. 'Lucille' is always what I've called the woman who supposedly gave birth to me. I'd be tempted to disbelieve we shared any DNA at all if it weren't for our similar bone structure. She's about as nurturing as a rattlesnake, and if it weren't for Matilda, I might have died as a child. If the kitchen staff whispers are accurate, I have to accept that my mother neglected to feed me much of the time.

"You coddle her far too much, Lucille," my father growls. "As the heir to our family seat, Delores will come without being instructed to do so. We will not tolerate her insolence after her animal emerges. She will behave as I command or suffer the consequences."

The last of Bruno's rant echoes off the marble walls of the foyer as I step onto the hideously expensive, endangered teak floor. Schooling my features into the mask of indifference I wear whenever I have to deal with them, I enter their den of drunken fights with my spine steeled for an emotional assault.

"I apologize for my tardiness, Father. I only wished to perfect the image I will present during my tour of Apex Academy. I realize it is imperative I impress the Headmistress and her staff."

The humanoid features of his face shift seamlessly, and the hungry crocodile inside of him gives me a toothy smirk. "You will impress them, daughter, or so help me… I'll send you to Bloodstone Isle."

My stomach drops like a stone as I barely suppress a shiver.

Bloodstone Isle is a reformatory school. It's surrounded by spells and enchantments to prevent students from escaping—a feat that has only happened once in its one thousand years of existence. The most feared cat group in the shifter world—the Khan ambush—runs the school, and they're rumored to consume errant students when the Council allows it.

It's the threat both rich and poor shifter parents used to keep their children in line. Wealthy parents like mine use it as a method of controlling any heirs that refuse to conform to the rigid structure of our society. Predators don't value the lives of those who are weak, and they label heirs who refuse to take their rightful place at the top of the food chain weak. Everyone knows Bloodstone is full of criminals, miscreants, and psychos, and even they don't seem to survive.

Bloodstone is a death sentence—pure and simple.

"Y-yes, Father. I understand," I croak out. As if the pressure of touring my new school isn't enough, now I worry the Dean will relay something to my parents that gets me shipped off to Death Island.

"Bruno, darling, if you scare her, she'll frown. That causes wrinkles. Delores, chin up and smile for us."

Swallowing the lump in my throat, I flash my mother my brightest smile. Her blood-red lips curve, and her leopard fangs burst free as she all but purrs. "I will not have you sullying the family name, Delores. It's bad enough that your education gave you ideas about your value beyond breeding stock. You will take the seat on the Council when it is time, but the husband we select will control the business—as nature intended. Do you hear me?"

My eyes narrow briefly, and for what is possibly the millionth time this week alone, I nod at my mother to appease her temper. "Yes, Lucille."

"Excellent!" The leopard fades as she claps her hands. "Matilda!"

The tiny woman steps up, her eyes wide behind her glasses. She's a pred, but the smaller size of hawk shifters puts her in the servant class. I believe she genuinely lives in fear of one or both of my parents deciding to eat her. "Yes, madam?"

"Fetch Bruiser. He will accompany Delores to the academy for her tour. Tell him to take the Escalade—it won't do for her to arrive in a tiny car—it will draw attention to her extra weight. We must make an impression."

Matilda nods, and I feel the fear radiating from her, and I don't blame her. Bruiser is one of my parents' bodyguards and our frequent chauffeur. He's a Komodo dragon shifter and the house staff are terrified of him. It's hard not to be, given that he prefers to play with his food, then eat it after it's dead. The kitchen crew believes he 'handled' the gardener that looked too long at my mother when I was ten. He disappeared without a trace.

Once Matilda scurries away, I watch my parents drink and bicker about their plans for the day. Bruno is going golfing with a congressman, and Lucille is going to the spa. We all know that both outings will include stops at the homes of their current pieces of ass for a quickie, but no one talks about it. The appearance of the loving couple has to be maintained, although neither of them has slept in the same room since I was a baby.

They don't give a damn about fidelity; I learned that at an early age. Children often discover things they shouldn't because of adults discount their ability to understand the conversations happening around them.

I stopped keeping track of who they're boning long ago, because I'd need an assistant to keep the affairs straight.

While my parents' marriage is a sham, I remind myself that my boyfriend, Todd, isn't like them. Yes, his parents only own half the live entertainment industry, but my father allows me to see Todd. The other parents will force the Heathers to accept an arranged betrothal, and I'm grateful I'm lucky enough to have found the perfect match on my own as my high school sweetheart.

"Delores, Bruiser is ready to escort you to Apex. He's pulling the car around now," the hawk shifter says softly.

Snapping out of my reverie, I smile at the trembling woman. Bruiser must have scared the living hell out of her. For no other reason than it amused him, I'm sure. He's as much a brute as his name implies, and I don't look forward to riding alone to the academy with him.

Something about that shifter gives me the creeps…

Sneak Peek: Children of the Moon

PROLOGUE

Twenty-one years ago…

A powerful wave of apprehension hits me as we approach Claridon's house. Pausing at the edge of the forest, I wait until we can see what awaits us. The silence is deafening as we take in the wreckage of what was once the home of our dear friends.

They splintered the heavy cabin door in pieces littered around their yard like an explosion sent the shards flying. When the wind shifts, the foul stench of death and rot slams into us, making my wife gag. Lights are flickering ominously in the shattered windows and another scent—burnt food—catches the breeze as we approach.

"Cast protection before we reach the porch," I murmur.

"Ego invoco deus ab mihi. Protego mihi ab hostili et malum.[1]"

I nod solemnly, repeating her words to invoke our Goddess' watchful eyes on me as well. The scene in front of the house does not inspire confidence about what we will find inside.

The air is thick as we step onto the porch and another smell wafts towards us—blood. Its metallic tang invades our senses almost to the point of tasting copper on my tongue. Climbing over the debris, I look at the once cozy living area. Shredded cushions, torn drapes, stuffing, and other destroyed furnishings lie scattered around the room. When I bend to examine the destruction, I find coarse animal hairs embedded in the remnants. I pick some up to sense the aura of the creature it came from, but all I feel is death.

The bloody hoof prints puzzle me—I do not recognize them as belonging to any creature I'm familiar with. Whatever came to this house was not a normal shifter, nor was it a common magic user. The level of malice and lack of emotion concerns me. Its aura is like that of a necromancer or one of their creations.

I follow a set of heavy prints to the hallway leading to the dining area and kitchen. Swallowing hard, I prepare myself for the carnage I know will appear. The rotten food and decomposition scents are so bad I have to raise my shirt to cover my nose before I vomit.

It is certain our friends are dead; no one can lose the amount of blood that coats the surfaces and walls while staying alive.

"What made those claw marks? I've never seen such deep furrows," my wife whispers.

I shake my head, holding a finger to my lips to keep her quiet. I've never seen that type of mark, either, but we don't know if there's anyone still here. We must stay silent while we explore. The food on the stovetop is burned and has flies on it—that's the rotting smell. Wood is barely burning in the oven, just a few embers remaining, but it tells me our friends were caught unaware.

It means the malevolent being that attacked the wolves did it within the past few hours.

My heart stops when I remember their baby girl. Feray had to be here when it happened; it's the New Moon and both of her parents stay home during the start of the new lunar cycle.

"Freya, forgive me. I almost forgot the baby," I hiss at my wife.

Her eyes widen and her hand flies to her mouth. I see the tears forming as she thinks about what the condition of this place means for a defenseless infant. Together, we leave the kitchen, intent on heading back through the outer room to the stairs.

Just beyond the landing, we stumble over the body of Claridon. His corpse is mutilated, but I recognize those battered hands anywhere. He clearly put up a hell of a fight to keep the intruder from making it past him. Despite that, it ripped his chest open and his intestines are hanging out. Blood spatter decorates the once lovingly decorated walls, painting them vermillion and signaling his desperation to protect his family.

Swallowing again as I look at Imogen, I tilt my head at the trail of bloody hoof prints that lead to the nursery. We were here when they found out they were expecting, when they assembled the room, and even after Feray was born. Now the beauty of that memory has been sullied by the scene before us.

We have to be strong…

Once we're both ready, we follow the prints to the door of the baby wolf's room. The sight that greets us is horrific: it splayed Lyra out as if nailed to a cross and impaled her head on a post of the baby's crib. Blood is dripping down the whitewashed wood, making its way to the pink carpet. Dead eyes stare sightlessly at us as we hold our breath and enter. The injuries to our friend are a testament to how hard she fought to protect her child, though in the end, she also failed.

I don't want to see what this monster did to the baby we considered a sister to our child. Forcing myself to approach, I stare at the empty crib in astonishment. There's no sign of Feray, nor that it harmed her in this room. I whip my head around to look at my wife in shock.

Was this a kidnapping? Why would they kill everyone so brutally instead of simply sneaking in to snatch the baby?

My eyes dart around the room until I reach the closet. I stalk over, throwing the door wide. There's a pile of dirty linens and blankets in the bottom, which is unlike Lyra. She always kept everything tidy, so much so that we all teased her about it. Tossing the clothes over my shoulder, I dig down until I reach the floor. I call for light and my magic brightens the dark space enough for me to see a tiny seam at the baseboard.

Claridon was always paranoid, and I never understood why. We both lived simple lives in a small town of magic users and shifters, well outside the dangers of the big city. He was a master craftsman and Lyra ran a bakery; there was nothing to worry about. Humans were far away from our little town and the stench of corruption from the gangs and Councils doesn't exist in Silver Falls.

But I recognize a bolt hole when I see one, so I search frantically until I find the lever that will spring the door open. It takes several tries to successfully open the door—Claridon was top-notch at his trade—but when it swings out, I gasp.

There, wrapped in her father's shirt and Lyra's clothing, is Feray. She has the warding amulet Imogen made for her on her chest, and I realize that even while scared for their lives, Lyra and Claridon ensured the beast wouldn't find their child. Between the magic of our amulet and their scent swaddling her, the baby is hungry and tired, but safe.

I lift the tiny infant out of the hole gently, my eyes filling with tears. Her baby scent makes my heart hurt for my fallen friends and I clutch her to me tightly. It's our responsibility to take care of her now; I know that. Imogen nods when I look at her with a sad expression, then walks over to the dresser, opening a drawer. When she hands me the baby sling, I know she feels the same.

Once I secure Feray to my body, we make our way back to the stairs and head out of the house. It will need to be burned to keep that creature or anyone else from following the scent trail to our home. We don't want anyone to know Feray is alive; she will be safe with us as long as we continue to have her wear the amulet that suppresses her wolf.

Raising her with our daughter, in a new town, is the only way to keep her alive.

I didn't wake up this morning knowing I'd have to abandon my entire life and our home, but I know as surely as the sun will rise tomorrow what we must do to protect this baby. Looking down at her curiously, I ponder the situation again. A magical beast used as an assassin seems like overkill if their target was the infant. Slaughtering her family was also unnecessary— that thing could have slipped into her room and killed her before anyone knew it was there.

Lifting the magic on her amulet for a moment, I wait until Feray opens her eyes. That's when I realize why my friends put it on her. My wife walks up beside me and runs a finger over her cheek. Her red hair looks very much like mine and as long as we keep the magic refreshed for the spell, she will look as though she is our natural daughter.

"We must pack up and move immediately," Imogen says as we walk out. "The capital city is vast, and no one knows us there. That will allow us to raise her as our own—a sister to Fiadh."

"Yes," I murmur. "I will send a message to the local council to inform them we are moving. The death of our friends and their daughter are too much for us to bear here. You simply need to keep her secret in our home until we leave."

She nods. "What about the monster who did this? Who would send it to kill a baby, and why?"

"Someone who scared Claridon enough to make a secret bolt hole in the nursery and forced Lyra to ask us for that amulet. I don't know what they were up to, but obviously, it was much bigger than our tiny town."

Imogen frowns. "We made three amulets, love. Why weren't Lyra and Claridon wearing theirs?"

"I don't know, Gen. Whatever the reason was, they took theirs off and someone powerful hunted down their daughter. Nothing is what it seems here, but we must protect Feray. We will keep her wolf suppressed for as long as possible—up to her Ascension if we can. She'll grow up and if she's destined for something bigger, she'll be able to assume that mantle when she's ready."

Taking this baby on and keeping her secret violates our coven laws; we both know it. Hiding her means we will always be on the run—we need completely new identities when we flee to the capital. It's a lifetime commitment, but the look on my wife's face tells me she's certain this is the right thing to do.

I know without a doubt that being was pure evil, and it came with one purpose: *assassination*.

Tomorrow, we begin our lives on the lam with two babies—there is no other option .

Get it now: **https://books2read.com/newmoonrisingCOM1**

1. I call on the gods. I protect myself from enemies and evil

Sneak Peek: Blood on the Ice

Killer Queen

Morgana

Looking around the campus with a critical eye, it isn't hard to notice the differences between the campus of Swallowtail and State U. The major difference is age, of course, but even secondary schools overseas are unlike the blatant marketing machines that are American universities. State U doesn't resemble the colleges I've seen in American movies or on TV, though much of that is the Society's doing.

However, banners, statues, plaques, signs, and even architecture are emblazoned with the school's motto—*Honoris. Veritas. Potentia*—as if constant reminders will enforce the virtues it extols. *That* differs from the places in Europe I attended or worked in.

"Getting used to the sales aspect of education here won't be your biggest challenge and you know it," I mutter to myself.

When the outcome of my trial led to a guilty sentence, I didn't expect the punishment they handed down. Instead of being jailed for the murder of my ex, they decreed I would replace him as the Dean at State U. I wasn't the only one who disagreed with my purgatory—the vote on the High Council was split down the middle until a mysterious figure cast a vote in favor of my exile. They summarily dismissed me from Swallowtail Academy and sent me home to pack my shit for a journey overseas to the nest of corruption created by the man I thought I would marry.

Not only am I the youngest Dean to ever hold the title, but I'm the only hybrid to head one of the Society's schools.

Placing me at the helm of the crown jewel of their American institutions made their unorthodox punishment even more bizarre, but I've never believed the group that guides our kind to be infallible. The irony of replacing the being responsible for all the university's current issues with the fiancee who killed him hasn't eluded me. It's like my penance for not blowing the whistle on him instead of taking my vengeance in blood.

They did not impress hard line elders with the eventual outcome, but that had to be expected. Some supernaturals don't believe in the young being given positions of power, especially when that young candidate is also a woman and a hybrid. Given that I believe Magnus had cronies at various levels of government he was paying off, some of them must be worried I'll expose them to prove I was right to remove him from this world. Either way, the assholes who are screaming I'll ruin their precious programs and reputation haven't shut up since I left the trial chamber.

Let them whine about their outdated, elitist standards. I'll show them.

I turn away from the greenery of the campus, leaving the balcony to take a seat at the enormous desk in my overly plush office. Knowing the way parents and donors behave in this country, I assume every inch of this space has been purchased not by the college, but by donors who had 'one little request' for my ex. Magnus Corona was well-known in academic circles for milking the wealthy Americans until they ran dry, but his lack of ethics couldn't go on forever. My greedy, dragon lover went on the lam after a series of scandals involving kickbacks, illegal sponsorships, sports, and sexual harassment. The last one is why I hunted him down and eventually watched the last breaths he took on this planet with vengeful glee.

I'll start looking for a decorator immediately. If it's not in the budget, my trust fund will cover it.

Like most lost ones, they left me on the doorstep of a very talented witch and her gargoyle mate. I never found my 'real' parents, but growing up on Swallowtail's campus was not a burden. It was different when my adoptive parents were professors there—three hundred years brings a lot of changes. When I graduated, I attended Oxford and came back to work there in administration because I missed the old buildings and libraries.

That's the gargoyle in me, I know.

My adoptive mother is blind—except for the gift of future sight. Being a beautiful, blind witch couldn't have been easy when she was teaching, but she met my father in college and they've been together ever since. When they graduated, they came back to Swallowtail to teach. Eventually, she became the head of the Witchcraft & Wizardry department at the Finishing School and my father was the chair of the Physical Education & Training program. Over the years, my mother's gifts made their investments and ventures fruitful enough to retire while they could still enjoy it. They live on a small island in the Mediterranean where supes of their caliber like to soak up the good life.

Once I get settled here, I might invite them to come tour the campus. My father would particularly enjoy the Gothic structure of the buildings; they were constructed to evoke the feeling of Oxford and he loves those old buildings. I give the picture of them on my cherry wood desk a half smile and sigh when I realize it's going to be awhile before I can extend that invitation.

First, I have to figure out how to get this ship back on course. Loyalty divides the staff; the students are due to arrive in two weeks, and I have a lot of house cleaning to do within these hallowed walls. It's going to ruffle feathers to do the things that are necessary to keep our supernatural accreditation *and* our human sports certification. I'll have to let some staff go, shuffle departments and assignments, and bring in new people to monitor certain aspects of the college's accounting to satisfy all the requirements we need to meet by the end of the semester.

State U has never been forced to toe the line quite as closely as we must now, and that is all because of Magnus Corona's lack of scruples and inability to think without his dick.

Not that any of his adoring fans will believe it for a second—and that is the rock I'll have to push up the hill for the foreseeable future.

"They'll have to get on board or get the fuck out," I say as I compare the list of coaches, trainers, and support staff for the football team. "I don't have a choice and neither do they."

When I finally finish going over the massive budget for the major boys' teams, my brain is damn near fried. I cannot fathom how colleges here justify the expenditures of these programs compared to the paltry sums I saw on the balance sheets for academic programs. Americans truly have lost their focus on education, and it doesn't surprise me at all that Magnus could manipulate this to his advantage. There's so many discretionary funds and black holes in the books that I'll have to find someone much more numerically inclined than myself to help me wade through this shit.

It's almost like it left room for loopholes and nefarious deeds.

Pushing to my feet, I rise from the high-backed leather chair and slip my shoes back on. I've been at this for hours and because I don't have office staff, no one was there to remind me I should eat or take a break. I had to fire everyone who worked in Magnus' immediate circle—both out of principle and necessity. I can't prove they knew what he was doing, nor that any of them would try to harm me as retribution, but I'm also not stupid enough to let someone with loyalty to my ex pour my goddamn coffee.

Coffee.

The word makes my blood hum and I know it's time to find sustenance— particularly caffeine. I locate my phone on the massive desk and slip it into the pocket of my suit pants. My appearance has been a topic of gossip on campus since I arrived—social media is a terrible curse when you're in the spotlight, even if it's for the right reasons. I've seen staff and alumni commenting on the 'uptight murdering bitch' strutting around campus dressed like someone from the *Addams Family* as if their vitriol isn't public when they post on Facebook.

My lips curve as I look down at the bespoke Tom Ford suit, Zegna tie, and Louboutin heels. Dressing the part has always been a theme of mine, but Magnus preferred the 'rumpled academic' look. He allowed the staff to run around looking like grad students and that will soon end. If they hate me for looking sharp compared to my frumpy ex, they're going to hate the new dress code when it rolls out in a week. I will not go as far as the Society schools did at home or in other countries, but I refuse to have the press haunting our grounds while taking pictures of grubby looking professors and coaches for their rags.

If this is the crown jewel, it needs more polishing than the Council realizes.

Before I go out, I shake my purple and black curls out of the messy bun, letting my hair settle over my shoulders. A quick check with the selfie mode on my phone tells me my makeup doesn't need to be freshened—thank hell —so I close the camera and put on my sunglasses to keep my sensitive eyes from the waning sun.

I'll need the State U app to find a place that's out of the way. I open it and cringe—the damn thing is hideous in form and function. I make a mental note to interview app designers and web developers; the website has to be as poorly maintained as this bullshit. Yet again, I marvel at the level of incompetence men can show without consequence. It finally loads the map and I scroll around until I find a coffee shop on the edge of campus. I don't want to go to a break room or the food court—there will be far too many eyes on me and I'd like to relax.

Noting the landmarks around the shop, I walk out onto the balcony and touch the amulet at my neck. My wings spring free, sprouting through the suit without a single tear, and I leap into the air. Catching a wind shear, I glide to the far end of the commons, then bank to the right towards the arts building. They nestled the little beanery I identified between the theater and the gallery, so I pull my wings back to descend slowly as I approach.

When I land, the magic of my mother's amulet helps me slip my appendages back in gracefully and walk towards the door without missing a beat. I open the door, take off my sunglasses, and stride in with confidence. I'm not here to throw my weight around, but I can't let anyone see me sweat, either. I look at the menu board before I lower my gaze to see the barista behind the counter.

Holy. Mother. Forking. Shit.

The guy behind the counter is beautiful, and I don't say that lightly. His long blond hair is pulled back in a ponytail, but somehow, it doesn't look douchey. Paired with his patrician features and thin silver framed lenses, he projects the air of a student, but not a new one. My guess is a grad or doctoral student and this is his side hustle. The muscled forearms and powerful hands tell me he's not just a bookworm, so I ponder what discipline this lithe, gorgeous supe is studying. When I finally drag my eyes back to his, the aqua color of his is mesmerizing.

"Can I take your order, ma'am?"

Yikes. That destroyed my brief fantasy.

"Um, yes, sorry. It's been a long day. I'd like a triple espresso and a club sandwich, please." I feel my cheeks heating not because I was staring—he's got to be used to it—but because I got caught checking out one of the students.

It's not forbidden at State U, but I am the murdering bitch with ice in her veins that's here to destroy everything the university stands for. Or, so the article in the *State U Review* said last night. There's no way this gorgeous coffee-serving man doesn't recognize me and I'm sure I'll get an earful about my evil ways once he's done making my order. In fact, I should continue watching to make sure he doesn't mess with my food for revenge.

Yeah, that's why I want to watch him.

"I don't blame you for coming here. It's not one of the campus hot spots. Mostly we get professors, arts kids, and the occasional normie who wants to hide from the masses."

I blink, realizing he's nailed my reason for choosing this shop without even trying. "I think it's rather cozy."

"You don't have to pretend, Dean LeCiel." His pretty eyes meet mine again and I feel that heat creeping up my spine. "I'm aware of how contentious your appointment was. It doesn't bother me, honestly. I've been a student through much of your ex's reign and since the music department was of little concern to him, I don't have any allegiance to the former administration."

Definitely a doctoral candidate. His thesis is probably massive.

Covering my mouth as the unintended double meaning of my words occurs to me, I wait until the urge to giggle like a teenager fades. It would be extremely unprofessional of me to comment on his… attributes… especially since that kind of bullshit helped bring Magnus down. Of course, that doesn't mean I'm not wondering now…

"Dean? Hello?" The hot barista is waving his hand as he looks at me curiously.

"I'm sorry to be so rude. I didn't catch your name?"

There we go. That sounded totally normal.

"I'm Slade," he replies with a slow smile.

That doesn't surprise me in the slightest, and I wonder if he might be part Fae. Not giving me his real name is part and parcel with them, and so is the ethereal beauty. "You may call me Morgana when I am here. I think titles are dreadfully stuffy, but…"

"Set boundaries early because you have mutinies to deal with."

Frowning, I tilt my head. "You aren't reading me with magic, are you, Slade? Even during my ex's time, that kind of invasion of privacy wasn't allowed."

"No, no!" He stops making the sandwich and gives me a sheepish look. "I inferred it. I mean, I don't run with the undergrads or the popular crowds, but I hear things. It wasn't hard to figure out that you're at the hole in the wall shop so you don't have to be on stage while you eat or that you're going to make big changes because of all the charges against the former dean."

I nod, observing him. "I believe you, though I probably shouldn't. Betrayal hides in obvious places; I'm living proof of that."

His features look sharper as he smirks. "There are those of us who don't believe what you did was unjustified, Morgana. Living here at State U will provide you with plenty of evidence to give the Council that will mitigate your actions."

"That's both my desire and my deepest fear, Slade. There's only so much bad PR this place can take before the Council shuts it down and moves on."

A coffee cup and a plate with my sandwich slide across the counter as he murmurs, "You'll have to decide if that's what you want when the time comes."

"I know."

Get it on Kindle Unlimited

Get Season Two on Ream

ABOUT CASSANDRA FEATHERSTONE

Cassandra Featherstone has channeled her lifelong passion for writing into a flourishing career, a journey that started when she first grasped a pencil as a gifted child with ADHD.

Her debut novel, born during the solitude of COVID lockdown in March 2020, draws on a tapestry of personal encounters and insights that resonate deeply with her readers.

An international bestseller, Cassandra has topped Amazon charts in categories such as LGBT Anthologies, LGBTQ+ Mystery, and Bisexual Romance, among others. Her works navigate the complexities of bullying, PTSD, body dysmorphia, mental health struggles, personal reinvention, and the empowerment of claiming one's own space. Importantly, Cassandra offers a thoughtful and respectful portrayal of LGBTQIA+ relationships, subtly reflecting her own connection with the community through her narratives.

Her literary repertoire spans sci-fi fantasy, urban fantasy, paranormal, and comedic genres in academy whychoose settings, with a strong commitment to portraying consensual, safe, and accurately depicted BDSM and kink lifestyles. Her books are an invitation to explore transformative stories that are both inclusive and engaging.

Often affectionately called 'The Muppet' for her wacky theater kid personality, she resides in the Midwest with her tech-savvy husband, their creatively inclined college student, a literary-minded dog, and four scheming cats.

READ MORE AT CASSANDRA'S WEBSITE OR HER FACEBOOK PAGE. SIGN UP FOR EXCLUSIVE CONTENT AND UPDATES HERE.

Join her Master List for promo and ARC opportunities by scanning the QR below:

Come Out & Prey (German)

Let Us Prey (German)

In Prey Trust (German)

DISCORDIA UNIVERSITY

Veiled Flame (Book One)

Quiet Burn (Book Two)

SECRETS OF STATE U

Blood on the Ice (Book One)

Suspicions on the Stage (Book Two)

FAETAL ATTRACTION

Hell on Wheels (Book One)

Book Two Title TBA

VILLAINS & VIXENS

Bloodthirsty (Book One)

Ruthless (Book Two)

Wicked (Book Three)

AUDIO OF THE VILLAINS & VIXENS SERIES

Bloodthirsty

Ruthless

TRIANGLES & TRIBULATIONS

Hoist the Flag (PQ)

Yo-Ho Holes (Book One)

**CHILDREN OF THE MOON-
WITH SERENITY RAYNE**

New Moon Rising (Book One)

Waxing Crescent (Book Two)

Waxing Gibbous (Book Three)

Full Moon (Book Four)

Waning Gibbous (Book Five)

Waning Crescent (Book Six)

RISE OF THE RESISTANCE

Ream Exclusive Prequels

Hooked on a Feline (Book One)

Peacock Me Like A Hurricane

Book 3 TBA Title

REAM SERIALS

Secrets of State U

Discordia University

Denizens of the Dark

Faetal Attraction

Agents of the Ouroboros

Rise of the Resistance

F.E.A.R. Academy

ANTHOLOGIES

Unwritten

Shifters Unleashed

Jingle My Balls

Love is in the Air

Silent Night

Snowed In

All Hallows Eve